30

D0269159

LIMERICK CITY LIBRARY

ل10

ie/library
.imerickcity.ie

The Granary,
Michael Street,
Limerick.

iss   subject   of the Library.
n   retu   the last date

AN INVITATION TO DANCE

Marion Urch is a novelist and writer of short stories with credits for film, radio and television. *An Invitation to Dance* is her second novel. Her first, *Violent Shadows* (Headline Review), was published to critical acclaim in 1996.

Her play, *The Long Road* won the LBC Radio Playwrights Festival Award and was broadcast on RTE (Radio Telefís Éireann). Short stories have been published in England, Canada and America.

An Invitation to Dance

MARION URCH

First published in 2009 by Brandon
an imprint of Mount Eagle Publications
Dingle, Co. Kerry, Ireland, and
Unit 3, Olympia Trading Estate, Coburg Road, London N22 6TZ, England

www.brandonbooks.com

Hardback ISBN 9780863223839
Paperback ISBN 9780863223952

2 4 6 8 10 9 7 5 3 1

Mount Eagle Publications receives support from
the Arts Council/An Chomhairle Ealaíon.

the arts
council
an chomhairle
ealaíon

Cover design: Anú Design
Typesetting by Red Barn Publishing, Skeagh, Skibbereen
Printed in the UK

For my father John Urch and my paternal grandmother Elizabeth O'Brien, who both ventured into the unknown at the tender age of fifteen.

"And after all, what is a lie? 'Tis but the truth in masquerade."

Don Juan
Lord Byron

Contents

Act II

Scene Eight
Indigo Cashmere
(Ripped and torn, blood-spattered and
caked with mud and manure)

Interlude

Act III

Scene Nine
A Set of Journals Bound in Dress Remnants

Scene Ten
Final Effects
(Addendum)

Epilogue

Acknowledgments

Prelude

*A*cross snow and ice it came, ruffling the surface of fallow fields and creeping into stark, frost-blighted gardens. It stole along muffled streets and slid beneath doorways. It slithered through thick layers of winter drapes, penetrating the tiniest cracks between wooden skirting and the walls. It blew out candles and unsettled cats. A brooding sense of unease lingered over the houses, an indeterminate restlessness dropping through the chill and frosty air.

Soliloquy

Lola stood at the back of the shrouded, unlit stage, soft glancing shadows settling around her like films of drifting soot. Soon the wall of dense maroon velvet would part with a swish in front of her, but not yet, not just yet. The tabernacle plush of the curtains rippled like water beneath a breeze, like skin rising beneath a lover's touch. She breathed more deeply. Beyond the curtains, she could hear a gathering impatience of voices. A violinist plucked a few strings; somebody coughed. As the rhythms of harp and timpani sounded, the curtains stirred. When the cymbals clashed, the drapes divided like the Red Sea parting in front of Moses.

She moved into the light, step by careful step, as if she had never walked before, as if all of her was held caged within each step. Two, three, four: she caught the rhythm of the harp and breathed the gut notes of the double bass. On the ninth note, she raised her castanets above her head. As she circled the floor, she wove an intricate web with the undulating movements of her arms, then wrists. In one moment, she was a woman blissfully in love, the next, scornful and proud. She was full of abandon, then rage, then desire—like a flicker book of emotions swirling around the stage. When she performed a drum roll of *zapateados* with her heels, the audience was jolted by the sound. With a bold gaze, she bore down on them, like the most powerful woman in the world.

That night, her performance encapsulated all the great moments of her career. Dresden, Warsaw, Paris, she danced them all again. She was in Berlin, dancing for the King of Prussia and Czar Nicholas I, the Emperor of all of Russia. In Munich, she conquered King Ludwig once more. She was twenty-three and making her debut all over again, on the stage of Her Majesty's Theatre in London.

When she took her final bow, the audience of the Broadway Theatre in New York rose, stamping and cheering, to their feet. Applause vibrated through her. Every part of her body tingled, from her fingers to the tips of her toes. She opened out her arms in supplication and the air filled with roses. After one kiss, she blew another. When a long-stemmed dewy rose landed at her feet, she picked it up and pressed the petals to her cheek. Deepest crimson, scarlet, damson, dusky grape—the buds spread in pools across the boards. By the time the curtains fell, roses clotted the stage. The trampled buds and bruised petals exuded the sweet, oily scent of roses. She began to feel dizzy. She worried that she might fall. The juice of crushed rose petals leaked across the floor.

After the show, Lola disappeared into chill, dusty corridors that stank of mothballs and the moist biscuity smell of unwashed feet. In her dressing room, she kicked off her shoes, and then let out a relieved sigh. A fire smouldered in the grate and steam rose from the bathtub. Across the room were flowers in every stage from bud to withering bloom. The air was steeped in the heady scent of dropping gardenia and the fetid, swampy stench of stagnant water. She unfastened her costume and allowed her skirts to drop to the floor. Sitting down at the dressing table, she reached for a cloth. Her perfect stage face had cracked and smudged and caked. Powder clogged the folds around her nose and mouth; the remains of greasepaint clung to glistening feverish cheeks; the black kohl around her eyes had seeped into a thousand tiny lines. On the tabletop beside her, the heads of tiger lilies splayed open on yellowing stems, their most intimate cores exposed, petals dangling and about to fall. Outside the dressing room, the sound of male footfalls echoed along the corridors. Springing up from her stool, she pushed three heavy brass bolts across the door. By the time she settled down again, she could hear an urgent pressing up against the walls. She took a last glance in the mirror, before setting to work with a bottle of rose water and a moistened cloth.

When she applied a thick layer of cream to her face and neck, her skin greedily drank it in. One perfectly executed *Oleano* was enough to exhaust her now, whereas once she could have danced all night. These days she applied her cosmetics a little more thickly and was happier in artificial light. Every morning, she plucked another twisted silver thread from her dark hair. She kept them in a tiny trinket box with a tooth and a ring with a red glass stone, alongside a set of journals containing her innermost thoughts.

The newspapers claimed that Lola was more beautiful than ever, but she knew that wasn't true. Genuine beauty was a kind of innocence; it gave off a certain kind of light. Those we think of as beautiful bear the lineaments of a child; they retain the same transparency of skin and mouth and eyes. What Lola had was allure, a witchy kind of glamour; it was a confidence trick, an ability to project.

She bathed quickly, then rinsed herself down with icy cold water. Rummaging among her dresses, she picked out a mossy green velvet that heightened her colouring and diminished her waist. She could hear voices calling her through the door now and she began to hurry. Youthful radiance came from a jar she had brought with her from Paris. Memories of a tender young lover brought a smile to her lips, a precise detail made her cheeks flush. She scrutinised herself in the mirror, then rearranged her hair. At last she was ready. Tonight she needed to capture at least one new patron, if not two; one to publish her memoirs and another to finance her new show. She glanced over at her pile of journals, each bound in a remnant of a favourite gown. She had already plundered their contents twice, but another idea was already beginning to form. Pushing up her breasts, she nodded at her reflection, then strolled over and unbolted the door.

ACT I

Scene One
TURQUOISE SILK THREADED WITH GOLD

Chapter 1

Let me tell you a story. Let me tell you about a little girl I once knew. About an infant in an attic room, eyes catching on glimpses of sky-blue curtains, a steely unyielding sky, flecks of amber in a pair of warm hazel eyes. Some dreams bud, then flower—others wither, and then fade. Sometimes fantasy mingles with reality, a lie with the truth. We live out other people's dreams, muddle hopes with fear, watch our own dreams become nightmares. Let me take you back, thirty-one, thirty-two years. Allow me to unpeel time like a spiral of shrivelled rind dropping from a still succulent fruit. Let me take you back, past that last great performance in Manhattan, past those heady and exhilarating days in Munich, past Berlin and Paris and London, all the way back to the beginning—to Ireland in the year 1820.

On a moonless December night, the clocktower in the middle of Cork city chimed twelve. In the back room of a tumbledown house in Main Street, a gang plotted an insurrection. At the top of the milliner's house, a fourteen-year-old Irish girl lay dreaming in her narrow bed. Down by the docks, an Englishman disembarked with a confident flourish. In their separate worlds, both the milliner's apprentice and the ensign were hatching rosy new futures for themselves. The following morning, heedless of frosted windows and icy toes, both sprang out of their beds with a jaunty swing in their steps. I can almost see my mother hurtling breathlessly down the attic stairs, still pinning up her hair, whilst my father strode out into the barracks yard with a masterful air.

Imagine a splendid castle complete with battlements and dizzying turrets, yet constructed entirely from tissue paper. I pieced together an image of my father from snippets of memory—the odd phrase, snatches of conversation, a touch, a gesture. Edward Gilbert was an illusion, a dream, initially of my mother's, then of mine. He was a handsome man as I recall, fine-boned and fair with a thin moustache and blond side-whiskers. My mother used to say that his pale curled lashes reminded her of a child's. Even his bones seemed to her to be quintessentially English and refined.

I pictured him standing in the barracks yard, tall and upright beneath a brooding Irish sky. In his red jacket and his narrow piped trousers, he would have felt sharp and neat and irresistible. It was a day full of possibilities, a bright morning for a fresh new start. Here in Ireland, his background need not hinder him. Pickings were rich, he'd been told. A young British ensign like himself could go far. He sniffed the air, expecting a dirty, unwashed, Irish kind of smell, but the odours drifting in the breeze were all too familiar—horse manure, polished boots, straw, composting vegetables, the reek of old cabbage water from the kitchens, the effluvia of a garrison anywhere. As he sauntered towards the gates, he imagined taking charge of the whole world, striding from one pink corner of the globe to the other in a single mighty bound. Saluting his lieutenant, he lined up with a squad of soldiers standing to attention by the gate.

As the heavily studded and reinforced barricades clanked open, his certitude evaporated into the sharp and frosty air. The first thing he saw in the widening gap was a gaunt girl in a ragged red petticoat tending to a pot over a smoky fire; the second, some rough, makeshift dwellings. For animals, he thought? Inch by rasping inch, foot by creaking foot, the gates of the garrison opened. On the other side lay a sprawling encampment cut from a field of prickly yellow flowering gorse. Blankets dangled from lines; fraying undergarments hung from spiky bushes; scrawny children with muddy legs ran in and out. The only animals in sight were one bony cow with sagging udders and a mangy half-bald dog. With the gates fully ajar, Edward counted thirty-five, forty women, and then lost count of the number of children. A wraith with hollow eyes peered out of one of the hovels, as others emerged blinking into the light. By the time the regiment emerged from the garrison, a bedraggled tribe had gathered by the side of the road.

"Come here to me now," cried a woman with jutting bones. "Wait'll you see what I have for ye."

The soldiers marched in formation, eyes focused on some far point in the distance. Edward tried to keep step, but a vein in his forehead began to twitch. He saw a woman bent as a crone, others with black teeth and gaping mouths: another, with a pockmarked face, had a child clamped to her breast.

"Can't they be cleared away?" he whispered.

"The wrens?" replied the lieutenant. "On the contrary, they're not permitted to leave. It's either here or the workhouse. Obviously they prefer to stay where they are."

"But there are dozens of them, sir. Surely it shouldn't be allowed."

The lieutenant snorted. "You haven't been in Ireland before, have you, Gilbert? There's a troupe of them in every garrison town. They make money doing the only thing they know how."

As the regiment marched towards the Town Hall, the women caterwauled after them. A girl with an angelic face and muddy feet fixed her eyes on a stocky young soldier; another tried to pacify a distressed child. When Edward glanced over his shoulder, a woman with an eye-patch jiggled a naked breast at him.

"Isn't my daddy English," called out a little boy with startling blue eyes. "That means I'm English, amn't I, just like you."

The regiment marched onwards, past town houses, municipal buildings and shops that bore a disquieting resemblance to an English market town. Edward tried to brush off the little boy's words, but they jangled the rhythm of his steps. On every corner, there were skulking youths and brooding groups of men who departed at their approach. As the squad turned from City Square into Main Street, Edward glimpsed a girl in a jade bonnet through the window of a milliner's shop. She looked fresh-eyed and innocent as a daisy, and the sight of her distracted him and dispelled his gloom. Perhaps life would have its pleasures after all. She smiled briefly, then disappeared. Edward retained an impression of bright piercing eyes and stormy brows, of dark colouring, offset by the deep emerald of her dress.

By day, Cork was quiet. At night, small fires flared up around the town. In December, a bucket of horse urine shattered the Courthouse window, and for weeks afterwards it smelt like a urinal on market day. Members of the constabulary were picked off one by one. Nobody saw anything; nobody admitted responsibility. Twice a day, the regiment patrolled the streets, but they had to watch their backs. For every welcome smile, there'd be a dollop of manure or worse thrown at their backs.

Every day my mother waited for the squad approaching Main Street. When my father peered through the milliner's windows, she drew back into the shadows so that he wouldn't see her. Once the soldiers had marched past, she craned her head out of the doorway and watched his retreat.

Eliza Oliver was a precocious girl with ambitions beyond her station. She had been apprenticed to the milliner since she was twelve, yet she thought of herself as grown-up and more than equal to the ladies who patronised the shop. Though she possessed all the essential physical accoutrements of a young woman, she had not yet had an opportunity to put them to the test. Men of sufficient class and means might consider her as a mistress, never a wife. The merchants and tradesmen who came courting, she regarded as beneath her. Already she was plotting her presentation at the annual Regimental Ball. The pale, refined features of the officer flickered across her mind. A British officer would never seriously contemplate a hat girl as a suitable spouse, but she could impersonate a lady without too much trouble. Hadn't she studied them often enough when they came into the shop?

At the barracks, Edward spent much of his time signing items in and out of books—convicts, deserters, provisions, arms. In the evening he joined the other officers and mixed with local dignitaries for soirées or games of cards. At night, he heard English voices coming from the encampment outside the gates. Within weeks, he was itching for a diversion.

At the annual Regimental Ball, the sight of a familiar face propelled him across the gleaming parquet floor. When the girl from the hat shop was introduced as Miss Eliza Oliver, the daughter of the late Sir Charles Silver Oliver, former Sheriff of Cork, Edward pulled himself up to his full height and smoothed invisible wrinkles from his freshly pressed waistcoat. Eliza was chaperoned by the wife of a magistrate who had been a friend of Sir Charles's. It had taken her more than six weeks to procure the introduction—her status hardly warranted it. She assumed that Edward was a man of means. He was an officer, wasn't he? To her untutored Irish ears, he sounded like the finest of English gentlemen. She didn't discern the West Country burr in his accent, nor that the higher ranking officers treated him with some reserve.

Eliza was wearing a lavender dress with an embroidered overskirt of voile; her shoes and gloves were of matching satin. As they danced, her skirt became a diaphanous lavender cloud that heightened the green glints in her otherwise dark eyes. Edward beamed with pride when he caught the other officers eyeing them as he swirled Eliza across the floor.

Edward didn't know that the gown belonged to Eliza's sister, Millie, who was a lady's maid. She, in turn, had been given it by her mistress who couldn't stand the sight of it. The lady herself had worn it but once, in the expectation of a proposal, only to find herself jilted instead. Eliza had pleaded with her sister to lend it to her. Millie finally relented, demanding in exchange an embroidered taffeta bonnet with a garland of silk roses. The hat had taken Eliza more than a month to make, and in the process she had badly strained her eyes. As Edward led her into another quadrille, she pressed her eyes closed and allowed herself a demure smile.

19

Cork simmered for almost a year, the bitterness of the native Catholic population bubbling up in small acts of rebellion. A local election sparked a riot. A tithe collector was shot on his rounds. Secret societies flourished. Men with white linen tied around their hats operated at night, stealing firearms from private houses and shooting policemen. In the encampment outside the gates, a foot soldier was found with his throat slashed from ear to ear.

Edward found himself handling the paperwork for deportations and the rounding up of deserters. In the evenings he courted Eliza. Far away from the familiarities of home, he never questioned the locations she chose for their meetings, and he put their lack of a chaperone down to sheer good luck. Eliza had a quality unknown to him in English girls, an almost unladylike sense of vibrancy and life.

After four months, rumours of redeployment began to circulate. Eliza had to think fast. Edward grew more ardent. She allowed him privileges she strictly shouldn't have. They fed each other lies like sweetmeats: tasty morsels, created lovingly from daydreams, spilled easily from their lips. She left her smell upon his fingers, and more than once the bodice of her dress slipped, but she always pulled back from the brink. When she rolled her head playfully in Edward's lap, he became so agitated he could hardly breathe. Once promises had been made, and a ruby ring slipped on to her finger, Eliza interrupted his fumbling and lifted up her petticoats herself.

Edward wasn't quite as impulsive as he seemed. Besotted, frustrated, aroused—he was all these things, but he was also a practical man. For almost five months he had dreamed of nothing but plunging into Eliza's petticoats, but in his mind there were bank notes and gold coins as well as heavenly pleasures tucked between the folds. Eliza's fortune would be more than useful, and as a married officer his salary would increase. Besides, who else would keep him entertained in some lonesome Irish town?

My own imminent arrival on the scene was marked by an endless letting out of gowns. My mother went to stay with my uncle in

Limerick. Humiliated by having to stay with a shopkeeper's assistant, above a hardware shop at that, she planned a triumphant return and a glorious wedding as soon as possible after the birth. Six months into her confinement, there was an outbreak of rebellion in Sligo, and my father's regiment was notified of immediate transfer. Eliza burst into tears when she received the news.

In Limerick it rained. It rained until there were rivers of it running through the streets. It rained in the morning and it rained at night. It rained until the wallpaper grew black and curled up at the corners. My mother blamed me for those endless months of waiting—hadn't she endured them purely on my account? Miles away from Cork and bloated as a whale, she worried that my father might abandon her. Swollen ankles, thickening waist, protruding veins: it was all my fault. In her mind, I was already a vivid little person. She pictured me blind, with the gaping, greedy mouth of a fish.

On the day I was born, evictions boiled over into riots. My mother was laid up in the front bedroom above the shop while the shouts grew louder in the streets outside. Her contractions came so rapidly that there was no chance of moving her somewhere quiet. Outside, women banged dustbin lids, men pulled up fence posts and railings, and the vast glass panes of the shop front shattered. My mother screamed, but the din outside drowned her out. While she strained and pushed and cursed, the Magistrate's Court across the street erupted into flames. As I pushed my head into the world, a brick sailed through the window and the room filled with glass. I stuck fast then and refused to budge. The midwife had to tussle to wrench me out. When my mother finally looked at me, she was crestfallen.

"My God, she looks like a servant," she cried.

She had been hoping that I would be an English-looking boy, fair and fine-boned like my father. But I was a strong-limbed, sturdy little girl with even darker colouring than hers. None of the Anglo-Irish strain of the Olivers seemed to have manifested itself at all. If anything, I looked more Irish than she did.

21

Three months later, the wedding took place in Christ Church, Cork. In the announcements in the newspapers, my mother was listed as the daughter of Sir Charles Silver Oliver; no antecedents were mentioned on my father's side. There were no relatives of his in attendance at all. My mother's few relatives obviously thought highly of themselves, but were hazy about their exact relationship to Sir Charles. The bride and groom looked deliriously happy, or was it just relief that each hadn't been found out? If either questioned the modesty of the ceremony, neither mentioned it aloud. Perhaps they were dazzled by love; certainly both had a youthful eagerness for its expression beneath the blankets.

They were halfway to Sligo before they remembered that they had left me behind in Limerick. I imagine them exchanging glances, before agreeing that they really should turn back. I was called Eliza by this time, or "the baby", if I was called anything at all. For obvious reasons, my birth wasn't registered. There is no proof that I was ever born at all. At the hardware store, my uncle, who had just found out about the wedding, refused to answer the door. My parents discovered me by the tradesmen's entrance, boxed up with a few illustrated books and a number of old gowns.

In Sligo, a sharp wind whistled down from the mountains through a few bleak streets huddled on a hill. Unrest rippled across the county, but without a clearly defined opponent, the army floundered. They could hardly mount a baton charge on a solitary farm-yard or an isolated road. As the numbers of deserters increased, their transportation took up more of Edward's time. He was also called in to oversee evictions on the larger estates. After a day of turning wretched women and bony children out on to the roads, he would be irritable at home. Eliza, who had imagined that they would be constantly entertaining, found that she had married a man who wished to spend a considerable amount of time alone. The baby cried; Eliza lost her bloom.

In order to placate her, Edward hired a local girl, and for a few weeks Eliza was happy ordering her about. Bridie was homesick for the mountains and cried herself to sleep night after night. Every week her mother came to collect her wages, and Bridie would plead to be taken home. When she lulled me to sleep at night, big tears rolled down her cheeks. As we rocked back and forth, I wrapped my hand tightly around her finger and stared intently into her face. Beneath the tears, I could see amber flecks sparkling in warm brown eyes. It took Bridie more than a month to become accustomed to wearing shoes; a corset she absolutely refused.

"My poor feet are imprisoned," she'd cry. "What is wrong with the feel of the ground? Soon folk will be refusing to go out of the door at all."

Bridie and I were largely confined to the upper rooms of the house. When I took my first few steps, it was with her. I still remember the curve of the ceiling, sky-blue curtains, a patter of rain against the windows and our four bare feet pacing across the floor.

My mother was fifteen years old, Bridie not much older; but when she found herself giggling with the servant girl, she quickly pulled rank. She could sign her name after all, whereas Bridie could neither read nor write. Years of grand ideas had built up in my mother's head, whilst every new thing took Bridie by surprise. My mother wanted the best of everything but had no idea of budgeting and costs. She tried to imagine what her father's house would have been like inside. When she saw an embossed wallpaper in the house of a lieutenant-colonel, she ordered the very same. When the major's family auctioned off their effects, she purchased much of their heavy mahogany furniture. It didn't seem to cross her mind that she should consult her husband first. Edward had conquered Eliza in much the same way his country had conquered hers. He was the one bewildered in a foreign land; she was the one wrestling covertly for command. When the bills started coming in, my father sat her down in the overstuffed parlour and forbade her to order anything more.

"I was only trying to give you the kind of house an officer deserves," she said.

My father bristled. "I am an ensign," he replied. "The most junior of officers."

"But an officer, after all."

"We must live within our means," said my father in exasperation.

My mother ran a wistful finger over the brocade upholstery of the armchair. "But the house is hardly finished. How can I be expected to entertain?"

"I have made myself clear," he said. "Now let that be an end to it."

Mama persisted. "What will people think?" she asked. "I am a daughter of the nobility, as well as being an officer's wife."

My father clenched one fist, then the other. When he spoke it was in clipped, icy tones. "In that case," he said, "I suggest you draw from your own funds."

Mama grew tearful. "Surely you want to live like a gentleman."

Papa jumped up from his chair and stood by the fireplace. "I am a gentleman," he said at last. "Let there be no doubt of that."

"Well, then," said Mama.

"My God, woman. Don't you understand?" Sweeping his hand along the mantelpiece, he sent a porcelain figurine crashing to the floor. "I am a gentleman, but without means," he whispered. "My salary is all I have."

Husband and wife stared at each other, the words hanging in the air between them. Shards of broken porcelain lay scattered across the floor.

After my father left the room, my mother fell back into her chair and twisted her ruby ring endlessly around her finger. Without means? How could that be? She sobbed until her body shook. With her wedding ring, she gouged angry, red lines into the back of her hands.

My father remained firm. When tradesmen called with new materials, he sent them away. Mama was reduced to asking for money for ribbons and buttons. Bridie set to work making candles and soap.

So eager were both my parents to improve their prospects that neither had properly verified the financial position of the other.

When a few months later, my father suggested they draw on Mama's funds in order to purchase a new carriage, more hard truths began to emerge. My mother had an inheritance—that much was true—but it was modest, and she wouldn't have access to it until she was twenty-one.

She blurted it all out piece by piece. Her expertise in the construction of hats had been more than a pleasant pastime. She had depended on it. She was the child of Sir Charles, but to his mistress, not his wife. His legitimate heirs would cross the street rather than acknowledge her. If one of the Oliver girls came into the milliner's, she would hide in the back of the shop. She refused to dwell upon her father's other illegitimate progeny. According to local gossip, the honourable Sir Charles had produced enough offspring to staff a large country estate, having sired bastards by a baker's wife, two servants and the daughters of a blacksmith.

My father was a gentleman without means, that's all my mother ever managed to find out. He refused to speak about where he came from or who his family was. My mother didn't press, afraid to discover the worst. She preferred to imagine that he came from genteel and ancient British stock, impoverished by some noble cause.

So there it was. From the heady heights of their courtship, both of them came crashing down. A gracious life would not be theirs. My father had married a bastard and a shop girl, of that there was now no doubt. My mother had married the most junior of officers, a man without means. Suddenly they knew too much about each other. The future was all too clearly mapped out. When the opportunity of an Indian posting came up, Edward had nothing to lose. What did either of them know of India except that it was the land of tea and spices and fine cloths? And what did India know of them? It was ideal. A blank slate. Here was an opportunity to start all over again.

Chapter 2

I was three years old when we left Ireland: knee-high to swishing skirts and tugging at coat-tails as my parents brushed back and forth. "Get her out from under my feet," instructed my mother, as Bridie bundled me out of the house. Halfway up the mountain, we collected water from a spring and tied red rags to a nearby hawthorn tree. "Heaven help us," Bridie whispered, as she sprinkled water in my eyes, and then marked a cold, wet cross on to my forehead. When I protested, she put a finger to my lips: "*Husha,*" she said. Threading a silver medal on to a blue ribbon, she strung it around my neck, and then tucked it beneath my clothes. With eyes tightly closed, she whispered, "May all the saints in heaven preserve us both."

I frowned, thinking of shrivelled vegetables swimming in jars of sour vinegar.

"Like pickles?" I asked.

She squeezed my cheek. "Like glorious juicy ripe plums in syrup!" she replied, with a wry smile.

When we got back to the house, a carriage was waiting outside.

In the course of a single day, "home" became a shifting, mobile place of cabins and suitcases and upended trunks, and "the world" developed a frame. The moment Bridie lifted me into the carriage, my perception changed. I remember endless movement from that point onwards: wind, steam, trains, boats, carriages. While other locations flew by, Ireland became a still, unchanging, timeless place in my mind. The rest of the world receded into a blur of pictures framed behind glass. It dripped and wavered and dissolved with drops of rain and splats of melting snow. It raced past carriage windows; it drifted away from the boat's deck.

We sailed to England, and then proceeded overland again, my father directing operations as if he were on manoeuvres. When he clicked his fingers, my mother and Bridie jumped. Poor Bridie had never so much as crossed a lake, never mind the sea, and she regretted it the moment she stepped off land.

"'Tisn't natural," she said. "If God had meant us to cross water, wouldn't he have given us all gills."

In Gravesend, the ship that was to take us to India reared up out of the water like a big, grey goose. The boarding plank rattled and creaked as we filed on, each clinging to the one in front. My mother clutched my father's hand, Bridie clutched hers, I clung tightly around Bridie's neck. On the decks, we squeezed through a bleating commotion of cows and sheep and wide-eyed apprehensive people. Beneath my chemise, the medal felt warm against my skin.

For four months, our world rolled and bobbed and rocked. Once or twice it broke the dishes. It made my mother queasy and threw us all about. Our tiny cabin, with its smeared window and its crooked floor, became our new home. The pale blue curtains from the nursery partitioned off the slop bucket. My cot, newly lined with remnants of embossed wallpaper, was hung from the rafters with ropes. In the daytime, my father read Pope's *Notes on Physiognomy* and my mother stitched cotton lace on to her petticoats. At night they slept behind curtains. Between themselves, they developed an excessively genteel manner; sometimes they argued through gritted teeth. Within seconds, gentle banter could turn sour. I could feel the tension between them like an icy breeze.

"Perhaps you might pour me a drink?" my mother would say.

To which my father would respond, with barely suppressed sarcasm, "I would give you the shoes from my feet."

"Indeed, I could not take them, for you have little else."

"There, at least, we are perfectly matched."

My mother bit her lip. "I have connections," she said, "which is more than can be said of you."

"I am a gentleman. You are a lady. Let us say no more."

My father would pour two glasses of Madeira and they would drink in silence. Or he would sweep me up and carry me on deck.

In the fresh air, he became jolly again. He called me his little princess; sometimes he named me after things you eat—his little pickle, radish, turnip, beet. If it wasn't too windy, he swung me through the air whilst I clung on to his side-whiskers or his hair. On the deck of the ship, he pointed out the names of seagulls or fish. Closer to land, exotic birds swooped in and around the ship. There were weeks of extreme heat, then weeks of ice and snow. I remember toddling along the deck in all weathers, hand in hand with my father, him solemn and upright as if he were escorting a proper grown-up girl.

After a month at sea, Bridie was acquainted with everyone aboard the ship. In the mornings she would collect me, then bring me back to our cabin at night. Her dormitory was packed with women, singing, crying, washing their hair. There were some in hammocks who never moved and others, like Bridie, who couldn't keep still. When Bridie wasn't praying, she told me stories. Didn't Moses part the Red Sea when the Israelites needed to cross it, and wasn't it a shame the captain couldn't do that now? And hadn't Jesus walked on water, but sure, that was only across a little lake.

Perched on her bed, with the bilge water swilling across the boards beneath us, other stories came alive before my eyes. Poor Jonah was thrown overboard and almost drowned. Then if that wasn't bad enough, wasn't he swallowed by a whale! And then there was Noah. After the whole world flooded and he saved all the animals, he spent the rest of the days worrying that the ark might sink, and he almost drowned himself in drink.

At that, Bridie would jump up, and we would go travelling down through the layers of the ship. I moved between people's feet.

I had begun to walk, but I wasn't very steady; the roll of the ship became part of my gait. After four months at sea, I walked with a permanent sway.

Inside the ship, we were cosy and dark as Jonah inside the whale. The deeper we went, the louder it became. Along dark corridors and tucked away in corners, we would come across huddles of people gambling or playing cards. Behind wavering canvas walls, I caught glimpses of entangled limbs, of the pale skin between a shirt and a belt or plump white thighs beneath dark skirts. There was a cheerful woman who lived in the corners of the stables with the horses and a wan, unhappy girl who stole the leftovers from the officer's table because she had nothing else.

Bridie regularly visited a man in the depths of the ship. His face black with coal, his arms shiny with sweat, he would come out of the steaming kitchens to catch her in his arms. Bridie would leave me in a corner while they embraced, his hands smearing her with coal dust, his body pressing her against the wall. As dark flames licked up and flickered behind them, the sound of their laughter crackled above the oven's roar, and their silhouettes merged.

I remember those four months in fragments of touch and sight and smell: the constant swaying of the ship, the sense of ploughing through the water, the proximity of bodies, the blast of heat. I remember my mother, too, cool and perfect in her pale dresses. She kissed me in the morning and she kissed me at night. If she was bored, she fixed ribbons in my hair and tried to teach me the names of fabrics: taffeta, chiffon, cotton, silk, lace. She smiled at me rarely, yet I warmed in her glow.

The stench of India hit us before we reached the shore. When we docked in Calcutta harbour, it drifted over towards the ship. It tickled my nose and I sniffed the air. Traces of crushed petals mingled with burning meat. I could smell the warm fleshiness of lots of people all jammed together. I could smell busyness and noise. It reminded me of the concentrated, indoor smell of a hot, busy kitchen, only it was outside.

Closer to land, brown men carried us on their shoulders as if we were kings and queens. Two brown hands threw me up towards the sky, then firmly gripped my wrists. The brown men waded through the cool water, while we wobbled about in the air with the sun pressing down on our heads.

As we journeyed up the River Ganges, the taint of disease rose up around the wide, flat riverboat. Though nobody spoke about it, it was a cloying sourness that lingered and increased. I heard the servants whisper, "cholera, cholera". It sounded like some special thing, an edible plant perhaps, or a fine delicate fabric for making hats. Two of the natives grew pale and clammy, then disappeared. Soon the stench of rotting and decay drifted up from the bilges. The day it cleared, a school of alligators appeared, leaping and snapping and circling around the boat. The adults fell silent. Bridie became clingy. Mama refused to leave the cabin.

My father scoffed at her fears.

"Fresh air can't kill you," he said as we took our daily promenade on deck. He drank water as usual, though my mother drank nothing but Madeira and beer. Within days he became brooding and quiet. Once or twice he clutched the rails, though the river was smooth and still as glass.

Within a week he was bedridden, and I wasn't allowed near him. In the few glimpses I caught of him, he looked as if he'd been coated in paper and glue.

"Hello, my little one, have you come to brighten my day?" he would call through the door, but my mother or Bridie would bustle me away.

From the cabin, the fug of sweat and vomit and diarrhoea assaulted my nose and throat. In less than a fortnight, he began to waste away. The next time I saw him he was so racked with pain he couldn't even see me. Bridie was constantly carrying in jugs of water, and I thought he must be trying to float himself away. He had grown so thin I hardly recognised him. I saw my mother holding his wrist and shaking her head, as if searching for something she couldn't find. Once I ran in and kissed him: his skin felt cold beneath my lips.

Outside the river went on and on. It was so wide you could hardly see the land to either side. The point ahead, where the two banks met, never grew any nearer. It seemed that it was a river without end.

My father became nothing but bones, then gradually his skin changed from white to blue. First his lips, then the colour of the skin around his eyes, deepened and grew mauve as old bruises. Even his fingernails turned blue.

An officer said to my mother that it was a miasma of the air that killed people. Another said simply, "It is India." But I think that it was the water, that he became one with the water, like Noah, who drank so much that he and the water became the same.

The last time I saw my father, there were clouds across his eyes. I pulled at his mouth to make him speak to me, but Bridie dragged me away. When I started to shout and cry, my mother slapped me until I was quiet. They closed the cabin door on me, and I never saw him again.

I tried to imagine him in the wisps of fragrant smoke spiralling up into the air, but there was a putrid undertow that thickened from day to day.

All around us, the Indians floated their dead on to the holy river. We passed bodies being laid out in white cloths on pallets lining the banks, their arms folded across their chests, necks festooned in garlands of orange and yellow flowers. When I looked back, the burning pyres had been pushed down the river banks, the bearers wading into the water until the current caught their cargo and swept it away. Poor Father, I would have liked to watch him float away.

In Dinapore, he was buried with the whole regiment around him. Two bugles sounded forlorn and defiant against the raging Indian sky. The soldiers marching and the sergeant shouting seemed like futile attempts to keep India at a distance. India overwhelmed us; India crept in all around. Great cones of incense burned at either side of the coffin, and the air was thick with dust and flies. I could feel my father settling over me like a second skin. Beggars without legs lay outside the gates. The stench clung to us like a shroud.

31

At the edge of the grave, I stood beside my mother, dressed from head to toe in a black mourning outfit that was an exact copy of hers. As I stared down into the hole cut into the ground, a tiny jewelled snake slithered across the bottom. I glanced at Bridie, who was standing with the servants. She caught my eye and winked. My mother held rigidly on to my wrist. When I looked up at her, I saw her eyes scanning the row of officers lined up on the other side.

Behind us, the officers' wives muttered among themselves: "It is the Indian disease. It is India that killed him. His poor widow, she's hardly more than a child."

Bridie left us soon after the funeral. In India, white women were outnumbered by men three to one, and Bridie blossomed under so much attention. She married an English sergeant from my father's regiment, who was more than pleased to have her. When she was leaving, she had to peel my fingers away from her skirts. I made her promise me that she would stay away from the river. Fat tears glistened on her cheeks. She was my second great loss after my father died. As I watched her leaving, I thought, *It's best not to love anyone; it only makes them go away.*

Chapter 3

My mother became a flickering mirage drifting in the heat, a brisk and busy figure in the distance, waving her arms around and issuing directives. As we travelled overland by elephant, then palanquin, then cart, she always seemed to be just out of reach. I waved to her, but she didn't see me. I called to her, but she didn't hear. I was parcelled up with frocks, hatboxes, saucepans, a year's supply of candlewax and soap. I was lifted up by officers, boatmen, small raggedy men with hardly any clothes. From snatches of conversation, I picked up recurring words. Calcutta, Dacca, I chanted, the sound clicking against the back of my tongue. I was tucked up in boxes, swaddled in muslin, daubed with calamine lotion. Wherever we went, my eyes remained firmly fixed on Mama. I studied the nape of her neck, her hands twisting patterns in the air, a bead of sweat trickling from her hairline to her chin. If she disappeared for even a second, I followed her. In my pitiful little attempts to please her, I stopped asking questions and tried very hard to be quiet. No matter what happened, I was determined not to lose sight of her. As the palanquin bearers hurried along, they made up little songs.

"She's not heavy, *cabbada,* little baby.

Carry her swiftly, *cabbada,* pretty baby," they sang.

From my lofty heights, a spinning kaleidoscope of strange and dazzling sights passed me by: tiny monkeys, flowers as big as dinner plates, naked holy men, tradesmen with bright bales of glittering cloth, dancers with red painted hands and feet.

If, in India, Bridie blossomed into a splendid flower, my mother became a rare and precious jewel—beautiful with sharp edges and many sides. Being an eighteen-year-old widow suited her, and as a four-year-old orphan, I was her ideal prop. Every afternoon, two or three gentlemen callers vied for her attention. Sitting demurely on the sofa, she would play them off against each other, whilst taking careful note of their rank and status. Junior officers were quickly dispatched; those with prospects were treated to Battenberg cake with their afternoon tea. Though it was much too hot, my mother continued to wear black because it made her look so opaline and pale. I had been taught how to curtsy and pour the tea, and at some point in the afternoon, I would be brought in briefly and displayed. My costumes were tiny copies of Mama's dresses, adorned with extra ribbons and beads.

"Take the gentleman his tea," my mother would say.

In my two little hands, a china cup and saucer became as cumbersome as a serving plate and bowl, and the room grew wider with every step. Staring at the steaming liquid swirling around inside the cup, I was terrified of its spilling over the rim. When I finally reached the officer, he invariably said "poor little mite", then continued to talk over my head as though I weren't there.

"That's all, darling," Mama would say. Then she would ring the bell, and I would be taken away.

Within months she was courting again. The British officers gradually gave way to a Scottish lieutenant with brown side-whiskers and a big round face like an egg. Mr Craigie looked directly at me when he spoke and never forgot my name. Using his hands, he could make the shadows of a fox or a donkey appear on the wall; he could even make them talk. If he paid me too much attention though, my mother would distract him and send me away.

One evening, Mama returned with Lieutenant Craigie and a small bouquet of pink tea roses in her hands. It was the lieutenant who explained that they were now husband and wife.

"Now that we're married," he said, "we're all going to live together in a big new house."

"Me, too?" I asked.

"Of course," he replied.

In the nursery, he knelt down beside me and offered me his closed, upturned fists.

"Does that mean you're my daddy now?" I asked.

"Will you have me?"

When I touched one of his fists, his fingers opened to reveal a pink sugared almond.

"I will," I solemnly replied.

"Then we have a deal," he said with a smile.

When he opened his other fist, there was another almond inside, this time sugared blue.

He winked. "Don't tell your mother," he whispered.

From the drawing room, Mama's voice rang out. "Don't pander to the child," she called.

In Sylhet we lived in a big white house with many rooms. Circling the outside were verandahs like the decks of a ship, and I ran around with my arms stretched out like a big bird. In the mornings, the servants let down the grass blinds, and we lived inside in the cool and shade. The blinds were sprayed with water, and the scent of vetiver permeated the house. When the water dripped on to the decks, it sizzled, then hissed and evaporated in a tiny cloud of steam.

In place of Bridie, we had an *aya* called Sita. Her eyes were brown like Bridie's, but where Bridie's were flecked with gold, Sita's were the colour of dark, smouldering coals. Like Bridie, Sita had come reluctantly from the mountains. Her white sari had a purple edge, and her hair was oily and black. She possessed more gold jewellery than my mother, and she wore it all at once. Even one of her teeth was gold. Like Bridie, she told me lots of stories, but in hers the river and the sea weren't dangerous, but blessed.

In the house in Sylhet, I had a large white room all to myself. My bed sat in the middle of it like a raft drifting out to sea. There were bars at the sides, and the drapes across the top were like sails. Each of the bed's legs stood in its own saucer of water. At the head and the foot, roses and scrolls and birds had been carved into the limed white wood.

"It is a bed fit for a princess," my mother said.

At night when I went to bed, Sita filled each of the saucers with water so that insects couldn't climb up the legs. When she raised the bars and drew the drapes across, I was cocooned as a silkworm. She took the lamp with her when she left. In the darkness, I could hear the sounds of tiny feet scurrying across the floor. I rattled the bars, but I couldn't get out. A lizard climbed up the wall. No one heard me when I called.

At the back of the house, the servants all slept together in one low room. Sita smelt of orange flowers and coconut and spices, her brown skin exuding warmth and heat. If I was lucky, she let me curl up with her and go to sleep. My mother resided in cool white rooms, and I rarely saw her. In the evenings, I was brought in to say goodnight and she smiled faintly. Even the sight of me exhausted her. Sita balanced me on her hip, whilst she made curries or prepared my mother's tea. She combed my hair for me; she cut mangoes into tiny pieces for me to eat.

Papa Craigie was often away. When he returned, he brought presents for Mama and me. Already she had found reasons to be ashamed of me. I was too tanned. I talked too fast. I couldn't keep still.

"Look at her," she would say. "She looks like a little Indian. I don't know where she gets it from. Her father was fine-boned and fair. She's so swarthy, she looks like a native child."

My stepfather watched her silently. The next time he went away, he returned with a green parrot for me, and we taught it how to speak. When my mother was critical, it said, "love Liza, love Liza," and I gave it more seeds to eat.

In the afternoons in India, when everyone was sleeping, the whole world became mine. Mama had given orders that I was to be kept indoors because she didn't want my skin to get any darker, but even Sita slept in the afternoon, and I could do whatever I pleased. I peeped into room after room. In one I spied a lady lying on a bed and a *punkah-wallah* kneeling sleepily in a corner. As the Indian boy operated the *punkahs,* the draped white cloths of the fans wafted the air back and forth. When I saw that the *wallah* was jealous of me, I stuck my tongue out, then ran away. I didn't really know where to go though, and I felt lonely all on my own.

At the end of the compound were the barracks where the soldiers lived; beyond that lay the Indian quarters. Down there the road became narrower, and some of the houses were made of dried mud. I slipped from corner to corner, peering around each one as I went. I saw an Indian woman leaning in a doorway. Two others danced languorously to pass the time, their hands and feet moving in strange angles with their bodies. When a soldier approached, their backs stiffened and they swayed their hips. I had never seen a native woman look directly at a white man before, nor seen a white man flinch beneath an Indian gaze.

When another soldier passed by, a little boy ran along beside him, pulling at his jacket.

"Soldier want *jig-jig,* soldier want *jig-jig?*"

The soldier brushed the boy away, and then glanced furtively about. He didn't see my one eye watching him. He thought he was the only white person on that dusty street. The soldier slipped into the doorway, and a woman in a red and gold sari followed him inside.

The little boy gestured for me to follow, but I shook my head. I wasn't allowed to mix with Indian children. Until then, I had thought that white people would never enter a native house.

The boy pulled me by the hand, and I allowed myself to be drawn inside. We crept along a gloomy corridor, and then peered into a shuttered room.

The soldier lay naked on the bed, and the woman was kneeling between his knees. She was pulling at him as if she were milking a goat or tugging up weeds. Her sari was a pool of red and gold beneath them. The woman straddled the soldier, but instead of play-ing "horsey", she gyrated in some weird kind of dance. The soldier didn't try to throw her off; he simply sighed. His white skin glis-tened; her dark skin glowed. The woman watched the soldier intently, as if she were trying to read his mind. The soldier shud-dered. Folding up his arms, he covered his face.

The little boy whispered excitedly to me and I ran away.

"You see *jig-jig*. You see *jig-jig*."

When he tried to follow me, I pushed him away and then ran until I was out of breath. In the jungle, I saw flowers with moist red tongues and lush bright orchids bursting from the crooks of trees. Monkeys were screaming and laughing at me.

Mostly, I spent my day with Sita. I went where she went, in and out of cupboards, up and down the steps. In the kitchens of our house, she taught me to dance. She moved her hands like birds, and I tried to copy her. When there was a new moon, she painted a red *tika* on her forehead, and I wanted one, too. Sita said it was my third eye and I would become wise. She put vermilion on my forehead and in the parting of my hair. When my mother saw it, she slapped me.

"Filthy child," she said. "Go to your room."

Alone in my bedroom, I closed my eyes and then touched my forehead, imagining my wisdom flowing from the tips of my fingers to each of my toes.

When I danced with Sita, she laughed because I couldn't move like her. Sometimes we were birds, sometimes a swaying tree. On her wrists and ankles, she wore bracelets which were sewn with tiny bells. When she moved, their tinkling followed her like the sound of cool, sweet water trickling over stones. Sita's hands could become a peacock opening out and displaying its tail, a conch shell, an eagle flying, a lotus bud opening into full bloom. I tried hard to copy her, but my deer stumbled and my little fish drowned.

Sita said that some of the dances were for love, but I didn't really understand what she meant. "Like this," she said, showing me how to grind up spices. "Love is when one thing is transformed into another." The mortar and pestle she used was made of smooth, worn stone. Love, she said, was the bringing together of two different, interconnected things.

When Sita wanted me to be quiet, she pushed betel nut into my mouth, and I lay back and dreamt. When I looked in the mirror, my lips and mouth were stained bright red. I showed Sita my tongue and she smiled. "You look like Kali," she said.

My mother was a remote queen to me. The garden was her unruly kingdom, and I looked for her amidst galloping creepers and over-ripe roses. In the early mornings, she endlessly pruned and trimmed and snipped. "Cut it back, cut it back," she ordered the gardener, but no matter how much they chopped, all the plants blossomed and spread. The bougainvillea tumbled down in bright papery waterfalls; thick vines twisted across the ground and strangled the roses. The yellow lilies were as big as trumpets, the scarlet hibiscus flowers in the garden as big as my face. When I pressed my nose into them, saffron dusted my cheeks.

Spying my mother in the distance, I ran towards her and threw my arms around her skirts. But she brushed me away as if I were a cobweb or a spider.

"Child, child," she said, with her mouth locked in a thin smile.

Holding me at arm's length, she surveyed her skirts. Orange stains of powdery saffron speckled the nubbed pale peppermint silk of her skirt.

"She's dirty, *Aya,*" she said. "Take her away."

I ran at her and wouldn't let her go. Mama unprised my fingers from her skirts as if she were flipping limpets from a shell or unpodding peas.

To Sita I was both precious and banal. She washed me in the river when she washed the clothes. "The holy water will cleanse your soul," she said, but she scrubbed me hard, as if I were a dirty old bag of clothes. If I had been troublesome, she plunged my head beneath the water again and again. "It's good for you," she said, with a grim little smile. Though the water stung my nose and filled my throat, I tried very hard not to mind.

My favourite times were watching Mama preparing to go out to a function or a ball. She put cream on her face, then a powder that smelled of roses. She added a glow to her cheeks and stained her lips red. Whilst she was sitting at her dressing table, she reminded me of Sita in the temple praying; it involved the same level of concentration. She powdered between her breasts and plumped them up as if they were pillows. When she kissed me goodbye, she kissed the air beside my cheeks. All I wished for was to lay my head on her bosom's warm rise and fall.

I loved my mother like Bridie loved her statue of the Virgin and Sita loved Shiva in the temple. To me, she was as distant and ideal as that. Mostly I was content to simply look at her. I made her dainty little offerings in the same way. I brought her tiny sweet biscuits made with almonds or coconut or wreaths of yellow flowers.

After my sixth birthday, my mother began to say that if I was good, I could go back to England, but all I could think was that she wanted to send me away. I didn't remember England except a sense of things retracting and closing in. I thought of grey—people, houses, sky, doors closing, little rooms. When my stepfather began to talk about it, too, I didn't know what to do. "You can become a lady there," he said. "You can learn Latin and Greek."

"Can Polly the parrot go too?" I asked. "Will someone teach me how to shoot?"

One morning, I was woken by my mother instead of Sita. When I went to look for her, I couldn't find her anywhere. The corner of the servants' room where she normally slept had been swept bare. The basket she used to store her clothes had disappeared.

"Where is Sita, where is she?" I asked, then shouted, then screamed.

"Don't be ridiculous, child," Mama said. "She's gone back to her village to look after her own children. Do you think she had nothing better to do than look after you?"

Whilst she was talking, my mother emptied the wardrobe in my room and folded my clothes into a large trunk.

"The boat for England sails in fourteen days," she said. "And anyway, your stepfather and I are moving away."

Chapter 4

As the temperature dropped and the months passed and the distance between India and me grew wider, I could feel my heart begin to chill, then freeze, then contract. Inside my chest, it creaked, then splintered, then cracked. Outside the carriage window, skeins of wild geese arced across a heavy, brooding sky. In the distance, grey washes of rain swept the mountains away. The tip of my nose, my fingers and my toes felt icy cold, the surface of my skin pinched into ruffles and folds. Attached to the lapel of my coat was a label inscribed with my name—Eliza Gilbert, my age—seven, and my destination—Provost Craigie, Montrose, Scotland.

Beyond the glass, the vast liquid sky constantly shifted and changed form. There were times when I couldn't see anything at all. I shivered, and then cradled my knees for warmth.

"What is it now?" I challenged the old gentleman travelling in the carriage with me.

"Rain, frost, dew, a fine shower," he would answer patiently.

"And this? And this?"

"Spray, mist, fog, drizzle."

He had a name for dewdrops, raindrops, wet papery snowflakes; he knew what everything was called.

"Now this," he said on the cold, wet morning we reached Arbroath, "is a *braw, dreich* day."

He tipped his hat as he took his leave, and I bowed solemnly back.

"Poor child," I heard him mutter.

"Aye," said the coachman. "She's been passed from hand to hand, like a parcel, the entire length of the British Isles."

Scotland was cool slate greys, damp hazy browns, stark chilly blues. In my drab new clothes, I merged with the landscape we were moving through. The clothes my mother had packed in India had been no use at all. In London, my step-aunt Mrs Rae had tutted over frothy gowns and vivid silk frocks in orange and scarlet and peacock blue before promptly replacing them. Beneath a stiff dress of bristly grey tweed, my vest and stockings were made of coarse unbleached wool, and my coat was a dull, slatey blue. The dress chafed the back of my neck; my stockings rubbed against my legs. I wriggled in the seat, and then scratched my knees. As one part of me stopped itching, another would start.

The further north we travelled, the colder it became. At each stop, I would pull on yet another layer of rough, hairy clothes. By the time we reached Arbroath, I was wearing three pairs of stockings, two pairs of gloves, a heavy coat, earmuffs and two woollen shawls. I had never felt so miserable or so cold.

As the coach twisted down away from the Angus Glens, a sharp, fishy stench arose. The coachman leaned into the carriage and grinned.

"Here's the Basin, there's Montrose, shut your een and haud your nose," he chanted through the window.

With my trunk upended on the pavement beside me, I was set down on the Harbour Road. Across the way, a lagoon of mudflats and seeping water stretched out as far as the eye could see. Huge white seagulls with hooked bills were screaming and crying and careering around my head. The woody smell of smoking haddock mingled with a rotting fishy stink. In the wake of ships, black-headed birds were fighting over entrails and discarded tails and scaly fins. Hundreds of pink-footed geese were spiralling down through a watery, windswept sky. There were dead fish everywhere. I closed my eyes, then my nose, then my mouth. With my hands I covered up my ears. One, two, three times I spun around.

"I want to go home.

I want to go home.

I want to go home."

On my fourth spin, there was a sharp tap on my shoulder. I opened my eyes. Looming down over me was a man with grey eyes and a thin blue nose.

"Well, Miss Gilbert," he said. "Welcome to Montrose, your new home."

"Hello," I replied, with a little bow. "Isn't it a *braw, dreich* day."

Provost Craigie was a tall, thin man who lived in a tall, thin house on High Street with his tall, thin wife and five of their tall, thin children. Four others, including my stepfather, had grown up and left Montrose. At one end of the street, in the far distance, a ship could be seen crossing the horizon. At the other, a towering steeple cast a lengthening shadow. My eyes moved up higher and higher, until, near the top, I spied a tiny window blocked in behind closed shutters and metal bars.

The inside of the house was gloomy and quiet. A clock ticked in the corridor. Every fifteen minutes it rang out. Later I discovered that on the hour, a tiny bell inside rang three times. The woman who met us crept about. When she spoke it was in a whisper. As she was talking to me, she kept her eyes fixed on her husband.

I met the rest of the household at teatime. They were all lined up in the dining room, in order of descending size.

"And this," said Provost Craigie, "is your new family."

There were two boys and three girls, all of them much bigger than me.

"Hello, hello, hello," I repeated, as I moved down the line.

At the end of the row was the youngest, Charlotte, who was twelve years old.

"Hasn't she got a peculiar accent," she said.

"I can't understand a word she says," said one of her brothers.

"I can't understand you either," I retorted.

"We will attend to her accent later," said Provost Craigie.

"Give me your shawl and your gloves, child," said his wife.

Wrapping the shawl tighter around me, I shook my head.

"Take them off," ordered Provost Craigie.

I shook my head again.

"At least take off your gloves," he said.

Provost Craigie offered up our meal in honour of the Lord, and we ate in a solemn, deathly silence. The cutlery screeched into contact with the plates. When a servant set down a bowl behind me, I jumped. I wrapped my shawl more tightly around me. When I glanced around the table, all my cousins were staring intently down into their dinner plates.

I slept in Charlotte's room, in a truckle bed in the corner. Immediately she made it clear to me that this was her room, her house, her parents. That night I lay awake and listened to her snuffles and snorts. Sometimes she whispered in her sleep, other times she tossed endlessly back and forth.

I referred to her as Cousin Charlotte, but really she was my stepaunt. She was my stepfather's baby sister, though she was almost fully grown.

"Little Miss Nobody," she called me. "Who do you think you are?"

After breakfast the next morning, Mrs Craigie sat me down in the kitchen. When she came towards me with a large pair of scissors, I screamed.

"Hush, child," she said, as she caught hold of my hair. "I won't hurt you. A wee trim is all you need."

My hair was thick and black like Sita's. Nobody had ever tried to cut it before. If I bent back my head, I could sit on it. Sita used to oil it when she oiled her own: whilst I laid my head in her lap, she would brush it in long sleek sweeps from the crown to the tip.

When I started to struggle, Mrs Craigie slapped me so hard I almost fell off the chair. Finally she ordered one of the servants to hold me down as she chopped off great hanks of my hair.

Big tears ran down my cheeks as dark locks piled up on the floor. When she had finished, the back of my neck felt cold.

"There," said Mrs Craigie. "Now you look like a proper little girl."

When she showed me my reflection, I didn't recognise myself at all. My hair hardly reached my shoulders. Above swollen, tearful eyes, I now had a dark heavy fringe. She had turned me into a charity child, a workhouse girl, someone who should be grateful and do as she was told.

In Montrose, every day unfolded in exactly the same way. Before a breakfast of salty porridge and lukewarm tea, we washed in bowls of icy water. In the mornings we studied mathematics and read the Bible; in the afternoons we exercised and learned Latin grammar. Provost Craigie constantly tried to straighten out the kinks in my accent; to flatten the sing-song flow of my speech.

"Order steadies the natural turbulence of a child," he would pronounce.

Learning was a new experience for me. It involved discipline, wooden rulers, the memorising of dates and sums. When Provost Craigie told me a story, I wanted to tell him one in exchange. He explained how God made the world in seven days, so I told him about Shiva making a river. Riverlets of Shiva's sweat had flowed from his body down the hills and taken the form of a beautiful woman, I said. I was just about to recount how the beautiful river woman married the ocean, Lord of the Rivers, when Provost Craigie marched me down to the kitchens and made me wash my mouth out with soap.

"You little heathen," he said. "Your stepfather sent you back just in time."

"What's a heathen?" I asked, but instead of answering he gripped my arm so hard it hurt.

"Repeat after me—mine is not to question, but to obey. Repeat

46

after me—my place is to listen, not to speak. Repeat after me—there is only one God, the Lord God Almighty."

I did as I was told (I didn't have any choice), but I was thinking of Sita. If there was only one God, he certainly had many different names and forms.

In Montrose, even walking was undertaken as a discipline. Part of every afternoon was taken up with marching through the park or down a country lane.

"Your daily constitutional," Provost Craigie called it.

He patrolled us as if we were his little army and made up lists of rules.

No dawdling.

No whispering.

No secrets.

"Soldiers for Jesus," he called us, as he exhorted us to march in step, to swing our arms and take deep breaths.

My stepfather wrote regularly from India; he even sent messages from the parrot. *Polly misses you. Polly mopes.* As soon as I saw an envelope with an Indian stamp and my name on it, my heart, which had become heavy as a stone, fluttered into life, as if a hundred drowsy butterflies had just woken up. I hid the letter in my pinafore until I could spend time alone.

In the dining room, I clambered into the window seat. When I drew the curtains, I was enclosed in a private world all of my own. Did you know that heat can come in a letter? That an opened envelope can hold the warm smells of spices and flowers? That a few scrawled lines could conjure up Polly and Sita and, deep within a tangled, overgrown garden, a mother beautiful and remote?

Beyond the curtains I heard first Mrs Craigie, then Charlotte calling me. Tucking my knees up higher, I quickly read the letter again.

Sita would send me biscuits if she could, my stepfather wrote, but she had to go home. I must try to understand that she wasn't with them any more. My mother's letters, when they came, tended to be stark and plain. *Be good, be quiet, be studious, be clean,* she

47

wrote. I posted drawings to Papa Craigie so that Sita could see what Scotland was like. I wished that he could put India in a little box and send it back to me.

Every day had a pattern, and so did every week. On Saturday nights, Mrs Craigie heated up pans of water, and the whole household queued up to bathe. Because I was the smallest, I was always last. By the time it was my turn, a veil of scum floated on the surface of the water.

"Why does everyone get hot clean water except me?" I asked.

"Why, why, why," she snapped back. "I've never met such a spoiled, precocious child. The shame of it is we can't cut out your tongue."

I didn't utter another word. I clenched my teeth so my tongue couldn't get out: it felt fat and warm in my mouth. My skin was scrubbed until it was pink, my hair rinsed in buckets of cold water until it squeaked.

After the first week I began to walk in my sleep. Three times Mrs Craigie found me dancing in the middle of the night, undulating like I had with Sita, my hands fluttering like flowers or birds. In my dream we were in the kitchen in India together. Once they caught me naked, dancing halfway down the street. After that my bed was fitted with bars. Mrs Craigie began to bandage my ankles and wrists together before I went to sleep.

"What were you doing?" asked Charlotte.

The next day I tried to teach her how to dance, but she had the most enormous feet.

"No, no," I cried. "You have to be graceful. You have to become like water; you have to learn how to flow."

It was because of the dancing that Grandfather Craigie first gave me the cane. "Discipline," he called it. I was nine and three quarter years old. If I stood up straight, my eyes were level with the fob watch in his waistcoat pocket. Catching me by the collar of my dress, he led me to his study. When he made me lift up my skirts and bend down, I felt naked and exposed. The cold air nipped my skin. The stick burned into me like a flaming brand.

"Humility purifies the soul," he said.

For days I couldn't sit down. The weals were there for more than three weeks. On the next two Saturdays, Mrs Craigie boiled up fresh water just for me.

After that first time, he disciplined me regularly. Between strokes he would pause and unbutton his shirt collar. Afterwards he wiped beads of sweat from his upper lip.

I caught one cold after another. I was always sniffling and sneezing. I became thin. My nose was constantly blue. I picked at dishes of boiled ham and cabbage or semolina, whilst pining for rice or the juicy taste of mango or pineapple. I missed the luxuriousness of India and its sumptuous all-enveloping heat. I missed my elaborate bed with the carved roses and birds. I even missed the saucers of water and the sound of lizards scurrying up the wall. On quiet afternoons, I would pull the trunk from beneath my bed and put on all my Indian dresses at once. In layers of scarlet and tangerine and vivid blue, I danced around the room.

Sullen Charlotte sat on her bed and pretended to be reading a book. I twirled round and round, describing my Indian bed to her, making it bigger and grander and draping it in damask and gold.

"It was a bed fit for a princess," I sighed.

"Well, you're not in India now," she snorted back. "If you're so special, why did they send you away?"

I ignored her and spun around again. When she complained to her mother that I was showing off, my trunk was taken away. I never saw any of those bright dresses again. The more the Craigies tried to stamp out my fantasy life, the stronger it became. For me, play-acting became a place to hide, another identity to try. One week I was an exiled Indian princess, the next a butterfly on a sunny leaf, lolling and dreaming and warming my wings.

Within months of living in Scotland, I began to develop a warmer, more colourful place in my mind. Montrose was just a location I was passing through, I told myself. I was destined for better, brighter things. I was already living in the future, in a place I hadn't yet found. Life was something that lay ahead of me, not this, not now.

"No good will ever come of you, my girl, until you learn to become a lady," said Provost Craigie.

But what is a lady beyond pretty manners and a demure frock? The Craigies tried to change my outward appearance, but nobody would meddle with my thoughts. When my stepfather sent me a journal covered with gold embroidered indigo silk, I began to confide between the pages.

On quiet afternoons, I would sit by the bedroom window and stare down towards the harbour, watching the fishing boats come and go. At the other end of the street, the tiny window at the top of the steeple remained resolutely closed. In my journal, I wrote about a poor little girl like me, who had been locked up inside. Every day, she sawed at the lock with a knife she had secreted away, until one day the lock finally fell into two pieces in her hands. Pushing open the doors, she jumped from the window without a second thought. She crashed through the air, plummeted downwards towards certain death on the cobbles below. But *then,* a split second before she was dashed, broken and bloodied, against the cold unyielding stones, she sprouted a beautiful pair of snowy-white feathery wings. In my story, she flew far, far away and was never seen in Scotland again.

It was November when I arrived in Montrose, the month when the wild geese came. I remember the sky was filled with their arrival. Perhaps to a wild goose, used to the Arctic wastes, Scotland was a mild and fertile homing ground, but to me it was a chill, unwelcome place. For four years I watched the arrival of the birds in winter, then waited until spring and watched them all fly away. Perhaps, like wild geese, there are people who need constantly to migrate.

I was eleven years old when the Craigies finally dispatched me to my step-aunt Mrs Rae. She, in turn, was to organise my education. As the carriage pulled away from the High Street, I vowed fervently that I would never set foot in Scotland again.

Scene Two

SPRIGGED COTTON

Chapter 5

Here is a fragrant bloom, its slender stem, its tender shoot. If you scrabble beneath the earth, you may find fibrous roots, a pod, a bulb, a tuber or a twisted husk. The seed may have been carried in on the wind or excreted by a bird. Perhaps it was trampled in with the mud from an old man's boot or selected from an illustrated packet by a child with golden curls.

I was eleven years old when I left Montrose. My step-aunt Mrs Rae bustled me down from one stagecoach, then waved as I was drawn away in another. What was I at that age? What did I know? I was a girl with a workhouse haircut and a pocketful of secrets, a girl bursting out of the seams of her clothes. One thing I knew for certain: my childhood was drawing to a close.

As Scotland receded into the distance and distant mountains flattened out into rolling green fields, I scrutinised the gloomy interior of the carriage. The dark leather upholstery had become worn and shiny with age, with a crumbling buff inner skin exposed along its seams. On the shelf above my head, my battered valise with its fading labels from India and Scotland was plastered with a crisp new tag bearing the address of the Aldridge Academy for Young Ladies, Camden Place, Bath. Inside the lid, bound up in parchment and red ribbon, were Papa Craigie's letters. My secret journal was wrapped up and hidden inside an old vest.

Stretching out along the length of the seat, I closed my eyes and pretended that I was still in India, with a warm breeze brushing against my face. In my imagination, I was being carried aloft in a wooden palanquin by four Indian bearers. They were hurrying through the jungle, making up a cheery little song as they went. Falling into a rhythm with the carriage wheels, I chanted my own special words.

> "When I grow up,
> I will travel the world
> and never stop.
> I'll live in a tent,
> instead of a house.
> I'll grow my hair,
> until it sweeps the ground."

I smiled quietly to myself as I pulled a corner of vivid silk from my pocket. When my bright Indian dresses were thrown away, I managed to retrieve a few tattered remnants before the ragman came. Secretly pieced together, then hemmed and stitched, it became a voluminous handkerchief of saffron yellow and peacock blue. When I shook it out, the Indian colours shimmered in the air. It was a flag, a dancing shawl, a magic carpet that could transport me wherever I wanted to go.

By the time we reached Bath, it was nightfall. Under the gaslights, the stone terraces glowed in sulphurous pools. I had never seen such elegant, empty streets. The carriage began to climb. When we reached the top of the hill, the coachman pulled up outside a four-storey town house.

My eyes were immediately drawn to the stone-carved elephant above the door. There was some continuity in life after all. I had ridden elephants from the earliest age. This one wasn't very big and his legs looked shrivelled and strange, but then India was a long way away.

The Aldridge Academy was at the end of a sweeping crescent built in grand, classical style. The central pavilion was topped by a coat of arms between two prancing lions and surmounted by Corinthian pilasters on either side. The entire façade was carved in the same glowing, honey-coloured stone. I was taking in the splendour of it all when the coachman tugged at the bell and two women emerged.

"You must be Miss Gilbert," said one.

"Welcome to the Aldridge Academy," said the other.

"I am Miss Aldridge," said the first.

"So am I," said her companion.

"That is to say," said the first, irritably, "*We* are the Misses Aldridge, though I, of course, am the elder. This is my sister, Miss Elizabeth. You are most welcome to our academy."

The Misses Aldridge nodded at each other and then at me, as if to say that that much at least was agreed. Both sisters had sharp features and tiny mouths. They were slight of frame with the same fine, sandy-coloured hair.

"And your journey?" enquired Miss Aldridge.

"Most agreeable, I hope," said Miss Elizabeth.

"Do let the child answer," scolded her sister.

As they ushered me into the school, the two women plied me with questions.

"Can you play the piano?"

"Sing?"

"Dance a quadrille?"

Beyond the foyer, the corridors became narrower. Behind the classical façade lay a maze of gloomy Spartan rooms. Over tea in a tiny drawing room, the sisters outlined the programme of the academy.

"We turn out young ladies with all the required accomplishments of society," said Miss Elizabeth.

"We try to develop their minds," said Miss Aldridge.

"Not overmuch."

"No, no," her sister agreed.

Both women blushed, as if they had said too much.

"And your French?" asked one.

"*Et ton Français?*" corrected the other.

The elder Miss Aldridge frowned. "It's not a competition, sister."

Miss Elizabeth looked forlorn, then rallied. "Are you familiar with satin stitch, herringbone, French knots? How is your tapestry? Your lacemaking? Your ability to make small, but essential repairs?"

Before I could reply, Miss Aldridge interjected. "Stand up, child," she said.

I acquiesced as first one, then the other, paced around me.

"Certainly she has potential," said the elder, surveying me.

Miss Elizabeth looked doubtful and clasped her hands around my middle. Though I was almost twelve, I still had the plump, undifferentiated torso of a child.

"Perhaps it's not too late."

"Oh dear," said the other. "I see what you mean."

The next morning, my first corset and I were introduced. It sat upright on a bench in the linen room, a forbidding construction of coarse linen and whalebone stays with a flat wooden panel fitted into the front.

"I don't know what they were thinking of in Scotland," said Miss Elizabeth. "They should have had you in a corset by the age of eight."

When my waist was measured, Miss Aldridge and the matron looked appalled.

"Imagine, and she's only eleven," said Matron, who was a stout, florid woman of late middle age.

"I am here," I said. "I can hear every word."

"Hush, child," said Miss Aldridge. "We've got her just in time."

Matron lifted my arms in the air whilst the maid held the corset in place. I looked at it, then down at my waist.

"You need a bigger corset," I said confidently. "That one will never fit."

Whilst I clung to the door, the maid pressed her foot against my behind and struggled to pull in the laces. My ribs began to hurt. Soon I could hardly breathe.

"Tighter, tighter," ordered Miss Aldridge.

The corset bones began to cut into my side. I began to sniffle, then cry. The maid jerked the laces tighter. Every few minutes, they would pause and measure my new waist. Twice the laces snapped and the corset had to be replaced.

"Twenty-two."

"Twenty."

"Eighteen."

At seventeen inches, I felt as if I had been cut in two. Whenever I took a breath my ribs felt crushed. I couldn't bend or sit down; I could hardly move. Any life in me had been squeezed right out. Ignoring my tears, the maid turned me gently to face the glass. The Misses Aldridge and the matron stood back and proudly smiled.

When I saw my reflection, I swiftly wiped my eyes. The loss of seven inches had miraculously produced the figure of a woman. I circled my new waist with my hands, then twisted and turned. Twirling my petticoats, I beamed with delight. With curves such as these, I could imagine what the life of a lady might be like.

After the corset fitting, I picked my way carefully back to the dormitory, only to find my trunk upended on my bed and my dismal shabby clothes scattered all over the eiderdown. A pretty dark-headed girl looked up as I entered the room. Her hair was dressed in ringlets, and she was wearing a dress of pale lemon silk.

"My dear girl," she said, "you haven't a decent stitch to wear."

As I opened my mouth to protest, the corset pressed against my ribs.

"Ouch," I said.

"You can call me Sophia, if you like," she said, as she continued to rummage through my clothes.

"Sophia," I stiffly replied, "I would be obliged if you would leave my personal possessions alone."

Sophia giggled. "My," she said, "don't you get cross. I could give you some pink velvet ribbon, if you like, or a length of sky-blue tulle."

I sat carefully down on the edge of the bed and began to gather up my clothes.

Sophia pouted. "May I have the pleasure of this cross girl's name?"

"Eliza Gilbert," I replied.

"That's a very sensible name," she said. "But are you a sensible girl? For myself, I was born with the name of Sarah. About my family name there is still some debate. Sophia is the title to which I aspire."

Whilst I gawped at her, she smiled, and then began to help me fold up my grey and sensible clothes.

"Eliza," she repeated. "Is that really the best you can do?"

A dozen possibilities were already bubbling up in my mind.

"You can be whomsoever you choose," she whispered.

"Bettina?" I offered.

Sophia shook her head.

"Too similar," she said.

I shuffled through a few more options, searching for something suitably romantic, or exotic, or melodramatic, until I realised that I already possessed the perfect designation, in the form of my hitherto unused middle name.

"Rosana," I decided, but in an instant, the name went from being too fanciful to too plain. "Rosana Maria," I added, with a flourish.

Sophia clapped her hands and smiled. "There you are," she said. "I knew we could be friends."

Inside the academy were fifteen girls ranging from the ages of ten to sixteen. Everything we did was watched over by Miss Aldridge or Miss Elizabeth. In the dormitories, there were seven or eight of us cooped up in each room. Our lessons all took place in the same large classroom.

In the mornings, one group of girls recited French, another memorised the words of philosophers or studied the arts, while a third group chanted from their Latin primers and a fourth wrote themes for the literature class. If I closed my eyes, the aphorisms of the philosophers became jumbled up with lists of Latin verbs;

French declensions merged with orations on etiquette or Ancient Greece.

The afternoon lessons were the important ones. "Preparations for life," the elder Miss Aldridge termed them. "The Necessary Accomplishments of a Young Lady of Society" was Miss Elizabeth's favoured term. Between dance steps and embroidery stitches, we learned how to walk and talk, how to sit down daintily or stand. We practised the piano or made sketches of bowls of fruit whilst Miss Elizabeth solemnly recited her list of magic rules.

"A young lady's gait should be neither too fast nor too slow. Her expression must be demure and modest. In conversation, she must be neither too animated, nor overtly loud. She should never run, nor giggle, nor frown."

Where Miss Elizabeth dreamily sighed, her sister busily came and went, slapping a crossed knee here or straightening a drooping back. "Deportment, deportment," she cried.

Outside the window, a constant stream of fine carriages and barouches passed by. From the briefest glimpse of their occupants, Sophia and I conjured up entire imaginary worlds. One evening we watched a lady in a frock of apricot tarlatan being handed down from a gleaming carriage and a young man skimming the pavement in a leisurely ironic bow. We imagined balls and assignations, a whole brimming, swimming world that one day would catch us up and carry us both away. The Misses Aldridge represented a severe warning of what we might become if we failed. We practised demure smiles intensely. Sophia taught me how to swoon. I coached her through the steps of the minuet.

"You have to be languid," I scolded. "You have to learn how to melt and droop and flow."

I wore my corset faithfully for a few hours every day. Gradually, I learned how to walk in it, then how to lower myself into a seat, then rise. Slowly I trained myself to bow in it, then to dance without wincing or clenching my teeth.

The sole masculine presence among us was the Latin master, Mr Humphrey Quill. Young Mr Quill, as the Misses Aldridge referred to him, was a slender man with fair hair and colourless eyes, who stammered except when on the subjects of Latin and Roman Bath. When he recited verse, his cheeks glowed and he waved his arms about. Sometimes he positively quivered with the excitement of it all.

"Pray tell, Mr Quill," Sophia would teasingly ask, "in what terms might one express a romantic attachment?"

"Latin," Mr Quill would reply, "is the language of the gods. What better place than Bath, the city of the Romans, to learn the language of love?"

It was Mr Quill who took us on our first extensive tour of the city, marching us through the streets in pairs, like little chattering ducklings, reciting Latin verbs. He would take us through the conjugations for "*regere*", and we would switch it back to "*amare*".

Steering us through the city, Mr Quill pointed out its more edifying aspects whilst we continued to chant. Future simple, imperfect, perfect, future perfect. By the time we reached the pluperfect, we had been escorted down the hill, past the Assembly Rooms and were circling the Abbey.

At the Pump Rooms, where the spa water was served, Mr Quill rather reluctantly allowed us to venture inside. Beyond the double-fronted doors, the interior opened up into a vast airy room. Corinthian pillars decorated the walls; stuccoed pediments surmounted the door. Light poured in from oval windows on every side. Chamber music drifted from the western apse. I drew myself up to my full height and happily sighed. Sophia squealed with delight. Fashionable ladies strolled arm in arm; gentlemen sprawled around tables reading newspapers. Proceeding directly to the pump, Mr Quill shuffled us all swiftly into line.

"Of course, it is only Catholics and primitives who believe in holy water. Here in the Pump Rooms, the partaking of mineral water is purely scientific. The magnesium, I believe, is particularly beneficial."

60

While Mr Quill extolled its virtues, we sipped steadily from our glasses. Beyond the pump, I caught glimpses of the King's Bath through the windows. The walls were stained a fiery terracotta, and the water was a simmering milky-green. On the arm of two maids, a florid middle-aged woman, dressed in brown sacking that billowed out in the water around her, was descending the slips. Behind her a stout, bilious-looking man circled stoically round and round, his face growing redder with every turn.

I tugged at Sophia's arm, and she giggled at the sight. Mr Quill became flustered and tried to block our view.

Mr Quill could not restrict himself to the scientific properties of the water for very long. By the time we were draining our glasses, he was in full and fervent flow.

"There is a temple to the goddess Minerva, below this very room," he pronounced.

Beneath the civilised surface of Bath bubbled an ancient pagan heart, it seemed. Where we were genteelly sipping water, the Romans had once plunged naked into hot and steamy pools. Mr Quill described a temple busy with scribes, drawing up charms on behalf of the good people of Bath.

"Imagine thousands of wishes," he sighed. "Weighted down with coins and tossed into the water, they sank to the bottom of the pool. The air would have been heavy with scented oils, with benzoin and sandalwood."

I came to think of Bath, with its fashionable town houses and bustling streets, as a beautiful backdrop to some graceful, elegant play. On our daily walks, we caught tantalising glimpses of it before we were bundled away. Thirteen, fourteen, fifteen; it seemed we would be for ever waiting in the wings. Our teachers constantly watched over us, as if we could be tainted by a look or easily bruised. In Cheap Street, there were noisy girls with grubby cheeks, apparently selling watercress. When the police approached, they picked up their ragged skirts and ran. Outside the Pump Rooms, there was one little girl of nine or ten, with a peaky face, a blue nose and liquid eyes. She hawked tiny bunches of violets with a voice that belied her size. If I looked at her too long, she stuck out her tongue. One day I noticed a gentleman in a frock coat beckon to her, and the pair of them disappeared into a nearby alleyway.

Within the academy, the daughters of the lesser aristocracy formed a natural elite. Below them were the daughters of members of parliament and the upper gentry. On the next rung came the higher ranks of the army, the daughters of major-generals and commanders. I was merely the stepdaughter of a captain. When I first arrived, my lowly status was quickly established, and I was patronised like some country cousin. Within a year, my stepfather had been promoted and my aptitude for dance noted. The slights grew less and my currency rose. For obvious reasons, I had neglected to mention any Irish affiliation. Then Amelia Seymour arrived from Cork, and a whole new difficulty arose.

As the daughter of landed gentry, Amelia had naively assumed that she would take her natural place at the top of the pecking order. Not only was she keen to declare her own connections, she was also familiar with mine. With Amelia busy making pronouncements, I suffered an instant drop in status. As far as the other girls were concerned, the Anglo-Irish were not only distant, but regrettable cousins. I could hardly say we were not really Irish, not Irish-Irish, not the brogue talking, rosary-bead waving, fighting kind of Irish. "I am from the ascendancy," Amelia pleaded. "I am from the ruling elite." Cork was a small place. Within days she had carved out a niche by establishing her distance from me.

"I hear your mother was nothing but a hat girl," she sneered.

"My grandfather was Sir Charles Silver Oliver," I said defiantly.

"But your grandmother was a whore," laughed Amelia.

Thank goodness Sophia remained my friend. Dear Sophia was the illegitimate child of the Duke of Clarence. As such, she was both above and beneath us all.

Sophia and I made pacts and promises. Formulating our wishes, we wrote them out on fragments of paper. We pulled in our corsets another degree tighter and prayed for smaller waists. Our bodies began to shift and mutate. Sophia developed breasts, then so did I. Patches of dark hair appeared in secret unexpected places. In private, Matron gave me napkins of layered linen, padded and stitched.

Sophia and I tried every new fashion, me improvising with muslin, Sophia with silk. In Paris, the ladies dampened their dresses so that the flimsy fabric clung to their breasts, but when we tried it, we just looked bedraggled and wet. Fourteen, fifteen, sixteen; the years passed in a tangle of etiquette and Latin grammar. We dreamed of balls and gowns, and of love that was boundless.

On one of our afternoon walks, I noticed a boy who lingered by the corner of Shire's Yard. He was a rough-looking fellow with a shock of black hair and an insolent stare. The sight of his square fingers and grimy nails made me shudder. I glared back at him once, expecting him to respectfully lower his eyes. Instead he looked straight back at me, and then bared his teeth in a wolfish grin. As we passed by, I could feel his eyes survey my neck and throat. In bed that night, I thought of him and lay awake, agitated and appalled.

When I was almost sixteen, I began to receive stilted letters from my mother, written in a childish hand. Compared to the sparse little notes that I was accustomed to, this new correspondence was positively fulsome. *How are you, my daughter?* she wrote. *We are so looking forward to welcoming you home.* At the same time, my stepfather's letters, which had lately become less frequent and more formal, began to refer to me as a young lady. Closing my eyes, I tried to conjure up my mother's face, but it was a bit like trying to see through water or a thick distorting glass. She was like a beautiful painting that had always hung in the drawing room—a rather formal portrait that one appreciates and admires. In her letters, she called me *darling* and *dear,* and I tried to respond in kind. I sensed that there was something she wanted or expected from me, and I puzzled and brooded over what it might be.

Once we turned sixteen, Sophia and I watched as girls dropped away from school like flies in wintertime. As news of engagements and weddings drifted back, we began to feel jittery. It was all very well to dream of a lover; it was quite something else to be thrown into some man's arms. In her letters, my mother began to write about Calcutta and the new gowns I would require. Her correspondence became a checklist of accomplishments and dance steps. *Perhaps*, she suggested, *you are ready to enter society?* A warm expansive feeling bubbled up in my chest. After all this time, it seemed that Mama wanted me to live with her and Major Craigie again. Imagine! I would be part of a family again! When I closed my eyes, I could almost feel the heat of the Indian sun against my skin. Towards the end of October, Mama wrote that she was coming to collect me in person.

> *Sailing from Calcutta 2nd November 1836. Arrive in Bath, God willing, by the beginning of May 1837. We will have such fun together, you and I.*

I had to read the letter twice.

"Imagine. Mama here in Bath!" I said.

When I showed Sophia the letter, she hugged me.

"I'm so pleased for you," she said. "Your mother will take care of everything."

"But what about you?" I asked.

"Don't worry about me," she said airily. "I will probably make my debut in London or Cheltenham."

My eyes widened. "Really?" I said.

"This is it then," said Sophia.

We stared solemnly at each other, before bursting into fits of nervous giggles.

I clapped my hands together, then made a pantomime bow like a gentleman at a formal ball. "May I have the pleasure?" I asked.

Sophia swished her skirts. "I will think of you every time I dance a minuet!" she replied.

We danced deliriously around the dormitory until we fell giddily on to the beds. After lights out, we exchanged specially made handkerchiefs. Mine to Sophia featured our two initials entwined; hers, to me, was embroidered with an elephant in the corner. In the darkness, we clung together, promising each other that no matter what happened, we would always write.

Chapter 6

All morning my ears had been alert as a cat's. Over the preceding weeks, I had meticulously charted my mother's voyage through the pages of the atlas—from the Bay of Bengal across the Indian Ocean, dipping down around the Cape of Good Hope. I had even mapped out her journey from Gravesend to Bath. Sophia was putting the finishing touches to my hair when we heard the carriage draw up outside. Peering out of the window, we saw an attractive woman in a voluminous cloud of pink brocaded silk adjusting her bonnet and smoothing out her gown. My heart swung like a pendulum. My mother, I thought, imagining a warm embrace, a guiding hand. My mother, I thought, remembering unanswered letters and my grubby fingerprints on the skirts of a pristine gown. I was accustomed to thinking of her as a distant and untouchable creature, I realised, not actual flesh and blood.

"She looks just like you," said Sophia.

"She does not!" I retorted.

Sophia raised an eyebrow. My response caught us both by surprise.

The woman outside had my dark hair and eyes. But were hers brown or blue? I sat down in front of the mirror and peered at my reflection. A moment before, I had seen a sophisticated young woman; now all I saw was a silly child with her hair piled up in a ridiculous adult style.

Sophia had spent the morning arranging it in the latest fashion. From a centre parting, the front sections had been smoothed down on either side of my head, and then looped over each ear; the rest was swept up into a knot at the back. I patted my coiffure anxiously, but Sophia smiled.

"You look very grown up," she said. "Your mother will hardly recognise you."

Downstairs, the door to the drawing room was ajar, and in my haste, I dashed through it and collided directly into Mama. Throwing my arms nervously around her, I kissed both her cheeks. She had hardly returned my embrace when I felt her draw away.

Holding me at arm's length, she looked me up and down.

"My dear child," she said. "What on earth have you done to your hair?"

Before I could reply, the Misses Aldridge came to the rescue with their echoing chatter about journeys and weather and cups of tea. The fine china had been laid out, and there was a small selection of dainty little sponge cakes. Whilst the two sisters quibbled over who should do the honours, my mother settled down and removed her bonnet.

To my astonishment, I saw that her hair was dressed in *exactly* the same style as mine, with the addition of pink fabric flowers inset in the knot on the top of her head!

I examined her with a critical eye. Her clothes were so new they squeaked. Yards of fabric had been used in her gown with its leg-of-mutton sleeves and ruffled neck. Even her shoes and her bonnet were made from the same pink brocade. Her eyes were plain brown, I noticed, not blue.

If I'm not good enough for you, I thought, *then you're not good enough for me.*

"The voyage was dreadful. You can't imagine," she said. "At least we shall have a little entertainment before we have to return. I've booked us a charming suite of rooms."

The elder Miss Aldridge coughed. "It is only May, Mrs Craigie. The end of the school year is not actually until June."

Mother frowned, then gestured from my dress to my shoes. "But we have so much to do. For goodness sake, child, look at you."

"But Mama," I pleaded.

I was thinking of Sophia. If I left school now, we would probably never see each other again.

"Very well," she said. "You may complete your studies, but you will stay with me in the rooms."

For the duration of the tea, she chattered about fellow passengers on her trip, her impressions of Bath, the charming acquaintance who had sorted out the rooms for her. The Misses Aldridge tried intermittently to discuss my education, but Mama would simply nod and then change the subject.

"I would be pleased to show you around," I offered. "I am acquainted with the Pump Rooms, and there's the Abbey and the Baths, of course."

"Not the Assembly Rooms?" she asked.

"My dear," said Miss Aldridge, "the girl is only seventeen."

"Indeed," said Mama.

That very afternoon, Mama and I took a carriage to our new quarters, which were located on the Circus, one of the most fashionable addresses in Bath. The plan agreed between Mama and the Misses Aldridge was that I would be allowed a few days to pack and make my goodbyes. A coach would then be sent for me and my belongings on Saturday morning.

"You poor child, being locked away with those dreadful spinster sisters," said Mama, as soon as we were outside.

The Circus bustled with carriages; on the pavements, neighbours exchanged nods and smiles. Mama strained this way and that, taking it all in. We had been driven round once, when she urged the coachman to go round again.

The apartment consisted of a spacious double drawing room, two bedrooms, a dining room and servants' quarters. Mama opened her arms as if to embrace the splendidness of it all, and then turned her attention to me.

"You must tell me what the latest fashions are here in Bath. And what are the gentlemen like?"

At this she laughed.

"But of course, you can't answer that particular question. Not just yet. So tell me about this school of yours. Though God knows, you have too much education for your own good."

I opened my mouth to reply, but Mama was already drawing up an extensive list.

"Ah yes, shoes, of course, and at least three dresses. How are your petticoats?"

I lifted up my skirts.

"For pity's sake. There is no need to show me."

She was a handsome woman. Of that there was no doubt. In my shabby, girlish dress and my patched petticoats, I felt like a lesser version of her.

"You always did like to display yourself," she said.

No, I didn't, I thought. *Or perhaps I did, but I was only six.* I stared at this beautiful woman who claimed to be my mother. *Perhaps she is an impostor*, I thought hopefully. *Perhaps she is not my mother at all.*

Within a week of her arrival, Mama had organised a soirée. "Regard it as a rehearsal," she said. As my new dresses were not yet ready, I was to wear one of her more modest gowns, a pale sprigged muslin with a draped neck, over a new corset which was lightly padded and heavily boned. It took the maid more than thirty minutes to lace it up, and then when we put the dress on over the top, my breasts were pushed up and exposed. I stared at my reflection in the mirror. On Mama, the dress had looked girlish and feminine, but on me, it produced a decidedly different effect.

"Well, you are uncommonly well-formed. I don't know where you get it from," said Mama, patting the sleek lines of her own slender figure.

Fanning out the muslin drapes around the neck of the dress, she pinned a silk flower to my décolletage.

"Whatever you do, don't breathe too heavily," she said.

"But, Mama . . ."

At that the doorbell rang. Blowing me a kiss, she left the room, and I reluctantly joined her by the door.

The first guest was a gentleman with wooden teeth, the second a thin, looming man with a wolfish grin. There were three plump ladies of indeterminate age, a man whose hair had been dyed a sticky-looking brown and a kindly man with a pink, shiny face. The one man who could passably be called young appeared to be about the same age as Mama.

When she introduced us, he scanned my chest.

"I see the fruits of the mother have ripened in the daughter," he beamed.

Mama proffered a sparkling smile, which didn't quite reach her eyes.

"We'll have no such talk in front of the child," she said.

I was mortified. Once all the guests had arrived, I ran to my room and draped myself in a shawl. In the drawing room, Mama stripped it away and then pushed me into the centre of the room. Goose pimples prickled on the tops of my breasts.

"Stand up straight and smile," she hissed.

Whilst the two hired servants offered glasses of pale, sweet sherry, Mama announced that I was about to play the piano.

"I am proud to present my daughter, who has just completed her education," she said. "Her father insisted upon it. It can't be helped."

My cheeks reddened as I struggled with a gavotte.

Throughout the evening, Mama whispered instructions to me in between mingling with her guests. "Watch me," she said. "All the crucial lessons in life are to be learned in mixed company." When the man with wooden teeth slid his arm around my waist, I glanced over at her. In one elegant movement, she wreathed the toothy gentleman in smiles and whisked me away.

"By all means, draw the gentleman out, reward him with smiles, a twinkle of the eye," she whispered. "But remember, there are favours men want, but not from a future wife."

Someone once said that my mother was like a turtle that lays her eggs in the sand, and then leaves them to nature or chance. Not for a moment had she considered that a daughter of hers might be anything other than a presentable young woman. Yet for all the care she had taken these past ten years, anything could have happened to me. I could have been lame or dead. I could have had squint eyes or the coarse thick ankles of a pit girl. I could have had a stammer or be covered in moles, and she wouldn't have known. As it so happened, nature had taken its course and given me hips and breasts and a not unpleasant face, and that was apparently all that concerned her.

"I really don't know why you want to stay at school any longer," she said. "We have such a lot to do."

It transpired that we were booked to sail to India in August, hardly three months time.

"You'll love it in Calcutta; you'll be the belle of the ball. Once we've sorted out your clothes, of course."

"It's only another month," I said. At least whilst I was still at school, I could tell Sophia all my news.

"Anyone would think that you didn't want to go to India," retorted Mama.

"Of course, I do. I can't wait," I said.

"Men don't look for education in a woman. It's the last thing you need," said Mama. "At your age I was married with a child of three."

Towards the end of the evening, Mama introduced the name of a certain eligible judge into the conversation. Such a marriage, she implied, would have any number of advantages. For her and my stepfather as well as myself. Not least, it would allow us to associate with the cream of Calcutta society.

"He is a fine gentleman, a widower," she said. "You could hardly wish for more."

"A widower!" I cried. "And how old, pray, is he?"

"What does age matter?" she asked.

"How old?"

"If you don't like the father, he has two sons."

"How old?" I persisted.

"Fifty-nine," my mother shrugged.

"Fifty-nine!" I squealed.

"But enough," she said. "We mustn't forget our guests."

So Mama would have me marry an old man, simply in order to fulfil her own social ambitions. Was that the sum of her regard for me? I glanced at the middle-aged men gathered together in the drawing room. I should have liked a young husband with strong white teeth and his own hair. Was that really too much to ask?

Over the coming weeks, Mama devoted herself to my transformation. We made trips to the dressmakers, the cordwainer, the glover. Petticoats, chemises and nightshirts were ordered in bulk. Measurements were taken for two day dresses, an afternoon frock and my first evening gown.

As we traipsed from one establishment to another, Mama passed on everything she knew. She taught me how to smile—slightly but often; when to withhold my opinion—most of the time; how to order shop girls about—with absolute confidence and authority; to distinguish between fabrics; and most importantly of all, to have an opinion on hats. In my mother's eyes, it seemed, the essence of a lady was displayed upon her head.

At the milliner's, her scrutiny of linings and stitches was enough to make me blush.

"Do you have to, Mother?" I protested.

"Nonsense, child," she replied. "I wish I made hats still. Millinery makes an outfit. It can turn a woman into a queen."

When she described her favourite hats, I hardly knew whether she was teasing me or not.

"In Ireland I made a hat with a tiny sailing ship on top and another piled high with exotic fruit."

The milliner and I exchanged glances.

When Mama settled upon a modest dinner cap of spotted tulle and two bonnets, one fabric, one straw, I let out a little sigh of relief.

Between assessing fabrics and sipping tea, I was becoming

acquainted with Mama's attitudes and ways. I wish I could say she took the trouble to understand me, but her attention never stretched beyond whether I suited pink or blue.

"You're my daughter, aren't you?" she said. "That's good enough for me."

Shortly after my mother's arrival, I had introduced her to Sophia, in the hopes that our friendship might continue. The next time I attended the academy, I discovered that Mama had made enquiries, then left instructions that Sophia and I were to be kept apart. "She is too feverish," Mama said, but I knew that it was her illegitimacy she couldn't abide.

Sophia and I gazed at each other longingly across the classroom. Without her, I had no one in whom to confide my greatest fears, nor from whom to seek advice. Though I told Mama repeatedly that I wouldn't marry the judge, she just laughed at me.

"How will you survive alone?" she asked. "Perhaps you'll sell posies in the street?"

Mama had been in Bath for almost a month when a new gentleman called. I was in the drawing room, half-heartedly embroidering a pattern of pale wisteria, when the doorbell rang repeatedly. It was a bright May morning and the room was filled with light. Beyond the windows, the Circus gardens were bursting with tulips and sweet william. In between stitches, I was composing a letter to Sophia in my mind. In less than three months, Mama expected me to be married off. Nothing I said could persuade her to change her mind. The very brightness of the day made me feel raw and sad. I thought of a young bud crushed in an old man's wrinkled hand. Of the petals of spent tulips splayed across the ground.

"A Lieutenant Thomas James," announced the maid.

The last thing I felt inclined to do was entertain.

"Surely he should leave a card," I said.

I was about to send him away when Mama came flying breathlessly into the room.

"Thomas James?"

I watched her with fresh interest. I had never seen her so flushed and disconcerted before. What manner of gentleman had so unsettled her, I wondered? My own troubles were momentarily forgotten, my curiosity aroused. While he was kept waiting, the room was swiftly rearranged and the maid sent out to buy a cake.

"I met him on the voyage over from India," Mama explained.

"You've never mentioned him before," I said.

We both listened intently for footsteps in the hall. It is in such slight moments that a life laid firmly along one route can suddenly waver, then change course.

Chapter 7

The drawing room crackled with energy. The maid looked nervous; Mama was unnaturally still. The full-length looking glass had been removed, the sewing hidden away. Three times, a vase of peonies had been repositioned around the room. When the lieutenant was shown in, he clicked his heels and bowed.

I glanced from Mama to our guest, but I could discern nothing in his appearance to explain her tremulous response. He was neither tall nor short. His chestnut hair was neither deep of hue nor fair. His eyes, though blue, were neither strikingly brooding nor pale. The red uniform jacket and narrow trousers were no more or less becoming on him than on any other officer.

In her violet gown, Mama looked pale as porcelain, the only colour in her face a glaze of pink across her cheeks.

When the lieutenant spoke, his accent betrayed Irish origins. His teeth, I noticed, were sparkling and white.

"Mrs Craigie," he said.

"Thomas," she smiled.

Mama's accent deepened in response to his. Their nationality hung like an intimacy between them. I recalled soft rain over a blue distant mountain. I had not thought about Ireland for a very long time. When Lieutenant James kissed Mama's hand, her cheeks glowed. Something passed between them that I couldn't comprehend.

"My dear lieutenant," said Mama, "I am so happy to see you. You are fully convalesced, I hope?"

"Indeed. A month in Ireland did me the world of good. It was grand to be home."

Mama nodded.

"This is my daughter, Eliza."

The lieutenant kissed my hand.

"You are almost as beautiful as your mother."

I attempted a smile. It was not quite the compliment I would have wished for.

Mama tilted her head. "I hope you can spend a little time with us, here in Bath," she said.

"Indeed," he replied. "I imagine we may be returning to India at about the same time."

Tea, that afternoon, drew on towards evening. A second round of refreshments was ordered, then a third. Though the conversation was restricted to niceties, some other form of communication seemed to linger behind the words. The next day, Lieutenant James called again. Two days later, he invited us to the Pump Rooms. Soon he was calling almost every day. He escorted Mama and me around the town, to the theatre and for promenades through the gardens. In the evenings, they would go to the Assembly Rooms together. Often they spent time alone.

One day a large, new trunk appeared in the middle of Mama's bedroom. Whenever the deliveries of my new clothes were made, she would allow me a chemise or a petticoat. The remaining garments were wrapped carefully in tissue paper and placed in the trunk. When my new gowns arrived, Mama insisted that they stay within their shrouds of protective muslin.

"They are for your trousseau," she said.

"But, Mama," I pleaded, "whilst we remain in Bath, I need something to wear."

"They are for India," she declared.

Two plain muslin frocks were quickly made up for me. One was a stark white, the other a pale pink that didn't flatter me at all. Sometimes, when Mama wasn't in, I would wistfully finger the elegant new dresses through their coverings.

"You have only to comply with my wishes and you can wear the new gowns whenever you like," said Mama.

As a rehearsal for the Grand Regimental Ball in Calcutta, it had been conceded that I might attend the Assembly Rooms at least once.

"But don't you be getting any ideas," said Mama. "You will marry the judge, let there be no doubt."

At the dressmaker's, my evening gown was slowly emerging from bales of creamy silk and yards of net and lace. At fitting after fitting, the seamstresses honed and refined their creation. The neckline was looped and draped around the shoulders; flounces were pinned into the skirt. As the waist grew smaller, the skirts seemed to billow endlessly across the floor.

Standing in front of the mirror, I swayed from side to side, enjoying the swish of silk around my feet. Any thoughts of our imminent return to India vanished from my mind.

"Keep still, child," said the dressmaker.

I raised my arms whilst two seamstresses, with pins clenched between their teeth, tightened the bodice. I was happily daydreaming about the forthcoming ball—everybody watching in admiration as I swirled elegantly across the floor—when my attention was drawn to a lacemaker working quietly in a corner. Her eyes were strangely unfocused and wavering. From between rapid, nimble fingers issued a stream of fine, creamy lace.

I nudged Mama.

"Hush, child," she said. "Can't you see that the poor woman is blind?"

The proprietress, noticing my distraction, directed the woman to lay the lace out on to the counter.

Turning to Mama, she said: "This is the Bath lace you ordered for the young lady's dress. Do you remember?"

The lace was a delicate tracery of silken threads caught up into a beautiful filigree pattern of birds, twisting vines, foliage and flowers. Whilst Mama was admiring it, the lacemaker returned to her seat and proceeded to create a fresh batch. The joints of her fingers were swollen, I noticed, the tips of her fingers raw.

My excitement about the gown disintegrated in front of my eyes. When the seamstress began to pin the lace to the neckline, I shuddered.

"I prefer it without the lace," I said.

"Don't be ridiculous," said Mama. "The lace has been specially made."

"I mean it," I said.

The seamstress tentatively continued. An assistant began to warily tack lengths of lace to the flounces of the skirt, until I couldn't stand it any more. Regardless of flying pins and loosening stitches, I tugged the dress from my shoulders. As I struggled out of the bodice, the pins scratched my skin, and a tiny drop of blood landed on the skirt. Before any further damage could be done, the seamstress helped me to climb free of the skirts.

Mama and the dressmaker exchanged perplexed looks. One of the seamstresses nodded towards the lacemaker, by way of explanation. But even after the wretched woman had been sent away, I could still see her busy twisted fingers endlessly spewing forth flurries of fine-spun ethereal lace.

The lieutenant became a regular part of our lives. At soirées, he and Mama would sit together exchanging confidential remarks. For the briefest moment, she would gently rest her hand over his. He remained gallant yet quiet. Mama became careless of the proprieties. The frequency of his visits became the subject of gossip. His protectiveness towards her did not go unremarked. I began to refer to him as Mama's cavalier because he attended to her every need. He picked up her shawl for her; he refilled her glass. He had a calming effect on her, I noticed. She was less brittle in his company.

For myself, I liked him well enough. He listened to what I had to say, and I was grateful to him for that. When he escorted me to school, we would talk of the events of the day.

Left alone, Mama and I had little flare-ups between ourselves.

When the lieutenant was visiting, we kept a polite distance. In his company, she would treat me as if I were a harmless, yet precocious child.

"Isn't it strange," I ventured one day, "that one young girl may become ruler of the whole country, yet women may not even vote?"

"A little republican," smiled Thomas.

"Don't indulge her," said Mama.

The lieutenant had brought a newspaper with him. Whilst he was waiting for Mama, I eagerly read the front page. King William was critically ill. If he died, his young niece, the princess Alexandrina Victoria, was next in line for the throne.

When Mama came into the room, she snatched the paper from my hand.

"Perhaps next time you could leave your newspaper in your club," she chided the lieutenant.

He raised an eyebrow, and then continued regardless.

"It is certainly ridiculous that a young girl of eighteen may conceivably became queen," he said.

"She has a mother to guide her," said Mama.

"Perhaps some young girls are more capable than will be admitted," I suggested. "If one may rule, then perhaps others might have some small say over their lives."

"Being opinionated is an ugly trait in a young girl," said Mama.

To the lieutenant she said, "Politics is hardly a fit subject for mixed company."

When the maid came in, Mama asked her to take the newspaper away.

"I'm sorry if I am unable to entirely confine my thoughts to gossip and embroidery," I snapped.

Taking my leave, I caught up with the maid. I spent the afternoon in my room, reading the newspaper from cover to cover. I pored over every boring detail, every laborious report. I even read the advertisements and the sports pages.

The trunk in Mama's room steadily filled. I was kept in my two plain frocks whilst the clothes in the trunk became steadily more refined. When some new garment was delivered, Mama would call to me, and I would hover by the doorway. When she went out, I would go and peep inside, before resolutely closing both her door and the lid of the trunk. Did she really think she could buy my acquiescence? At the sight of a pair of embroidered blue brocade slippers with yellow silk lining, my resolve weakened. I could picture myself gliding across an elegant drawing room in slippers like those, inviting guests into my very own ballroom. The contents of the trunk promised a rarefied and cosseted life. What other real choice did I have? I recalled the little girl outside the Pump Rooms disappearing with the man in the frock coat. When I had pointed them out to Sophia, she had scoffed at me in disbelief: "I don't think the gentleman is interested in buying violets, never mind watercress!"

A month after leaving school, I made my debut at the Assembly Rooms. I wore the cream silk evening gown; Mama wore a shimmering icy pink. Overhead, the chandeliers hung like huge glittering cities. The walls were a vast expanse of aqueous blue. Light blazed from candles, jewels, diamond-encrusted gowns. I saw a flushed young girl in a puffed skirt that looked like a meringue and a young gentleman whose starched collar was so tall that, when he moved suddenly, it chafed his cheeks.

Passing the ballroom mirrors, I caught delicious glimpses of myself. My shoulders rose from a neckline of tucks and drapes, my skirt frothed out in creamy flounces from a tiny waist. I was all curves and plumage. I was voluptuous as a swan. The lieutenant parted the crowds, whilst Mama and I nodded and bowed. My eyes were caught first by the décor, then by the gowns. I was so dazzled that I hardly noticed the gentlemen signing my dance card. My eyes flitted from one sight to another like a pollen-drunk butterfly in the height of summer. Plaster garlands and laurel branches were festooned across the ceiling; palm leaves and rosettes decorated the fireplaces. I saw a woman whose head was crowned with arching ostrich feathers in baby blue and a grinning man with two metal plates instead of teeth.

By the time we took our seats, my dance card was almost full. I glanced down the list of names, but only the first was familiar.

Lieutenant James bowed and we took to the floor.

"You look charming," he said.

"Almost as beautiful as Mama?" I asked.

As we moved into the opening dance, both of us glanced at Mama, who was being partnered three couples down the line. She was lovely, of that there was no doubt. Everything about her was delicate and neat. She was like some exquisite, finely crafted doll. I straightened my back. Mama may be pretty, I thought, but I have youth on my side. As one star fades, another rises. I have a woman's shape whereas she still has the slight figure of a girl.

As we danced, I gathered up admiring glances and hugged them to myself. What would it take, I wondered, to break the bond between Mama and her cavalier, to keep his attention entirely focused on me? At the conclusion of the dance, the lieutenant placed his hand on the small of my back. I felt his touch tingle through me as he led me from the floor.

When the lingerie for my trousseau arrived, Mama offered to demonstrate how each intimate item should be worn. In her bedroom, I watched her rummaging greedily through the tissue paper, then swooning in front of the mirror with another sumptuous scrap of lace held up in front of her; a camisole in fine cambric muslin trimmed with parchment lace, a morning gown of white piqué with a cape collar, a gauzy negligée trimmed with Valenciennes lace. Her eyes were hooded with pleasure, like a woman dreaming of her lover.

"Let me show you," she said.

I gritted my teeth. "That is very kind of you, Mama," I said, "but we are neither the same size nor shape."

She turned sharply towards me, tossing the negligée into my arms.

"You don't know how lucky you are," she snapped. "When I was first wed, I had to make do with a borrowed gown. The only new things I had were a crocheted bonnet and a square of cotton lace."

The days flew from the calendar. The tickets for our passage to India arrived. On those days that Mama could spare him, Lieutenant James continued to escort me to school. Sophia had recently been removed from the academy and, without her, I had no one in whom to confide. I had arrived at school one day to find a letter and a length of sky-blue tulle (now faded). She was staying in Cheltenham with an aunt who hoped to arrange a suitable marriage for her.

"Embrace the future!" she wrote.

Perhaps it was the walking that made me open up. It brought back memories of endless strolls up and down the decks of ships, my tiny paw caught in the palm of my father's reassuring hand.

"You must call me Thomas," Lieutenant James would say. But I couldn't, he was so much older than me. Instead, I would reply that I thought of him as a father, that he would always be Lieutenant James to me.

As the date of departure drew nearer, I could think of nothing else.

"Am I just a chattel of my mother's?" I pleaded. "Do I really have to go?"

"You have to marry sometime," said the lieutenant.

"But I am only seventeen; would you leave me in the hands of some old man?"

"An older man may be kinder."

"Some old man pawing me? Is that all I am worth?"

"Your mother only wants what is best for you, you know that."

"Mama would listen to you."

"I don't know," he said.

"Do you want me to get down on my knees?" I said.

"Don't be so dramatic, child."

I turned on him in fury.

"Don't call me child," I said.

I could feel my breath catching fast—in my chest, in my throat, in my mouth. I glared at the lieutenant, and he stared back with a strange, puzzled look. For a moment neither of us spoke. I could feel his breath on my face. At last, he cleared his throat. His chestnut hair was glossy and thick, I noticed. His eyes were the softest blue.

One evening when Mama and the lieutenant were out, I stripped off my clothes and slipped into the lace negligée. It was semi-transparent, revealing the outline of my body. Panels of lace across my breasts and thighs made patterns against my skin. In it, I felt more naked than if I had been wearing no clothes at all.

Perched on the edge of Mama's bed, I tried to imagine that it was my wedding night. The gauzy fabric brushed my skin. I felt a quiver of unease between my thighs. I imagined waiting. But for whom? And what was meant to happen next?

As my eyes traced the intricate patterns, I recalled the sight of lace issuing from between twisted, arthritic fingers. In the corner of some dark, cramped room, some miserable wretch was producing, for a pittance, an endless flow of these intricate gossamer veils. I felt as if I had been caught in some deadly, silken web: imprisoned by the contents of a trousseau. Throwing off the negligée with a shudder, I scrabbled into the safety of my own chaste, girlish clothes.

June was a traditional month for weddings; on Saturday after Saturday, bells rang out and brides issued from churches. Even the trees were decked out in their bridal best. After my last day at school, I pleaded with the lieutenant once again. We had taken a diversion through the botanic gardens. The rhododendrons were draped in masses of papery flowers. The fallen blossom from the cherry trees lay scattered across the ground, like a trailing nuptial gown.

"Please don't let her take me back to India," I cried.

"But what can I do?" he asked.

"I beg of you," I said.

When a tear rolled down my cheeks, he gripped my shoulders. "Please don't cry."

Tentatively he put his arms around me. One teardrop fell after another, until the shoulder of his jacket was wet. As my sobs receded, I found myself listening to his heartbeat. My own heart was thudding, but the lieutenant's outpaced mine. Gazing up at him, I saw that his face was flushed. His lips were parted, as if he couldn't breathe.

"Why don't you take me away?" I whispered.

"You don't know what you're saying."

"No," I said.

I knew that I felt safe within his arms. I knew that our hearts were beating in time. With my head on his shoulder, all my troubles had flown away. I looked shyly up at him, and he seemed to glow in the warmth of my helplessness. When he kissed me gently on the mouth, I placed myself entirely in his hands.

Scene Three

A LENGTH OF SKY-BLUE TULLE

Chapter 8

Imagine an unfurling bud on a mysterious tree in a strange, yet beautiful garden. My mother fully expected a gorgeous bloom that would reflect well on her and fetch a good price—a sweetly scented and luscious Persian rose perhaps, or a delicately tinted magnolia. Lieutenant James, on the other hand, presumed that he had acquired a fresh and malleable young shoot that he could train and constrain and prune.

When I look back upon my seventeen-year-old self, I see a dormant creature striving to break free. I was all impulse and reaction, bouncing around like a reflection in a hall of mirrors. In one glass, I saw myself through my mother's eyes; in another, I glimpsed a sweetheart for Thomas; in a third, a schoolgirl in patched petticoats. I acted instinctively, and then waited breathlessly to see what the outcome would be. I didn't know it yet, but I was stuck fast in a sticky web—the more I struggled, the more entangled I would become.

It was an argument with Mama that propelled me into action. Early one morning, in the week preceding our departure for India, she stormed into my bedroom and shook me awake. I had been fast asleep, dreaming of a glowing young suitor with fair hair and twinkling blue eyes. Though it was barely seven o'clock, she was already in full flow. As she swept back the curtains, I clutched the counterpane and shielded my eyes.

"I have your best interests at heart, that's clear for anyone to see," she said, as she darted around the room, straightening a cushion, adjusting a gown on its padded satin hanger, rearranging a chair.

"Except you, of course. What kind of daughter are you anyway? You don't take after me, at all."

I reached for my dressing gown. "Well, thank goodness for that," I retorted. "Hopefully I am my father's daughter, more than I am yours."

Mama threw a bundle of pressed linen on to the bed, and then stalked out of the room. Five minutes later, she was back. I watched her in the dressing-table mirror as I continued to brush my hair in long strokes from the roots to the tips.

"May you be as tawdry as your father," she cried, as she slammed a jewelled ring down on the marble surface of the dressing table. "You might as well have his betrothal ring. I don't know why I kept it. He promised me a ruby. And what do you think this is? It's red glass. Not even a garnet. And the setting is plated brass. If you take after your father, God help you. All your dreams will turn to dust, all your promises to ashes. I only want what's best for you. A place in society, security. I don't know why you can't see that. Romance is as counterfeit as this useless bauble. Believe me, it quickly wears thin."

I looked from Mama to the ring. The intricate casing looked like pressed gold. The square-cut, faceted stone was the colour of deep smouldering claret and was unusually large. Had it been a genuine ruby, it would undoubtedly have been extremely valuable.

"How do you know it's worthless?" I asked.

Mama avoided my gaze.

"Because I tried to sell it," she whispered.

When she was gone, I held the ring up to the light. The red stone glowed, a pool of rich dark liquid frozen in time. As I examined its detail, a beam of crimson light bounced off the mirror and the walls. Mama might consider the ring a cheap fake, but to me it was tangible proof that I was born of love. It was the thought that counted, wasn't it? My father would have bought her a ruby if he'd been able to afford it, I was sure of that. Perhaps somebody cheated him, I thought. Maybe he'd bought the ring in good faith, not realising he had been duped. He wouldn't deliberately have lied to her, would he?

I remembered my father's smiling face, his thin moustache and blond side-whiskers. I remembered him throwing me up in the air and then catching me and spinning me round. I must have been three, four years old. Had he still been alive, he wouldn't have been insisting upon this marriage. He would have desired my happiness; I was certain of that.

I slipped the ring on to my wedding finger and held out my hand to admire it. Had Mama cared for my father a little more, who knows? He might still be alive. She should have loved and cherished him, not been so eager to diminish him, I thought. In that moment, I decided that Mama's dashing cavalier would become mine. If he was good enough for her, then he was good enough for me. Let her take the judge, if she desired the marriage so much.

On my last evening in Bath, I wrapped the jewelled ruby ring in the embroidered handkerchief that Sophia had given me, and then slipped it inside the length of sky-blue tulle. No matter how often my mother insisted upon the ring's worthlessness, it would always be precious to me. How could she be so cynical? Disappointment has made her bitter, I decided. Possibly she had lied to me, in a last desperate attempt to win my acquiescence. Even if the ring wasn't quite as valuable as she had once imagined, I was convinced that it wasn't simply a piece of coloured glass. As I closed the lid of my little Indian trunk, I vowed that I would never turn into such a cold-hearted, unromantic and calculating woman. No matter what happened, I would never resemble my mother in thought or in word or in action. Not even in the slightest hint of a trait or mannerism, nor in the shadow of a look, or a glance, or in the echo of a sigh.

Chapter 9

I had very little to pack—a few trinkets, my patchwork silk handkerchief, now faded and full of holes; the length of sky-blue tulle to remind me of Sophia. I left my plain, ill-fitting school dresses hanging in the wardrobe. The new trunk had been moved down from Mama's room to the hallway, where it was waiting, along with three others, to be shipped to India. I took one last peek at Mama. She was sleeping soundly with a black satin mask across her eyes. Her dark hair was laid out neatly across the pillow. I didn't write her a letter; she would find out soon enough. I never doubted, not even for a moment, that the lieutenant would come for me. At precisely three o'clock, I heard the horses approach.

Outside the door, I looked around me one last time. The whole world was asleep. Even the buds of the flowers were closed up against the night.

In the carriage, the lieutenant pulled me into his arms and wrapped us both in a fur rug. I was cocooned and warm and held; for the moment that was enough. Strapped to the back of the carriage was the trousseau from my prospective wedding; at my feet was my little Indian trunk. The rest of my life I gladly left behind.

My head was full of romance, of tales of highwaymen and lovers. The lieutenant was a fugitive who had been misunderstood. I was an innocent who had been stolen away. His love was primitive and fierce. He wrapped me in his cloak and we galloped away.

The horses sped on through the night until their necks strained and their hooves stumbled. A swollen moon streaked across darkened windows, shone up from puddles, led us along winding roads. Every sound—a twig breaking, the cries of an owl, the wind in the branches of a tree, the wheels across the ground—intensified in the dead of night. I could hear the fall of the horses' hooves, the cut of the whip, the coachman's cry. By the morning, the horses had slowed to a somnambulant pace, and the coachman had to spur them on with lashes and harsh words. Inside the carriage, the curtains were drawn against the light. In our snug little cocoon, I remained oblivious to the world.

At intervals, the driver would protest that the horses needed to rest.

"Soon, soon," Thomas would say.

Perhaps he feared that I might have a change of heart, or perhaps he shrank from my mother's wrath. Whatever the reason, we travelled over thirty miles in record time. When there was more than a day between us and Bath, he finally allowed the coachman to call a halt.

It was a twilight summer's night when we pulled up at a coaching inn on the outskirts of Bristol. The coachman was tight-lipped, the horses exhausted. Sweat glistened on their flanks, the bits foamed in their mouths, their coats were white with salt. They fretted and stamped until a stable boy unshackled them and led them off one by one. Whilst the coachman unpacked the carriage, a stout man in a filthy apron came out and shook Thomas's hand. Across the yard, the stable boy crooned to the horses as he rubbed them down with straw.

The coaching inn consisted of an ancient warren of tiny rooms. Thomas and the innkeeper had to bend their heads to get in through the doors. Upstairs, we were shown into two adjoining bedrooms. The floorboards were bare, the ceilings beamed, the heavy furniture of a dark, carved oak. Two candles threw shifting silhouettes around the room.

Supper consisted of a rough meal of red meat, bread and a thick, heavy wine. Though both the fare and the accommodation were rudimentary, I had Thomas's full attention, and I felt very giddy and grown up. I was seventeen; Thomas, who was in his thirties, was about the same age as Mama. *At last I have a papa to take care of me*, I thought. Death might have taken the first, and Mama monopolised the second, but nobody would snatch this one away. Across the table, Thomas's blue eyes twinkled back at me. I had never felt so safe and cosy and secure.

After we had finished our meal, the innkeeper brought a flask of port and two glasses. In a brief exchange, it became apparent that Thomas had stayed here before. Their laughter grew coarse, and I did not appreciate the way the innkeeper was looking at me. Taking my leave, I bade them both goodnight.

The door to the adjoining room was heavy, and it was with some effort that I pushed it shut. Once I was inside, the room was snug. The walls were so thick I could hardly hear the murmur of voices on the other side. Changing into my nightshirt, I clambered into the vast bed and lay with my hands folded neatly over the blankets. I was half asleep when niggling thoughts of Mama crept into my head.

I pictured her alone in the apartment. Once she had discovered that I was gone, she would have called upon Thomas, only to find that he, too, had disappeared. Perhaps we should have left a note, I thought a little guiltily. Then I glanced at the two trunks across the room and my heart hardened. She will probably miss the lingerie more than me, I thought resentfully. Her pride would be hurt, that was all.

On the table beside me, the candle flickered and a huge shadow reared up across the wall. All the angles in the room were crooked. Dark beams loomed over the bed. Outside I could hear the wind whistling through the trees and the roar of the stream. I could have been anywhere. In a woodman's cottage in an enchanted wood, miles away from society. I thought of the lieutenant in the next room and smiled dreamily. Wrapping my arms around a pillow, I curled up and fell into a deep sleep.

In the early hours of the morning, I was woken by the creaking of the door. Swinging open, it banged against the wall. I sat up in bed with a start. There stood Thomas James, swaying in the doorway, his face flushed, his shirt-tails flying. In one hand he held a lamp, in the other a half-empty glass of port. But for his unbuttoned shirt, he was completely naked.

"My precious girl," he said.

I couldn't drag my eyes from the protuberance rising up towards his navel. What did I know of the nature of men? I had seen naked little Indian boys and statues made of marble; that was all. In either case, the emblem of masculinity was modest and could easily be contained. But what I saw of the lieutenant could not have been adequately covered by a fig leaf. *My God*, I thought. *Is this what lurks beneath the breeches of every gentleman?*

"Lieutenant," I said.

"You must call me Thomas."

"Thomas," I said.

Before I could say anything more, he was pressing down on me, his mouth devouring mine, his hands ripping open my nightshirt. Pinned down beneath his weight, I couldn't move. I could feel his manhood throbbing against my thigh, like some independent ferreting animal nosing its way in the darkness.

I had to think quickly. Slumping back against the pillows, I sighed. His movements were slow, his reflexes fuddled by drink. As soon as he loosened his hold on me, I slithered from beneath him and withdrew to the other room. The key was still in the lock, and I swiftly turned it. Retiring to the other bed, I dragged the blankets up to my neck.

From the other side of the door, Thomas begged and pleaded.

"My petal, my darling," he called. "I didn't mean to frighten you. Come on now, cherub, open the door."

At first he tried endearments, then he issued threats.

"I'll send you back. Your mother will be waiting for you. Stop this nonsense now, do you hear me? I demand that you unlock the door."

In response, I said little, beyond, "I'm tired, I need to sleep."

The big brute, I thought. Does he think that he can use me as if I were some sort of servant girl?

The next morning at breakfast, Thomas would hardly speak. It was left to me to keep up the proprieties. I was determined that at least one of us should remain civilised.

"I hope you slept well," I said. "I am so looking forward to Ireland. I haven't been there since I was a child."

Thomas sulked and brooded and pushed his food around his plate. I had to sweet-talk him into speaking to me at all.

Across the counties of Wales, we had the same tussle three nights in a row. In Monmouthshire, Glamorgan and Carmarthenshire, I was kept awake by an urgent knocking at the door.

On the fourth night, I believed that I had escaped his attentions altogether. We had stopped at a small hotel in Pembrokeshire. Thomas was quiet over dinner. I had retired early, being careful to turn the key in the lock. I drifted off to sleep in the safe knowledge that I would not be disturbed.

It was hardly midnight when I heard the key fall, then the handle turn. Thomas, who was all sweetness by day, became a different creature at night. After he had locked the door, he dangled the key mockingly in the air, and then kicked the other one across the floor.

"Well, my pretty little one, did you think you could so easily escape me?" he crooned.

My eyes darted round the room. There was no quick means of escape. The windows were tiny, there was no adjoining room, and the only exit was locked.

Sitting beside me on the bed, Thomas stroked my hair. His mouth traced kisses along my neck.

"We have given up so much to be together," he said. "Why hold back now?"

Before I could fend him off, he wrapped me tightly in his arms and smothered me with kisses.

"Please, Lieutenant," I pleaded with him. "Will you not let me go?"

"I love it when you beg," he said.

When his hand found my breast, my breath caught in my throat. Despite my fear, my nipple swelled between his fingers.

"Come on, sweetness," he coaxed. "You know you want me."

His thighs were locked around my legs, and I couldn't move. His urgency was startling, the depth of his ardour communicating itself directly to me.

When he loosened the drawstring of my nightgown and cupped my breast, I could hardly breathe. He put my nipple in his mouth, and then sucked until it rose up against his tongue.

"What fine fruit," he said.

I was almost lost entirely, but fearful of where his mouth might venture next.

"Tell me you don't like that," he said, as his tongue slid across my breast.

In the lamplight, he looked ancient and lascivious.

When he felt me yield, he loosened his grip. Quickly I twisted round and pushed him away. He chuckled as if it were a sport and pinned me face down on the bed. My head was buried in the pillows, his mouth closed on my neck, like a beast upon its prey. In the struggle I felt my nightgown rise up around my waist.

"Please don't," I said.

Thomas sighed and grasped my buttocks in his hands. Before I could move, his fingers slipped between my thighs. With startled surprise, I felt a finger slide inside of me.

"Like a key in a well-oiled lock," he crowed.

I struggled violently, elbowing him and kicking at him with my feet. I had almost shaken him off when I felt something pressing into me. With horror, I recalled the size of his member. He couldn't be trying to put that inside of me, could he? I bit his arm but he pushed deeper. When I screamed, he undulated against me, pressing deeper with each thrust. Something inside me stretched, then tore. I couldn't breathe. I felt as if he was filling up my lungs, my throat. I lay there. What else could I do?

"Eliza, Eliza," he moaned.

A farmer ploughs through a field, breaking up dry clods of earth after a rainless summer. Through wild brambles and wayward shrubs, he cuts a virgin path. He hacks a tunnel through a chalk mountain. He chews through bone. Why had nobody explained this to me? Why hadn't I believed Sophia's lurid tales? How could I not have known?

In the morning, Thomas looked sated and happy. He brought me breakfast in bed and gently brushed my hair. I kept very still, afraid the slightest move on my part might encourage him. Oh, where was Sophia now? I wished so much to talk to her. When she had whispered the facts of life to me, I had refused to believe her. It was typical of her to make up such things to tease and torment me. Was this really the future? To have my nights disrupted by a lifetime of assaults and whispered apologies?

For the next three days I hardly spoke. I expressed no excitement or curiosity. I asked not where we were going, nor showed any interest in the passing surroundings. At night, Thomas kissed me tenderly goodnight, then retreated to his own room, but I understood from the expression on his face that he was only biding his time. We boarded the ship to Ireland and then disembarked the other side, and still I passed no remark. From Wexford we travelled by coach along muddy, rock-strewn roads.

On the fourth day, Thomas said gently, "We could get married in Rathbeggen. My brother could perform the ceremony."

From my corner of the carriage, I looked at him with flat, cold eyes. My dreams hung in tatters before me. I had no choice in anything. I never had. No matter which way I had turned, the outcome would have been the same. I had been shocked to see the blood on the sheets, whereas Thomas had looked elated and proud. I was so angry with everybody. In my innocence, I had never envisaged anything beyond the intimacy of kisses. In all the talk of love and romance, at school and with Mama, no one had ever divulged the brutal reality of the relations between men and women. I thought of all the women who had kept me in ignorance, especially my mother. She had encouraged his affection. This was all her fault. His frustration with her had simply been transferred to me.

Thomas talked of marriage as if the ceremony would placate me. As if my silence was an attempt to force his hand. In reply, I wanted to spit in his face. But in the cold light of day, I knew that I had no choice. I was ruined. No one else would want me now. I could not go back. Thomas was my family now, whether I liked it or not.

Chapter 10

On the night before the wedding, I tried on my white ball-gown one last time. As soon as I saw my reflection, tears welled up in my eyes. The gown was such a fanciful creation, evoking a world of grand balls and broughams and the pavements of civilised streets. In the archway of the tiny Rathbeggen church where the ceremony was due to take place, the gown would have looked ostentatious and absurd. I remembered the glow of anticipation when I had worn it in Bath. I remembered all my hopes and dreams. When I examined myself in the mirror, I already looked more steady and grown up. Being a married woman carried distinct advantages, and, leaving aside the circumstances, Thomas probably wasn't such a dreadful catch. He was relatively youthful, and he had his own hair and teeth, at least. For days now, he had been unfailingly tender and solicitous—helping me into and out of carriages, guiding me by the elbow, taking my hand. He could have just abandoned me altogether, after all, and then what would have become of me? Sometimes when he smiled or told me a silly story, I remembered why I had liked him in the first place. Life might be a series of rude awakenings, but it was better than living in a world of make-believe, I persuaded myself. I wiped my eyes, then wrapped the pristine white gown carefully in tissue paper and folded it away. Thomas was right. The modest merino gown was sensible and warm.

On our wedding day, rain fell in grey sheets like gloomy veils, and I had to run across the churchyard to avoid getting completely drenched. Inside the church, there were no flowers, except a jug full of yellow gorse and the full-headed white chrysanthemums more usually associated with funerals. Thomas's brother officiated over the ceremony. His wife and child were the only witnesses. Thomas wore his military uniform, I, the blue merino gown, with a wool chemise underneath.

As I skipped down the aisle, I was swept away by the drama and excitement of it all. We had eloped together, after all! What could be more romantic than that? At the altar, I smiled up at Thomas and then clutched his hand. The vicar kept sneezing. I stifled a giggle. After we had exchanged vows, we shivered in each other's arms. "My husband," I whispered to myself, enjoying the sound of the words. The celebrations consisted of an iced sponge cake and a second pot of tea. For all the modesty of the occasion, I was contented enough. If I had wanted a grand society wedding, I could have married the judge.

The James family seat in Wexford was a solid, four-square house misleadingly named Ballycrystal. Mount Leinster loomed over it; for half the day the house was in the shade. My father-in-law was a widower, and though there were constant visitors, he essentially lived alone. Without the regular attentions of a mistress, a pall of neglect hung over the rooms, and a gentle layer of dust coated the surfaces. The instruments of sport—fishing rods, guns, saddles, boots—were evident in every room.

From all over the country, the James family came in platoons to meet me. I was paraded past cousins and the local dignitaries; the magistrate, the vicar, even the doctor came to look at me. There were times when I fully expected someone to examine my teeth. Thomas took great pleasure in describing me as being of good Anglo-Irish stock, and I could feel myself being knitted into the web of society, integrating with my family connections, becoming absorbed into an actual grown-up married woman's life.

"This is my wife, Eliza," Thomas would proudly proclaim. "Her mother was one of the Olivers of Cork."

Heads would nod, eyebrows raise, impressed glances be exchanged. "Not *the* Olivers of Castle Oliver?"

"The very same," beamed Thomas. "Eliza's maternal grandfather was Sir Charles Silver Oliver."

The vicar clasped my hand; the magistrate bowed; the doctor stroked his moustache.

"Indeed," he purred.

"Sir Charles was High Sheriff of Cork," Thomas preened. "As was his father before him."

Thomas would expound at length, unless a visitor happened to enjoy direct acquaintance with Cork society. Then he would be overcome with modesty, and the conversation would abruptly change course. He neglected to declare my mother's illegitimacy, and of the Gilberts' dubious antecedents there was no mention at all.

Life at Ballycrystal drifted by in a haze of hunting and endless cups of tea. The James women were pale, insipid creatures, whilst the men would shoot at anything at all. I can hardly be of the same race, I secretly thought. When I was out riding alone, I would come across the local peasantry and be disconcerted to find my own colouring mirrored in their black hair and blue eyes.

One day I almost trampled over a young couple who were walking along the road. I had to rein in the horse when they did not automatically step aside. They were barefooted and wild. The woman wore a shawl around her face; the man was carrying a creel of turf. Both had the same thick lustrous hair and bright, enquiring eyes. They simply looked at me until I demanded they allow me to pass. Though they were thin and dressed in little more than rags, they seemed inordinately proud. Shaking off my disquiet, I spurred the horse before galloping rapidly away.

To all outward appearances, Thomas and I were like any other newly wedded couple. If I was sometimes sullen or Thomas authoritarian, nobody commented or enquired. The scene of my seduction hung between us, reminding me that I had little choice but to surrender to him, both in public and in private. He was all charm and smiles, as long as I was compliant.

Within weeks of our elopement, Thomas began to speak of another subject of which I had little experience. Intimacy and finance were, it seemed, inextricably entwined. Before we married, Thomas had asked me to write to Mama asking for her approval. A second letter, also ostensibly from me, hinted that she might make me an allowance or that I was owed some kind of dowry. When Mama denied us her blessing, Thomas began to make outright demands.

"Your stepfather is a captain, for goodness sake. Of course they must make a settlement."

Occasionally he switched tone. "You have standards to which you are accustomed, my precious, that I can't possibly meet. If I could shower you with gifts and pearls, you know I would. It's only natural that your parents should wish to assist."

As the weeks passed, I became more familiar with the comings and goings around the house. Whispered conversations in the kitchen and between sisters became clearer. There seemed to be threats to the house both from outside and within. There was talk of cattle being stolen, agents being attacked along the roads, of threatening anonymous notes pinned to the stable door. One day I came across Thomas's sisters, Jane and Amelia, in the hall. They were carrying a laden tray towards an unused wing of the house. I demanded to know their business. They exchanged glances, then allowed me to follow them.

"Understand, sister," said Amelia, "we may have to tolerate the attentions of men, but some women pay a terrible price."

"Prepare yourself," said Jane, "to meet Sarah, Michael James's wife."

Sarah's room was at the end of a neglected corridor. When Amelia opened the door, the force of the smell felt like an assault. Inside, the stench of bodily functions pervaded the room. As soon as she saw me, Michael James's wife looked distraught.

"Don't fret," said Jane. "It is only Thomas's young wife."

Sarah was a small woman with a peaky face and nervous, twisting hands. Her hair was a warm honey blonde, her dress a pastel brocade stripe. She would have been pretty, had she not been so thin. Attempting a polite smile, she beckoned to us to sit down.

"I'm sorry," she said. "It can't be helped."

Whilst we maintained a stilted conversation about the latest fashions in Bath, Sarah compulsively smoothed down her skirts. If she were able, the gesture seemed to say, she would have wiped the odour away.

"I love my children," she said. "I cling to that."

"But why should you have to hide away?" I blurted out.

Jane placed a restraining hand upon my arm; Amelia shook her head.

If I was ignorant of the mechanisms of childbirth, I wished fervently that I might have remained so. What had happened to Sarah was not unusual, it seemed. Indeed, she was lucky to be alive. Whilst she was giving birth to her second son, her internal organs had ruptured. No matter how much she washed, the fetor of bladder and bowel pervaded her person. Her husband sent a regular allowance but rarely visited. When her children came to see her, it was only a matter of time before they, too, were repelled. Poor Sarah lived in isolation within a suite of empty rooms. When we were about to leave, she caught my arm.

"Thomas is a good man," she said, "but you may have to learn tricks to keep him away. There need be no hurry for children, no matter what he says."

That night after Thomas's exertions, I washed myself rigorously in the hopes of rinsing any risk of impregnation away. I puzzled over what Sarah had said. What tricks might possibly keep him at bay? Whilst Thomas was asleep, I scrubbed myself until my thighs were raw.

I was not unhappy with Thomas. Curled up in bed at night, I felt warm and secure as a dormouse—drifting into sleep with my husband beside me, waking up the next day to find him still there. I enjoyed the small intimacies of marriage: brushing down his shoulders for him, leaning against his arm, holding hands. He amused and surprised me. I think he was as restless as I after a time. There was only so much hunting to be done, so many visitors to be received. When he began to talk about returning to India, I was pleased. I began to feel a little more relaxed. I grew familiar with him in company. I would tease him and answer him back. One evening the family were gathered around playing cards. Thomas had a full house and looked gleeful. I laid down an ace and trumped him. His father chuckled; Amelia repressed a giggle. A flicker of irritation swept Thomas's face. Throughout the rest of the evening, he remained monosyllabic and tight-lipped.

When we were alone in our bedroom, he stripped off all his clothes. I was already in bed when he climbed over me and pushed my book aside. He knelt over me, naked and clearly aroused. Thrusting his manhood towards me, he demanded I take hold of it.

"Do as I say," he ordered.

When I recoiled, he clasped my hand around his member. It was the first time I had touched him so intimately. I could feel the blood pumping against my hand. Thomas closed his hand tighter over mine and began to move it up and down.

"Don't ever try to humiliate me again," he said.

"It was only a game," I hesitantly replied.

"Harder," said Thomas.

"In India the women can satisfy a man with their mouths," he said.

When I looked horrified, he laughed.

"Go on," he said, thrusting himself in my face.

The opening at the top of his penis stared at me like a greedy eye. A drop of pearlescent liquid formed on the tip, then dropped. Before Thomas could force himself on me, I pushed him away. Suddenly I felt a hard, resounding slap across my cheek. Thomas's face pulsed and twitched.

"You'll learn," he said.

Pulling on his clothes, he stumbled out of the room. Minutes later, I heard the sound of horses' hooves. I lay in bed and cradled my cheek. My face burned hot beneath my hand. I remembered giggling with Sophia over what our future husbands would be like. When Thomas had come along, I had thought, If I have to marry someone, why not him? Presumably all husbands imposed themselves upon their wives. Somehow I must learn to swallow my pride. I closed my eyes and tried to sleep. This was married life, and I would just have to accustom myself to it. Thomas would try to mould me, whether I liked it or not.

When Thomas came back the next morning, he was contrite. He kissed my eyelids and my cheeks and the tip of my nose.

"I am so, so sorry, my darling. Nothing like that will ever happen again. I need to be busy. I need to be occupied. When we get to India, life will be perfect, I promise. You will have your own house to attend to; I will have my work."

Though I asked where he had spent the night, he neglected to reply.

As we were leaving Ballycrystal, I saw the wild, dark-haired couple by the side of the road. They pulled in to allow us to pass. On a cart beside them, two grubby children were huddled among scraps of furniture and rags. In the distance the thatch of a cottage burned.

"What has happened?" I asked.

Thomas shrugged.

"Father is clearing the estate," he said. "The tenants bring in a pittance; it's better to put livestock on to the land."

As the carriage passed, I looked back one last time, expecting to be confronted by angry, defiant stares. Instead the couple averted their eyes. I felt strangely disappointed, as if I had desired their fury. For some reason, I wanted them to wave their fists and shout. Instead, the woman pulled her shawl over her head. The man bent his back beneath the weight of the cart. Neither of them would look at me.

Chapter 11

The smell of India swept me up in a warm embrace, filling my nose and entering every pore. As the ship drew up alongside the Calcutta shoreline, I took a deep, lingering breath. Garlic and tobacco mingled with jasmine and cow dung; wafts of chillies and sandalwood thickened in the still, hot air. As we disembarked, I smiled up at Thomas, and he squeezed my hand. We stepped on to the dock, anticipating a leisurely life amidst British society, only to find that Thomas had been posted to a far-flung corner of northern India.

Whilst the travel arrangements were being made, we tried to establish contact with my stepfather and Mama. After I ran away with Thomas, she had returned to India; in the two years since then, I had received only one letter from her. For more than a fortnight, Thomas sent letters, dropped calling cards and left messages. After a week, my stepfather replied with a note stating that he would be happy to receive us, but that ultimately the decision was my mother's. The day before our departure, she finally agreed that we might call on her. That morning, I dressed with special care, in one of the day dresses she had chosen for my trousseau.

In her drawing room, she greeted us without a hint of warmth or affection. When I went to embrace her, she held out a cool, limp hand.

I could feel my heart pounding in my chest as if it might burst. A small voice inside me wanted to plead for her forgiveness. I wanted to squash her in my arms, to crease her gown and ruffle her perfect hair.

Her response to our news was a barely suppressed smile.

"It is a promotion," she said. "You should be pleased. Your stepfather had to pull quite a few strings."

I sank back into the chair.

So this is your revenge, I thought.

Thomas bristled, then stood up. "No doubt, we owe a debt of gratitude to you," he said. "I will give you a few moments alone together.

Once he was gone, Mama looked inquiringly at me.

I coughed.

"Perhaps we might become friends," I hesitantly suggested.

"Let us not pretend," she replied. "You have scorned my wishes to your own detriment. You will receive no financial assistance from your stepfather or myself."

I was stung by her words. "You deliberately misunderstand me."

Mama picked up her embroidery hoop and stabbed her needle through the cloth.

"Your husband will be waiting for you," she said.

We spent another four months on the Ganges, traversing the entire length of India in a flat-bottomed paddleboat. The river was three miles wide; in places the currents were so strong they pulled the boat backwards, and we had to set down anchor and then be towed. Venetian blinds threw slatted strips of light across the cabin floor. At night, we lay together in the languorous sticky heat, idly teasing each other. Perhaps it was the sense of drifting, of timelessness—whatever it was, I was becoming receptive to the pleasures of love.

Travelling with us was a sergeant-major and his wife. Evelyn was a fine-boned Englishwoman, with mousy hair and grey eyes. She had never been to India before, and the slightest incident unsettled her.

One day, as we were taking tea, the charred remains of a funeral pyre floated by. The blackened corpse was still garlanded with orange and yellow marigolds; wisps of smoke rose from incense cones. Evelyn became hysterical.

"I can't stand it," she cried.

"There, there, Evelyn," I said, comforting her as best I could.

She never did grow accustomed to life on the river. A naked holy man, a crippled child, a dozing alligator: each new sight tested her nerves.

"How could they?" she would cry as another funeral pyre drifted by.

"It is their way," I replied. "To them the river is holy."

Evelyn was inconsolable. At each new outrage, she turned her face to one side. To me, little had changed. I watched the passing country through the eyes of a woman and the memory of a child. As we approached Dinapore, where my father was buried, I thought of him more and more. When Thomas encouraged me to visit his grave, I shook my head, preferring to imagine him beneath endless fields of poppies and Indian corn.

Beyond Dinapore, we passed through the holy city of Benares. The riverbanks were lined with temples and the whole place smouldered with incense and prayers. Thousands of people thronged the water's edge. The sounds of weeping and lamentations washed over the boat. In the water, the living mingled with the dead. Evelyn retired to her cabin and drew the blinds. It seemed to me that we had reached India's heart. We had come so far, I couldn't imagine ever going back.

At Benares, the river whispered to me. *Accept your fate*, it seemed to say.

As the Holy City receded into the distance, the Ganges narrowed and the currents grew stronger. For the last part of our journey, we travelled overland. Held aloft in palanquins, we passed through fields of capsicums and castor oil plants. As a child, I remembered the bearers singing as they hurried along, but this time, there was no laughter, no made-up songs. Instead the bearers were sullen and quiet. Whenever I looked at them, they averted their eyes.

It was May when we arrived in Karnal, and the days were sweltering and humid. Our six-roomed bungalow had high ceilings; the whitewashed walls were more than a foot deep. From the verandah, I could see the Himalayan foothills in the distance. Standing there, I could almost feel the mountain air like a cool breeze across my skin. The first thing I did was purchase plants I remembered from childhood. Soon the bignonia was producing masses of amber flowers, and the passion fruit was laden with white and purple blooms. The twisting tendrils spread rapidly. Within a month, the flowers threatened to envelop the house.

Inside our bungalow, I could neither think nor breathe without a row of brown faces watching me. The housekeeper, the table servants, the cook, the cook's boy, the sweeper, the gardener, the messenger and the maid all paid attention to my every move. Whenever I tried to do anything remotely resembling manual work, they would look embarrassed on my behalf. If I picked up a lamp and moved it across the room, the table servant would very slightly shake his head; if I dressed myself in the morning, the maid would look infinitely disappointed with me.

Within days, I realised that it was the housekeeper who made all the important decisions. Jaswinder was a regal woman of indeterminate age. Everything about her, the delicate bones of her wrists and her ankles, the incline of her head, her pristine white sari, indicated a woman of natural grace and majesty. It was she who determined the exact way in which the household should be run, not me. I had to repeatedly remind myself that I was the mistress of the house. Though I prepared menus and issued orders, Jaswinder wouldn't necessarily comply.

"If it pleases you," she would say, but by the slightest flicker of her eyelids, I knew that she did not approve.

In the first few months, one domestic catastrophe followed another whilst she stood blithely by. The piano was eaten by termites. A procession of white ants marched through the bungalow, devouring the rush matting on the floor. One week I ordered an excess of flour, the next too little. Inadvertently, I upset the servants by asking them to complete tasks outside their caste. I asked the Muslim cook to prepare pork and the Hindu cook to prepare beef. If I wasn't constantly vigilant, the sugar and the salt simply disappeared.

"Why didn't you warn me?" I demanded.

"*Memsahib* did not ask."

I soon learned that a harmonious domestic life in India consisted of adherence to a strict set of rules, the only problem being that I didn't know what they were. Soon I was reduced to consulting Jaswinder at the beginning of each day.

"Leave it in my hands," she would reply with a tight little smile.

Within weeks I was completely dependent on her. I found myself wanting to please her, but despite my best efforts, I continued to make small errors of etiquette or judgement, and she would admonish me with her eyes. It took me months to understand what was required of me. Only when I relinquished the idea that I was actually in charge did the household begin to run smoothly. Once the hierarchy was established, the servants settled down. They had run the household without me and would do so again. One white *memsahib* was much like another, their silent exchange of glances seemed to say.

In the next bungalow, Evelyn fared worse than I. Her servants intimidated her. Mosquitoes had made a pincushion of her pale English flesh. Her legs and feet swelled in the heat.

"I want to go home," she wailed.

"Please don't cry, Evelyn," I entreated her.

I suggested that she stop wearing stockings, at least during the hot weather, but she looked appalled.

"I can't do that," she said. "What on earth would people think?"

She lay motionless for hours in the shade of her verandah, pouring jugs of cold water over her stockinged feet.

One morning I found her weeping at her desk, desperately trying to hold down papers with her elbows and her hands. Letters and invoices were flying around the room. Suspended from the ceiling, the *punkah* continued to send great gusts of air back and forth. Pens and books were swept to the floor. The *wallah* continued to operate the pulleys until I ordered him to stop.

"You have to weigh everything down," I explained, showing Evelyn a small pile of brass weights piled up in the corner of the room.

"I never thought of that," she said.

"You're going to have to take the servants in hand."

At this, she sighed.

"The servants hate me. And I can't sleep for the insects and the noises at night. The frogs, the cicadas, some terrible yacking bird."

"Brain-fever, brain-fever," I chirped.

Evelyn wiped her eyes.

"Heaven help me," she cried.

"Isn't that what you hear?" I asked. "It is the cry of the brain-fever bird."

She pursed her lips. "Well, why didn't you just say so," she snapped.

Once I found her sitting solemnly at her desk, beneath a muslin tent that completely covered both herself and the desk. Her legs were bare, her feet sitting in a bowl of cold water.

"Don't laugh at me, Eliza," she said. "I cannot bear to be bitten, and that is all that counts."

When Thomas came home, our marriage was played out in front of the servants, in a strange kind of strangulated code. There was hardly a conversation between us that was undertaken alone. I never knew how he would react. One moment he could be all charm and smiles, the next brooding and silent.

"What's the matter, Tommy?" I would ask.

"Isn't it obvious?" he would reply.

If he was brusque, I wanted to win him back; if he was angry, I wanted to make him smile. If he was in a playful mood, I indulged him and drew him out.

He was responsible for enlisting and training Indian recruits, and though it was a promotion of sorts, he took little pleasure in his work.

He would appear in the late afternoons and slump down in a chair.

"Three desertions, missing shoes, multiple thefts. I do believe that your stepfather is punishing me."

"A difficult day?" I enquired.

"Damn natives," he muttered. "They nod and bow, but they don't take a blind bit of notice of a word I say."

Once the day had cooled, he would ride out with the other officers and shoot at anything that moved. Afterwards, he laid his spoils at my feet: he was never happier than after a successful shoot.

"Look at that," he beamed. "Cook could prepare a feast from that little catch, eh?"

Jaswinder and I exchanged glances. In matters concerning my husband, we were generally united. The partridge and the hare looked tough, the peacock bedraggled and scrawny. Jaswinder and I both knew from experience that the former would be tasteless and the latter fit only for Mulligatawny stew.

"See what you can do," I whispered.

When supper was served, Thomas tucked in heartily.

"Is this the partridge I caught?" he asked. "There's nothing like hunting for your own food."

During the long drowsy afternoons, I began to update my dresses with new collars and petticoats, just in case Mama relented and decided to invite me to Calcutta. I monogrammed the bed linen and the handkerchiefs. The antimacassars required embellishment, I realised; the cushion covers were really much too plain. Soon my world had shrunk to the size of my embroidery hoop. My *pièce-de-résistance* was an elaborate bedspread made from individual sections, each embroidered with an Indian scene. It began sedately enough, with gentle scenes of mountains or rivers, before progressing to views of temples and wildlife. Soon I found myself stitching more turbulent scenes. My needle jabbed back and forth through the cloth. An Indian lion devoured a British officer; a demure matron was lost in the jaws of a crocodile; an elephant carried a young woman away.

We had been married for two years when Thomas began to enquire about a child. We were lying in bed, after spending a tender and leisurely morning together.

"It may be just what you need," he said, gently stroking my stomach.

When I tried to get up, he gripped my shoulders.

"Lie here with me," he said. "Allow the baby a little time to settle and take hold."

Even Jaswinder began to look sorry for me. I could see it in her eyes.

"Still no sign of a baby *sahib*?" she enquired. "We must feed the *sahib* more fish, I think, and eggs."

"I don't want a baby," I said.

"Of course, you do," she said. "All women do."

Thomas began to dwell on the subject more and more: "Do you think there is something wrong with you? I could take you to see a doctor in Calcutta, if you like, to check that everything is in order."

I made no reply. I was still only nineteen; the last thing I wanted was a child. Slowly it had dawned on me what Sarah, Thomas's poor sister, had meant by tricks. If I pleaded a severe headache, I might be left alone. The slightest hint of women's troubles, and Thomas would blanche and then retire to his own room. Despite my best efforts, his attentions became more regular and determined. After he had been hunting, he grew amorous. If I danced with someone else at a function, he became aroused. It was after a military dinner that the inevitable occurred. I had woken in the middle of the night to find Thomas labouring over me. Some instinct notified me that the moment of conception had occurred. *Please God*, I prayed, *don't let this be true*, but a knot tightened in my belly, and I knew that something had taken root.

Soon afterwards the monsoon came. The skies grew pale with dust. Clouds piled up and the sky darkened. Thunder rumbled and the rain came crashing down. The house began to leak. At night we slept under giant green umbrellas. At a stilted dinner party, the air was thick with insects. Huge moths fell in the soup. Evelyn's husband was pontificating about the natives when a dung beetle flew into his mouth. After dinner, I caught Thomas and the captain's wife alone together on the verandah. Mrs Lomer, who was a matronly thirty-five with firapple cheeks, was picking dragonflies from his hair. I smiled to myself when I saw them. *Imagine flirting at her age*, I thought.

Next door, bright green mould appeared overnight on Evelyn's books and shoes. Her pictures rotted on the walls.

"You have to put everything away," I said.

"Everything?" she wailed.

There was nothing unusual about the evening. The rains had passed, and gazing out from the verandah, the world looked fresh and new. Thomas had come home from the officers' club, his cheeks flushed from one too many whiskies. We were sitting down at the table. Dinner had just been served. For the main course, fresh chicken had been cooked in the stock and gravy of a guinea fowl.

"*Bon appetit,*" I said.

Thomas swallowed a few mouthfuls, then moved the food around the plate with his fork.

"You're making a fool of me," he said. "This isn't the bird that I caught."

I didn't know what to say.

"Please," I said. "Not in front of the servants."

"I don't give a damn about the servants. Is it or isn't it?"

"Thomas, please."

He glared at me, and then swept his plate from the table. It broke into two clean pieces and the gravy trickled across the floor.

Both of us stood up. Thomas was breathing heavily.

"You think there is something wrong with me, don't you?" he said very quietly.

"What on earth do you mean?"

"You know very well."

"Thomas, you're frightening me. I don't understand what you're talking about."

"Why the hell aren't you pregnant yet?"

I swallowed hard and sat down.

Over the weeks, I had felt the baby growing inside me, small and hard and solid as a walnut. For some reason, I had neglected to tell Thomas.

"Get the hell out of my sight," he snarled.

I was about to blurt out the news when Jaswinder came into the room. The servants stood rigidly by the wall, their eyes fixed on some distant point outside. Jaswinder remained by the door.

Thomas continued to breathe down over me.

"Thomas, please," I whispered.

The force of the blow jolted my head and stung my cheek. When I looked up, I saw the appalled look in Jaswinder's eyes. If Thomas had lashed out at me before, it was behind closed doors. If he forced himself upon me, I tried not to be surprised. I assumed that for every marriage, there was a price. But to humiliate me in front of the servants? Matters could hardly be worse.

The next morning I woke up with a fever. Every bone in my body felt as if it were being relentlessly twisted by an unseen hand. Though I was shivering with cold, my head burned. Soon I was vomiting blood. When Jaswinder came to attend to me, I couldn't bring myself to look at her. By the afternoon, my fever broke and I began to sweat, then the whole cycle began again.

Jaswinder wiped my brow and ministered extra quinine. The doctor diagnosed malaria and recommended fasting, then bleeding. When Thomas came to see me, I turned my face away.

I remained in bed for three weeks, so weak that I could hardly move. On the fourth week, I woke in the middle of the night with a sharp ache in my stomach. Needles of pain shot through me over and over again. In the bathroom, I clutched the tub, then crouched down on the floor. My stomach muscles churned of their own accord. As the pain increased, I stifled a scream. Suddenly my thighs were drenched, and a slimy creature emerged from between my legs. I stared down at it before tentatively reaching forward. The baby was roughly formed, like the early stages of a figure emerging from the clay. It was a little girl. She was warm, but dead, her flesh a mottled livid mauve.

In blind, unthinking panic, I wrapped her up in a linen sheet and hid her beneath my clothes. By the time a servant appeared, I had bundled up the soiled sheets and mopped up most of the blood.

In the hours before dawn, I rode out towards the woods with strips of cotton bunched between my legs. I pushed the soiled sheets into the hollow of a tree, and then dug a hole in the earth beside a kapok tree. I buried the baby without unfolding the sheet, hoping that would be an end to it. But once I had patted and smoothed down the soil, I could see tiny, intricate baby's fingers in front of my eyes, waving at me. Another month passed before I was well again. When I rose from my bed, I was thin and empty and yellow.

Chapter 12

In October, the cold weather set in, shrouding the house and the trees in a dense, smoky fog. I began to sneak off on long aimless walks, but nothing tired me out. Often, for no reason at all, I would break down and weep. One day, when I had roamed beyond the boundaries of the garrison, I came across a wild cat caught in a trap. The animal became a hissing ball of raised fur and sharp teeth as soon as I approached. Its paw was bleeding badly; part of the bone had been exposed. The trap had monstrous jaws like some Neolithic creature. As I tried to prise it open, the cat sank its teeth into my hand. Despite the animal's assaults, I managed to wedge my crop into the trap and it sprang open. The cat leapt towards me so abruptly that I fell backwards into the bushes. I was left tangled up in the undergrowth whilst the cat limped steadily away. As I struggled to free my clothing from brambles and vines, it sloped off. I had twisted my ankle, and every step was painful. When I eventually got home, I hobbled stiffly past the servants without saying a word.

Sitting down in front of my bedroom mirror, I examined my face. My dress was torn, teeth marks punctured my hand, and there was a slight cut across my cheek, yet for the first time in months, I felt vital and alive. When the wild cat had slunk away, I had wanted to follow it. I wondered where it was going and whether it had a home. That evening, Thomas and I sat down to dinner as usual. He didn't notice the scratches on my hands nor the cut upon my cheek.

After dinner, I retreated to my desk, pulled out my best writing paper and gazed at a blank white page. I was barely twenty years old. There had to be more to life than this, I thought.

As schoolgirls in Bath, Sophia and I had gleefully invented new names, parents, even nationalities. "You can be whomsoever you want," she had whispered, and we had imagined ourselves as actresses, as Russian princesses, as elegant English heiresses. The future had been unknown territory, a place full of adventures and delicious possibilities. I often wondered what had become of Sophia. Though I wrote regularly to the address she had given me, I received no reply. I imagined her happily married to a viscount or a duke, with the busy life of a London socialite. From the sky-blue tulle she had given me, I made a luxurious petticoat. Whenever I wore it, I gave off flashes of bright summer sky.

When I finally put pen to paper, my hand trembled. *My dearest Mama*, I wrote.

Her response was swift and brusque. *Maybe next year*, she replied; *now isn't a good time*. Somehow she must have read between the lines.

Next door, Evelyn had borne a pale, sickly infant. Both mother and child wore stiff, white canvas knee-high boots and spent their days beneath a mobile gauze cage. Nobody talked to me about babies any more. Evelyn might try to persuade me to come visiting, but I would rather have ripped out my tongue than make small talk. The care of the household was left entirely in Jaswinder's capable hands, and it ran more smoothly than before. Despite protests from Thomas, Evelyn and Jaswinder, I began to ride out, alone, every afternoon.

"It is dangerous," said Jaswinder.

"I forbid it," said Thomas.

"What will people say?" said Evelyn. "You need an escort; you can't possibly go alone."

At first I rode side-saddle. Later, I straddled the horse so that I could gallop off into the hills. On each trip, I travelled further and further afield.

There was one particular temple ruin I returned to again and again. The main entrance had been bricked up, and the walls had been defaced with layers of European names. I circled the building, searching for another way in, my eyes tracing the incisions. The names of soldiers, officers, sweethearts had been carved into the soft white rock, almost obliterating the intricate, twisting carvings underneath.

One day I was clambering over the stones when I discovered a second entrance hidden beneath twisting vines and blocked by a rotting wooden gate. With a single push, I found myself inside. Huge, branching trees had pushed their way up through the temple floor. Green parrots screeched through the leaves. Monkeys swung down through the branches and stole pins from my hair. I could hardly believe what I saw. Erotic stone carvings reared up on every side. The figures looked like dancers; the limbs of men and women seemed to undulate with desire. Each intimate coupling seemed rooted in the earth and tangled up in the trees. The lasciviousness of the carvings shocked and repelled me, yet I couldn't drag myself away. Every possible union had been portrayed. With their swaying hips and full high breasts, the female figures were as powerful as gods. There was such joy and life in their embraces, it rendered them utterly strange. The wantonness brought prickles to the surface of my skin. For reasons that I could hardly understand, I stretched out my arms and spun round and round. I wanted new experiences, fresh challenges. There was so much I didn't know, whole worlds that remained utterly mysterious to me.

On my way back to Karnal, I was riding through a copse of trees when I saw a European couple standing by the river. They were wrapped in each other's arms beneath the shade of a banyan tree. Their horses were tethered near by. Then I looked again: the pair seemed familiar. As I drew closer, I peered through the trees. The woman was Mrs Lomer, but I recalled that her husband was dark, not fair. My curiosity was piqued, but I realised that I must not be seen. As I was turning the horse, I caught a glimpse of the man's face. Though it was a face I knew intimately, it took me a second to comprehend. I watched him cup her chin in his hands, as he had once cupped mine. Mrs Lomer gazed lovingly up at him, and my hands began to shake. As Thomas's face moved down towards hers like a lizard's tongue around a fly, I turned my horse and galloped away.

On the outskirts of the garrison, I rode past the kapok tree. Every time I passed by, I would gaze down at its roots, half-expecting to see the baby lying there, plump and alive and waving her little hands and feet. In my mind, she was as blue as Krishna, with exquisite fingers and toes. That day, I saw that the tree had lost all its leaves, yet it was neither dead, nor dormant. The bare branches were laden with huge, scarlet blossoms. I looked down at the tree's roots and saw nothing but fallen leaves. As I stared at the bright flowers adorning the leafless tree, I knew that it was time to leave.

Chapter 13

I would love to say that I abandoned my marriage without a second glance, that I walked proudly away without tears or scenes or recriminations. But in truth I screamed and shouted and ripped up most of Thomas's clothes. Going through his wardrobe, I poured honey over his finest pair of military trousers until they were swarming with white ants and tiny black flies. Pacing the verandah, my head spun with anger and jealousy and hurt. When Thomas finally returned, I refused to allow him to enter the house.

"If she is your mistress, then go to her house," I shouted.

"What on earth are you talking about?" he said.

"I saw you, I saw you," I cried.

"My dear Eliza," he said.

"Don't you dare patronise me."

"Let us go inside and discuss this in private," he said.

When he tried to force me into the house, I pushed him down the steps. Hot, angry tears were streaming down my cheeks.

"How could you?" I cried. "She is old enough to be my mother."

"Eliza, Eliza," he crooned. "We are friends, that is all."

"I saw you!" I shouted.

Then he turned the tables. "And what kind of wife have you been to me?"

Lifting me off my feet, he marched me into the drawing room and then threw me into a chair.

"You are overwrought," he said. "Since the attack of malaria, you have not been yourself."

I hesitated. An image of the baby flashed across my mind. I really should have told him I was pregnant, but I had hardly faced up to it myself. Had I said the words aloud, it would have meant admitting that I didn't want his baby any more than I wanted him. What kind of unnatural woman was I? Perhaps if I had confided in him, the outcome might have been different. It was only after the miscarriage that I had felt the loss. A small, precious, unformed, inarticulate part of me died then, and nothing I said now could bring it back.

It was Thomas who suggested I go to stay with my mother for a while.

"The break will do you good," he said. "It's been too much for you, being isolated up here."

"Perhaps you're right," I conceded.

I had already begun to layer my dresses between tissue paper when Thomas discovered his ruined clothes. Waving his uniform in front of me, he shouted: "Damn you, woman! What the hell is wrong with you? When are you going to admit that this is as much your failure as it is mine?"

I continued to pack in silence. I had no intention of arriving at my mother's house with bruises or a black eye.

Of course, Jaswinder already knew about Mrs Lomer. When I told her I was leaving she simply nodded, then said: "Give yourself a little time. These things pass. It is a small matter in a lifetime of dealings between a man and his wife."

Next door, Evelyn wept. "Your life is ruined," she spluttered between tears. "What will become of you?"

"Don't be ridiculous, Evelyn," I retorted. "It is Thomas's loss, not mine."

"My poor, dear Eliza," she cried.

I departed for Calcutta as the sun was coming up on a brisk, bright, almost English morning. At the stage-post, Thomas oversaw the loading of my luggage, and then insisted upon airing the carriage before helping me inside. I looked at him through the carriage window, and he smiled defensively. Within three years, deep creases had already begun to etch themselves on to his face. His mouth was punctuated with two cupped lines, his brow crumpled into a permanent frown. Though I knew his features intimately—the fall of his hair, the crinkle of lines around his eyes—they had ceased to hold any emotional significance for me. Any lingering feelings I had for him had seeped away the moment I made my decision.

"You'll be back in no time," he said. "You know what your mother is like."

As he leant forward to kiss me, I clasped his face between my hands.

"It is over between us," I whispered.

He pulled abruptly away from me. "Nonsense," he snapped.

As the carriage trundled away, I knew that I would never come back, and though he was loth to admit it, I was certain that Thomas knew it, too.

I arrived at my mother's house with two trunks and my small valise, which was now so covered with labels that the original leather could hardly be seen. Though I had written to Mama notifying her of my arrival, when the carriage drew up at her house, she wasn't there. The servant who answered the door obviously didn't even know that Mama had a daughter.

"Do you wish to leave a card?" she asked.

When I insisted upon waiting, I was shown into a formal drawing room with stuccoed walls and furniture upholstered in a dark regency stripe. Except for the *punkah* wafting cool air across the room, I could have been in London, or Bristol or Bath. As I surveyed the room, I allowed myself to imagine a brand new life in which we attended balls and concerts together and Mama proudly introduced me to all her friends. Thirty minutes later, she swept into the room.

"I was not expecting you," she said.

"I sent a note."

"I would not normally expect a guest whom I had not personally invited."

"I have left Thomas," I said.

"We'll see," she said.

We sat down in opposite chairs, each warily examining the other. Any thoughts of reconciliation evaporated. It had been a year since our last meeting, but nothing had changed. If I had been a grave disappointment to her then, I was doubly so now. Mama was looking elegant in a gown of shimmering fuchsia silk. Only the slightest puckering of skin on the backs of her hands and around her throat betrayed her age. My thoughts returned to Mrs Lomer. Then further back again, to Thomas and Mama in Bath, their heads bent close together.

At least Major Craigie was pleased to see me. When he came in, he clasped me warmly by the shoulders.

"Let me look at you," he said, before wrapping me in a warm embrace.

"My beautiful little girl," he smiled.

It was as if thirteen years hadn't passed. Papa Craigie stroked my hair. I gazed up at him with a broad childish smile.

"She says she has left her husband," said Mama.

"Let's not talk about that now. Can you still dance? You must have a vacation. Rest, relax, enjoy yourself a little. We will hold a soirée tomorrow in your honour."

The following evening, a dozen military officers arrived with their daughters and their wives.

"Remember," said Mama. "There will be no talk of leaving your husband. You are visiting, that is all."

Major Craigie proudly introduced me as his daughter. Mama remained aloof and unyielding throughout.

"If one more person says how much Eliza is like me, I swear I'll scream."

122

Major Craigie smiled mildly. "She is your daughter, darling. Do try to be proud of her."

Throughout the evening, Mama's attention flicked constantly back and forth between her guests, her demeanour changing according to whom she was addressing. In Ireland, I had noticed the same tendency amongst Thomas's family. They behaved in one way among the British, in another among the Irish. It was a quality I recognised in myself. *Perhaps it is a characteristic of the Anglo-Irish*, I thought, *of being betwixt and between.*

When the dancing began, I could feel Mama's eyes upon me.

"Is it true that your mother was once a professional dancer?" enquired my partner. "The lady herself will neither confirm nor deny it."

"Are you suggesting that Mama was once less than respectable?" I teasingly replied.

The officer looked flustered, then apologised profusely.

She probably started the rumour herself, I thought. Though the story flattered her, such a career would have been out of the question. Even if it were true, she was hardly likely to admit it.

After the soirée, Mama refused to allow me to attend any other functions, nor were any held in the house.

"You have your marriage to think of," she said. "There is nothing else to be said."

When a number of officers began to ask after me, she became fractious. I was reduced to watching her dress then leave the house, as I had done when I was a child. She began to update her wardrobe and to dress with especial care. I bided my time, hoping that she might soften towards me. Within a month, she had written to Thomas suggesting that he travel down from Karnal to collect me.

Every afternoon, he called at the house, but I refused to meet with him. Mama received him in her drawing room, while I resolutely remained upstairs. After a week of his visits, Mama asked me to come and see her.

"He is willing to take you back," she said.

"Is he, indeed?"

"You have no choice. He is your husband. It is time for you to leave."

I took a deep breath. "Let me stay," I whispered.

"You can't turn the clock back," she replied. "You have only one chance at marriage, and you have taken yours."

"The marriage is over," I said.

Mama laughed aloud. "Don't be ridiculous, child. A marriage is for life. Women cannot divorce their husbands; you know that perfectly well. You're not Henry VIII who could divorce then marry again. You are dependent on your husband, whether you like it or not."

"I will not go back," I said.

"I would be careful, if I were you. If you give Thomas grounds for a divorce, you will be left with nothing at all."

"I have made up my mind," I said.

"Ungrateful girl!" exclaimed Mama. "You had everything and you threw it away! I arranged a good marriage for you, but you rejected it. You wanted Thomas, well now you're stuck with him. At twelve I was earning my own living, whilst you were spoilt at school until you were sixteen. Why on earth should I have any sympathy for you?"

"I do believe you are jealous of me," I burst out. "Is it my fault he wanted me instead of you?"

Mama flushed bright red from her throat to her forehead. For a moment I thought she might strike me.

"If you refuse to return to your husband, then you leave me no choice."

"What are you saying?"

"The only other option available to you is to go to relatives in Scotland."

"Scotland?" I cried.

"It is up to you," she said.

Having arrived at Mama's, it had not occurred to me that she might send me away. I had used up all my courage leaving Thomas. I had not made any plans beyond that.

"Your husband will continue to provide for you," she said.

"You have already discussed it?"

"Thomas has been very generous."

"What does Major Craigie say?" I asked.

Mama stood up, her face ashen, her hands shaking.

"Understand this," she said. "You will not be staying here."

The *Larkins* was due to sail from Calcutta at the beginning of October. Thomas and Major Craigie came down to the docks to see me off. Mama said goodbye to me in front of the house, kissing both my cheeks in a formal embrace. I searched her face, but there was no tenderness in it. Framed in the doorway, she stood there with a strange, fixed expression. She shivered, and then glanced away, before retreating inside. As the carriage pulled away from the kerb, I realised it was the expression of a woman who felt grievously betrayed. I felt overwhelmed with guilt and shame. I was her only daughter, and I had disappointed her, not once, but twice. I should have tried harder, I thought. Clenching my fist, I banged it repeatedly against the side of my head. *No, no, no*, I thought, my eyes smarting with hurt perplexity. It couldn't be entirely my fault, could it? What about her? She was meant to be my mother, after all. If, by my actions, I had shamed her, she, by hers, had failed me a thousandfold.

At the dock, Major Craigie clasped my hands.

"Your mother does love you," he said. "She is a proud woman; she can't help it."

When he hugged me, I didn't want to let him go. He had offered me more love than Mama ever had.

"If ever you need anything," he said, "obviously, you have only to write to me."

As the ship pulled away from the dock, I watched him recede into the distance, his cheeks glistening with tears.

For the sake of appearances, Thomas sailed part of the way down the Ganges with me.

Once he had finalised the arrangements with the captain, he joined me on deck. We both watched silently as the boat that was to take him onshore drew up alongside. As he took his leave, he looked awkward and shamefaced.

"You will always be my wife," he said. "You know you can come back whenever you like."

When he caught me in his arms, I remembered our first embrace.

"It is not too late," he whispered.

The thirteen years that lay between us yawned open like an unbridgeable gulf. I had used him to escape from an unwanted situation, without a thought for the consequences. But I was no longer a naive seventeen-year-old. Thomas had made sure of that.

"It's time for you to go," I said.

As he climbed down the rope ladder, he paused. "You never gave me a chance. You never wanted me, not really. You wanted a father, not a husband."

I bit my lip.

"I'm sorry," I mouthed.

As I watched the boat rowing him towards the shore, I felt as though the whole of my life was drifting away from me. The small part of me that was wild and untrammelled had its roots in Indian soil. I thought of the overblown, luscious blooms of the kapok tree. Of my father's grave in the cemetery at Dinapore. I thought of Evelyn and Jaswinder, Mama and Major Craigie. Above me the canvas cracked. The banks of the Ganges began to widen out towards the sea. The wind caught in the sails, and the ship began to gather speed.

Scene Four

GREY MERINO WOOL

Chapter 14

After the bud flowers and the petals fall, the stem may bear hips or attract bumblebees. If there are seeds, they may be eaten by birds or scattered in the breeze. Should the fruit ripen, it may shrivel against night frosts, or attract blight. The leaves may be eaten by weevils; caterpillars burrow tunnels through succulent fruit. A falling harvest bruises, blackens, ferments. The tree may wither from the roots to the tip.

As the ship sailed away from India, I watched the lamp swing from the ceiling and listened to the sound of the sea. Though I was barely twenty years old, my future looked bleak. In the middle of the Indian Ocean, in a windowless cabin aboard the *Larkins,* I slid my wedding ring repeatedly on, then off, my index finger. The waves pounded the side of the ship, and the cabin walls vibrated. A spider swung from a thread above my head. A rat ran along the edge of the floor. I felt a tear slide down my cheek. With every crashing wave, Mama's parting words kept coming back to me.

"What makes you think you're so special?" she'd said. "One day, somebody will knock the dreaminess out of you, mark my words."

Ordinary unhappiness was common enough; why couldn't I have settled for it like everyone else? I wouldn't have been the first woman to swallow my pride. "You must cut your cloth to suit your purse," Mama had said before laying down a list of rules. Silk frocks would no longer be considered appropriate attire; a modest grey merino or a simple muslin must suffice. She might as well have arranged to bury me alive. How could this be happening? I lay down on the bed and closed my eyes. Outside, the sea broke endlessly against the hull of the ship. I had left Scotland at eleven, swearing that I would never set foot in the wretched country again. Did I really have to endure it all over again?

Hours later, I woke to a persistent knocking. The lamp had burnt itself out, and I had to stumble across the cabin to the door. The captain's wife introduced herself, whilst I was still rubbing my eyes.

"My dear girl," she said, "are you missing your husband already? Well, you mustn't fret. I have given him my solemn promise that we will take good care of you."

Behind her, the dinner bell rang three times.

"Are you ready?" she asked.

"I'm not hungry," I replied.

Mrs Ingram smiled. "Of course you are. A slip of a girl like you. Best make the most of the meals whilst you can. Within a month, there will be nothing but salt-fish and biscuits."

In the dining cabin, she ushered me over to the captain's table, where we were joined by a middle-aged American couple and the captain himself. Mr Henry P. Sturgis, from Boston, Massachusetts, insisted upon introducing himself in full. His wife, Mary, merely smiled. Within minutes, it became apparent that Thomas had already spoken to all of them.

"Your poor husband was most anxious about leaving you alone," said Mrs Sturgis. "We were only too happy to reassure him."

"We will escort you," said Mr Sturgis.

"And I will act as your chaperone," said his wife.

"You need never be alone," said Mrs Ingram, cupping a hand over mine.

I managed a faint smile.

"Your husband tells me that you are not quite well, my dear. Indeed, the climate in India is too excessive for many young women."

"Indeed," I replied.

"Such a shame about your accident," said Mrs Sturgis.

"My accident?" I enquired.

"There, there, my dear, don't agitate yourself."

By way of explanation, she leaned over towards Mrs Ingram and lowered her voice.

"The poor girl has not recovered from a riding accident," she said. "She fell from a horse in Meerut and sustained a back injury. Her husband hopes that a period of convalescence at home might help."

"You will sorely miss your husband."

"Sorely," I replied.

"And to be so far from your mama."

"Distance hardly matters in a relationship such as ours," I dryly replied.

I looked around the room, at the passengers from other tables. Among the entire company, I couldn't see anyone who might possibly rescue me. When my attention came back to the company, I found Mrs Ingram and Mrs Sturgis were peering anxiously at me.

At the port of Madras, the captain announced a dance in honour of the new influx of passengers. As usual, I had spent most of the evening trapped between Mrs Ingram and Mrs Sturgis, who were competing to cosset and protect me. After dinner, a raggle-taggle band of sailors began to play. A pianist of sorts was accompanied by a fiddler, a horn player and the cook's boy playing a flute.

While we were lining up, both the captain and Mr Sturgis caught me by the elbow.

"A married woman alone is so vulnerable," cautioned the captain.

"Especially one so young," said Mr Sturgis, sliding an arm around my waist.

"You could so easily become a target of gossip," said the captain, snatching me away.

I was pinned between the two men, when Mrs Sturgis approached. For my part, I was oblivious to their deliberations. The door to the captain's cabin had opened, and my attention was entirely taken up by a young lieutenant who was being escorted across the floor.

"Excuse me," said the captain.

The new passenger was a compelling blend of youth and authority. He was a tall, slender figure with fair hair and pale, deep-set eyes. As the captain shook his hand, the lieutenant noticed me watching him. I blushed and averted my eyes.

Turning my attention back to Mr and Mrs Sturgis, I found them continuing in the same vein.

Oh, why hadn't I worn my lilac silk or the green shot taffeta? I thought. And why couldn't I have taken a little trouble with my hair? I had been so utterly convinced that my life was effectively over that I had neglected my appearance. My hair had been haphazardly arranged, my dress was serviceable but plain.

Throughout the evening, the lieutenant seemed to be circling the room. Every time I looked up, he would be somewhere else. I would catch sight of him at one table after another, talking to someone else. My eyes followed him until I began to feel dizzy. In every glimpse of him, I took in another detail. His moustache and eyebrows were darker than his hair. His eyes were grey. Or were they blue? The captain, then Mr Sturgis, talked continuously whilst we danced. I nodded and smiled without taking in a single word.

Chapter 15

As everybody knows, a lady may not introduce herself to a gentleman, nor may a gentleman impose upon a lady until formal introductions have been made. In the circumstances, there was nothing I could do but be patient and wait. Every afternoon at four o'clock, dinner was served in the cuddy. The passengers were grouped in clusters, with the more privileged guests being seated at the captain's table. On alternate days, the place settings were reshuffled. On the third day, the lieutenant and I were finally seated at the same table.

Captain Ingram did the honours.

"Mrs Eliza James: Lieutenant George Lennox. 4th Madras Cavaliers."

The lieutenant bowed and took my hand. His generous mouth broke readily into a smile. His hand felt warm around mine. His eyes, I noticed, were a warm, slatey blue.

Suddenly I no longer felt hungry. My body had become a substance of light and air. When the waiter placed a bowl of brown soup in front of me, I hardly remembered what I was supposed to do with it.

Over dinner, Mrs Ingram and Mrs Sturgis plied the lieutenant with polite but insistent enquiries, which he answered with a wry smile.

It was his privilege to be the aide-de-camp of Lord Elphinstone, the governor general of Madras. He imagined that his uncle, the Duke of Richmond, was, indeed, very proud of him. After three years in India, this was his first return home. No, he had not yet had any thoughts of marriage; he was only nineteen, after all. Yes, he fully expected to return to Madras. India had been kind to him, and his future prospects were very good. Of course, he would be pleased to call upon Mrs Sturgis and her niece should they ever visit Madras.

A dish of boiled pork and rice was followed by roast chicken and potatoes. By the time a yellow semolina pudding had been served, the focus of the conversation had taken an unwelcome turn.

Whenever the lieutenant turned his attention in my direction, my escorts became fastidious in their protectiveness. Before I could reply, one or other would take it upon themselves to interject. When I heard myself described as a happily married woman, I could hardly object. When Mrs Sturgis expounded at length upon the tragic separation of such a loving young couple, I almost choked upon a mouthful of semolina. It was left to Mrs Ingram to explain that I had fallen from a horse and had not yet recovered from my injury.

"The poor child," she said. "I understand that you were out riding alone, dear, and not even side-saddle. Your husband should never have allowed it."

By this point, I could hardly eat anything at all. One course followed endlessly after another. What on earth had Thomas told them, I wondered? Can there be anything more?

Later that evening, I was partnered by the captain, then Mr Sturgis. The lieutenant danced with Mrs Ingram, then Mrs Sturgis, before it was my turn.

"Your escorts are very thorough," he said.

"I am as closely guarded as the crown jewels," I smiled.

When our palms touched, I felt my cheeks burn. As we moved into the dance, I couldn't look at him; even the mingling of our breath seemed an intimacy. The lieutenant was an assured dancer, and he led me easily around the floor. Though we began at a suitable distance from each other, by the end of the first waltz we had drawn close.

"You dance very well," he said.

My mother's few gifts, I thought. *Dark hair, nimble feet.*

133

"So do you," I replied.

"For a woman with a back injury, your dancing is nothing less than miraculous."

The next day, I was taking the air on deck when the lieutenant fell into step beside me. We had a few moments alone before Mrs Ingram slid between us and firmly linked my arm. The rest of the week followed the same pattern, until I realised that neither of my chaperones emerged from their cabins before noon. When I began to take an early morning walk, I found that the lieutenant would already be strolling the decks.

"Might I accompany you?" he would ask, and I would smile and take his arm.

Our youthfulness made us natural allies. We were the conspirators of the early morning, whilst the guardians of etiquette slept. After three years with Thomas, I realised how much I had missed talking to someone my own age. An easy, relaxed manner quickly developed between us. Hanging over the rails of the ship, we would point out any strange fish or birds and try to guess their names.

"What's that?" I cried.

"It's an African darting fish."

"No, it's not. It's a blue glistening fish."

"I think you'll find that it's a splendid example of an Atlantic wriggler."

"Nonsense. It is most definitely an azure stickler."

One morning we woke to find a shoal of flying fish floundering on the deck. They were twisting and writhing and suffocating in the heat.

"Are they edible?" I asked, but the lieutenant shook his head.

Whilst I was soaking them in water, he caught them by the tails and threw them back into the sea. On another day, we watched an albatross soaring overhead, its shadow gliding across the deck.

There were times we forgot ourselves completely, like two naughty truanting children, caught up in the excitement of it all.

"Look! Look!" I cried, pulling him by the hand towards the

rails. Alongside the ship, a school of porpoises were swooping in and out of the sparkling blue water.

"They've come to say hello to us," I laughed.

"They are almost as playful as you," the lieutenant replied.

Impulsively, he pulled me towards him, then remembering himself, he abruptly dropped his arms.

"I'm so sorry," he muttered.

Before I had a chance to respond, he swung round and marched away. He didn't turn up for supper, nor for the evening's entertainment. The next morning I waited vainly on the deck. At dinner that afternoon, there was still no sign of him.

"Is Lieutenant Lennox ill?" I asked.

"He has requested that all his meals be served in his cabin," the captain replied.

After supper that evening, Mrs Sturgis came to my cabin. She hovered in the doorway, her eyes brimming with anguished solicitude.

"You might as well come in," I said.

"You can't go on like this, Eliza," she burst out. "There has been all manner of talk."

"What on earth do you mean?" I asked.

"You have danced with him three times in a row. Now he has hidden himself away. What on earth is to be assumed by such behaviour?"

"You are talking about the lieutenant, I suppose."

Mrs Sturgis sat on the sofa, looking plump and flustered and concerned. Though she was only a few years older than Mama, she was matronly in a way Mama would never be.

"Please, Eliza, I beg of you to put a stop to it now."

"If you don't mind, I was about to get ready for bed," I said.

"I am only thinking of you," she pleaded.

I showed her the door. "I appreciate your concern," I said.

It was two days before Lieutenant Lennox reappeared. Throughout dinner, he seemed distant and embarrassed. Beyond an initial acknowledgement, he wouldn't even look at me. When I saw him leave the table, I, too, made my excuses.

I found him on the upper decks of the ship, leaning on the rails. I approached him quietly, slipping my arm through his. When he began to pull away, I tightened my grip, folding my hands over his. Silently, we gazed out across the surface of the water.

It was a clear, still night, and the moon was a fine crescent in the sky. Above it, the Southern Cross glowed. The reflection of the star and the moon rippled across the sea. As the ship moved forwards, a trail of silver followed in its wake.

"We must keep a distance, Mrs James."

I kept my arms firmly linked through his. Our faces were only inches away from each other.

"Why?" I asked. "You are my only true friend aboard this ship. I cannot be parted from you. Nor can we spend four months avoiding each other."

The lieutenant turned to me and grasped my hands.

"You are the wife of an officer. I wouldn't make you the subject of any gossip for all the world. The captain has already spoken to me about the inappropriateness of our behaviour."

I looked into his eyes.

"I am the wife of an officer in name only. He doesn't deserve to call himself my husband. By his actions, he has given up any rights over me."

"What on earth do you mean?"

"I will be my own woman soon, you'll see."

This was wishful thinking on my part. I knew perfectly well that I would never be free of Thomas, either financially or in law. Just for a short time, though, I wanted to pretend that my life might magically change course.

For a few long moments we stared at each other, then hesitantly we embraced. When I lifted my chin from his shoulder, he shuddered, then his lips brushed mine.

"It is sealed then, the bond between us," I said.

We were both aware of the boundary we had crossed.

From that moment onwards, we were inseparable. If the other passengers were talking about us, I didn't care. We spent the afternoons lounging together on the deck in two basket chairs placed side by side. We sat together at dinner; we danced with each other again and again and again. In the long, hot evenings, we strolled arm in arm, seeking out the dark and unfrequented corners of the ship. Long after the decent hour, when all the other ladies had retired, we lingered on the poop deck. After I was seen visiting the lieutenant's cabin, my self-appointed guardians came to call on me.

With Mrs Ingram beside her, the soft-hearted Mrs Sturgis became sterner. For her part, the normally congenial Mrs Ingram gave off the impression of black, thunderous clouds contained within a very small, neat frame.

"I really must protest," she said.

"Anyone can make a mistake in the dark," I casually replied.

"Believe me, we are only thinking of you," said Mrs Sturgis.

"His cabin has a window, mine does not," I replied.

Both ladies responded to my offer of a seat with marked distaste.

Mrs Ingram looked jittery. "Everyone knows that by night the sofa becomes a bed," she said.

"Really, Mrs Ingram," I protested. "What exactly are you implying?"

That evening, the lieutenant and I were tucked up on the very same sofa, when I caught Mrs Ingram peering in through the window. When I went over and drew the Venetian blinds, she jumped back, looking embarrassed and annoyed.

Within days, the captain and his wife had announced that they could no longer receive me. Initially, I was moved from the captain's table, then later it was made clear that I was no longer welcome in company at all. From that point onwards, I was excluded from all the ship's functions, and my meals were sent to my cabin on a tray.

George and I celebrated Christmas and New Year alone together in the intimacy of his cabin. When we heard the music drifting up from the cuddy, we pushed back the furniture and waltzed slowly around the floor.

I could no longer imagine life beyond the drifting confines of the ship. Every evening, Lieutenant Lennox came to my cabin, and we gazed happily at each other for hours. I could see clearly only what I could touch—his face, his mouth, his fingers. Everything else was a blur. We hypnotised each other with our eyes. How long could kisses be enough, the feel of his arms around my waist, his face beneath my fingertips?

"Lieutenant?"

He smiled. "Mrs James?"

"Please call me Eliza," I asked.

His smile grew broader.

"Eliza?"

I stifled a giggle. "Yes, Lieutenant?"

"Please call me George," he said, kissing the tip of my nose.

"George?"

"Yes, Eliza?"

I pulled him closer. "Kiss me, George, please kiss me."

His mouth slid from my neck to my throat.

"Where, Eliza? Here or here?"

We were sitting in his cabin. The lamp swung gently from the beams, glancing shadows across the walls. Beyond the porthole, the darkening sky glowed in swathes of copper and purple. His mouth slipped from my throat to my chest.

"There is so much more of you beneath this gown," he whispered.

As my breathing became faster, the whalebone in my corset creaked and my dress strained at the seams.

"Will you help me, George?"

Turning my back to him, I indicated the hooks and eyes that secured the bodice of my dress. His hands shook as he clumsily unfastened me. Once he had undone the last one, I slipped one arm, then another from my sleeves.

Beneath my bodice was my corset and beneath that a transparent chemise which barely covered my breasts. My nipples strained against the fabric. My breath caught fast in my throat. George's hands trembled as he loosened the drawstring of my chemise. When he cupped me in his hands, I could hardly breathe. I sighed with pleasure when he buried his head between my breasts.

"George," I whispered, "you can do whatever you please."

We fed on each other's love, like hummingbirds from the deep throats of lilies. But the more we ate, the hungrier we became. One day we were lounging on the sofa in my cabin. I had removed my shoes, my overskirt, the bodice of my dress. George's shirt was dishevelled, his buttons undone.

Sliding down between his thighs, I began to carefully unbutton his trousers. I was curious about him; there was a part of him I had not yet seen. George held his breath.

"What are you doing?" he whispered.

His penis was taut and proud as a tall mushroom. I held it in my hands and it seemed a sweet and grateful thing. George watched me through hooded eyes whilst I examined all the minutiae of his manhood—its tip and lip and rim, its responses to the slightest movement of my hand or tongue.

"It won't bite you," he said.

"Won't it?" I replied.

With a bowl of water and a wet cloth, I washed and attended to him. Kneeling between his thighs, I moved the cloth up and down, and his penis throbbed against my hand.

George was in thrall to the paraphernalia of femininity. Corsets and stockings and cosmetics fascinated him. One day when I was powdering my face, he picked up the sponge. Once I had made up my own face, I powdered his, applying rouge, then carmine to his lips. When I showed him his reflection, he looked pretty as a girl. Afterwards, we kissed and smooched until powder and paint were smeared all over our faces, and we looked like a pair of delirious clowns.

We were pulling off each other's clothes when there was a knock at the door. Stifling our laughter, we waited for the knocking to stop. Later, I found my dinner congealing on a tray outside on the deck floor.

Mrs Ingram began to send out spies. There was always someone peering through the window or listening at the door. More than once, her maid caught me in my underclothes. She would wait for the cabin door to swing open and then take a peek inside. Once she caught me putting on my stockings in front of George; another time, she saw him lacing up my corset.

We resolved to be more careful. I was dependent upon my husband whether I liked it or not. Though it was sweltering inside my cabin, George and I began to bolt the door. I continued to delude myself that our transgressions were minor in nature. After all, no matter how intimate the exchanges between us, our relationship remained unconsummated.

Late one evening, I was reclining sleepily on the sofa and George was sitting on the floor, his head on my lap, one of my stockinged feet in his hands.

"It is time I retired," I said.

"Can I help you undress?" he asked, tracing a finger along the inside of my ankle. I lay back dreamily as he lifted up my petticoats and traced my silk stocking up to the tops of my thighs. I suppose I had imagined that he would loosen my garters and begin to unroll my stockings. Instead he manoeuvred through the multiple layers of my underclothes. When he found the opening of my drawers, I let out a startled cry. Suddenly his fingers were stroking my most intimate flesh.

"Ssh," he said.

His hands gently parted my thighs and his head disappeared beneath my petticoats. As he continued to probe, I felt myself open like a clam. He explored the oyster, then the pearl. As his fingers moved over it, it swelled beneath his touch. He teased and probed and licked me with his tongue. I covered my face with a layer of my petticoats, but I didn't ask him to stop.

For the first time in my life, I understood passion, compulsion. I wanted to try everything; I could hardly leave George alone. I remembered Bridie and her lover beside the ovens deep within the ship. I recalled the erotic figures in the temple. I remembered the sight of an Indian woman gyrating above the British soldier when I was a child.

Moving my hips slowly round and round, I danced over him as he lay. I was wondrous at the sensation, dazzled to have a man lying helpless beneath me. Whilst I was teasing him, he was steadily loosening first my underclothes, then his own. When I started to giggle, he tumbled me around. My chemise gaped open; his penis sprang free of his clothes. He paused. I pulled him to me.

"Don't stop," I whispered.

His first thrust made me solemn; his second made me cry out. As he moved inside me, his eyes never left my face. I opened my thighs wide, and George hooked my legs over the crook of his arms. Locked together we moved backwards and forwards in rhythm with the rolling sea. If the ship had begun to sink, I wouldn't have cared. In that moment I would happily have drowned.

As we were approaching the Canary Islands, we discovered a butterfly pupa on the rafters in George's cabin. First one wing, then another burst forth from the shell. It clung to the ceiling and hardly moved. It was a beautiful creature, the size of a tiny bird. Its wings were a bright cerulean blue with a vivid yellow eye in the centre, their edges tipped in a silver filigree pattern, the tips trailing tiny veils.

The next day, the butterfly's wings trembled, then they began to flap, as if growing accustomed to their purpose. When it began to fly around the room, battering its wings against the walls, we didn't know what to do.

"What do butterflies eat?" I asked.

"I've no idea," said George.

"If we keep it here, it will die," I said.

"But what will happen if we let it go?"

"Who knows?" I replied.

As the ship passed Madeira, I opened the cabin window. George caught the butterfly in his hands, then shooed it up into the sky. Together, we peered out of the window and watched its progress. The butterfly fluttered in the air for a moment before being swept up in the breeze.

Portsmouth approached. After Morocco, the weather had turned decidedly cold. I switched from silk to wool stockings and pulled out a couple of knitted shawls. As we sailed from the Bay of Biscay into the English Channel, January gave way to February. The future loomed up, unbidden, in front of my eyes. I retreated to my own cabin and closed the door.

When we landed at Portsmouth Docks, my step-aunt, Mrs Catherine Rae, would be waiting for me, along with Mrs Sarah Watson, a widowed sister of Thomas's. After an overnight stay in Blackheath, Mrs Rae and I were to take the steamer direct to Scotland, where I was to reside with her brother in Leith. It would be like staying in Montrose all over again. The ticking clock. The silent meals. The empty parlour. Like Montrose, Leith was a harbour town. There would be the same grey mudflats, the same stink of fish.

Twice my mother had sent me away. One thing was certain: I wouldn't give her the opportunity to do so again.

Chapter 16

At Portsmouth Docks, I descended the gangplank with downcast eyes, like a condemned woman resigned to her fate. Instead, a coachman handed me a letter, then promptly departed. As I opened the envelope, George leant over my shoulder, and we read its contents together.

Mrs Rae had caught a chill on the journey down from Scotland and regretted that she was unable to meet me. She enclosed the address of Mrs Watson in Blackheath and directed me to make my own way there.

"My carriage awaits," George grinned.

I hesitated for only a moment.

The same thought obviously crossed both our minds. George caught my hand, and we almost ran towards the stagecoach. He swung me up on to the seat, then ordered the coachman to load my luggage alongside his. As the horses pulled away, we peered out of the window in time to see Captain Ingram and his wife hurrying breathlessly after us.

"Mrs James, Mrs James, wait, wait."

Behind them, Mrs Sturgis was ruefully shaking her head.

Inside the carriage, George and I fell back against the seats and giggled like ten-year-olds. Once we were properly on our way, I scanned the letter again.

"What will you do?" asked George.

I folded the letter up carefully and replaced it in the envelope.

"What do you suggest?" I asked.

We looked into each other's eyes. A flicker of uncertainty scudded across George's face, and then he cupped my face in his hands. When we kissed, I felt as if we were falling through feathers. That night, we booked into a local inn. Wrapped up in each other's arms, we fell deeply and happily to sleep. It was the first time that we had spent the entire night together. By the morning, we had decided that we wouldn't be parted.

Looking back on it now, I realise that the Imperial Hotel in Covent Garden formed the backdrop to my spectacular fall from grace. The moment I clapped eyes on it, any lingering concerns for my reputation slipped gently away. The creamy stucco façade was embellished with festoons of flowers and classical columns, each surmounted by the fierce, looming head of Jupiter, and a suitably imposing sweep of steps led up to double-fronted, glass-panelled doors. Two footmen in top hats and gold-trimmed frock coats stood on either side of the entrance, ready to loop back a red velvet rope. As I tripped lightly up the steps, I clasped George's hand with oblivious pleasure. We were only a stone's throw away from the Royal Italian Opera House, the most fashionable theatre in England.

In our two adjoining rooms, tall engraved mirrors and heavy damask drapes hung from deep ruby papered walls. I was utterly thrilled with the sumptuousness of it all. As soon as the porter departed, I span George exuberantly around the room.

Both Major Craigie and Mama had expressly forbidden that I spend any time in London, and now that I was actually here, I was determined to find out why. George and I occupied our first afternoon promenading the pavements. Everywhere cafés, music halls, cigar divans and supper clubs opened out on to the pavements. When we passed the Opera House, we booked tickets for the following night. The streets teemed with elegant horses and smart carriages. Fashionable people alighted at every turn. There were also, I noticed with some curiosity, a number of well-dressed, yet curiously brash-looking women who were promenading the streets alone.

On our second night in London, we went to the Royal Opera House, and I fell in love all over again. I was dazzled by the whole experience—the lights, the music, the bustle, the glitter. A fellow officer and friend of George's, Lieutenant Charles Hewitt, picked us up and acted as our guide.

Marching up the steps and through the porticos, he negotiated a path through the jostling crowd.

"Every human vice is here," he pronounced, "from the squalid to the exalted."

Though he was fresh-faced and sandy-haired, he had a world-weary quality about him, as if a cynical old roué had occupied the body of a youth. At regular intervals, he would whisper something to George, and the two of them would bellow with laughter.

Inside the auditorium, we joined the couples parading the aisles. Leaning from the velvet ledges of the opera boxes above, I noticed a number of gorgeously attired women surrounded by men in fluted shirt fronts.

Before the performance had even begun, I was captivated by the interplay in the auditorium. All eyes were upon a striking, dark-haired woman in one of the boxes. I studied her through my lorgnettes. Her ripe mouth and lustrous Japanese eyes seemed to feed upon the attention of the audience. Swathes of diamonds encircled her neck and one of her wrists.

I tugged at George's sleeve.

"Who is that lady?" I asked. "She is wearing far too much jewellery."

"That lady, as you so kindly refer to her, is a *grande cocotte,*" he replied. "She is so far beyond society that she may do whatever she likes."

"Do you mean she has a lover?" I whispered.

George snorted with laughter. "Be sure, a woman like that can calculate a man's worth at a glance. Look at her," he said. "No respectable woman would survey the audience in so bold a manner."

"The vamp with the jewels goes by the sobriquet of the Brazen Bellona," confirmed Lieutenant Hewitt. "She is Italian, they say.

Rumour has it that she spent the entire fortune of her previous protector in under two years. Whilst the poor man languishes in a debtors' prison, Maria Bellona goes from success to success."

Such talk made me feel uneasy. I was about to admonish my companions when a trumpet sounded and the curtains swung open. In the romantic ballet that was being enacted on the stage, the dancers wore short diaphanous skirts, their exposed legs encased in pink fleshings to create the illusion of nudity. I wish that I could tell you the name of the ballet or the identity of the principle dancers, but my attention kept sliding away from the stage. Throughout the performance, the sirens in the opera boxes were courted by a constant flow of admirers.

In the interval, Lieutenant Hewitt gleefully identified them.

"The woman in lilac is known as the Venus Mendicant; in the next box is the Mocking Bird; on the other side of the auditorium is the White Doe."

"You mean these ladies are all . . . ?"

"*Poules de luxe,*" said Lieutenant Hewitt.

I glared at him, then George.

"And you're an expert, I suppose," I retorted.

In truth, I did not think that he should be talking to me of such things, and I was indignant that George had not interjected.

After the performance, we passed Madame Bellona in the foyer. Lieutenant Hewitt bowed graciously and she paused. When she smiled, her eyes twinkled—as if the whole world and everything in it had been laid on solely for her amusement. In a moment, Lieutenant Hewitt was presenting her to George, who blushed like a girl. When Lieutenant Hewitt turned towards me, I was utterly furious. I nodded very slightly, then pulled George away.

"How dare you allow me to be introduced to a courtesan?" I hissed. "What does your friend take me for?"

When George didn't reply, I tugged on his arm. "Why don't you say something in my defence?" I asked.

Overhearing this, Lieutenant Hewitt raised an eyebrow. "Ahh! The foibles of love!" he drawled.

146

For days, I played hide and seek with Mrs Watson and Mrs Rae. When they received no word from me, they began to make enquiries all over London. By the time I had moved into a suite of rooms in Great Ryder Street, Mrs Watson had tracked me down.

"Please listen to reason," she pleaded, but I shook my head and turned her away. I determined to move without leaving a forwarding address, but the very next day, she returned with Mrs Rae.

I had little choice but to show them into the drawing room and offer them tea. Both women looked painfully embarrassed. They kept darting encouraging looks at each other. Neither of them seemed to be able to look directly at me.

"These are very pleasant rooms," said Mrs Rae.

"Let us come to the point," said Mrs Watson.

"Indeed," said Mrs Rae.

Mrs Watson was a stout, buttoned-up woman of indeterminate age, with an unfortunate resemblance to her brother. Mrs Rae sat with her hands twisting in her lap and her eyes brimming with concern. Both women perched uncomfortably on the edge of their seats, as if they were afraid of catching something. How could they possibly understand how I felt? I had a nightmare vision of myself in the future, sitting in an eminently respectable drawing room in Leith, with plump little hands and cheeks, and a marked predilection for cakes and puddings over headier, more sensual pleasures. I thought about the exotic courtesans in the theatre, who clearly had no need of chaperones. Unless I put my foot down now, my life wouldn't be my own.

"What exactly is the point?" I asked.

Ignoring Mrs Watson, who obviously had her brother's interests at heart, I directed my question to Mrs Rae. When I was a child, she had rescued me from Montrose; I had lived briefly with her before I was sent to school in Bath.

Mrs Rae paused.

"You are destroying your future," said Mrs Watson.

"What future?" I cried.

"If you persist with this . . . this entanglement, you will be excluded from decent society," said Mrs Rae.

"You will be no better than some strumpet who walks the streets," said Mrs Watson.

"Hush," said Mrs Rae. "There is no need for such talk."

"It is best to speak plainly," retorted Mrs Watson.

Mrs Rae turned to me.

"It's not too late," she said.

"I will not be buried alive in Scotland," I cried.

"Come and live with me in Edinburgh," she pleaded.

I hesitated for a moment. She had always been kind to me, but I was no longer a child.

"I cannot leave George," I said.

"Very well," said Mrs Watson.

Mrs Rae looked distraught.

"Oh, Eliza," she sighed.

"But what should we inform your husband?" asked Mrs Watson.

I shrugged. "Whatever you like," I replied. "It is of no consequence to me."

George and I swiftly became an established part of London society. For the most part, we were discreet—I, a married woman, and he, simply my escort. Every evening we dined out or attended the theatre. In the afternoons, I went riding in Hyde Park in a barouche drawn by two white horses.

Between three o'clock and five, the park filled with chic phaetons and landaus as fashionable society rode back and forth. There were unaccompanied women in tight, riding costumes riding side-saddle on cantering horses, and others in carriages emblazoned with the coats of arms of their protectors. The *grandes horizontales* certainly came out in style. I watched them out of the corner of my eye, with a mixture of fascination and revulsion.

Often I caught men looking at me. Something blatant had grown in me. I knew that the intimacies of our bedroom were written across my face. Desire grazed the surface of my skin. George had only to touch my neck or stroke my arm and I would be ready for him. I was saturated in his caresses. I was honey to his touch. There wasn't a moment in the day when I didn't think of him.

In March, George rented an apartment for me in Half Moon Street, Mayfair. My elegant new chambers occupied the middle floor of a house which had been stuccoed in duck-egg blue and decorated with swags of ribbons and flowers in white relief. It looked like a love nest, and I wanted it straight away.

Within days of settling in, Mrs Rae paid me a visit. It was not yet noon, and I was only half dressed. George had arrived shortly before-hand, and I had been padding around in my bare feet, dressed only in a chemise and a petticoat. I asked the maid to send my step-aunt away, but instead I heard her calling my name from the hallway. George looked startled. I was determined to ignore her and locked the door.

The constant reiteration of my supposedly fallen state both oppressed and aroused me. My need for George became urgent. My desire pulsed beneath my skirts.

Unbuttoning my chemise, I beckoned to him. When he came over I pulled up his shirt and loosened his trousers.

Outside, Mrs Rae began to knock on the door.

"I am only thinking of you," she called.

George pressed me against the wall. Reaching inside his cloth-ing, I felt his penis spring up in my hand. He buried his head in the crook of my neck. His heart beat next to mine. His breath was in my hair.

"Ruin me," I whispered, winding my legs around his back.

Negotiating his way through my petticoats, George discovered that I was slippery and wet. When he pushed into me, I felt myself close tightly around him, like the blind, greedy mouth of a sea anemone.

We both fell back against the wall for support.

From the hallway, my step-aunt continued to call through the door.

"Men can do what they like, but it is women who pay the price."

"Ruin me," I whispered again.

George's mouth closed over mine. Whenever I tried to speak, he silenced me with his mouth, his lips, his tongue.

Mrs Rae banged on the door. "He will leave you with nothing," she shouted.

I tightened my grip around George's hips. Waves of pleasure radiated between my legs. At times we stumbled and almost fell.

"Eliza, Eliza," she called.

At last, we heard the sound of retreating footsteps. When the front door closed, we toppled to the floor. George's cries grew faster. I wrapped my legs around him. I was suffused in a warm, pulsing glow that swept upwards and engulfed my head. I was drowning in a blissful sea. I sighed: "I'm dead, I'm dead."

One day I was out riding in Hyde Park when I heard a familiar voice calling me. When I glanced up at the occupant of a racy white carriage, I could hardly believe my eyes.

"Is it really you?" I cried.

I had not seen Sophia for six years, since we were schoolgirls together in Bath. We had written to each other intermittently, but after I eloped with Thomas, we lost touch. There, in front of me, were the same almond eyes and shiny ringleted hair, but her round cheeky face had become sleek and sharply defined. She was wearing a soft blue velvet riding costume that she had obviously been sewn into. There was a new quality about her, an air of barbed sophistication that hinted at the possibility of cruelty.

We exchanged addresses, only to discover that we were living a few streets away from each other. Within the hour, we were both sitting in my drawing room, taking afternoon tea.

"Are you married?" I asked.

"Are you?" asked Sophia.

I outlined my situation.

"So you are his mistress," she said.

I had never heard myself so bluntly described.

"We love each other," I primly replied. "One day we will marry."

Sophia laughed out loud.

"My dear Rosana," she said, using my old pet name from school.

It transpired that Sophia was currently the mistress of the Duke of Argyll, who owned estates in Berkshire, Scotland and the West Indies. Previously she'd had a number of admirers. She had received offers of marriage, but from men she considered beneath her.

"Your mother was right. You shouldn't have thrown yourself away on a mere lieutenant. What on earth were you thinking of?"

I avoided her gaze. "I was naive and unworldly," I said. "What did I know?"

Sophia seemed to be entirely happy with her situation. I could detect no shame in her at all.

"But you're a kept woman," I protested.

"I have friends that support me, that is all."

"Nobody will ever marry you now," I said.

"A wife is a kept woman compelled to obedience and restrained by convention, whereas I may do whatever I please. If my protector leaves me, I can easily get another."

"But what about love?" I asked.

"Love fades."

"Not ours," I replied.

"I hope you're right," she said.

For months, George and I lived behind the drawn curtains of Half Moon Street, in a blissful, twilit world of our own. Often he would arrive early in the morning and stay until midnight. The intricacies of his body were imprinted upon my fingertips. A faint scar beneath his lip. The outline of his lower rib. The down of fine hair on his belly, that grew coarser further down. The slight curve of his penis, its jaunty cap, its width in my hand.

In public, George continued to introduce me as Mrs James. In the privacy of my bedroom, he persisted in calling me that, too. I think it tantalised him to think that I belonged to somebody else.

One afternoon we were making love, when he paused.

"Don't stop," I said.

As he moved slowly inside of me, he watched my face.

"What was Lieutenant James like in bed?" he asked. "Did he do this and this?"

I froze.

When the questions continued, I pushed him off me and wrapped myself in the sheets.

"Why are you behaving like this?" I asked. "I will never go back to him. You are my husband now."

"Come back here," grinned George, disentangling me from the sheet.

"I *am* going to divorce him," I said.

George frowned.

"Don't be silly," he said.

In one swift movement, I ripped the sheets from the bed, then jumped up and got dressed. How dare he speak to me like that? It was the first inkling I had that George regarded me with less than absolute respect.

When I was alone, I began to fret. Mrs Rae's words would echo in my head. What would become of me if George left me? Without him, nothing in my life would make any sense. If he ever had to leave London for any reason, I would have moments of sheer panic, imagining that he would never come back. When we were together, I wanted him all the time. Anxiety became confused with desire. When he was inside of me, I felt fed and reassured. I made him promise that he would never leave me. I wanted him more and more. By the summer, he was calling at Half Moon Street later and later each day. Occasionally a day would pass when he didn't visit me at all.

One day, towards the end of July, he arrived at four o'clock in the afternoon. When he came into the drawing room, I feigned surprise. In response, he looked formal and shamefaced.

"We have to talk," he said.

For weeks I had been persuading myself that nothing was

wrong. But when I looked at him now, I knew that the inevitable could no longer be avoided.

He had to clear his throat before he spoke.

"I have been posted back to Madras," he said.

I searched his face, but he seemed incapable of returning my gaze. We both knew that the decision had been made in order to separate us. His senior officers had been pressurising him to stop seeing me for some time.

"I could come with you," I suggested.

"You know that isn't possible."

"I am not good enough for you, is that it?"

George remained silent.

"Evidently, I am good enough to be your mistress, but not for anything else."

"Oh, Eliza," he said at last, "you know I will always love you. But there is no future in it. If we continue, it will damage my career. You are already an officer's wife. It cannot be undone."

Kneeling at my feet, he clasped my hands in his.

"I am so, so sorry," he said.

When at last he looked up at me, I pushed him away. I was shaking so much that I could hardly open the door.

"I can continue to pay your bills for some time," he offered.

"Get out," I said.

"But what will you do?" he asked.

At that moment I hated him with all my heart. Did he really think that he could salve his conscience with money? I looked at him one last time and saw him for the weak, cowardly man that he was.

I shook my head. "I don't ever want to see your face again," I said.

The next day, I visited a discreet and reputable jeweller in Bond Street and sold an emerald brooch. When I came home, I found Ellen, my maid, sitting in front of the mirror in my bedroom. She made no effort to get up when she saw me. Her hair was piled up on top of her head, and she was wearing a necklace of mine around her throat. I had never looked at her properly before. Her hair was glossy and conker brown, her skin pale. Her eyes reminded me of Bridie's; they were the same hazel flecked with gold. A little money and attention could transform her into a dashing proposition, I thought.

"Two months wages you owes me," she said.

"I will pay you soon," I replied.

"I've heard that before."

"What can I do?" I asked.

"You can pay me in kind," she said, indicating a rose pink taffeta gown that was thrown across the bed.

It was Ellen who suggested Islington. She found the cottage in Hornsey Road via a previous employer. I agreed to retain her services, paying her in dresses and trinkets. I had no illusions about her loyalty. I knew that her allegiance was to my wardrobe and my jewellery.

Islington was more than an hour's drive from Picadilly, the streets were muddy, and the smell of manure and silage wafted in the breeze. Opposite the cottage was a field of lugubrious cows. I tried to put a brave face on it. If I had fallen, it was among decent and honourable people. The fresh air and open spaces would be good for my health, I persuaded myself. The cottage was compact and clean: I decorated the rooms in a bohemian style in the hope that they might look original rather than simply meagre and shabby.

Once my predicament became known, I received a number of gentleman callers offering me assistance. I settled for the Marquis of Salisbury because I thought he would be easy to manage. He was a plump, round man in his late twenties, with unruly black hair and a shiny pink face. Though he took it upon himself to pay my bills, I endeavoured to keep a distance between us. After an evening of theatre, then dinner, it became more difficult to fend him off. When he became too passionate, I reminded him of the delicacy of my nature. Malaria had permanently debilitated me, I explained, and I was under doctor's instructions not to exert myself in any way.

Soon my excuses began to run out. Whenever the marquis was visiting, I arranged for Ellen to disturb us every ten to fifteen minutes. When her interruptions became ludicrous, the frustrated marquis stamped off in a huff.

"You'll have to get yourself another gentleman," said Ellen, but I shook my head. I knew I didn't have the stomach for it.

In my cramped little parlour in Hornsey Road, I reviewed my finances. The money that Major Craigie had given me had finally run out. At the jewellers in Bond Street, I had discovered that a pair of diamond earrings that the marquis had given me were paste. At the bank, the manager had refused to sanction any further withdrawals until Thomas sent another payment. When I returned home, Ellen had chided me. The rent was overdue. Three more bills had been delivered that very afternoon. Counting out the remainder of my money, I found that it amounted to little more than a few notes and a handful of coins.

Over the next week, I watched as my brief attempt at independence was stripped away. The horses and the carriage were returned to the stables and the furniture sold. Ellen accepted the paste earrings and a jade silk gown as payment. One thing I knew for certain: I would never wear pastels again. Love had a price, and I had paid dearly for it. With a final sale of goods, I paid the rent and settled most of the bills. Then, with the last of my funds, I took a stagecoach to Edinburgh and Mrs Rae.

Scene Five
SCARLET SILK

Chapter 17

My first impressions of Edinburgh were of a bleak, unyielding place, with the castle looming over the city, as if to say, "You are only a step away from entombment in some dank, subterranean place." It was an overcast October afternoon, and dusk was already settling over the houses like a fusty voluminous old cloak. On the streets, the inhabitants were huddled in dark heavy coats, their faces pinched and closed. As the carriage rattled over the cobbles, I remembered the cerulean blue and silvered wings of the Indian butterfly that had hatched in George's cabin on the *Larkins*. We had given it up to chance and the warm winds, rather than the certainty of watching it perish. Now, here I was, delivering myself up voluntarily.

When I arrived at Mrs Rae's house, she received me kindly and apparently without surprise.

"You are young," she said. "We shall say no more of what has occurred."

My eyes smarted with unexpected tears. "Your sympathy is more than I deserve," I said.

Life at Mrs Rae's consisted of a mind-numbing round of afternoon tea, church functions and embroidery. Her social gatherings had the hushed tones of parish meetings. If, on one of these occasions, a man engaged me in conversation, my step-aunt would appear beside me in less than a minute. She recounted a sanitised version of my life repeatedly, as if she hoped that by repetition, it might become true. When I was fully convalesced, I would rejoin my husband in India, apparently.

If I protested, she led me rapidly away.

"Your reputation is not the only one at stake," she reminded me. "There are also your husband and your stepfather to consider. And, not least, my own good name."

Mrs Rae's prohibitions were concise. No talk of politics, no newspapers, no novels. When I enquired about a horse and the possibility of riding, she shook her head.

"You hurt your back, remember."

"But you know I didn't really fall from a horse," I pleaded.

"Let us not quarrel," she said.

Needlework took up an inordinate amount of time. Mrs Rae regarded it as the ideal way to occupy the mind.

"Idle hands make mischief," she said.

If only, I thought.

Between us we stitched the trousseau of a slight, pallid girl who was betrothed to a young officer. If ever there was a bride destined to die in childbirth, it was she. To give her a little luck, I embroidered sprigs of white heather along the inside seams of her petticoats.

On the rare afternoons that I left the house, it was for desultory walks in the botanic gardens. Icy gravel crunched beneath my feet. Webs dewy with raindrops were slung across the bare branches of bushes and shrubs. Strolling between dripping trees, I pondered my options. I could be a governess or a lady's companion. Within the realm of the respectable, there was nothing else.

My needle dipped in and out of the canvas; first with green wool, then with a russet, then with a pale coral pink. I was happiest when I had a large section to work. Whenever I switched colours, the rhythm of my stitches broke and I became irritable. Three times I had changed wool, and it was not yet afternoon.

For the past four months, I had been helping Mrs Rae with her tapestry. As yet, she hadn't noticed that the segments I had stitched were becoming slightly overblown. Fruit seemed to ripen and bloom beneath my needle; a pear bulged from the canvas, the skin of a bright plum dulled, an apple looked bruised. When Mrs Rae wasn't looking, I amused myself by embroidering tiny flies and spiders amidst the fruit. A worm emerged from an apple, a peach sagged and oozed, a fruit fly crawled over a leaf. Soon there was a teeming, tiny world lingering around the solitary bowl of fruit.

It was the beginning of March, a few weeks after my twenty-second birthday, when the summons came. In the drawing room, Mrs Rae had just discovered my secret embellishments to her tapestry.

"Whatever next?" she exclaimed. "Goblins, dragonflies, elves? You just can't help yourself, can you?"

Her deliberations—should she demand that I unpick my handiwork, or should it be allowed to remain?—were interrupted by a loud knocking on the door.

When Mrs Rae discovered the identity of the caller, she turned white as a sheet.

"Oh, my dear," she whispered.

Behind her stood a gentleman of the courts.

"Is your name Mrs Eliza Rosana James?" he asked.

When I nodded, he continued.

"You have been summoned to appear before the Court of the Arches in London on the 8th December 1842."

"What on earth for?"

The officer shuffled his feet. "You are charged with adultery, Madam," he replied.

When he was gone, I sank back into my chair.

"How could he do this to me?" I asked.

"Oh, my dear," said Mrs Rae, "Lieutenant James has obviously been informed of your adventures. I swear he did not hear it from me."

"But he was the one who was unfaithful," I protested. "That is why I left him in the first place."

"It does not signify," said Mrs Rae.

"But I am the one who has been wronged," I cried.

"You know perfectly well that a man may do whatever he likes."

"I will stand up in court and tell the truth. I will counter sue!"

Mrs Rae bit her lip.

"You couldn't possibly afford it," she said. "The only grounds on which you could divorce him would be extreme physical cruelty."

"He was physically cruel."

"You're not dead," she said. "Any husband has the right to discipline his wife."

"Then the law is unjust," I cried.

Mrs Rae sat down heavily and shook her head.

"You have insulted his pride," she said. "He cannot ignore that."

I had a terrible thought.

"But how will I live?" I cried. "If he divorces me, my allowance will be cut. I will be left with nothing."

Mrs Rae wrung her hands.

"I don't know what to say," she said. "This is the end. Matters could not be worse."

"He can't do this to me," I said.

Mrs Rae pulled a handkerchief from her sleeve, then dapped her eyes. "Oh, my dear," she sighed. "My poor, unfortunate child."

In my bedroom, I sat very still. Dear Mrs Rae was even more upset by the news than I. I had brought shame on her when she had tried so hard to save me from it. She had not said as much, but I knew that I could no longer remain beneath her roof.

By divorcing me, Thomas would place me entirely outside society. I could almost picture his cold and vengeful rage. In citing adultery, he obviously intended to shame me publicly. Every detail of my relationship with George would be dragged through the courts. My name would be trampled through the mud. Once the courts had finished with me, my life would be in tatters.

I thought of George and the time that we had spent together. Of tentative kisses between glimpses of dolphins and flying fish. Of falling asleep in each other's arms in a ruby-papered bedroom in the

160

Imperial Hotel in Covent Garden. In those brief, glorious months of freedom, I had abandoned myself to love.

Suddenly, I felt defiant. How many times can somebody be ruined, after all? I was a resilient young woman of twenty-two, not some dilapidated and neglected building. When I had eloped with Thomas, people swore that I had destroyed my prospects. When I fell in love with George, ruination had been whispered again. Now my husband sought to finish me, once and for all. I had survived certain ruin twice; I would do so again.

I glanced around my rose-sprigged prison, my pretty little room. If nothing else, I could save Mrs Rae from further embarrassment. I would ask only one thing of her, that she supply me with the means to get to London. After I had packed up all my possessions, I went downstairs.

"But where will you go?" she asked. "What will you do?"

I kissed both her cheeks.

"You mustn't worry," I said. "I will take care of myself, I promise you."

We stood awkwardly in the hallway until Mrs Rae pulled me into her arms. I clung to her for a moment, not wanting to ever let go.

"I'm so sorry," I said.

Mrs Rae brushed a strand of hair from my cheek.

"Don't ever forget that there are people who love you," she said.

When I left Scotland, it was to the sound of beating rain. Beyond the Moorfoot Hills, the River Tweed had broken its banks and the water splashed up over the road. The wind buffeted the carriage perilously about. The driver wanted to turn back, but I refused. I urged him to go faster, faster against the wind and the rain.

Chapter 18

In the back of the jolting stagecoach, I peered at the envelope that Mrs Rae had pressed belatedly into my hand. Two letters with Indian postmarks had been delivered shortly after the court summons, but in all the upset and confusion, they had been left unopened on the hallway table, until I was about to leave. (Why hurry to read letters that would merely underline what we already knew?) Whenever the carriage paused, I took the opportunity to examine the envelope further. The once crisp white paper was scuffed and the corners were dented and curled. It had been posted in Calcutta on 12 December 1841, a full three months before. Every time the pace of the horses slowed, I looked at the envelope again. On the front, my mother's handwriting looked jagged and cramped, as if she had made a considerable effort to contain herself. I could imagine her righteous anger pouring on to the paper, then steaming onwards from Calcutta to Edinburgh, via Bombay, Portsmouth and London. I could almost hear her accusations bursting through the envelope. *How could you do this to me? To your stepfather? To poor Mrs Rae?* Why even bother to open it, I thought. Why didn't I just throw it away? My mother's chastisements were already resounding inside my head; I really didn't need to see them written down on paper.

I turned over the letter and contemplated the seal.

Three hours later, I broke it open.

Inside the envelope was a single black-edged card printed on thick dimpled white paper. There was no accompanying letter, no angry words. I withdrew the communication in puzzlement and confusion.

Though I read the inscription once, twice, I had some difficulty comprehending the meaning of the words. I could feel myself falling, sinking, the walls of the carriage floating up, then down. Though I clung to the armrest, the words swam in front of my eyes. Embossed in small, neat black letters across the centre of the card was the formal notification of the death of Major Patrick Craigie.

It can't be true, I thought.

I reread the card again, trying to find further meaning in the paucity of words. Surely there must be something more? Some softening words or phrases, a piece of memorabilia, some mention of last words, a final thought, a fond memory? How could this stark card signify such an unimaginable loss? According to the inscription, my stepfather had been buried in the military cemetery in Dinapore, where my father also lay. I vividly recalled standing next to my mother there, dressed in a black gown that was identical to hers, though I hardly reached her hip. In front of us, a deep rectangular hole had been cut into the dry, dusty ground, and the smoke from vast cones of incense coiled up against the sky.

I squeezed my eyes closed. My temples throbbed. My chest ached.

The possibility that I might have driven my stepfather to an early grave hovered in my thoughts. With every turn of the stagecoach wheels, I could hear my mother's words: "Reckless, hotheaded girl. You'll get what you deserve." *It can't be true*, I thought. *It can't be*. Inside my head, a small insistent voice kept whispering: You have already lost one papa, how have you managed to lose another? Why would anybody want a troublesome girl like you?

In a vain attempt to hold back my tears, I banged my head repeatedly against a strut at the back of the carriage. Images from early childhood flashed through my mind. Papa Craigie making shapes with his hands and then casting the shadows of a rabbit and a donkey on to the walls. Papa Craigie offering me a pink sugarcoated almond or a blue one, and promising that we had become a family. Papa Craigie coming home with Polly the parrot and teaching it to say, "love Liza, love Liza."

I drew the soot-blackened curtains of the carriage closed and pressed my eyes shut with my fists, but all my griefs and sorrows came back to me. When I began to cry, my sobs were those of a small defenceless child. I was a four-year-old who had lost her father, I was an uncomprehending seven-year-old sent far away from home. I cried until my throat hurt and my eyes were swollen, until my face was awash with mucus and tears.

Through those long years in Scotland and later at school, it was Major Craigie who had written to me. He had been the one continuous thread connecting the fragments of my life together. I remembered his reaction after I arrived in Calcutta, having left Thomas. "My beautiful little girl," he had said with a broad smile. When we said our last farewells at the dock, knowing that we were unlikely to meet again, I had felt ashamed that I had let him down. No matter what I did, I trusted somehow that he would continue to love me. He had been my guardian angel. I had taken him for granted, as one might a mountain or a lake. Without him, yet another fragile string to the past had been broken, and I felt newly alone in the world.

Wiping my eyes, I reread the black-edged mourning card one last time. I hadn't been able to see him laid to rest in India, but I could still honour his memory now. I pushed a corner of the card between the grilles of the stove until it crackled, then ignited. When I held it in the air, tongues of yellow and orange devoured the words printed on the pristine white paper. Once the letters making up his name had been completely eaten away, I tossed the burning card from the carriage window and watched it float away. Caught in a gust of wind, it was swept upwards, before vanishing in a final burst of flame.

Chapter 19

Within a matter of days, I had acquired a newly decorated apartment in a fashionable part of London and a maid in a black silk dress to answer the door. Never mind that the new drapes were from a dubious source, that Ellen's dress was on extended loan, or that I had barely enough funds to last for a month. There was no time for delay. Soon a number of gentlemen of my acquaintance would each receive a note stating that I would be pleased to receive them.

Ellen had been my first port of call. After my departure for Scotland, she had returned to Half Moon Street. Bidding the coachman to pull over, I had waited outside. The moment she stepped on to the street, I beckoned for her to get inside.

"Them earrings was paste," was the first thing she said.

"Were they really? The marquis swore they were rose-cut diamonds," I replied. "To think I put my trust in such a man."

When I asked her to come and work for me, she narrowed her eyes.

"What's it worth?"

"What is the going rate?"

"Six shilling a week. If you can't pay me in cash, you can pay me in kind."

"I can offer you a brocaded rose silk gown if you could start straight away. What do you say?"

"Has it got matching slippers?" she asked.

"It has," I smiled.

"Done," she replied.

Once I had sworn her to absolute secrecy, I outlined my plan, and the meagreness of my funds. Mrs Rae had given me fifty guineas. The last payment from Thomas had been lodged in the bank. A few pounds remained from the cheque Major Craigie had given me. Beyond that, I had no other income. There were the contents of my jewellery box, of course, but I had no idea what any of it was worth. Once Ellen knew my means and requirements, she agreed to help me, but only if I increased her wages.

"Eight shillings and sixpence," she said.

"Seven," we agreed.

I suggested lodgings in Islington, but Ellen shook her head.

"You'll never attract the right class of gentlemen," she said.

Whilst Ellen was seeking out suitable accommodation, I paid a call to a jeweller's in Bond Street. During my last sojourn in London, I had become a regular visitor, and the proprietor and I were on friendly terms.

Mr Smallbone was a dapper little man with slender, meticulous fingers. His discretion could be relied upon: he would never ask six questions where one would do.

"Ah, Mrs James," he said, ushering me into the privacy of his workroom.

When I presented him with a betrothal ring, he pursed his lips and weighed it in the palm of his hand.

Every time I looked into my jewellery box, I would see the ring lurking accusingly in the corner. With a gleam in its shiny black eye, it squatted there like a bulbous nocturnal toad. It was a cumbersome piece of jewellery: set within a ring of tiny gems was a gloomy, square-cut stone.

"It is obviously an heirloom," said Mr Smallbone. "Are you sure you want to sell it?"

"Absolutely," I replied.

Any associations I had with the ring were entirely negative. On her deathbed, Thomas's grandmother had apparently pulled it from her finger. "For your future wife," she had said. Some months after our wedding, Thomas had given it to me, almost as an afterthought. He neither asked whether I liked it, nor troubled to find out whether it fitted. I wore it once or twice to please him, before dropping it into the back of my jewellery box.

Mr Smallbone fixed his magnifying glass in his eye and began his examination.

"Interesting," he said. "The central stone is a dark tourmaline, and the lesser stones are diamonds."

"Is that good?" I asked.

"It's satisfactory," he replied.

We were both happy with the deal we struck. Ellen had already suggested a starting price, and Mr Smallbone had more or less agreed. According to Ellen, the price the ring fetched would keep me in London for at least a month.

The very next day, we moved into a modest apartment in a quiet, residential street in Covent Garden.

"Well, what'd you reckon?" she asked. "I know it's not Mayfair, but it's a start."

"Can I afford it?" I asked.

"You'll have to," she said.

Ellen knew the price and the value of everything. Talking to her was an education in itself. In the streets, she would point at a woman, then estimate the cost of her clothes.

"That there gown is worth about twelve pounds," she said.

"What about that one?" I asked, indicating a very fashionable lady descending from a carriage.

"Fine silk velvet, ermine trim. I'd say it probably cost about twenty pounds. Secondhand, you'd be doing well to get ten pound for it, 'less you knew where to go, that is."

Behind the woman, a young servant girl was carrying two large hatboxes.

167

"Now she, on the other hand, is wearing a cheap but serviceable cotton frock that probably set her back about twelve shillings. Or the best part of three weeks' wages."

As we crossed the Haymarket, my attention was taken up by a streetwalker who was wearing a familiar peach taffeta dress. The usual costume of the dollymop was an ill-fitting crinoline beneath a merino gown; if her head was covered, it would be with a porkpie hat sporting a waving feather. This girl looked almost ladylike, except she walked with a swagger and glanced boldly about. Before leaving for Scotland, I had given Ellen a similar dress in lieu of wages. As the girl drew nearer, I scrutinised the detailing.

"That *is* my gown," I said.

"It's very similar," Ellen conceded.

"It's the very same," I insisted.

"Is it?" she asked.

"Look at the fine pleating around the hem," I said. "I would recognise it anywhere."

Ellen remained tight-lipped.

"Why didn't you keep it?"

"What good would it be to me? A servant can't wear a lady's gown. Besides, a dress lodger will pay a very good price for a gown like that."

"How much?" I asked.

"Can't I keep a few secrets to meself?" she pleaded.

"I was just curious," I said.

"Put it this way," she said; "wearing your dress, that girl can get five pounds off a gentleman. In her own clothes, he wouldn't pay more 'an five shillings."

"You seem to know an awful lot about it," I said.

"There's very few women doesn't have a price," she replied.

Of course, I had a protector. A woman in my position would not get very far without one. The Earl of Malmsbury was well known for his patronage of the arts, and his connections were extensive. An association with him would do me no harm at all. Once I took him into my confidence, he was only too happy to assist. The fact that he was happily married only added to his charms. Not only was he discreet and undemanding, but he also spent a considerable amount of time out of town. Despite all evidence to the contrary, I persisted with the idea that he might nurture and protect me.

Everything was going according to plan. I had been in London for less than a month when I enrolled at Miss Fanny Kelly's Theatre and Dramatic School in Dean Street. On my first day, she interviewed me in a private room.

Miss Fanny Kelly's fame preceded her. Having made her debut at the age of seven, she later became one of the great actresses of the day. Her reputation was ferocious.

"How can I help you?" she asked.

"I wish to go on the stage," I replied.

"What can you do?"

"I have the usual accomplishments," I said. "I can play the piano and sing. My French is fluent."

"The usual accomplishments will not get you very far."

"Madame, that is why I came to you."

"Very well," she conceded. "Come back tomorrow and we will see what we can do."

I recognised Miss Kelly's type straight away. The aspirant Irish could always be found on the margins of society, whether it be in India or treading the boards. Miss Kelly reminded me of some wild hybrid of my mother and a chorus girl. Her appearance was overblown, yet regal, and her manners seemed lately acquired. At forty-eight, her hair was an extravagant white cloud around her head. The hooped costume she wore was more appropriate for the stage than for everyday wear.

When I arrived the next morning, she took me into a large drawing room and indicated the piano.

"Play me something," she said.

One of Chopin's mazurkas was the first thing that came into my head.

"So you are fond of a lively dance tune," she said afterwards. "Now stand over there and give me a little speech."

I had hardly begun before she interrupted me.

"You have the strangest accent," she said.

No matter how much I tried to restrict myself to a refined English accent, the faintest imprints of the places of my childhood always gave me away. There were strange dips in my speech, vowels elongated where they should have been more precise. My intonation contained something of the singsong tone of Indian speech, as well as traces of an Irish accent, with my mother's affectations layered over the top.

"Try again," she said.

By the second line she stopped me.

"Your voice is very small."

I started again. This time I got to the third line, before Miss Kelly shook her head in dismay.

"I don't know, I really don't," she said. "I will do my best, but I can't promise anything more."

When my attendance at Miss Kelly's establishment became known, attitudes towards me began to shift. It was little things I noticed. A certain kind of matron would withdraw or grow silent at my approach. Young girls would be led away. As my esteem with the ladies declined, my popularity amongst men increased a hundredfold. I knew that society had begun to whisper about me, but I had no choice but to brazen it out. The court case was not yet common knowledge, and there was still five months before the trial, but the news was bound to slip out at some point. Until then, my married title offered some protection, but I knew that time was running out.

"Hopeless, hopeless," Miss Kelly cried.

I was taking a class in the Royalty Theatre that was attached to the school. Miss Kelly was standing at the back of the auditorium, and I was on the stage. She had been trying to teach me how to project, but no matter how many times I tried, my voice, instead of increasing in volume, became more high-pitched. In the hollow empty space of the theatre, a squeaky little noise echoed back.

"My dear Eliza," Miss Kelly sighed.

"I am doing my best," I replied.

"That is what worries me," she said.

She beckoned to me, and I sat down next to her in front of the empty stage.

"If only there were a call for silent actresses," she said. "Your appearance is very good; there is no doubt about it. Love and tragedy come easily to you. You are very expressive, if a mite theatrical. And you are charming to look at, of course. But whenever you open your mouth, well, you can hear it yourself."

"I will work harder," I said.

Miss Kelly shook her head.

"There is no easy way to say this. You may have all the appearance of an actress, but you will never make the grade. We will have to think of something else."

I stared morosely at the empty stage. *What else is there?* I thought.

Miss Kelly clapped her hands.

"I've got it," she said. "Why didn't I think of it before? You must dance!"

"I haven't exactly got the figure for it," I said doubtfully.

We both looked down at my bosom.

"You certainly know how to fill a dress," she said.

"And I'm much too old," I protested.

Miss Kelly smiled.

"To be a ballerina, maybe."

Day after day, the newspapers were filled with stories of Fanny Elssler's success in America; her stage presence was so elemental they called her "the Pagan Ballerina". When she introduced a Spanish cachucha into her repertoire, it caused a sensation.

"Character dances are very popular. And they do not require endless years of training," said Miss Kelly. "Think of Fanny Elssler in Coralli's *Le Diable Boiteux.*"

My eyes lit up.

"It's true," I cried. "There are any number of dances—the gavotte, the tarantella."

"There is a wonderful fandango in *Figaro*," said Miss Kelly.

I clapped my hands, jumped up on to the stage and tapped out a few steps.

"At school we learned the bolero, the mazurka and the minuet. In India, I learned some native dance. I'll show you," I said.

Bending my knees as Sita had taught me, I twisted my hands into birds, then blossoming flowers around my head. As I began to move my hips, my eyes flicked from left to right.

Miss Kelly burst into laughter.

"You look like a simpleton. Or the temple whore."

"You don't think it's beautiful?" I asked.

As I undulated from side to side, I realised that the movements were not unlike those of the gypsy in Mazilier's opera, and I began to pull the two elements together. I had already played the part of a gypsy at a military masquerade. *Yes, yes*, I thought, as I danced across the stage.

"You certainly have talent," observed Miss Kelly, "but I am not sure that it is the right kind."

In the realm of my own drawing room, my dramatic skills were already being stretched. There was even some advantage in possessing a small, childlike voice. Earl Malmsbury was clearly enchanted by my ability to fill a low-cut gown. On my accent, he made no remark. When he began to make unfatherly demands, it required all my talents and ingenuity to keep him at arm's length.

I practised my pieces in front of him, lingered over my dying swan, allowed my gown to slip in the role of an ambitious courtesan, titillated him as a country wench, offered him an occasional glimpse of ankle or calf. Whenever he drew too close, I flattered him and appealed to his sense of honour. If I enacted the part of a trusting and impressionable young actress, eternally grateful for his paternal protection, he found it difficult to argue.

Señor Antonio Espa was a native of Spain. It was said that he was a quintessential Spaniard—romantic, fiery and passionate—with the dark hair and flashing eyes of his type. Backstage at the Italian Opera House, he was very much in demand. Should a new production require a knowledge of Spain, Señor Espa would be called in to add some authentic flavour. He would teach the ballerinas the intricacies of Spanish dance and try to inject some fire into their performances. If he felt so inclined, he also took the occasional private student. So it was that I arrived at his studios in Covent Garden with a letter of introduction from Miss Kelly.

I was greeted by a middle-aged man with dyed black hair and a thickening waist. If I was a little disappointed, I endeavoured not to show it. Señor Espa's stout body was packed into tight black breeches, a short jacket and Cuban heels. He had fierce eyebrows and the intense self-regard of a girl.

Inside the large mirrored studio, a guitarist sat idly in a corner.

"*Aqui*. Stand up straight," commanded Señor Espa, stamping a stick on the ground.

As he read the letter, he circled sternly around me.

"Señora Kelly thinks you have some talent," he said.

"She is more than kind," I replied.

Señor Espa glared at me and stamped his stick.

"Can you dance, *sí* or *no*?"

"Yes," I said.

"*Es serio?*"

"My life depends upon it."

"*Muy bien,*" he said. "We will begin straight away. Allow me to demonstrate."

He clicked his fingers and the guitarist began to play. The señor may have been a small man with a barrel chest, but when he danced he was transformed. He could switch from fury to tears within seconds. His eyebrows collided in the furrow of his brow. His hands were as eloquent as dipping birds. As his heels tapped out tattoos of longing and rage, he even became handsome. When the dance came to an end, his inky black hair fell in damp clumps across his glistening face.

173

"Now *es* your turn."

He indicated the centre of the floor.

"Forget you *es* a lady," he said. "We must begin all over again."

He tapped my back lightly with his stick.

"Stand up straight, straighter," he ordered. "Hold your chin higher, higher."

"Look at me in the eye. *Aqui,*" he said. "Do not look away."

"Raise your arms above your head."

"*No, no,*" he said. "Not like that. Like this."

When I was standing as he directed, he said: "*Ahora,* stay like that. *Ahora,* follow my eyes."

He began to walk around me, his eyes locked on mine.

"How does the pose feel?" he asked.

As soon as I raised my arms, my breasts were thrust forward and my diaphragm opened. A deep breath filled my lungs. It made me feel like some powerful, primitive creature. Yet without my arms to protect me, the whole of my torso felt exposed.

"Splay your fingers," he said. "*Bueno, bueno.* But next time, you must leave your corset at home."

Week by week, Earl Malmsbury's sense of chivalry was being overwhelmed by his feelings of lust. My appeals to his paternal aspect began to wear thin. I extended the range of my favours. I allowed him access to my hands and wrists and a portion of my neck. All in all, I considered that I was infinitely generous. I flattered and entertained him; that should have been enough. How could he possibly imagine that I desired his kisses?

Whenever his mouth brushed mine, I would be filled with an aching sense of sadness. After an evening of skirmishes on the sofa, I would lounge disconsolately about.

"When passion is at its height, collect jewels," advised Ellen.

"I am not a courtesan."

"Be practical," she said.

"Go away," I cried.

When I was alone, I emptied my jewellery box on to the bed.

There among the baubles was a love token, wrapped in a square of sky-blue silk. Inside it was a jewelled butterfly brooch that George had given me.

Unwrapping it, I examined its fine detail. It was an exquisite piece of work in silver and lapis lazuli. In the centre of each blue wing was a bright topaz eye. Tiny diamonds were inset along the trailing wing tips. It was an almost exact replica of the butterfly we had seen on the ship.

After our last meeting, I had tried to banish George from my mind. Occasionally I would hear news of him. Sometimes I woke from dreams of sweet, delightful kisses. He had recently departed for India, I heard.

I held the brooch in my hand. How long does a butterfly live, I wondered? Was it a matter of days, weeks? I had no idea. I smiled mournfully. I had thought our love would last for ever. In my naivety, I had imagined marriage and a whole new life together. In those happy times, I had given of myself freely. Now each tawdry exchange had a price. An intense love burns brightly, but quickly flickers out. I knew that now. I must be practical. Ellen was right. Rewrapping the brooch, I pushed it to the back of the box. The earl's embraces might not arouse me, but they paid the bills.

Every day I arrived at Señor Espa's studio with the fervour of a religious convert. There in the middle of his creaking wooden floor, he demanded that all the attributes of femininity be stripped away. Day by day, I felt I was becoming more myself. Señor Espa worked at paring each emotion down to its basic element. What Miss Kelly had referred to as my outrageous overacting began to make sense. Those aspects of myself that I had always had to restrain were now allowed full play. I could be dramatic, impulsive, unruly, sad. Even my memories of dancing in India found a place. When Señor Espa began to show me the serpentine movements of hands and fingers, I surprised him with the suppleness of my wrists.

As we went through the different dance styles, I realised that the dances I knew were, in fact, diluted and modified forms.

"All this must be thrown away. We must begin all over again," said Señor Espa. "*El baile de España* is not civil, it is not polite. When you leave here, you can do what you like. But until then, you must learn the authentic form."

After four months of daily classes, Señor Espa suggested I go to Spain.

"It will help with your *expresión,*" he said. "I have given you the groundwork. I can help you no more."

Towards the end of summer, I heard that Lieutenant Lennox had been summonsed to appear before the Consistory Court. I had refused to even think about the divorce proceedings, but now they could no longer be ignored. Thomas had filed an action against George, who had been charged with criminal conversation.

"Poor George," I said.

"Poor you," said Ellen. "It is your reputation which will be dragged through the courts."

If I stayed in London, the scandal would explode around my head. My name would be all over the newspapers. There would be any amount of talk. I would be branded an adulteress, a divorcee, worse. Any last shreds of respectability would be plucked away. I would be left unprotected and exposed. As the court dates loomed nearer, I resolved to disappear.

Once I had made all the arrangements, I finalised the details with Ellen and the earl. After a discreet call to Mr Smallbone, I paid a last visit to Señor Espa's studios. Over the past months, we had fought over steps and interpretation, and I had grown immensely fond of him. When I told him my itinerary, he clutched his heart and swore me to secrecy.

"*Niña,* I have a confession to make," he said.

"What is it?" I asked.

"Promise you won't laugh at me."

"You have my word."

"What nationality am I?"

"Why, you're a Spaniard, of course."

He shook his head. "I am not really Spanish at all."

I was utterly astonished.

"But how can that be?" I asked.

He thumped his chest. "I have a Spanish heart," he said. "You will understand soon enough."

Señor Espa was, it transpired, a tailor's son from the East End of London. When he was eleven, he had fallen for a Spanish dancer at the Vauxhall Gardens. At the age of fifteen, he had travelled to Spain.

As I was leaving, a tear rolled down his face. When we embraced, he kissed me on both cheeks.

"It is the Spanish way," he said, with a wan little smile.

Chapter 20

For me, Spain was an enchanted place: the scent of jasmine in a sultry breeze, sweeps of blue jacaranda tumbling across a courtyard, splashes of pink oleander, the sun casting a warm glow across a parched field in the late afternoon. In Cordoba, Ellen and I saw a bleeding statue being paraded through the streets. In Seville, we slept in an old *palacio*. In a courtyard in Cadiz, I saw a single red hibiscus flower on a bare branched bush. It reminded me of India, and I luxuriated in the sight of it. Overhead, a woman in a black shawl peered down from a tiny window in an ancient tower.

Through the narrow winding streets of Granada, the sounds drifted up into the air: a canary singing in a cage, a few notes from a guitar, a deep-throated lament, the tinkling laughter of children. In doorways, beguiling women hid their faces behind veils. On street corners, beneath a statue of the Virgin, *hombres* with swishing capes strutted and posed.

On the Calle de San Juam de los Reyes, the *damas* paraded the streets with an innate majesty. Embroidered shawls draped their shoulders; tall ivory combs decorated their hair. Their faces were vivid portraits, ropes of ebony hair hanging beneath black *mantillas*, alabaster skin offset by carmine-painted mouths.

Ellen and I would sit in the cafés and watch them strolling by, free and impervious as queens. Sometimes, a man would approach and the *dama* would bow, then link his arm or depart with him in some lavish carriage. I scrutinised every detail of their attitude and sense of style; within weeks, I had adopted a proud demeanour and a flounced and swirling skirt.

I would like to say that I knew exactly what I was doing, that I had a plan. But one blind step led me to another, and then on to the next. The mornings were taken up with dance lessons, the afternoons with language classes. In the evenings, I observed the *Granadinas* in the cafés and on the streets. I refused to reflect on the past, nor speculate on the future. Like a true Spaniard, I would savour the moment.

Ellen had become my honorary companion. I was tired of relying on men, but I knew that if I appeared alone in public, I would be subject to unwelcome attention. With Ellen beside me, I could do as I pleased. In one of my old gowns, she could almost pass for a lady. It was only when she opened her mouth that she gave herself away. I gave her strict instructions on how to behave. If any men approached, she was to acknowledge them with a slight bow of the head; otherwise she was to remain silent.

For a paltry sum, we lived in sumptuous, though faded splendour in apartments that had once housed an Arabian prince. Every day, the Spanish maid would arrive with a handful of flowers or a few pieces of fruit—a pomegranate, a persimmon, a few figs.

"From the *finca*," she would say.

Dolores was a good-looking, swarthy girl with a sweet smile and a playful manner. Her name, she said, crossing herself, referred to the Sorrows of the Virgin.

One day I was practising a fandango in the drawing room when she came in with a jug of yellow lilies. No matter how many times I repeated the dance, I faltered over a few linking steps. Dolores set the flowers down on to the table and closed her eyes, and then with startling ease, she demonstrated the difficult central section. When she had finished, she stamped her heels and gave me a big, happy smile.

"I didn't know you could dance," I said.

She shrugged. "No more or less than anyone else," she said. "My family is *gitano*. It is in our blood."

I danced the fandango again.

"What am I doing wrong?" I asked. "What is missing?"

"Your heart is not in it."

"My heart?"

"I mean no offence," she said. "Come with me and I will show you."

The following week, Dolores took me to visit her family in the gypsy caves of Sacromonte. An old woman nodded to me, once she had scutinised the contents of the envelope I had given to Dolores; otherwise my presence was largely ignored. Among the flickering shadows, a dozen or so people were celebrating the first Holy Communion of Dolores's younger brother. The remains of a meal lay scattered across a table. Little children were running about. From among a huddle of people sitting in the middle of the room, a fat man with a handlebar moustache stood up. Silence fell, then a youth tapped out a simple beat and the man began to sing. His voice was crude and raw. His song was a deep cry, a wail of anguish, almost a howl. He sang with such a depth of feeling it ripped at my heart. The other gypsies began to clap out a series of rhythms and counter rhythms, and the singer plunged deeper into his song. With the intensity of religious fervour, the entire room stamped and clapped, as if they were calling up some strange, dark god.

When the song was over, the attention moved to a rotund, middle-aged woman with a pock-marked face.

"Carmen, Carmen," they called.

"*Es mi tia,* my aunt Carmen," said Dolores. "Watch her carefully."

The gypsies clapped, some called, another beat out a rhythm with small sticks. Carmen stood within the group. One hand on her hip, the other grasping a large, lacquered fan, she began to tap her heel.

Had we been in England, the focus of all this attention would have been considered comic or grotesque. Here she held her audience with ease. Her plump, ridiculous body was encased in a garish scarlet gown; her chubby fingers were decked with elaborate, gold filigree rings; her black hair stuck in stiff rings upon her cheeks. With a swish of her skirts, she took a few steps with a confident, fluid sway.

When the others urged her on, she waved her fan and pretended to ignore them. Then Dolores danced across her path, as if taunting her with her youth and beauty.

"*Guapa, guapa,*" the gypsies cried.

The *palmas* grew more persistent. Two men beat out a rhythm using short wooden sticks.

Carmen laid down her fan with a flourish, then stood very still, one foot slightly forward. She tapped out three or four steps with her foot and the room grew quiet. Very slowly, she brought her hands above her head, clicking her fingers as she went. Her wrists were supple as willow, her face a solemn mask. She seemed to know exactly when to pause, when to vary the pace, when to splay her fingers, when to cut curves through the air. My attention was glued to her every move. Between the wailing of the song and the whirl of skirts came a story of grief and deep sorrow. In a flurry of *zapateados*, she tore at her clothes. The dance was a fierce battle against death's gloomy cloud.

In the second *cante*, the dance became lighter and more festive. Carmen's *alegria* was full of sweet oranges and swooping birds. All my ideas of beauty fell away. As Carmen danced, her body spoke a rich vocabulary of love and desire. In one moment, she was graceful as a young girl; in another stately as a queen.

When a young man began to echo her steps, she responded with mild humour. This is a woman, she seemed to be saying; what you saw before was a slip of a girl. In one moment she was gently mocking him; in the next she became loving and maternal. As they danced, the flirtation between them was in turns sensual and playful. During the last *copla* I realised, with astonishment, that the slender youth was her son.

Afterwards, Dolores brought her aunt over to meet me.

"But this is not what I have been taught," I said.

Carmen shrugged.

"There is Spanish dance and there is flamenco," she said.

I repeated the word, enjoying the sound.

"What does it mean?" I asked.

She shrugged again.

Flamenco was an attitude, a certain style. It was full of bravado. It had ancient roots and a deep sense of pride. It was of the moment. It was loud and flashy and bold.

Carmen was a severe, unforgiving teacher. Though I paid her extremely well, she would never let me forget the gift she was offering me. For a time, nothing else mattered. The gypsies knew how to tap some elemental source, and I wanted to understand how they did it.

Carmen made me repeat the same steps over and over again, whilst little children came and went, giggling and mimicking my every move.

"Your dancing is good," said Carmen. "But without *duende,* the form is an empty shell."

"What is *duende?*"

"It is the dark sound, the mystery. It is a matter of blood, of roots. To dance with *duende,* you must find the core. You must strip everything away. When you find a raw quivering thing, then you can begin."

She clapped her hands.

"Now try again."

I began the opening movements of a *farruca.*

Carmen shook her head.

"You are too English, too stiff."

"I am not English," I retorted.

Carmen snorted with laughter.

"You dance as if you have water in your veins instead of blood. You dance like an old milk cow in a field. As if you have a fat green frog in your heart, instead of fire."

She clapped her hands. "Again."

Infuriated by her insults, my *taconeos* were razor sharp. My arms cut swathes through the air, my fingers became knives.

When I completed the last *turneo*, Carmen applauded.

"That's better," she said.

Whenever I went to Sacromonte, Ellen felt obliged to accompany me.

"I don't know why we have to go there," she said. "They are such filthy people. Everything they eat is drenched in oil. And not only that, they are robbing you blind."

"You don't have to come," I said.

"And let you go there alone! Anything could happen to you."

"Very well, it is time to go."

As we strolled towards the caves, she continued her refrain.

"It won't come to nothing," she declared. "All that stamping and wailing. It's so crude and undignified. You can hardly call it dancing at all."

"Perhaps that's why I like it," I replied.

"Well, no one will pay to see it," she said. "There certainly isn't a living to be had from it."

"We'll see," I said.

Towards the beginning of spring, one of Dolores's cousins got married. Carmen had invited me to the wedding party and suggested a suitable wedding gift, a purse full of coins tucked inside a canteen of silver cutlery. As the afternoon wore on, the singing and dancing began. Sometimes the men and the women danced opposite each other, like two combatants in a deadly fight; at other times they were all laughter and smiles.

Ellen sat stony-faced in a corner, as if she were in one of the lower circles of hell. Whenever anyone offered her food or wine, she shook her head.

"You are being very rude," I said.

"I don't care."

Over the past few months, most of Dolores's family had become tolerant towards me. I think that it amused them that I should want to learn from them. Only Dolores's grandmother refused to acknowledge me.

Mujer Irlandesa, they called me. Or *niña India* or *gitanita.*

At regular intervals, glasses of *fino* were handed out, a thick golden sherry that fired the belly and oiled the throat. By the evening the dancing had become passionate and wild.

After another toast, a girl called Immaculata began to circle the floor. Beneath fierce eyebrows that joined in the middle of her forehead, her black eyes cast about. Somebody gestured towards me, but I rigorously shook my head. Ignoring my protests, Immaculata dragged me into the middle of the floor. She moved into the opening steps of a fandango, her body twisting and undulating from left to right, her arms curving into arabesques. I echoed her movements, but my body felt stiff and awkward. Immaculata thumped her foot down until the dust rose. She thrust my chin up into the air. The clapping vibrated inside my head. Immaculata shouted at me. Everyone around us clamoured and stamped their feet.

The *fino* and the clapping began to do their work. The noise and heat swirled around my head. By the end of the second *copla,* my body surged with energy. Sweat glistened on my brow, the back of my dress and between my breasts were soaked with sweat. Something elemental had awakened in me and would not lie down. Immaculata cajoled me. She stamped out the rhythm. Her *palmas* forced the dance into life. I could feel its beat in my stomach and my heart and my throat.

After the fandango, I danced a *solea.* Love pierced my breast. It created the movements of my arms. It animated my hands. I carved out the beginnings of love, then its end. There were deep shadows, and then sudden shafts of light. A single rosebud in spring. A wreath of desiccated lilies left in front of a catacomb. The patter of rain upon cracked earth. A departed lover. The bare branches of a tree. An un-baptised infant buried beneath a kapok tree. By the end of the dance, all my losses had come back to me. My hair unravelled itself around my neck. Sweat poured down my face. My dress was ripped. My ankles were coated with sweat.

Afterwards, Immaculata patted me on the back. Carmen wiped my face and brushed my hair from my eyes. Someone handed me a glass of sweet wine. In a far corner, I saw Ellen's mouth curl in disgust.

The next day, a couple of letters came from England. The first, from the Earl of Malmsbury, contained a bank draft and a number of newspaper cuttings. The second, from the Courts of the Arches in London, had been forwarded via Mrs Rae. According to the official documentation, Thomas had been granted a divorce "*a mensa et thoro*". The previous week, George had agreed to pay him damages. Had I bothered to read the small print, I would have noticed that the terms of the divorce were partial, allowing no rights of remarriage. Lieutenant James and I were stuck with each other, whether we liked it or not. Because of my family connections, the case had appeared in many of the newspapers. In his summing up, the judge pronounced that I was guilty of behaviour that would make an alligator tremble and blush. There was much scurrilous gossip and speculation about the exact nature of our "criminal conversation". In the theatres and society drawing rooms, my love affair was apparently being paraded like some cheap romance. People would be whispering: "Adulteress, slut." Very well, I thought. I have nothing left to lose.

"Does this mean we can go home?" asked Ellen.

I nodded.

"As soon as the dust has settled," I replied.

It was time to take stock, to make a firm assessment of the facts. Ellen was right. If I tried to dance flamenco in London, I would be laughed off the stage. What the British theatregoer wanted was a flavour of the exotic, not the whole dish. They wanted Mazilier's *La Gypsy* or Florinda in *Le Diable Boiteux*. They wanted an interpretation, an essence of Spain that had been thoroughly filtered, diluted and drained. Very well, I thought, I will create a fantasy. Within the gilded and refined world of London theatre, I would present such a spectacle that the audience would not know whether they shuddered with pleasure or disgust.

I stopped going to the caves. I ordered three Spanish dancing dresses. I practised the slow stately quality of the classical dances, then learned to perform without breaking into a sweat. I simplified the steps. I halved the intensity, and then slowed the pace. I practised with castanets. I learned to use a fan, then a shawl. From Sita I took the exquisite, undulating use of the hands, from Miss Fanny Kelly some dramatic effects, from Señor Espa a sense of theatre.

The gypsies of Sacromonte would have been dismayed to see what I had done to their art, and Carmen felt utterly betrayed. Yet for me, it was not a complete travesty. No matter how faint it was, an echo of flamenco still remained. It was buried in my heart; I had not thrown it away.

Early one morning, Ellen discovered a single rosebud that had been left outside the window. The next morning there was another. Every evening, Dolores would quietly place a crystal glass full of water on the windowsill. The next morning it would be filled. Ellen was determined to unmask the culprit, but no matter how early she awoke, she never saw anyone in the courtyard. Every day, she would rush to the window, to find yet another perfect rose. At first the rosebuds were white, tinged with pink, the bud tightly closed. As the days passed, the petals of the rose would be slightly more open, and the blush on the petals deeper. On the seventh day, the rose was in full bloom, the velvet petals deepening to lush, muted carmine at the tips. Ellen, Dolores and I inhaled its heady perfume.

"I obviously have a secret admirer," I said.

Dolores and Ellen looked at me with startled surprise, and then Ellen shook her head.

"The rose has been left for me," she insisted.

Dolores smiled a shy, secret smile. "I think it is for me," she said.

As the day of our departure approached, I assembled a whole new wardrobe. Soon afterwards, Dolores announced her engagement. At my insistence, Ellen gave her one of my old gowns.

"Do I have to?" she asked.

"Yes," I said.

At the drapers I also found myself buying a lavish white lace mantilla made up of an intricate filigree pattern of orange blossom and roses. I persuaded myself that it was a gift for Dolores to wear on her wedding day, but I never quite managed to give it to her. When my new clothes were delivered, I tucked the mantilla away, then handed on the contents of my old wardrobe to Ellen, who couldn't believe her good fortune.

"Are you sure?" she asked.

I nodded. "They belonged to Eliza James," I said.

One day, we were sitting outside a café on the Calle de San Juan de los Reyes watching the *damas*. I was dressed in my latest finery, Ellen in one of my cast-offs. In Sacromonte, one of Eliza Gilbert's old dresses was being adapted into a wedding gown for Dolores.

As I watched an exchange between one of the grand *damas* and an admirer, I had a sudden realisation. I whispered my revelation to Ellen.

"That much is obvious," she sniffed.

"But they are so discreet," I protested.

Ellen looked at me curiously, and I laughed out loud. The grand Spanish ladies I had so carefully modelled myself upon were courtesans. I looked down at my new costume. I only hoped that in London the majority of society was as naive.

Scene Six

SHIMMERING ORGANZA OF CRIMSON, VIOLET AND BLUE

Chapter 21

On a crisp, frosty morning in April 1843, the passengers from Cadiz disembarked in Southampton Docks. Among them, an exotic young woman shuddered delicately against the cold and pulled a cashmere shawl more tightly around her shoulders. Señora Maria Dolores de Porris y Montez—for, like a true Spaniard, she insisted upon her full title—was from a noble Spanish family, recently impoverished during the Carlist wars. In the tender bloom of youth, and barely married, cruel circumstance had already deprived her of a husband. Dressed from head to foot in mourning clothes, the widow was a picture of desolate grief. Her raven hair was caught up in a Spanish comb, her dewy eyes veiled behind a mantilla, her demeanour sorrowful, yet upright and proud. Unusually for a Spaniard, who were generally of the swarthy type, Señora Porris y Montez had the most startling azure eyes.

As I lingered among the thronging crowd on the docks, I observed the effect I was having. Nobody doubted me for a moment. As I passed by, there were admiring whispers; I caught attention, but nothing untoward. I watched with bated breath. Behind me, Ellen scuffed her heels. Following my strict instructions, she kept her mouth shut throughout.

At Her Majesty's Theatre in London, the gala performance of *The Barber of Seville* was *the* society event of the year. Tickets were already changing hands at inflated prices when a new star was announced. Between acts, Doña Lola Montez, a leading dancer of the *Teatro Real,* Seville, would perform the original Spanish dance—

El Oleano. Rumours were rife. The demand for tickets doubled. On the opening night, the theatre hummed with excitement. In the royal box, the aged King of Hanover was seated next to the Dowager Queen. Downstairs, gentlemen were crushing into the lobby, pleading for tickets.

It was the Earl of Malmsbury who secured the audition. Though he had recently transferred his affections to an aspiring actress, he could never resist an opportunity for amusement and mischief. In the box office afterwards, he scanned the list of forthcoming events, and then pointed to the imminent royal gala performance.

"That would be very bold," said the director. "But are you sure that our little *señorita* can carry it off?"

The earl smirked. "It will be scandalous," he said.

Before the first evening's performance, I mingled with the audience, dressed in an old dark dress and bonnet of Ellen's and carrying a basket of oranges. The Earl of Malmsbury had certainly been busy; the early edition of the *Morning Post* had carried a glowing preview, and tonight's debut was the talk of every notable soirée and coffee house in London. With each retelling, the gossip had acquired another colourful flourish and a further layer of intrigue. In both the stalls and the boxes, everybody was speculating about the mysterious Lola Montez. I eavesdropped from left to right, savouring each delicious remark.

At the back of the stalls, two off-duty actresses, with painted faces and perky little hats, leaned over the publicity flyer.

"I see she's dropped the formalities," said one.

"And her fleshings," said the other, with a sardonic arch of an eyebrow.

"Orange?" I asked, proffering a fruit.

"Psst," hissed Ellen behind me. "You're needed backstage. It will take more 'an a few minutes preparation to pull off this pretty little masquerade."

190

After the interval, the curtain steadily rose, and the sound of Spanish music filled the auditorium. Against the backdrop of a Moorish chamber in the Alhambra, a closed door dominated the stage. As the tempo of music increased, the door slowly opened. I stepped forwards, in a swathe of sumptuous black lace. A hush rippled through the audience. I paused. Then, with one dramatic gesture, I stripped off my mantilla, threw up my arms and clicked my castanets. An appreciative murmur swept the theatre.

This was my perfect moment, my masterpiece. The music, the timing, the attitude, the choreography—I had a complete vision of how it would be. My gleaming black hair was drawn tightly back, my face a mask of fierce intensity. Three blood red camellias adorned my coiffeur. My figure was cast into silhouette, my arms and throat pale as alabaster. The tight black velvet bodice accentuated my waist, its low neckline, the swelling of my breasts. A shimmering skirt with tinted flounces of crimson, violet and blue floated around my calves; my legs were scandalously naked. To the stark rhythmic beat of my castanets, I stepped dramatically into the light. At the sound of a solitary violin, my arms circled the air and I began to dance.

I inhaled a deep intake of air, and any last shreds of pretence slipped away. As I clapped out the rhythm with my castanets, my breath filled my throat, my lungs, my heart. As I began my *El Oleano,* I became Lola Montez and she became me. I followed the sound of the violin, stepping to the left, then to the right, my arms circling the air, the opening steps flowering across the stage. My hands became hovering birds, then gently falling leaves. I could feel the power of the dance flow through my body, my neck, down my spine. The orchestral music made me more fluid, it made me glide. A feeling was beginning to take root, deep in the pit of my stomach, that I could do anything, be anything.

The lights of a thousand candles flickered in front of me, the light of a thousand eyes. As I danced around the stage, my body swayed with the impulses of the wind. My arms branched from left to right. My wrists twisted and undulated into the strange and myriad forms of anguish, then desire. Delicate *paseos* became jumps, then turns. I could feel the applause, like a warm balmy sea washing over me. Inwardly I smiled, and then raised my chin a little higher.

Amidst the audience, I glimpsed a familiar face, staring at me in disbelief. It was the Marquis of Salisbury, who had once attempted to buy my affections with paste earrings. I flicked my castanets. The marquis's plump face quivered with indignation, his black hair flopping over his eyes, his cheeks growing redder. It was too late for him to stop me now. The past was cast away. I was no longer my mother's neglected daughter, my father's orphan, no longer a disgraced wife. I was none of these things.

What is power? Not money, not land, nor kingdoms. But this. The audience was entirely in my hands. I could make a flash of Spain erupt in front of their eyes. I could send shivers down their spines. I shook down clusters of rhythms with my hands. I stamped my feet.

The marquis jumped up from his seat, but the rest of the audience was swept away. He cried out in protest, but his words were lost beneath the applause. I smiled. *I am Lola Montez*, I said to myself, *and the world is mine*. I gazed at the women in the audience hemmed in by restraints I had left far behind. I soared high up into the sky. As the dance drew to its close, the men in the audience went wild. I could see adolescent girls clutch their hearts, their cheeks grow pale. For the encore, I performed *El Oleano* once again. This time I could feel Lola's power from my toes to the tips of my fingers. Where I grew timid, she lifted my skirts. Where I hesitated, she performed a furious *zapateado* with her heels. She would never leave me now, I knew.

The marquis continued to wave his arms and shout. In a quiet moment, his voice could finally be heard.

"Why that's Mrs Eliza James!" he cried.

The words echoed around the auditorium. Heads turned.

I paused. Then in a gesture of scornful outrage, I shook out my skirts. I thought of every man who had ever preyed upon me, of every unwanted touch. I rose up on a crest of applause. Like Venus, I was reborn. A man who had once insulted me shouted out, then another who had mauled me. Like tiny crocodiles, my castanets ate up their words. I was beyond them now as the sun. I took a final bow. I knew that I had won. When I blew kisses, it was to the entire world.

The next day, the newspapers were filled with ecstatic reviews. I felt triumphant, unstoppable. Unfortunately for me, my spurned suitor chose to exact his revenge. The marquis had important friends, and together they challenged the theatre with promoting a fraud and adulteress. Earl Malmsbury protested, but to no avail. Soon one of the newspapers began a campaign. When a prominent journalist threatened to print a full exposé, the theatre cancelled all future performances. Though I swore blind that I was not the disreputable character that my enemies claimed, the director would not take the risk of allowing me to perform again.

London was full of impostors. But to me, Lola was not one of them. The moment I stepped on to the stage, she became entirely real. For the first time in my life, I was my own woman. It was Eliza Gilbert who was the impersonator, Thomas's wife who was the implausible fake. Lola Montez was more alive to me than they had ever been. Do you remember poor Eliza Gilbert? She took her mother's name and her mother's lover. She was hardly her own person at all. Then there was Rosana, a romantic schoolgirl with her head in the clouds. She walked up to the altar with Lieutenant James, and then I never saw her again. And Mrs James, the officer's wife? She vanished in a puff of smoke, along with her flowered bonnets and her demure sprigged gowns.

In Spain, the bullfighter and the dancer go hand in hand. Both struggle with matters of life and death, and Francisco Montes was the bravest bullfighter in the whole of Spain. As for my mother! I gave birth to myself. I was born in a cave in Granada, out of dust and sweat and fire. First the birth, then the christening: my name, with its resonance of the grief of the Virgin, was almost too fitting, too apt. Every servant girl in Spain might answer to Dolores, but in the arms of her lover, she will always be Lola. The name brims with sadness, yet the diminutive is playful and full of joy. It was a name made for me. Amidst the blackest of sorrows, are there not moments of pure delight? Though I wore a widow's weeds, my only loss was of my former self. Lola Montez was wild and impulsive and free. She was everything I wanted to be. If circumstances give you a name that doesn't suit you, take another! If your life conspires to diminish you, throw it over and start again!

After the triumph, the fall. After the defeat, the rallying cry. If I could not dance in London, then I would continue my career abroad. I planned my mode of operation like a military campaign. Before leaving London, I studied the *Almanach de Gotha* and mapped out a tour that took in every court in Europe. I had danced in front of royalty; I would do so again. I imagined theatre doors swinging open and plush red carpets unfurling before me.

Only Ellen sounded a cautionary note. When I asked her to accompany me, she shook her head.

"Meddle with the truth at your own expense, not mine," she said. "When you tire of being a Spaniard, what will you become next? You can't build a future upon every whim and impulse. Believe your own lies, and I dread to think what will become of you."

"Don't you dare speak to me like that!" I snapped.

"I'll speak to you however I like," she snapped back.

Alas, she was right. I had been more dependent on her than she on me, and we both knew it. I bit my lip. "I'm sorry," I said. "I'm disappointed, that's all. However will I manage without you?"

"You'll cope."

"You won't reconsider?"

"I'm going to open a dress-lodger's shop," she said.

I laughed. "Really! I'm sure you'll do very well."

I turned back to the map spread out across the table. "I'm going to make my fortune, you'll see."

"I don't doubt it," said Ellen. "Just remember to keep your feet on the ground. Money isn't everything, you know."

At that, we both guffawed with laughter. "It helps, I know," she said.

"Is that you giving me your blessing?"

"It's as close as you'll get. You won't be needing this dress, will you?" she asked, indicating a leftover pastel gown.

The day before I left for Hamburg, Sophia came to see me.

"I just wanted to wish you good luck," she said.

"Who told you I was leaving?"

She nodded towards Ellen, who was dividing my wardrobe into two neat piles, one destined for the trunk, the other for her new shop in South Molton Street.

"Why do you think you have to do everything on your own?" asked Sophia.

"Don't tell me you want to come with me?"

Both she and Ellen smiled. "I meant, you're not alone. Your pride will be your downfall," she said.

"What else have I got?" I asked.

"Friendship," said Sophia.

"All right then, I'll write."

"You promise?"

I nodded.

"Let's see who settles down first!" she said.

We both pointed at each other at the same time, then burst into fits of giggles.

"It's not funny!" said Ellen.

"It certainly isn't," I said with a broad grin.

"I think I may be the only sensible person in this room," said Ellen, patting the growing pile of discarded pastel gowns.

Chapter 22

In a cramped corner of a Hamburg dressing room, amidst smeared bottles and pots of grease, I traced a determined finger across a map of Europe. Buxom *frauleins* with flaxen plaits squeezed past me to get to the mirror, a baritone practised his scales, and a horrible yapping little dog ran by with the wardrobe mistress following close behind. I had succeeded in securing a provisional contract to dance at the Stadttheater, but not, alas, the privilege of my own dressing room. Whilst I was waiting for the interval in *Der Dorfbarbier*, I pored over my pocket atlas and tried to ignore the bustle and chaos erupting all around me. The names of countries I had never visited whispered to me from the pages. The vast expanse of Russia was tinted green, neighbouring Prussia was a pale orange. Beneath Prussia, Germany was a patchwork of tiny kingdoms. In my journal, I mapped out a route. *Dresden, Berlin, St Petersburg*, I wrote. A swift glance around the dressing room—at the *fraulein* caking her face in sticky white powder, the baritone turning purple, the dog piddling on a pile of abandoned costumes—strengthened my resolve. Inking in a series of lines across the page, I circled all the major cities en route to St Petersburg: Prague, Warsaw, Riga. Beneath my feet, the grand European cities would become my stepping stones. I pictured myself like a daughter of Gulliver striding the globe.

In Hamburg, I danced a tarantella. In Dresden, I performed a sevillianas and a bolero. Then, having used up my repertoire, I moved on towards Prussia. A fictitious letter of introduction from a distant

German relative of Queen Victoria opened the door of the first *kapellmeister,* and the rest soon followed. After one performance, it was easy to secure further engagements. I collected letters of introduction like playing cards, each one bringing the promise of another of higher value.

As I clambered into yet another carriage, I smoothed a lavender mohair shawl across my knees and pressed my hat down upon my head. Opening my battered old portmanteau, I unwrapped my lucky talisman and clutched it tightly in the palm of my hand. On my frequent trips to Mr Smallbone, I had often taken my mother's betrothal ring with me, then at the last moment proffered some other trinket instead. Perhaps I did secretly fear that he might declare it a worthless fake; nonetheless, to me, it was priceless beyond measure. No matter what Mama said, the ruby ring was tangible proof that I was born of love. It was also my only memento of my father—its pool of faceted red like a drop of blood linking us together.

The rhythm of carriage wheels lulled any lingering feelings of panic and anxiety. Movement suited me. Stagecoaches and cabins felt like home; the mid-point between departure and arrival was always my happiest time. Through the windows, I watched the world swirling by. Any feelings of abandonment or vulnerability belonged to Eliza Gilbert, not me. Whenever I caught myself feeling clingy or dreamy, I pictured my mother in India, prising my hands from her skirts. Eliza Gilbert was grubby fingerprints in peppermint silk; she was a pathetic residue that needed to be swept firmly away.

Beyond the fashionable boulevards, I stumbled through narrow tenemented streets, the stench from the pothouses mingling with the odour of baking bread. I marched purposefully onwards, ignoring the jibes of street urchins selling pins and the whores in pink stockings who strutted the pavements. Outside my run-down hotel, I eyed a chocolate seller with mercury stained teeth, and she eyed me. I knew perfectly well what she was selling, and I suppose she assumed the same of me. The spectre of poverty dogged my every step. I saw fallen women everywhere.

197

Often my lack of a chaperone was interpreted as an open invitation. I was vulnerable to advances of every kind. In Hamburg, a gang of children chanted obscenities at me. In Leipzig, a drunken man pushed me into a dark alleyway and grappled with my skirts. In Dresden, Potsdam and Berlin, I was accosted and manhandled. In response, I quickened my impulses and sharpened my tongue. For my own protection, I armed myself with a small pistol, a dagger and a gentleman's rawhide horsewhip, which I lovingly maintained with beeswax and saddle-soap.

I was staying in Berlin when a bundle of letters was forwarded from England. Among them was a black-rimmed card announcing the death of Mrs Eliza James, *née* Gilbert, daughter of Mrs Craigie of Calcutta, India. I studied the card in genuine puzzlement. It had been more than a year since I had used my married title, never mind my original maiden name. There must be some mistake I thought. The card that I was staring at clearly announced my own death. It took me some minutes to comprehend, and then I shuddered. Any thoughts that I might one day be reconciled with my mother vanished. What kind of woman sent out a formal notice declaring her only living daughter dead?

The covering letter was from Scotland, from my step-aunt, Elizabeth Rae.

"Your mother has taken the news of your stage debut very badly," she wrote.

Poor old Mama, I thought. She had strained so hard for respectability, only to be besmirched by ruin and scandal. The speculation that the eminent Mrs Craigie might once have been a dancer had truly come back to haunt her. I imagined her closeted in her drawing room, refusing to venture out. If I was a heartless and ungrateful daughter, it was no more than she deserved. She had been willing to sacrifice my future happiness to her own ambition. Yet instead of fulfilling her sweetest dreams, I had become the very embodiment of all her fears.

Mrs Rae also enclosed a letter from my late stepfather, Patrick

Craigie. It was dated November 1841, almost two years earlier. Major Craigie must have written it in the month before he died.

I clutched the letter to my chest; then, swallowing hard, I forced myself to read it.

> *There is nothing to be done for her now*, he had written. *My sweet little Eliza has thrown herself at the mercy of the world. Tell her that though her mother is still angry with her, it is largely on my account. She worries so about any possible damage to my career. Of course, Eliza's actions are regrettable, but we will always love her. She was always head-strong; in that she resembles her mother. May God help her.*

Towards the end of her correspondence, Mrs Rae offered to intercede. *Surely*, she wrote, *there can be no bond greater than the love between a mother and her daughter?*

I laughed bitterly to myself. I knew my mother well enough, but on this occasion, at least, I happened to agree with her. I surveyed the card proclaiming the death of my former self. You're right, Mama, I thought. Eliza Gilbert is well and truly dead.

Chapter 23

On the day of the Grand Parade in Berlin, I summoned the hotel seamstress to stitch me into my riding costume. "Tighter, tighter," I whispered, until my silhouette was curved as the figurehead of an ancient ship. The parade was the finale of the state visit of Czar Nicholas I and had been billed as the most significant event in the Prussian calendar. I had remained in Berlin especially for the occasion. As I made my preparations, I tried not to dwell on any niggling doubts. A Prussian diplomat had faithfully promised to escort me into the royal enclosure. I only hoped he wasn't having second thoughts. Establishment figures happily consorted with dancers after dark, but a society event in broad daylight might well be a different matter.

I had been dancing my way from Hamburg towards St Petersburg, but I was often penniless, and my dance slippers were rapidly becoming threadbare. A personal invitation to dance at the Russian Imperial Court would not only launch my career across Europe, it might also give me a little financial leverage. The Czar's passion for dancers was well known. At an Imperial banquet, he had astonished his guests with Marie Taglioni's slippers, served up on a silver platter and gently simmering in a fine Madeira sauce. (How the guests must have looked askance at each other across the table! Mercifully, they were only required to consume the sauce.)

The Grand Parade was my last chance to make an impression. From breakfast to mid-morning, I paced my hotel room, waiting for my Prussian diplomat. By eleven o'clock, I realised that he had reneged on his promise; at half past, I knew that if I wanted to attend the parade, then I would have to go alone and unchaperoned.

I emerged from the hotel stables at midday, straddled across a sleek black Cordovan stallion with the apt and splendid name of Fury. My riding costume, which was made of plum velvet with a trim of the softest suede, fitted like a second skin, and Fury's immense muscles rippled and glistened beneath his coat. As we proceeded down the Unter der Linden, I patted his flanks and we fell quickly into step.

It was a fine October morning, and the sun glimmered in the linden trees. Gleaming cannon trundled by, patriotic bunting fluttered in the breeze. As we rode out to Friedrichfelde, Fury and I settled into an easy rhythm. On foot, on horseback, in carriages, piled on to the back of ramshackle carts, the entire populace seemed to be streaming out of the city alongside us. Gangs of chattering housemaids with white-painted faces strolled arm in arm. In the back of a milk cart, five dollymops tapped brass-heeled boots, their pale, goose-pimpled breasts spilling from gaudy low-cut dresses. As I passed by, one of them winked at me and rubbed her fingers together as if she were rustling banknotes.

I pressed swiftly onwards, anxious to avoid any taint by association. In recent police sweeps, overzealous Prussian gendarmes had twice stopped me, demanding to inspect my papers.

As we neared Friedrichfelde, the numbers swelled to a hundred thousand. Families huddled in small groups. A mother warmed her child's tiny hands with her breath. A thick fog obscured the ground. I kept a tight rein on Fury. As he high-stepped along the cobbles, people moved briskly out of the way.

Thirty thousand soldiers marched in formation, then stopped. The infantry, then the cavalry and the horse artillery paraded past. The Prussian army, in their uniforms of black, red and gold, stretched as far as the eye could see. The boisterous cheers of the crowds rolled back and forth. Two riders galloped across the parade route. When a gang of boys ran out in front of them, the smooth regimented lines of the troops began to waver, then break. The seething crowd pushed forwards, and the police struggled to retain control.

Fixing my eyes on the royal platform, I skirted the enclosure. Riders and carriages had already begun to break through the cordons. A Prussian officer with grey side-whiskers was lashing out with his riding crop in an attempt to hold back the crowd. As an artillery salute rang out, I spurred Fury directly inside the royal enclosure. Casting about for a familiar face, I moved through the élite as if I had found my natural place. When the side-whiskered officer galloped over and grabbed Fury's bridle, every muscle in my body tensed.

I fixed my sights on the Czar in the distance, raised up on the Imperial platform, then surveyed the Prussian officer who was blocking my path. I glared at him, determined to press on, whether he liked it or not.

"Let go of me," I hissed, but the officer, with his thin authoritarian face and flinty eyes, tightened his grip.

As he struggled to establish control, I cracked my whip. Within a split second, two distinct images flashed through my mind. One moment, I was reacting against Thomas, my husband; the next, I was a ten-year-old cowering beneath the stern, looming face of Provost Craigie. There were droplets of sweat beading his upper lip, and I felt overwhelmed by a queasy feeling of humiliation and dread.

Fury reared up against the officer's restraint, his hooves flashing in the light. In all the confusion, I raised my whip.

Since I had left England, I had been mauled and insulted at every turn; this side-whiskered officer was the very last straw. I lashed out, all the hurt and rejection of the past year erupting in a single devastating blow.

The whip cracked through the air.

The officer flinched.

I recoiled from the impact.

The milling crowd gasped. Those within the enclosure averted their eyes.

Red welts swelled up on the officer's neck and cheek. Then minute drops of blood broke the surface of his skin. The lash had sliced through his cheek like a blade.

"You will pay heavily for this, Madame," he said.

My mouth opened wordlessly, then closed. I had to force myself to respond.

"I suggest you let go of my horse," I whispered, the words dropping from my mouth like stones.

All around us, riders and pedestrians were pouring into the royal enclosure. The Prussian officer glanced at the marauding crowd. I stared at the officer and tried not to panic. He could prevent me from crossing over, but what about all the others? The officer cursed, and then let me go.

As I rode away, I patted Fury's sweat-drenched neck and whispered reassurances. I could feel my cheeks throbbing and my heartbeat thundering in my ears. Inside the royal enclosure, a Russian aide invited me to join his party. I mustered a faint smile, but the image of my whip piercing the officer's cheek remained fixed in my mind. When the Prussian diplomat caught sight of me, he studiously avoided my gaze. The royal box shimmered tantalisingly out of reach. Inside it, the Czar, surrounded by an impenetrable cordon of military bodyguards, stifled a yawn.

The next day I was charged with assault.

Of course, I should never have lashed out like that. The moment a drop of blood flowered on his cheek, I regretted it. I replayed the scene over and over again, as if I might be able to change the course of events. I understood that I had crossed an invisible line into unknown and dangerous territory, but I didn't know how to get back to safer ground. It took more than six weeks for the furore to die down, and the charges to be quietly dropped. I was permitted to leave Berlin, but I was never able to shake the story off. Everywhere I went, the tale of my whipping the Prussian officer preceded me. Once it had been picked up by the foreign press, the incident became larger than life. Newspapers printed satirical cartoons in which whole regiments fled my whip. Best-selling print runs featured me brandishing a riding crop. In the speciality brothels of Europe, queues of men apparently clamoured to pay for the privilege of a "Lola Montez". Whenever I performed, journalists would revive the story.

Chapter 24

By the time I arrived in Poland on a bleak November evening, a reception party was already waiting for me. Sometimes I felt like Minerva, who had sprung, adult and fully formed, from the brain of Jupiter. At the mention of my name, a certain type of person actually backed away. Strangers hesitated to interfere with me; admirers were less inclined to take liberties. Instead of quibbling over my fee, theatre directors readily agreed to pay half the box-office takings. Sometimes I felt immortal. Sometimes I felt that I really could do whatever I pleased; the newspapers had published so many wildly exaggerated stories, it was almost expected of me. Outside the Hotel Rzymski, a huddle of journalists in black cloaks hovered like crows around carrion. Smiling magnanimously, I swept past them without uttering a single word.

Warsaw reminded me of Dublin, with the air of the countryside enlivening city streets. Jammed between grand classical buildings were squalid blocks of ramshackle wooden cottages. Dray horses and wagons rumbled over the cobbles. Girls in cross-tied shawls swept up mounds of golden leaves with brushes made of twigs. On street corners, the urchins sold gaudily painted tin.

Warsaw society, I soon discovered, divided into two distinct camps. If the Russians lingered by the door, the Poles tended to cluster around the fireplace, and vice versa. The occupying Russians treated me with some caution, I noticed, whilst the Poles, with whom I shared an immediate feeling of warmth and kinship, were more inclined to playfulness. At the first soirée I attended, I was introduced to Piotr Steinkeller, a wealthy Polish industrialist with an intense passion for both his country and the theatre. Soon the two of us were watching the manoeuvres in the room and hatching a gleeful plan.

At the Grand Theatre, the Russian director stroked his military side-whiskers and his mouth broke into a slow lascivious smile. After a cursory glance over my letters of introduction, he tossed them aside.

"I see you have danced at the Schauspielhaus. That is good enough for me," he said. "You and I shall become the best, the most intimate of friends."

I raised a quizzical eyebrow.

Colonel Ignacy Abramowiwz was a tall, lean man in his early fifties. He had very long, bony hands, like some kind of pre-historic spider.

Once we had agreed upon dates and terms, he clamped his fingers around my forearm, and insisted upon escorting me back to the hotel. In his carriage, he examined me with shrewd, glittering eyes.

"I am the eyes and the ears of this city," he said.

"I hope my little dance does nothing to offend," I replied.

The colonel laughed, and then gripped my knee.

"How charming you are. What harm could a sweet little creature like you possibly do?"

For my first performance the theatre was filled to capacity. From the moment I clicked my castanets, I was showered with roses and constant applause. Afterwards, I flung open my dressing room door expecting a deluge of admirers. Instead I found one wrinkled little gnome of a man, attired in the uniform of a general and carrying a bouquet of lilies in his hand.

"And who might you be?" I asked.

Before I could say anything more, Colonel Ambramowiwz stepped in to make the introductions.

I winced, then dropped into a curtsy. The little man kissed not only my hand, but the entire length of my arm. His lips were nuzzling my shoulder, before I succeeded in disentangling myself from his grasp. My formidable new admirer was, it transpired, none other than Prince Ivan Paskievitch, the viceroy of the Czar.

For the past twelve years, the prince and the colonel had ruled Poland with a vice-like grip. After the virulent suppression of the nationalist uprising of 1831, Paskievitch had been made Prince of Warsaw, and Abramowiwz his chief of security. Everywhere the secret police were the silent, watching eyes of the Russian state. Ten thousand activists and intellectuals fled the country. Writers and poets languished in gloomy cells or were exiled to Siberia and never heard of again. The very worst dungeons of all were directly beneath the prince's ballroom.

Within days, both men had declared themselves. When the colonel invited me for a ride in his velvet-lined carriage, I knew that my contract was dependent upon it. On the way to Lazienski Park, I accepted his compliments with good grace. Outside, a persistent wind was gradually stripping the trees of their leaves. We were passing through the looming cast-iron gates of the park when the sky grew dark. As the rain thundered down, Abramowiwz caught me in his arms and pressed his thin cold lips against my neck. I tried to push him away, but the struggle only aroused him further. When he began to tussle with my skirts, I sank my teeth into his cheek.

The colonel sprang back, clutching his face.

"Madame," he said, "you will pay dearly for this."

"You are mistaken, sir. If Prince Paskievitch hears of it, the cost will be yours."

Abramowiwz raised his hand, then coughed and apologised. I smoothed down my skirts. All the way to the hotel, the carriage shook with the force of the storm.

That evening, over sweet wine and Polish pastries, I embellished the incident for the amusement of my Polish friends, casually remarking that I had thrown the colonel out of his own carriage into the pouring rain. When the story got back to Abramowiwz, who was trying to disguise the wound to his cheek, he began to plot his revenge.

Having despatched one pursuer, I became complacent about the other. A few days later, I was hosting a small supper in my hotel suite when Prince Paskievitch arrived, uninvited and unannounced. As the evening wore on, the Prince of Warsaw lingered after the other guests. At one point he gazed at himself in the mirror and adjusted his moustache. Following the slightest nod of his head, the remaining guests made their excuses, then left.

Prince Paskievitch moved closer. I calculated the distance between myself and the door. Every time the prince spoke, he revealed the artificial gold roof of his palate. When he slid his arm along the back of the sofa, I recoiled.

Rolling another cigarette, I blew a cloud of blue smoke in his face, then another. Nothing dimmed his ardour. As the prince declared his love, a gnarled hand gripped mine. His sunken eyes hovered over the swell of my bosom. With each rise and fall, he offered me something else—furs, diamonds, a country estate.

When his thigh brushed mine, I jumped up from the sofa, indicating the door.

"If you want a pet, Your Highness, I suggest you buy a parrot," I spluttered. "Not for all the wonders of the world would I submit to your withered embrace."

Prince Paskievitch drew himself up to his full height, before taking his leave.

"You will be sorry, Madame."

"That is what they always say," I replied.

For my fourth appearance at the Grand Theatre, I danced *La Saragossa,* then *El Oleano,* between acts of Aubers's *Fra Diavolo.* My admirers were out in force, and so were their employees. A dozen typesetters from Piotr's printworks had been paid to whip up the enthusiasm of the crowd. Scores of his factory workers were dotted throughout the audience.

Colonel Abramowiwz had also been busy. Secret policemen in plain clothes were stationed in almost every part of the auditorium. When I began to dance, the policemen began to hiss as ordered.

When my admirers rose to their feet, the hisses of the police grew louder. Soon jeers mingled with whistles and cheers. I paused, and then swept across the stage. With elegant twisting movements of my hands, I echoed the tapping of my feet. The two rival groups glared at each other. With a flourish of my skirts, I followed one *paseo* with another. The applause grew louder. The jeers became shouting. Soon the orchestra could hardly be heard beneath the din. Those members of the audience who were not directly involved glanced at each other in startled bemusement.

I danced on. My feet stamped the stage. My eyes narrowed to slits. At the close of the dance, I bowed defiantly. By the time the curtain had fallen, a fight had broken out in one of the stalls.

I burst through the drapes, then strode to the footlights, my cheeks burning with righteous indignation. The hisses and the cheers faded away. Everyone stared at the stage.

I took a deep breath, before thrusting a finger towards Abramowiwz, who was sitting in the director's box.

"*Messieurs et Mesdames,*" I cried out, "I owe this unworthy insult to that gentleman! There is the scoundrel who thus attempts to revenge himself upon a poor feeble woman! First he bombards me with debauched and infamous proposals. Then, when I refuse to submit, he tries to ruin my performance! *Messieurs et Mesdames,* this is too much!"

The audience fell into astonished silence, and then first one man, then another began to clap. Soon most of the audience were shouting.

"*Bis! Bis!* Again! Again!"

"*Brava,* Lola, *brava!*"

Colonel Abramowiwz stared at the crowd in horror. The secret policemen looked askance at each other. Twelve years of defeat rose in the throats of the audience. Young Poles were jumping up and down. Even the ladies shook their fists and shouted out. The few Russians made a speedy departure. I surveyed the tumult, and then withdrew behind the curtain, leaving the theatre in uproar. The commotion worsened. Abramowiwz cancelled the second act of the opera, before calling in uniformed police to clear the auditorium.

News of the public denunciation of Colonel Abramowiwz spread rapidly throughout the city. Within hours, there were outbreaks of rioting. A firebomb flew through the window of Namiestnikowski Palace. Russian carriages were overturned, and hundreds of people were arrested. During the night, underground bulletins printed the story, reporting that I had turned my *derrière* upon my detractors, and cried out: "All people everywhere deserve the right to be free!" By the morning, I had become a heroine of Polish liberation.

At the Hotel Rzymski, I was placed under immediate house arrest. When the officer on guard refused to let me out, I slapped him, and then slammed the door in his face. I sank down to the floor, on the other side of the door. They couldn't make me disappear, could they? I had a nightmare vision of myself locked up in the dungeons below the prince's ballroom, crouching down there in the darkness, with chains clinking in distant corners and the sound of dance steps echoing above my head.

When the colonel arrived with deportation orders, I barricaded myself in, shouting through the door that I would shoot dead the first man who dared to break in.

Outside the hotel, there were already groups of lurking Poles. The slightest hint of an altercation inside the hotel would inflame an already volatile situation.

First the colonel shouted through the door, then I heard Piotr.

At the sound of his voice, I pulled back the furniture, and he tumbled through the door on the butt-end of a rifle. He sank into a chair, his face ashen. When he invited me to visit his country estate, I understood that I was being offered a way out. I struggled to keep the panic out of my voice.

"They won't throw me in jail?" I asked.

"It's lucky for you that you're not a Pole," he ruefully replied.

Within the hour, I had packed my bags and gone down to the

waiting carriage. As Piotr helped me alight, I clung to him. "I can't just leave you here," I whispered. As I repeated my apologies, a group of young Poles formed themselves into a guard of honour. When a street urchin presented me with a painted wooden plate, I graciously accepted, then pressed my fur hat upon his head. As we all paraded through the streets, I saw Russian soldiers gathering on every corner, and smoking pyramids of damp, smouldering leaves.

Chapter 25

The grand finale of my European tour was a symphony of closing doors. In St Petersburg, my usual mode of operation failed me. My letters of introduction did not impress. Theatre directors shook their heads; strange men lurked in the corridors of my hotel; journalists refused to meet me. I was followed, and my calling cards were ignored.

When I protested to one newspaper editor that I had been compared to the great ballerina Marie Taglioni, he laughed in my face.

"I know all about that," he said, pulling out a Berlin newspaper: "If it is said of Taglioni that she writes history with her feet, so can it be said of Donna Montez that she writes Casonova's memoirs with her whole body."

I would dearly have loved to slap the man for his impertinence, but I was too lacking in friends to risk creating another enemy. Instead, I summoned up a confident smile.

"It is not a bad comparison," I said. "*The Memoirs of Casanova* are not without merit, I think. Operas have been based upon it, why not a dance?"

"Here in Russia, we do not encourage licentiousness."

"In Russia, it seems, you encourage nothing at all," I said.

"I would advise caution, Madame. A Spanish passport is not the strongest form of defence."

"But I have danced in front of the Czar," I pleaded.

"It is from the Czar that we have received our instructions."

After five fruitless days in St Petersburg, I had to concede that my dream of dancing there was over. The news from Poland hadn't helped. As a direct consequence of my sojourn in Warsaw, over three hundred people, including Piotr, had been imprisoned. According to the newspapers, the Grand Theatre had been closed for a month whilst new guidelines for censorship were drawn up. Every performance was weighed with the greatest of caution; even the most harmless ballerina was seen as a potential subversive. As I folded my stage costumes between layers of tissue paper, I tried to console myself. I might have failed, but at least it was on a grand scale.

For a week, I travelled non-stop, day and night, across Russia, through the Baltic states of Pomerania towards eastern Prussia. The weather was miserable; animals were coming into the villages in search of food. The flat, desolate landscape unfurled perpetually before me, a barren waste of ice and snow. In the distance, I saw chimney smoke curl up from a solitary wooden cottage, then a forlorn, crumbling castle with a broken tower. A starving wolf staggered by the edge of the road. Even in the brief hours of daylight, the moon hung heavy in the sky. A never-ending blanket of glistening whiteness seemed to cover the entire world. Huddled inside my carriage, I felt outcast and alone. My leather-bound folder, which usually contained letters of introduction, was empty. The idea of Paris loomed, but without contacts, I had little hope of success.

As a child, in moments of doubt, I had looked for a sign. Little things had sustained me: the thought that the door on the tower in Montrose might finally open and release a beautiful bird, my stepfather's letters from India, an embroidered handkerchief from my school friend Sophia. I decided to trust in the fates once again. But which country first? And where to start?

At the Prussian border, the coachman stopped to change the horses. In the post house, I ordered a coffee and a *cognac*. Beneath the watchful eyes of the other customers, I rolled a cigarette and then picked up a newspaper that had been left lying on a table. A man immediately removed his wife and daughter from the premises. A solitary gentleman retired to the other end of the room. The proprietor grimaced. Inhaling from my thin black *cigarillo,* I blew a plume of blue smoke into the air.

With a mouthful of *cognac* warming my throat, I remembered my mother's admonishments and Thomas's indulgent smile. There was a whole world of ideas contained within a newspaper; no wonder men (and mothers) sought to keep them to themselves.

Rattling the newspaper open, I scanned the headlines. On an inside page, I found an article about the romantic composer Franz Liszt, who was about to embark on a new programme of recitals. Everywhere I went, the pianist had been there before me. In Stettin, Danzig, Konigsberg, Tilset, then Riga, I had found remnants of his visit. Among my Polish friends, the Hungarian nationalist had been especially popular. He had been in Warsaw six months before me. On the newsstands in St Petersburg, I had seen a print of his face, dark eyes burning from the frame. I had been following in his footsteps for months. *What would happen*, I wondered, *if we found ourselves in the same place?*

After his tour of Germany, the pianist was due to return to Paris. My eyes lit up. What better introduction to Parisian society than a letter from Franz Liszt? I scanned the dates and locations of his concerts, and then circled one of the smaller venues in southern Germany.

Chapter 26

It was the middle of February, and the roads had become a treacherous roller-coaster of deep puddles, flying mud and the exposed roots of trees. Inside the carriage, I was constantly being jostled and thrown about. Wrapping a chinchilla rug more tightly across my lap, I pulled my astrakhan down over my ears and buried my hands in my muff. By the time I arrived in Upper Saxony, I felt like a loose assembly of bones with a pink nose and extremities of stone. When I took my seat at the concert hall that evening, I still hadn't been able to shake off the chill in my bones. My stomach rumbled, and I yearned for my snug cloak and warm muff, which were languishing forlornly in the cloakroom downstairs. Trying not to shiver too visibly, I rubbed my hands together until my fingertips were no longer blue.

I had travelled from Russia in record time and in the process used up the last of my meagre funds. It was only when Franz Liszt finally appeared on the stage that I remembered why I had gone to so much trouble. With flowing hair and deep-set eyes, Liszt, who was wearing a loose full-sleeved white blouse, really did look like a figure from a romantic sonnet. As he took his place at the piano, a thousand static prints and impressions sprang into dazzling life. He raised his hands, then paused. With the piano jutting out before him, he performed like a man possessed. His face was transfixed, his hair tangled and wild, his wrists cutting patterns through the air. As his *Devil's Waltz* filled the auditorium, it was as if three men were playing, not one. The audience gaped open-mouthed. A woman fainted; others wept.

Afterwards, I almost ran down to the stage, but at the sight of the gathering crowd, hovered momentarily on the stairs. Two women were fighting over Liszt's handkerchief, another kissed his hands, a fourth ran off with his gloves. When at last he looked up, Liszt's eyes caught mine. Amidst all the pale women dressed in pastel gowns, I was the only one dressed entirely in black. My costume was cut from a stark velvet with a matching bolero braided in the Spanish style; my hair was caught up in a tall carved ivory comb on the back of my head. Anybody who regularly read a newspaper would recognise me.

Liszt bowed, and then his mouth curled into a smile. I tilted my head slightly. Before departing, I sent a note inviting him to call.

Back in my hotel room, I ordered a plate of sandwiches and then downed a large balloon glass of brandy to steady my nerves. Earlier that evening, I had offered the coachman full payment and a generous bonus if he would only wait until we reached Paris, but he had declined my offer. Perhaps he sensed my air of desperation. Sticking out his hand, he stubbornly waited. I reluctantly emptied my pocketbook and parted with a fistful of banknotes in different currencies. The coachman counted the notes, then stuck out his hand again. I had to give him a pair of pearl earrings and a silver pendant before he would leave me alone. I had gambled everything on my success in St Petersburg. Without it, I had enough funds to get me exactly this far, but no further. If I wanted to eat out or pay my hotel bill, I would need to find a pawnbroker's in the morning.

Surveying the hotel room, it suddenly didn't seem adequate for my purpose. "Courage, courage," I whispered. I swiftly rearranged the furniture, then appraised my handiwork. A froth of snowy lace protruded from between drawn heavy damask drapes. Two upholstered armchairs were positioned on either side of the fireplace; a guitar propped up beside one, an embroidered Spanish shawl draped over the other. The lamps were dimmed; the coals smouldered in the grate. On a nearby chiffonier sat a half-empty decanter of brandy, two gold-rimmed crystal balloon glasses.

Perfect.

The plate of half eaten sandwiches was relegated to the bedroom along with various items of furniture.

At ten o'clock, I was picking out a wistful tune on my guitar when I heard a discreet knock. I took a deep breath, and another mouthful of brandy, before opening the door.

Liszt, who was a little drunk, fell happily into one of the arm-chairs in a loose-limbed sprawl. As he did so, his kidskin gloves fell to the floor. In the flesh, he seemed to emanate a warm golden glow. His eyes were lively beneath the deep set of his brow; his unruly hair was flecked with gold.

We both reached for the gloves at the same time.

I suppressed a smile.

"Your admirers would pay a small fortune for these," I said, placing the gloves on the chair arm beside him.

"I lose three pairs a week," he replied. "Those I manage to keep are rare as hen's teeth."

I poured him a glass of brandy.

"I lose silk camellias; it's much cheaper," I said.

Liszt chuckled, then clinked my glass.

Within half an hour, we were matching each other story for story. When he recounted his tales of the Magyar gypsies of Hungary, I described the gypsy caves in Granada, in Spain.

"I am half gypsy, half Franciscan!" he cried.

"I am half gypsy, half queen!" I countered.

As the evening flew by, we kept interrupting each other.

"Let me finish," I protested.

"But I must tell you this," said Liszt.

As we leaned close together, I took one of the pianist's hands in mine and examined his palm. His skin was soft, the tips of his fingers square and broad.

"You're cold," he said. "Let me warm you."

Cupping my hands between his, he blew softly upon my finger-tips. Any thoughts of patronage or letters of introduction (or even the slightly more pressing matter of the hotel bill) slipped completely from my mind. For the past three years, I had been so busy fending off admirers that my own desires had become almost dormant. All my sensuality had been channelled into my dancing, my passions expressed upon the stage. I shivered involuntarily, feeling the heat of his breath penetrating my fingertips.

"Which am I? A creature of reason, or desire?" I asked.

Looking at his tender, almost girlish mouth, I wanted to taste each lip and run my tongue across his teeth. In the fireplace, the embers were fading. On the mantelpiece, the clock chimed three.

Liszt raised my hand to his lips. "There is only one possible answer to such a question, but the choice is yours."

Whilst he heaped more coal on to the fire, I spread a chinchilla rug across the floor. He kissed my ears. I buried my fingers in his hair. He unfastened my gown; I pulled off his blouse. I could feel his hot breath on my throat, his flesh pulse beneath my fingertips. I nibbled his mouth; he parted my lips with the tip of his tongue. When I sank into his arms, I felt as if I had been immersed in a pool of molten light. We stumbled into the bedroom, clambering over the drawing-room furniture that I had so hastily piled up inside the door.

The next morning, we travelled to Leipzig, then to Dresden. With Liszt picking up the bills, any immediate concerns about finance faded, and I quickly secured engagements at all the leading theatres. My jewellery collection remained intact, and I started to build up my funds for Paris. (The trick to accumulating money is to give the impression that you don't actually need it, I realised. One whiff of desperation, and you might as well lie down in the gutter.) Every morning, Franz and I woke up in our canopied bed at the Hotel de Saxe, the linen crumpled, our limbs entangled. Every evening, Franz played to ecstatic audiences, while I danced intermezzo at the Court Theatre. During the afternoons, whilst Franz practised, I lay beneath the piano, enveloped in layers of sound. Sometimes I sang a Spanish folk song for him or picked out a dance tune on my guitar. Often we did not get dressed until late afternoon. We were Byron's children: impulsive, creative, inspired. We had been plucked from the same storybook—he was my *compañero,* my brother, my twin. Within a week, he was determined to visit Spain. Whilst he wove the Spanish folk songs I had shown him into endless variations, I began to draw up an itinerary of my favourite locations.

Within a fortnight, my euphoria had already begun to wilt and fade. Liszt might have been a genius, but he also had feet of clay. The passionate and creative sparks between us had quickly degenerated. The very qualities we found attractive in each other became a source of irritation. In a certain light, Liszt's golden glow could easily be mistaken for smug complacency.

When I interrupted him at the piano, he banished me from the room.

"I will not tolerate tyranny," I cried.

He burst out laughing, then pushed me out of the door.

"I demand to be treated as an equal," I said. "Otherwise I would rather be alone."

"Music is my only equal," he replied.

I slammed the door shut, then stormed out into the street.

When Liszt began to spend entire afternoons at the piano, I felt deeply wounded.

As the days passed, I draped myself over the piano, and then tried to seduce him. When I walked naked across the room and he didn't even notice, I realised that it was time to leave.

After five weeks in Dresden, Liszt's programme of concerts had drawn to a close and he was expected in northern Prussia; my destination was the Paris Opéra. With my pocketbook now bulging again, I estimated that I had sufficient funds to set myself up until I could start making a regular income. On our last morning together, we ordered breakfast in bed. Over cups of steaming coffee and crumbling slices of poppy seed cake, we exchanged gifts. I presented Liszt with a songbook of Spanish melodies and a hand-drawn map of Spain; he gave me a set of silver guitar strings and a handful of letters to influential Parisians.

Among the introductions to critics and journalists, an envelope addressed to the author Alexandre Dumas had been left unsealed.

Liszt smiled. "Open it when I am gone," he said.

I felt blessedly relieved to be the centre of my own universe once again. As the carriage trundled across the cobbled streets, I spread my belongings across both seats until I had entirely filled the coach. On the outskirts of Dresden, I noticed a scrawny little urchin in cracked wooden sabots, hawking barley-sugar sticks. I remembered another little girl in Bath who sold watercress as a pretext for something else. Halting the coachman, I bought a single barley stick, and then dropped all my silver thalers into the girl's grubby upturned palm. As the carriage drew away, I watched her eyes sparkle with wonder and pleasure and counted my blessings. Sucking on the sticky orange confection, I contemplated my future. After St Petersburg, Paris was the cultural capital of Europe. With my letters from Liszt, my future was assured. As the coach pulled out of Dresden, I opened the envelope addressed to Alexandre Dumas.

Chapter 27

Outside the Paris Opéra, on the rue Le Peletier, the first buds were ripening on the chestnut trees. At the side of the stage, a trapdoor led down to a small brooding lake. Within the confines of my dressing room, I trembled like a fledgling on a lofty branch. My entire future rested upon a single performance. I could soar triumphant, or plummet. I looked at the peeling yellow paint, the mottled old mirror, the grimy paint-splattered floor. I could leave now, I thought. I could simply walk out of the door. Through a tiny window, I could see bright unfurling leaves; directly beneath my feet, I could feel the damp seeping up from the cold and inky depths of the underground lake.

On the first day of rehearsals, the janitor had pointed out the trapdoor and waved a bunch of keys.

"Many years ago," he said, "a prima ballerina drowned herself. Now I have to be very careful with the key."

"The poor creature!" I cried. "Why on earth did she do such a thing?"

"It was because she realised that she would never be truly great," he said, with a doleful shake of his head. "You know these dancers."

In my dressing room mirror, I readjusted my costume for the umpteenth time. The Opéra was the foremost ballet stage in the world. Marie Taglioni had performed here. Fanny Elssler had danced her famous cachucha. *Be brave*, I told myself. *Le Bal de Don Juan* had attracted a full house: in the auditorium, extra seats lined the aisles.

As the curtain rose, the audience broke into rapturous applause. I stood motionless in the centre of the stage, silvery skirts billowing out from a tight bodice, a lace mantilla flowing down from a high comb in my hair. On the first note from a violin, I raised my castanets above my head. Twisting my wrists, I clipped out a staccato beat, and then followed the rhythm with the tapping of my heels. I swooned from left to right, imagining the sun warming my skin and the scent of orange blossom in the air. I was a woman dancing for her husband. I was the full red petals of an opening rose. My body arched, my arms swept through the air. My heart smouldered. My veins coursed with desire. With three bold steps, I was at the footlights. Eyes flashing, hands on swaying hips, I sashayed boldly around the stage.

After the initial excitement, the audience grew fidgety. By the middle of the dance, they were shifting in their seats. When the murmuring became audible, I grew hesitant.

As I circled the front of the stage, my satin slipper flew from my foot. I stopped mid-pirouette. The audience began to titter. I glared at the entire auditorium, then in one deft movement, swept down, caught up the slipper and threw it to a young officer in one of the boxes. The audience were flabbergasted. Flushed and defiant, I kicked off my other slipper and finished the dance. With a swish of my skirts, I prowled the stage. A dozen people walked out in disgust. A small number rose to their feet with cries of *Encore!* Twisting my wrists into a final flourish, I thrust a naked foot forwards, and then took a closing bow. Three red roses landed forlornly on the stage. The applause was distinctly muted.

The next day the rumours started. One newspaper reported that I had thrown a garter, another that I had stripped completely naked. Despite my protests, word spread that I would never dance at the Opéra again.

At the shooting gallery in Lepage, I unleashed my frustration in a match against my new friend, Alexandre Dumas. In India, a sergeant had taught me how to handle a pistol, and my shooting was confident and precise. Firing in rapid double *coups,* I left a card entirely perforated with pistol balls. Dumas looked on in astonishment. The next day, the incident featured in *La Presse.* By the following week, it had been syndicated around Europe.

Though I vehemently denied it, my little setback at the Opéra was a major fiasco. The stark fact was that I was no Elssler or Taglioni. How could I possibly compete with prima ballerinas who had trained from the earliest age? And though I insisted upon the essential Spanishness of my dancing, I wouldn't have been foolhardy enough to perform in front of a Spanish audience. I had aimed high, but now I needed to find some middle ground.

In the autumn, my gaze fell upon a young man with grey-green eyes. Alexandre Dujarier was a close friend of Dumas, an impetuous, sharp-witted man with a cleft chin and a wide easy smile. Though he was only twenty, he was already the proprietor of *La Presse,* the most successful newspaper in Paris. Tall and thin, with dark hair and a prominent brow, he cut an elegant figure in the salons of Paris. In our own ways, we were both essentially self-made. The first time we were alone together, we toasted each other with champagne.

"You are an *arriviste,*" smiled Alexandre.

"And you a *parvenu,*" I laughed.

Of all the admirers, Alexandre impressed me most with the tenderness of his wooing. Where others plied me with bouquets of roses, he presented me with a nosegay of dewy violets. One day he gave me a single daisy, the next, the delicate skeleton of a leaf. Within a matter of weeks, I had moved into the apartment adjoining his.

"Is that wise?" cautioned Dumas. "Why take a mistress, then keep her beside you like a wife?"

At 39, rue Lafitte, we settled into a new life together. Where I was intense, Alexandre was languid; when I grew agitated, he remained calm. For the first time in eighteen months, I began to drop my guard. When the truth came tumbling out, Alexandre merely chuckled in amusement. We were lounging in my apartment after dinner, the curtains drawn, the fire blazing, two glasses of Madeira glowing amber in the lamplight.

"I'm not really a widow. I'm divorced," I confessed.

"I wouldn't care if you had a dozen husbands," he declared.

"In Prussia, I was charged with assault."

Alexandre's face broke into a wide smile. "You're famous for it, *ma chère*."

I bit my lip.

"But they say I'm an adulteress and a fraud."

"You're a woman of flesh and blood. What's fraudulent about that?"

"You know I was ejected from Poland."

Alexandre caught me in his arms and kissed my neck. "We published the story in *La Presse*. What can I say? Their loss is my gain."

I persisted. "My husband is a British captain in India, not a Spanish hero."

"Then it is no wonder you left him."

"You're not taking me seriously," I burst out. "You don't care about me, at all!"

Alexandre pulled me closer, kissing my eyes, then the tip of my nose.

Though I told him everything, he swore that his love was boundless. Not even the deception over my nationality deterred him.

"It's you I love," he insisted, "Not your country."

Instead of compulsively dreaming of the future, I began to savour every day, every hour. I loved to gaze at Alexandre as he slept, his dark eyelashes curling against his cheek. I loved to watch his long-limbed silhouette moving through a crowd. The sight of him sleepy-eyed over his breakfast coffee brought a warm glow to my cheeks. Watching his gesticulating fingers as he discussed politics in a café, I wanted to reach out and stroke his fingertips.

When I planned another expedition to the shooting gallery, I assumed that he would wish to accompany me.

"Why should a woman be shooting pistols?" he asked.

I looked at him in surprise.

"I can defend myself," I said. "What about you?"

"I don't know how to shoot," he replied. "And I hope I never have to."

I became insistent. Affairs of honour were common, especially amongst the fourth estate. For a man in Alexandre's position, it was only a matter of time before he was challenged.

At the shooting gallery, huddles of men parted as we approached. It had been raining all afternoon, and large puddles had appeared between the stalls. Servants held large black umbrellas aloft whilst their masters took aim. Some practised with rifles, others with pistols. In a white marquee, two men circled each other with fencing swords. The air was thick with the sharp smell of gunpowder and damp sawdust; the red and white-banded targets were pitted with shot.

Alexandre had not been exaggerating his lack of skill. Where I hit every target, he was able to hit a mark as large as a man only twice in fourteen times.

"Let me teach you," I said.

Alexandre shook his head.

"At least learn to fence," I pleaded.

He shrugged. "If I am challenged, so be it. Then I will bow to the inevitable."

That winter, Sophia arrived in Paris on a shopping trip. Alexandre and I had dinner with her and the Duke of Argyll, who also had interests in a couple of newspapers. Throughout the evening, the two men held forth on the dangers of communism, a radical new theory that was having a considerable impact in both London and Paris. I smiled complacently across the table at Sophia, who was looking sleek and beautiful in an ice-blue silk outfit trimmed with ermine. Her nose twitched for a moment, before her lips parted into a wide unguarded smile.

The following morning, she called at the apartment, and we congratulated ourselves on our good fortune. We had moved beyond the confines of respectable society, and despite all the dire predictions, nothing terrible had happened to us. Among the artists and intellectuals we mixed with, petty concerns with morality dropped miraculously away. We were young and desirable and carefree. What more could we possibly ask for?

In my boudoir, we clinked glasses of sparkling champagne, though it was not yet afternoon.

"Here we are in Paris!" said Sophia.

"It is not quite what we imagined in school. Will it do?"

"Oh, this will more than suffice," said Sophia.

"The Misses Aldridge would be proud that we are putting our French to such good use," I suggested.

"You don't sometimes feel a little insecure?" asked Sophia.

"You're not thinking of marriage?"

"It's out of the question, of course. Charles already has a wife," she replied. "But marriage is certainly one way to take care of the future. What about you?"

"I like to think we might marry one day," I said.

Sophia looked a little surprised. "Isn't Alexandre a Catholic?" she asked.

I shrugged. "We haven't actually talked about it, but I am sure Alexandre would marry me if he could."

"I wouldn't be so sure his mother would allow it."

"A mere detail," I said, with a wide grin.

I refilled our glasses. "Let's drink to the glorious present," I said. "Let's drink to every precious moment!"

We clinked glasses, but I noticed that Sophia's smile didn't quite reach her eyes.

After she was gone, the conversation played on my mind. Of course, I could have asked Alexandre about marriage outright, but why spoil the moment? We were perfectly happy as we were, I reminded myself.

The following spring, I was engaged by the Theatre de la Porte St Martin. On the opening night of "*La Dansomanie*", the audience went wild, whooping and applauding and stamping their feet. So many flowers were thrown on to the stage that there was hardly room to move. I danced an exuberant polka, then a voluptuous mazurka. I had put in a year of rigorous practice with a strict ballet master, and there was a new level of precision in my dancing, with balancing moments of lightness and grace. Murmurs of approval swept through the audience.

In my dressing room, I blew a playful kiss at my reflection. Life could not have been sweeter. The previous evening, Alexandre and I had toasted our first six months together with oysters and champagne. As a member of the Porte St Martin company, I could settle in for a long run. I dared to imagine a long, happy life, like a shiny pink satin ribbon unravelling endlessly before us.

When Alexandre came to see me after the show, I greeted him with a broad smile.

"How shall we celebrate?" I asked.

"I'm sorry," he said. "I have an engagement at the Trois Frères Provençaux."

My smile faded.

"Then I will come with you," I said.

Alexandre shook his head.

"Why on earth not?" I asked.

"I forbid it," he said.

I looked at him in puzzlement.

"If the company is fit for you, surely it is good enough for me."

"You are above them all," he said. "This will be the last time. I promise I won't leave you alone again."

I reluctantly let him go. I had understood what he was implying. My reputation might be scandalous, but I had no desire to sully it further by contact with the *demi-monde*. Sitting back down at my dressing table, I brooded over the conversation. For weeks now, he had been highly strung and excitable.

Over supper the following evening, Alexandre was shaking so badly he could hardly pick up his knife and fork. Though I plied him with questions, he was evasive. Where he was usually happy to weave amusing anecdotes out of any time we spent apart, on this occasion he was irritable and quiet. When I finally guessed the truth, he couldn't deny it.

"I knew I should have gone with you," I cried.

Alexandre poured himself another glass of brandy.

"It was bound to happen sooner or later," he said.

"For goodness sake," I pleaded, "tell me who has challenged you. I will put a stop to it."

Alexandre snorted with laughter. "And how would you propose to do that?"

"I would fight on your behalf if only you would let me," I cried.

Alexandre wrapped me in his arms.

"I know you would," he said. "But this is a baptism to which I must submit."

When I quizzed him about the details—the location, the choice of weapon—he became incensed.

"For goodness sake," he shouted, "leave me alone! We will talk about this in the morning."

Reaching up on tiptoes, I reluctantly kissed him goodnight. He clung to me for a moment, and then stroked my hair.

"There is nothing to worry about, I promise you," he said.

I woke at six o'clock. At seven, I sent him a message. Whilst I was waiting for a response, I gazed out of the window. It had snowed during the night, and a blanket of whiteness softened the ground. The world looked still and peaceful. A few snowflakes spiralled down, then settled upon the windowsill. At last, there was a knock at the door. I ran out into the corridor expecting Alexandre; instead his valet handed me a letter.

As I broke open the seal, I heard a commotion in the street outside. From my window, I caught a last glimpse of Alexandre's carriage. In its wake, the grubby tracks of wheels and hooves were trammelled across the virgin snow.

I scanned the letter. The hand that wrote it had obviously been shaking, and the words slanted across the page.

I am leaving to fight with pistols. At ten, it will
be over and I will run to embrace you, unless . . .

The letter fell through my fingers.

"God help him," I cried.

I raced back and forth across Paris, hammering upon the apartment doors of everyone I could think of, but nobody could tell me where the duel was to take place. In his house on the Chausee d'Antin, Dumas shook his head.

"For pity's sake," I pleaded.

"These matters must take their natural course," he said.

"At least tell me the name of his opponent."

When I steadfastly refused to leave, Dumas admitted that the duel was between Alexandre and Beauvallon, the drama critic of *La Globe*. That night, at the Trois Frères Provençaux, the two men had pitted their antagonism into a game of lansquenet. In the early hours, they argued over a gambling debt. Beauvallon, who was known to be a superb shot, had issued a challenge.

"My God," I cried. "Alexandre is lost."

At 39, rue Lafitte, I read the letter over and over again. When the church bells struck ten, the hour the duel was to take place, I clasped my heart. Ten became eleven, then twelve. There was still no word. I ceaselessly paced the floor. I could almost see the two men turning to face each other. One man raising his pistol, then the other. One standing motionless, the other crumpling to the ground. I could imagine it all too clearly. I covered my ears and clenched my eyes shut.

At half past twelve, I heard horses in the rue Lafitte. As the carriage drew into the courtyard, I flew down the stairs and pulled open the door. Alexandre's limp body slumped into my arms, his coat wet with melted snow. At the sight of his mangled face, I began to wail. Blood trickled from his mouth. The bullet had entered his cheek, leaving a ragged bloody hole. As I rested my forehead against his, I could feel the cold seeping out of him. His friends had to wrench the body away.

I stood in the middle of the courtyard, my arms held out hopelessly in front of me. Blood smeared the front of my pale blue morning dress. Tears streamed down my cheeks.

"The one man I truly loved," I wept.

I allowed myself to be taken upstairs, but when my maid tried to persuade me to undress, I clung to the bloodied gown. When I began to tear at my clothes, she summoned the doctor. After a large dose of laudanum, I collapsed in an oblivious heap on the floor. Less than an hour later, two officers of the king began a formal investigation into Dujarier's murder.

"He's dead, he's dead," I wept.

At the funeral, in the church of Notre Dame de la Lorette, neither Dujarier's mother nor his sisters would acknowledge me. After the service, Dumas asked me, for the sake of the family, not to attend the burial. From the church steps, I watched helplessly as four white horses drew the coffin away.

When Beauvallon was brought to trial, I was called as a witness. In the courtroom of Rouen, I shielded my face behind a black veil and shrouded myself in a black cashmere shawl, which fell from my shoulders to the floor. When I was questioned about the circumstances leading up to the duel, I cried out, "I would have taken his place!"

At this, the public gallery broke into nervous laughter, which rapidly fell away upon the realisation that I meant exactly what I said.

I nodded towards Beauvallon.

"Had I taken aim, that gentleman would be dead," I said.

I stared at him until he looked sheepishly away. For months he had been pressurising me to sleep with him, suggesting that it was only a matter of time, but I had simply laughed at him. I hadn't told Alexandre because I was worried he might think I had invited the attention. Now because I had failed to take Beauvallon seriously, Alexandre was dead.

Beauvallon's bullet had not only killed Alexandre; it almost destroyed my career. How could I continue to dance when I was saturated in thick, glottal tears? Ten days after the funeral, it was announced that I was no longer a member of the Porte St Martin. Alexandre had left me seventeen shares at the Palais Royale, but it wasn't enough to live on. I moved into a hotel on the Boulevard des Italiens, tried to evade my creditors, and became reliant upon the kindness of a diminishing circle of friends.

Among those who turned against me was Alexandre Dumas. In his grief, he coined a new phrase, *"femme fatale"*, citing me as the true cause of the duel. My need for financial security became paramount. When an admirer offered to take me on a tour of the spa towns of Belgium, then Germany, I accepted.

On the day of my departure, I rode up to the cemetery at Montmartre. It was a fine spring morning, and the air smelt fresh and clean. Standing beside Alexandre's grave, I remembered our last evening together, his trembling hands, his fatalism, the way he'd clung to me. Barely six months had passed since our first meeting, our first tentative kiss. I remembered the first time I had woken up beside him, his head on the pillow next to me. Must everything good be snatched away, I thought? Dumas was right, my love *was* a deadly curse. On Alexandre's tombstone, I placed a single white rose. Then, with dry eyes and a brittle heart, I bade farewell to Paris.

Chapter 28

After Alexandre's death, I travelled constantly, swapping companions as often as carriages. There was no longer any need for letters of introduction. Often I didn't even need to announce myself. My black mantilla and three red camellias had become my insignia. Though I continued to call myself a dancer, I repeatedly broke contracts and cancelled appearances. I had become a hollow, scooped-out version of myself. Whenever I tried to rehearse, I felt unable to move. My heart slowed, my limbs became wooden, my fingers and toes, strange, alien appendages which refused to follow directions. How could I celebrate joy, vibrancy, life? I had tasted happiness and then lost it in a duel that should never have taken place. I could have danced a petenera bursting with grief and loss and rage, but nobody would have paid to see it.

I travelled from Ostend to Heidelberg, then Homburg. From Stuttgart, I headed down across Bavaria, with the mountainous snow-tipped Alps shimmering in the distance. As I travelled towards them, I was reminded of the Himalayas in India. Six years earlier, I had left my husband with no inkling of what lay ahead. I tried to recall myself as a young wife, but it was poor Evelyn who came vividly to life. I remembered her weeping in her drawing room, the *punkah-wallah* sending her papers flying through the air. If I had developed a taste for performance anywhere, it had been in northern India. With a row of brown faces constantly watching me, it had been easier to act out the part expected of me. At least Evelyn had been genuinely, pathetically, straightforwardly *herself*. When I tried to conjure up Mrs Eliza James, I saw only an empty shell. It was no wonder I ran away.

On my first afternoon in Munich, I strolled idly through the Innenstadt with my white lapdog Zampa. It was the beginning of October, and a sharp wind nipped at my fingers and toes. All around me, the pavements thronged with the black robes of religious orders. On every other corner, there loomed a church, a monastery or a religious school. Within minutes of leaving the Bayerischer Hof, I had attracted a hostile response. Two ladies pointedly crossed the road, a group of boys shouted obscenities, a man caught my arm, another whispered my name to his companion.

I bristled, and put a swing in my step.

"Does Munich smell any better than it looks?" I asked Zampa as she sniffed a tree, then a post. "Perhaps we should try our luck in Austria. They say Vienna is the second capital of Europe."

I heard hurried footsteps behind me.

"*Fraulein* Montez, *Fraulein* Montez!" a man breathlessly called. "Perhaps we might have a few words."

Everywhere I went, I was followed by journalists. No sooner had I arrived in a new city than a lurid version of my life would appear in print. At Beauvallon's trial, Alexandre's letter, revealing that we usually slept together, had been read to the entire court, and then widely reported in the newspapers of Europe. In reviews, my critics were either breathless or condemning. Admirers declared themselves consumed by passion, burnt by my touch, abject beneath my feet. Women avidly read about my exploits, whilst professing outrage. What on earth would happen to society, the newspaper commentators asked, if the female sex followed their impulses and did exactly as they pleased? As for me, I fed on the attention like a caterpillar gnawing through leaves.

"What is your purpose in Munich?" asked the journalist.

"To create a stir," I replied with a smile.

"Will you dance?"

"Only if the king insists upon it!"

In two suede albums, one scarlet, one aquamarine, I kept all my newspaper cuttings, regardless of whether they were blatant lies or hymns of glorious flattery. Whenever I was feeling low, I would read through them to give myself a boost, or to prepare myself for tackling the world.

The journalist sneered. "They say that Dujarier died in a vain attempt to defend your honour. How many other men have died because of you?"

Scooping up Zampa, I turned on my heels.

"Is it true your love is a deadly curse?" he shouted after me.

For the past eighteen months, I had worn nothing but black, adopting the high neck and simple sleeves of a mediaeval costume. On the day that my grief gave way to an appreciation of the dramatic and flattering qualities of mourning dress, I liked myself a little less. I had embarked upon my career in the guise of a widow, without giving it a second thought; now life seemed to be taunting me. I recalled my mother, at my father's grave, scrutinising the faces of the officers on the other side. I had travelled halfway around the world, yet I had not entirely escaped her influence. Lately, I had detected a certain brittleness in myself. My dreams began to seem foolish, my thirst for new experiences reckless. A querulous, nagging little voice urged me to be practical, to think of the future. The only way I could shake off a gathering sense of fatalism was to keep on moving to the next city, the next court theatre.

Sometimes I felt like a grotesque figure on a merry-go-round, spinning endlessly in circles. I wanted to say, "Sshh, be still, be quiet." In dreams I found myself falling through dank, gloomy basements, through bottomless chasms, into deep abandoned wells. I needed to dance again. I needed the stage, the glare of the footlights. Only in dancing was I truly myself.

As I circled Max-Josephplatz, the winged seed from a sycamore tree spiralled through the air and landed at my feet. I swooped down and picked it up. *By a simple act of chance, an immense tree may flourish*, I thought. Perhaps my luck was about to change. Perhaps the gloomy cloud above my head was about to disperse. Since leaving Paris, I had been waiting for a fresh sense of purpose or for my life to take a different course. I glanced over at the palace. Beneath the bone-white October light, the buildings glistened like a new veil over an ageing bride.

Scene Seven

MIDNIGHT BLUE VELVET

Chapter 29

I magine a perfect rose in an enclosed garden: a damask rose on the cusp of full bloom, its lush petals tinged from the palest blush to a hint of deepest carmine at the soft curl of the petal tips. A soulful youth might pass by, happy to imbibe the scent; another reach out to gently stroke the velvet petals and sigh with pleasure. A poet might eulogise, an artist paint, a musician create a symphony. Without a second thought, a merchant would snip through the thorny stem and calculate a price. Another might press the petals between the pages of a book, or distil them to extract a heady perfume. A dandy would throw the rose to a dancer on the stage, a gardener take a cutting. Determined to improve upon perfection, the assiduous collector would almost certainly graft the cutting on to another shrub in order to create a hybrid, a brand new rose.

King Ludwig I controlled almost every aspect of life in Bavaria, from the theatre programme to the colour of the garlands for *Oktoberfest*. In order to dance at the Court Theatre in Munich, I needed to secure his personal permission. In the royal chambers, my eyes swept the Italianate interior with its vast mirrors and gilded rococo embellishments, before settling upon the elderly clerk shuffling papers at an imposing central desk. I was about to enquire upon the whereabouts of the king when I noticed that the clerk was wearing a large ring imprinted with the Wittelsbach insignia. The man in the frayed and faded green housecoat *was* the king, I realised. He rose to greet me, long legs unravelling beneath the table—a surprisingly imposing figure, despite pockmarked skin and the large, disconcerting cyst in the middle of his forehead.

"I am one of the last true kings of Europe," he pronounced. "I am an autocrat. My authority is absolute, my word is the law."

I dropped into a deferential little curtsy, endeavouring to hide my confusion. I could feel my eyes widen, and I struggled to contain an irresistible little twitch in my upper lip.

"I am a Spanish dancer come to perform my native dances upon your illustrious stage," I managed.

Ludwig scrutinised me with grey appraising eyes, as if he were making a thorough and detailed inspection.

"*Encantado,*" he said.

"*Habla Español?*" I replied in astonishment.

Ludwig beamed. "*Muy bien,*" he said, signing the relevant papers. "You may dance in the intermissions. And make sure you're wearing Spanish costume."

During my first performance at the Court Theatre, I could feel Ludwig's eyes watching my every move. When I performed my bolero for him, he drank me in like a ravenous man sucking on soup. Afterwards he greeted me in loud idiosyncratic Spanish with a declaration of his passion for all things Hispanic. At the end of the evening, he asked me to pose for the court painter. Soon he was calling at the Hotel Bayerischer Hof, sometimes twice in the same day. When I began to sit for my portrait, he insisted upon accompanying me.

Every year, Ludwig commissioned a portrait of a beautiful woman; in one particularly fruitful year, he had commissioned three. His Gallery of Beauties, which was housed in the north wing of the palace, included likenesses of an English woman, a Greek, the wife of a chicken merchant and the towncrier's daughter. Ludwig intended the collection to be a monument to his intellectual and spiritual appreciation of art and feminine beauty. Whenever he heard it referred to as his harem, he bitterly resented it. That his appreciation had occasionally found physical expression, was, he insisted, entirely incidental.

In the draughty studios of the court painter, amidst neo-classical props and oil-soaked rags, I perched on a dusty red velvet sofa and warmed my hands in front of a charcoal warming pan. Across the room, the artist scowled, then wiped his hands on his apron. With one eye shut, he brandished a paintbrush in the air.

Beside me, Ludwig loudly recited one of his Spanish poems. The price of immortality, I realised, was an aching neck, a piercing headache and feet that had fallen asleep. When Ludwig had finished one poem, he turned to another. The fixed smile on my face became strained.

"Keep still," snapped the painter.

The artist's studio was a cavernous white space with curving steps leading off into obscure corners. Antiquities grappled for floorspace with driftwood and sea-smoothed stones; the heady odours of linseed and turpentine mingled with incense and burning charcoal. Propped up on every wall were canvases in various stages of development, from rough sketches to rejected paintings marked with crosses of stark black paint.

In the middle of it all, Ludwig and I gazed at each other in mutual admiration. Beneath the watchful eye of the court painter, we communicated in whispers and snatched glances. From the beginning, we spoke to each other in Spanish, evolving a heightened and emotive pidgin language that excluded everyone else.

"*Serenissimus,*" I said, using the formal address.

"Call me Luis," he insisted.

"I couldn't possibly," I replied.

He clasped my hands.

"*¿Me extrañó?*" he asked. "Did you miss me?"

My eyes twinkled with pleasure and amusement. "*Mas que peudo decir*, more than I can say," I replied.

Perhaps Ludwig was so in thrall to the ideal of beauty because his outward appearance didn't reflect his inner perception of himself. Popular cartoons depicted him with an outsized ear trumpet and the beady eyes and long snout of a ferret, yet Ludwig regarded himself as a passionate man with the heart of a poet. He felt deeply hurt by the images and kept trying to ban them. Art held out the possibility of perfection, where mere physical beauty inevitably failed him. If a painting didn't meet his exacting standards, he could simply order another.

When my own portrait was nearly finished, the artist mounted it on an easel in the middle of the Gallery of Beauties for inspection. Ludwig stared at it with rapt attention, before turning to me.

"Don't leave me," he said. "*Estancia en Munchen. Estancia con mí.*"

The artist coughed, then made his excuses.

I tried to concentrate on the incomplete canvas, but my eyes were drawn to the dozens of elaborately framed portraits lining the walls. There were women of every type—matrons, girls, sophisticated women of the world. Swarthy, buxom, ethereal, blonde, some looked esoteric, others more down to earth; one looked compliant, another distinctly malicious. I dragged my eyes back to my own portrait. From a handful of sittings, the artist had produced a masterpiece in chiaroscuro and red. In it, I emerged with a faraway look in my eyes and more sharp-chinned than I would have liked.

"*Bien?*" asked Ludwig.

"*No sé,*" I replied.

Why not stay? a little voice whispered. Since Paris, I had travelled from one court theatre to another, but without any real sense of ambition or purpose, except to keep on moving and to earn a living. Perhaps it was time for a change, but what exactly did Ludwig want from me? My eyes swept the portraits circling the gallery, and I thought of the stuffed trophies gathering dust in the officers' mess in Karnal in India.

There, the moulting heads of an Indian tiger, a bull elephant and a startled deer were probably still staring down from the mess walls with glassy, baleful eyes. Whenever I'd been obliged to meet Thomas there, I had always tried to avoid looking at them.

The portraits in Ludwig's Gallery of Beauties were certainly lined up like spoils of conquest, whether they were or not. Exactly how far did the royal prerogative stretch? How many of these women had simply submitted to Ludwig's every wish, before allowing themselves to be dismissed?

I shook my head.

"I don't know," I said.

With a wave of my hand, I outlined plans to journey onwards to Vienna, dancing at the principal cities en route.

"Which do you suggest?" I asked. "Salzburg perhaps, or Linz?"

"*Estancia,*" whispered Ludwig.

There was a marked sense of movement in the painting, I noticed, as if I were about to jump up and rush away.

At the final sitting, Ludwig burst in to the artist's studios and dropped three lavishly bound editions of his own poetry into my lap.

"*Yo te quiero,* I love you," he declared.

On the red velvet sofa, I flipped through the leather-bound volumes and weighed up my options. Ludwig was a firm believer in the power of platonic love. He was married, the father of eight children, and had recently turned sixty. I was barely twenty-six, claiming to be an ingénue twenty-one. Ludwig had begun his Gallery of Beauties before I was even born.

"I have my reputation to think of," I said.

"I love you like a father," he persisted. "Let me take care of you."

Why not stay? I could settle down for a while. Relax. Create a home for myself. Kick off my dancing shoes. Unwind.

"It will be hard to wrench myself away," I conceded.

Ludwig looked hopeful. "I've never felt like this before," he said. "The love you inspire in me is pure and sacrosanct. I feel positively reborn."

In the Gallery of Beauties, a prominent space had already been cleared for my portrait. "But you're different from all the others," Ludwig had insisted. Lined up along the walls, there were almost forty reminders, lest I forget, that I was only the latest in a long line of royal muses.

"I won't let you go," he whispered.

Stacking the three volumes of poetry in a neat pile beside me, I turned my full attention towards him.

"It's true that in the past few weeks, I have grown immensely fond of you," I said.

His voice trembled. "Without you, my heart is dead," he said.

I looked into his eyes, and then gently stroked his face.

"I would willingly give up everything for you, *cariño*," I said, "but how will I live?"

Ludwig promised me a house, a title, a coach and horses, and a guaranteed annual income. Whenever I mentioned my career, he doubled the figure. When his offer topped ten thousand florins, I had to sit on my hands and bite my lip in order to contain myself. Few members of the aristocracy could claim such wealth. If Luis kept his promise, I need never worry about money again.

Behind his easel, the court painter applied the finishing touches with deft, angry strokes.

"So you'll stay?" said Ludwig.

"We have a pact, my *Luisito,*" I replied, kissing both his cheeks.

Within three months, I was sitting in my own box at the theatre, in the circle reserved for members of the nobility. A subtle shift had taken place in my consciousness, and in my wardrobe. Seeing myself filtered through Ludwig's divinely appointed eyes, I had thrown myself wholeheartedly into my elevated new role. Much of my time was now occupied with the refurbishment of a small mansion in central Munich. Every day I pored over catalogues and architects' plans. During the production of *La Sylphide,* I gazed nostalgically at the stage. Folding my gloves neatly in my lap, I repressed a fleeting desire to kick off my shoes. By outward appearances, at least, I was now a respectable member of the Bavarian elite.

During the interval, Luis came to call on me. When I neglected to curtsy, a scandalised hush swept the auditorium. "Who does she think she is?" they whispered. "Surely she doesn't think herself equal to the king?"

Luis coughed, and then indicated that I should rise up. I barely heard what he was saying. "Which bath taps should I order? The gold set from Paris or the marble inlay from Vienna?"

When the renovations were completed, I slid the heavy iron key in the lock of No. 7, Barerstrasse. As I turned it, I paused for a delicious lingering moment, before pushing open the door. In my euphoria, I brushed any residual feelings of disquiet aside. I had never owned more than the contents of my luggage before, never mind an entire mansion.

Inside the neo-classical façade, light from the tall windows fell dramatically across each room. From the first glance, I beamed in rapt, childish pleasure. "My house, my house, my house," I whispered. The walls of the salon were decorated with murals in the Pompeian style; in the courtyard was a fountain with four dolphins; leading up to the boudoir was a staircase made entirely from crystal. If a house reflected its owner, I thought this one conjured up a beautiful princess in a courtly romance. Walking from room to room, I luxuriated in every detail. I stroked the doorknobs and ran a finger across the white marble fireplaces. Nothing had been left to chance. Rose-coloured glass had been installed in the bathroom windows. The bath, which was carved from a single block of creamy marble, was an antiquity from Rome. The mirrors were Venetian, the furniture gilded. The one detail that slightly marred the light, sensual appearance of the house were the heavy iron shutters, which looked as if they should have been cladding a fortress, not a palace.

In the drawing room, I sat beside the window, enjoying the weight of the keys in my hand. At my feet, Zampa stretched out and warmed herself in a pool of sunlight. A moment later, the air filled with broken glass. A pebble landed at my feet. Zampa began to bark.

The life of a mistress is an insecure one, dependent upon bonds of obligation, should those of desire falter. But I was not a mistress; I was a muse, a goddess, a living, breathing work of art! That evening,

I led Ludwig on a guided tour. In the salon with the Pompeian murals, I presented him with a sumptuously wrapped gift.

"Close your eyes," I said.

Luis fumbled with golden cord and folds of crimson silk and fine tissue before opening his eyes. There on the table before him stood a life-sized alabaster model of my foot. He pressed it breathlessly to his lips, covering it with kisses, from the curve of the arch, to the sole, to the toes pressing into a pillow of yellow marble.

"*Te gusta?*" I asked.

"Your foot has no equal," he declared. "It appears to be an antique ideal."

The sculpture became a paperweight on the royal desk, keeping all the important documents of state firmly in place. When I saw it there, I smiled. Without even realising it, Ludwig had begun to involve me in every decision he made.

For a brief, happy time, we inhabited a charmed world of Spanish ballads and romances. In the midst of a chilly Bavarian winter, we retreated into a land of jacaranda and bright sunlight, of long shadows and guitar serenades.

"I feel like Vesuvius!" Ludwig declared. "Everybody thought that I was burnt out, but look at me now! I have erupted into full glorious life once again. I have the vigour of a man of twenty!"

Oblivious to growing public unrest and sporadic outbreaks of rioting, we memorised lines of Spanish verse together. In the Nymphenburg Gardens, we strode through avenues of bare, leafless trees, quoting verses about grape-heavy vines and gypsy queens. When the government resigned over my naturalisation, Luis simply appointed another. *Absolute monarchy certainly has its advantages*, I thought. For the first time since leaving Paris, I began to sleep for a full eight hours every night.

With the coming of spring, green buds appeared on the trees and the sap began to rise. Despite his protestations, Ludwig found himself wanting to possess more than my affections. Vesuvius took on an alarmingly physical aspect. In a vain attempt to curb his desires, Ludwig ordered one portrait after another, so that he might possess me in the oil, if not in the flesh. When he finally broached the subject, it was in terms of artistic appreciation. Was not the nude the ancient classical ideal? Could I not offer him a glimpse of my calves, my thighs, the splendour of my breasts?

"What!" I cried. "You would expose me naked in front of the world! I know your subjects think little of me; it's clear you feel the same."

"Surely you could pose for me," he implored. "You could be an exquisite, breathing sculpture for my eyes alone."

I threw my slipper at him, and then stalled whilst I decided what to do. As long as Luis had idealised me, I had returned the favour. Now that he was making the same demands as any other man, I felt the first stirrings of loathing. As his kisses grew more fervent, I visibly cooled. I allowed him to kiss my ankle, my knee. Once when I was in the bath, I allowed him to sponge my back. Hardly acknowledging it to myself, I granted fleeting favours, leaving him in a state of agitated arousal, which he was forced to satisfy alone.

Two days after the queen had departed for the summer, Ludwig pressed for consummation. Having made every excuse, I could not think of another. I took a deep breath, and then led him towards the crystal staircase. The steps sparkled in the lamplight. From every surface, myriad reflections bounced off the mirrors and the walls. It was like ascending a staircase of shimmering light. I looked at Luis's crumpled face, his rheumy eyes, his mottled hands. Then, with a wistful sigh, I climbed the last few stairs. In my dressing room, I slowly divested myself of my clothes, goosepimples springing up on my arms and chest. After pulling on a chaste nightgown of broderie anglaise, I joined Ludwig on the bed. Lying back against the pillows, I closed my eyes. The coupling was brief and incomplete, Ludwig fumbling and apologetic. I thought of Alexandre and wanted to weep. Afterwards, I reassured Ludwig of my affections, then fell promptly into a feigned sleep. The king was a connoisseur, I thought bitterly. He had acquired me, as he might a pedigree horse, or a rare antiquarian book. I had been the worst kind of fool. I had tried to play him at his own game, and lost.

It had taken a mere six months for Ludwig's lofty ideal of platonic love to so messily implode. But I was not a painting, or an orchid or a rose. He might have gained access to my bedroom, but he couldn't possess my thoughts. He had upped the stakes, that was all.

Chapter 30

At the top of the central staircase, at the far end of the corridor and accessible through a small unprepossessing door, was a modest cocoon of a room, decorated in shades of buttermilk and ivory. My bedchamber was the one place in the house that I had designed for nobody but myself. I could close the door upon the world and forget about pleasing Ludwig, or winning the acceptance of his subjects, or worrying about what the future might hold. I could relax and unwind and loosen my clothes. It was an essentially private place for me alone. The walls were hung with alabaster silk, and the drapes were a creamy watered taffeta. From the windows, the light filtered in through layers of gauzy fabric trimmed with Sicilian lace. Unlike all the other rooms, this one contained no mirrors and very little in the way of furniture. The small double bed was carved with roses and scrolls and birds, just like my little bed in India, and the milky-white coverlet was of an Indian design, embroidered with threads of gold. In the corner stood a small rosewood desk, which housed writing paper, a handful of old love letters and a set of journals covered in remnants of my favourite dresses. Often I would retreat with Zampa curled up beside me on the bed and read a novel or, if I were in the mood, write the occasional letter to Sophia or fill in a page or two of my most recent journal.

Whilst Ludwig continued to bombard me with erotic love poetry, an accumulating sense of fatalism pressed down on my head. Vesuvius awakened was not so easily subdued. As Luis's demands grew, I retreated further into the house. But no matter how deeply I recoiled, he followed me. No matter how many tawdry compromises I made, he wanted more. Once he had climbed the crystal staircase, there was nowhere left for me to be completely alone. Sometimes I felt as if my life was slipping between my fingers; small items seemed to go missing, objects weren't where I left them, trinkets were misplaced. More than once, it crossed my mind that one of the servants might even be stealing from me.

Barely a month after sleeping with Ludwig, my beautiful bedroom had been reduced to little more than a sanatorium, reeking of foul breath and the stench of sickness. I lay there between damp sheets, helpless as an infant, every inch of my skin coated in a thick, sticky layer of sweat; the table next to the bed was littered with blue medicine bottles and sopping towels.

At moments of crisis, the malaria I had first contracted in India had a tendency to recur. First, Sita appeared beside me, and then Jaswinder came, mopping my brow and chastising me. "I'm so sorry," I cried, "but what else could I do?" There she was, standing beside the bed, an expression of disappointment and resignation on her regal oval face. I lay back against the pillows and sighed. At the foot of the bed, Zampa barked at me in frustration and confusion. Between the curtains, I glimpsed a bright summer sky. July came, and then went. *What have I done*, I thought. *What have I become?*

Everywhere I looked I saw the imprint of Ludwig; every surface seemed soiled by his touch. As soon as I had recuperated, I was determined to redecorate, if I had to strip the alabaster silk from the walls myself. A recurring memory of Ludwig's face, straining over me, remained etched in my mind. Every dint and dimple on every surface recalled his touch. I could see traces of his footprints everywhere. I might as well turn it into a tart's boudoir, I thought bitterly. I could decorate it with gaudy scarlet wallpaper and lots of gilded mirrors. *Damn him*, I thought, *and damn myself.* Every day I asked my maidservant Susanne to change the bed linen in the hope the memory of that night might fade.

Every morning Ludwig called, but I sent him away. Susanne delivered his anxious little notes and his outpourings of poetry, but I refused to look at them. The fact that he would give me whatever I asked for merely emphasised my feelings of hopelessness. I should go away, I thought, but where to? London, Paris, Berlin? Every option was the scene of some scandal or disgrace. I had promised myself that I would never retrace my footsteps, but where else was there for me to go? The thought of being trapped for ever in Munich filled me with dread and panic. Though I was richer than I had ever been, my dissatisfaction deepened.

The moment I made any signs of recovery, Ludwig appeared beside me eager as a puppy. If I didn't physically prevent him, he would follow me into my dressing room or the bathroom. In an attempt to keep him at arm's length, or at least out of my bedroom, I pleaded the delicacy of my health. When that didn't work, I cited the long-term debilitating effects of malaria, a fear of pregnancy, the possibly injurious effects of any vigorous activity.

"Don't make me speak of such things," I pleaded, as I rifled through racks of shoes.

"My precious Lolita," said Ludwig, "you must tell me everything."

In his methodical way, he began to keep a chart of my menstrual cycle and then to employ a specialist to build up my strength with diet and herbs.

One evening, after a dinner engagement, he came up to my dressing room, and I didn't have the heart to ask him to leave and then to watch his face droop with disappointment. I was sitting at the mirror, returning my jewellery to its casket. Without thinking, I kicked off my shoes, which were of blue brocade lined with golden yellow satin. Ludwig's eyes widened and his cheeks turned pink. I watched with curiosity as he stared at my stockinged feet. I was about to giggle, then tickle his nose with my toe, when I felt the intensity of his gaze. After years of dancing, my feet were well-formed and muscular, almost masculine. I flexed the arches of my feet and wiggled my toes. Though I no longer danced, my feet retained their suppleness, but they were neither pretty nor feminine. The tension in my dressing room thickened into a murky soup. My eyes locked on Ludwig's face; his eyes remained glued to my feet. A tantalising idea began to take shape in my mind: such an attachment would certainly provide a means of keeping Ludwig at a distance. I lifted up my petticoats and began to unroll my stockings, but my fingers became as clumsy and unwieldy as twigs. I closed my eyes, in order to focus all my attention on the task at hand. When I had completely removed my stockings, Ludwig fell in front of me, flicking his tongue joyously between my toes.

I squirmed beneath his attentions and tried to keep a clear head. "Have you no dignity at all?" I wanted to scream. "How can you claim to be a divinely appointed king, and yet worship at my feet? Doesn't that make you an idolater, at the very least?"

Resting the ball of one foot firmly against his chest, I pushed. Ludwig stumbled backwards, and I caught him in my arms to soften his fall.

"Oops," I murmured.

Ludwig looked hurt and confused.

I giggled, folding my arms around him and kissing his cheek. "Is my dear old Luis really so insatiable?" I asked, with the gentlest of smiles. "The pressures of monarchy must weigh heavily. But when we're alone together, why shouldn't you unburden yourself? Your secrets are safe with me."

Having debased himself so thoroughly, Ludwig seemed to bask in his own degradation as if he had discovered a strange kind of freedom. It startled me, the depths to which he would sink. Whenever we were separated, he got into the habit of giving me two pieces of flannel to wear next to my skin.

"You know where," he said.

Later, when I handed him the moistened cloths, he pressed his nose into them in ecstasy. I began to spray the material with musk or civet. Ludwig didn't register the difference. Cynicism thickened around my heart like scar tissue. Why couldn't he just love me in the pure platonic fashion he had promised me? Why did he have to reduce any semblance of friendship to this sordid exchange of soiled cloths and groping sticky fingers? Why couldn't he behave with the dignity befitting a king?

Hardly had I recovered from one bout of malaria, than I was afflicted with another. In rare moments of lucidity, I recognised that I had built my empire on shifting sands. Every act of intimacy felt like a small betrayal; each tawdry exchange made my skin crawl. In a dream, the glimmering salivous trails of snails were marked across my belly and my breasts. All that I thought was pure was corrupt. On my sickbed, I was filled with horror and disgust.

Snatches of conversation with Ellen, my maid in London, kept coming back to haunt me. I remembered one altercation, at a time when I hovered between success or ruin.

"All women have a price," Ellen had insisted.

"You sound just like my mother," I had protested.

I spent much of that second winter in Bavaria confined to my room. Whilst the city was knee-deep in snow, my temperature soared. In the midst of my fever, I hallucinated that Ludwig had opened my ribs like a cupboard and found an empty cavity where my heart should have been. In a nightmare, I was in India again, eloping with George, only to find him transformed into Thomas, the husband I had been trying to escape from.

One morning I woke from a particularly virulent bout to discover a half-written letter lying on the bed beside me. I glanced at it with genuine puzzlement. The handwriting was shaky, and much of it was crossed out and then rewritten, but it was immediately recognisable. The many hours I had spent labouring over it, at the insistence of the Misses Aldridge, had produced a delicately looped and flowing feminine hand. It was unmistakably mine.

The letter, which I had no memory of writing, was addressed to my mother, and contained many corrections and crossings out. I tried to read it, but found it difficult to extract any sense from it. I had to reread it again and again.

~~My dearest Mama,~~

~~My dear Mrs Craigie,~~

Dear Mrs Craigie,

Some time ~~almost five years~~ has passed since we were last in contact. We did not part on the best of terms, I know, and I am sure that you had reason to be angry with me, but we are both alone now, with no kin but each other, it seems a shame not to reach out to each other ~~in some small way~~. Perhaps we might make some attempt at friendship. ~~I miss you.~~ You are my mother after all. When I left Thomas, how could I have possibly known what the future might hold? Once the genie was unleashed, my life developed a momentum of its own. ~~Am I really so bad.~~ The papers make up stories. Can't you find it in your heart to forgive me? ~~It's not my fault~~. Surely we are not entirely unalike? You once owned a hat with a tiny sailing ship on top, don't you remember? And another piled high with exotic fruit. Don't you recognise the tiniest part of me within yourself. ~~You were obviously an ambitious woman. You cannot deny that I get my nimble feet from you.~~ Can it really be true, that you would prefer me to be dead, rather than acknowledge me? ~~What do you want from me?~~ An apology? ~~It's too late for respectability.~~ Isn't there anything I can do? Spare me a thought. Just a few lines perhaps. A few words.

The letter was unfinished, the words trailing off on the last page, as if even I in my fevered state realised their futility. As my eyes scanned the pages, I could almost hear its pleading tone mocking me. My God, did I have so little pride? Tears prickled my eyes. I crumpled the letter into a tight ball in my fist, and then sank back against the pillows in exhaustion.

I was loth to admit it, but my thoughts had begun to return to my mother more often of late. Whenever I found myself ruminating upon our relationship, I pushed my thoughts away. In dreams I sometimes sought her out, only to find myself looking into an ornate and beautiful mirror that reflected nothing back. I caught myself clinging to little snippets of possibility. If only I had reached out to her, touched her shoulder; if only I had pleaded with her one last time . . .

I smoothed out the crumpled letter and stared at the words until my eyes were blinded with tears. Deep inside my chest, my feelings of hurt and rejection tightened into a small aching coil. If only she had allowed herself to love me a little, perhaps my life might have turned out very differently.

Catching the sentimental flow of my thoughts, I pulled myself up short. On the few occasions that I had really needed her affection, she had always backed away. She would despise any weakness as much as I did. I remembered the words she had written when I asked for her help after my marriage to Thomas. *You have made your bed, now you must lie in it,* she wrote. *If you discover it is made of thorns, not roses, it is nobody's fault but your own.*

I shook my head and picked up the letter. Then, with great care and deliberation, I ripped it into a thousand pieces. As the fragments scattered across the bedspread like so much cheap confetti, I resolved never to think about contacting my mother again.

Within half an hour, I had rewritten the entire letter from memory. Perhaps I will send it, I thought hesitantly. What harm can it do? A fresh feeling of hope rose in me. You never know, I thought. Perhaps we might conduct a distant but friendly correspondence. There is no point in being unrealistic. I cannot expect any more than that.

I emerged from my sickbed a month later, considerably weakened. The bouts of chills, then fever had left me as wrung out as the sheets that soaked up my sweat. My bones ached; I looked drawn. Whenever I spent any time by myself, I sank into brooding and melancholy. Often I was overcome by a blind, seething rage. Most of all, I hated Ludwig for thinking he could buy me, and myself for naming a price. *As always, my mother was right*, I thought. *I have made my bed in Bavaria, now I must lie in it.* When I was seventeen, she had tried to marry me off to an old man. I had run halfway around the world to avoid that, only to find myself in exactly the same position. Only this time I was allowing myself to be mauled without even the security of marriage. How my mother would relish the irony of it all! I could imagine a small bitter smile of triumph briefly lighting up her neat little face. Perhaps I was truly her daughter after all. Somehow I would learn how to contain Ludwig's demands. In the meantime, I needed to consolidate my interests and secure my position. I needed to be practical. *I need to think of the future*, I thought.

Chapter 31

Deep within the labyrinthine corridors of the palace, a secluded courtyard opened out on to a glasshouse, which housed Ludwig's prized orchid collection. We often spent the afternoons there, lounging idly on a striped brocade sofa amidst the cactus plants and the palms and the delicate quivering fronds. When Ludwig was preoccupied with governmental matters, he tended to his root and flower stock, and I would watch him check the moisture levels or sprinkle seeds around a mother plant. There was a rare violet and magenta orchid from Sumatra with a tiny internal callus in the shape of a human skull, a pure white hybrid from east Africa, and an exotic flame-orange specimen with frilled variegated petals and long curling sepals in imitation of an exotic Asiatic butterfly.

Whenever Ludwig focused his full attention in my direction, I was inclined to indulge him, as long as his passion remained on a higher plane. At the slightest signs of more physical ardour, I switched tactics. An ageing man, no matter how powerful, is deeply vulnerable. I could see it in his eyes.

"How much do you love me?" I teased him, whilst nibbling his ears and licking his nose.

Brushing my breast against his arms, I picked imaginary fluff from his shoulders. If his embraces grew too urgent, I had only to mention politics for him to recoil. Once he pushed me so hard, I almost fell off the sofa. For split seconds at a time, I was convinced that I could persuade him to do whatever I chose. For some reason, the unfortunate incident in Berlin regularly crossed my mind. I could almost see my beautiful rawhide horsewhip unfurling through the air. In my little reveries, the tip of the lash curled around Ludwig's ankle, bringing him down to his knees with a heavy thud, directly in front of me.

"How much do you love me?" I teased.

When the newspapers began calling me the most powerful woman in Bavaria, Ludwig instituted a nationwide censorship programme. Often, the newspapers appeared with large sections blocked out with black ink, and the police scoured the streets at dawn pulling down any newly erected posters. Though the majority of Bavarian society remained staunchly Catholic and conservative, a significant minority were rallying for change. As my influence over the king became known, a steady procession of radicals and students began calling upon me, some asking for favours, others whispering conspiracies. In Ireland, India and occupied Poland, the most heated discussions had always revolved around the mechanics of power; in Paris, liberalism and democracy were hotly debated; yet in Bavaria, church and state were still linked in an almost mediaeval system. For twenty-one years, Ludwig had ruled unchallenged. The temptation to meddle was irresistible.

During our afternoon liaisons, I began to make a few minor suggestions. If the church had less of a stranglehold over the government, I reasoned, it might make me more acceptable to the people of Bavaria. Ludwig endeavoured to ignore me by spraying his orchids and trimming back withered roots. When he was ruminating over possible appointments to the new government, I pulled out my own list of candidates.

"There are those who question the divine rights of the monarchy," I meekly suggested.

Ludwig tightened his grip on his magnifying glass and moved determinedly on to an amber and violet speckled slipper orchid from Brazil.

His eyes narrowed. "That's treason," he said.

He continued to inspect the flower's internal curlicue structure, his hand visibly shaking.

I leaned back against the sofa.

"Perhaps you should introduce a Napoleonic code," I teased.

Ludwig slammed the magnifying glass down, and the orchid head quivered on its slender stem.

"Never in Bavaria!"

I giggled. "Allow the common people a vote?"

Ludwig turned to me, his face trembling. "A woman cannot be expected to understand these things," he said. "I refuse to discuss the matter any further. Now if you don't mind, I need to attend to my orchids."

I jumped up and ruffled his hair. "Poor thing," I said, with a playful little pout. "You know I'm only toying with you."

For my twenty-seventh birthday, Ludwig presented me with a title, and I became formally known as Marie, Countess of Landsfeld. For my own protection, I began to appear with two liveried lackeys, in the manner of the queen or the crown princess. If any noble ladies refused to acknowledge me, I greeted them with a few choice phrases in colloquial French.

As the year was drawing to a close, an unexpected visitor called at the house. When Susanne showed me her card, I could hardly believe that it might really be her. I ran into the hallway to greet her, and we warmly embraced. Stepping back for a moment, we both examined the other, then grinned.

"I am so pleased to see you," I said, leading her into the drawing room.

Once we had settled down, I felt suddenly self-conscious. "I suppose you've come to gawp at me," I said.

The new Duchess of Devonshire fixed her grey eyes on me, so that I wouldn't doubt the sincerity of her words. "I told nobody that I was coming to see you, not even my husband. And I will tell nobody when I return to London. I promise I haven't come to fuel the gossips."

Sophia's new rise in status clearly suited her; I sensed that nothing I said could possibly faze her. Though her relationship with Charles, the Duke of Argyll, had fizzled out soon after they left Paris, she had very quickly attracted a new admirer. She had only been married for a month or so, but she already emanated a more solid and commanding presence. An air of confidence and prosperity softened the slightly jagged sense of sleek sophistication that I remembered. In a sumptuous taupe alpaca costume with a matching cape and velvet-trimmed hat, my old school friend managed to look both chic and eminently respectable. She was undertaking a grand tour of Europe with her new husband, she said, and she had decided to call on me *en route* to Vienna.

"So we have both done very well," I said.

She smiled. "I heard that you are now a countess," she said.

I grinned back. "Even in that you've trumped me," I said. "Is a German countess obliged to curtsy to an English duchess? I really can't remember."

"My dear Rosana," she said, suddenly looking serious. "I can call you that?"

I nodded.

"I had to come and see you. The newspapers print such stories, and I was a little worried about you."

"Worried?" I said.

"You must know you're playing a very dangerous game."

"I would have thought you would approve."

"You don't seem to understand. Your life could be at risk. All over Europe, the situation is very volatile. The people could rise up."

I scoffed. "Don't be so dramatic," I said. "I have the love and protection of the king. Look around you. What more could I possibly need?"

"What about happiness?"

"Happiness!" I could hear my voice crack. "I can't believe you said that!"

"You know what I mean," she persisted.

"I tried happiness, remember? In fact, I tried it more than once. The first time robbed me of any possibility of a normal, respectable

258

life. The second ended in a duel in Paris. You probably read about it in the newspapers."

Sophia nodded. "I was very sorry to hear about Alexandre's death. You did seem so blissfully contented with each other."

"So you finally got yourself a husband," I said quietly.

"The dear duke wanted to keep me all to himself," she said with a complacent little smile.

"I am very pleased for you. I am really. But that kind of life was never for me. When I was living with Alexandre in Paris, I did sometimes fantasise that we might one day marry, but it was just a silly dream. I think I always knew that really."

Sophia hesitated. "I do wish you would listen to me," she said. "Europe is not as safe as you seem to think. You only have to look at what is happening in some of the smaller principalities."

I rang the bell to summon Susanne.

"Please, can we change the subject?" I asked.

We spent a stilted hour together, the chink of china cups echoing in the silence between us, until Sophia took her leave. At the drawing room door, she turned back and looked at me one last time. "Be careful," she entreated me.

"There really is no need to worry about me," I assured her, but I couldn't quite summon up a corresponding smile. On the doorstep, I found myself clinging to her for slightly too long. Back in the drawing room, I listened to the sound of carriage wheels over cobbles. All of a sudden, I felt intensely irritated. Sophia might have become a duchess by marriage, but that really didn't give her the right to patronise me. Why did she have to come here with her solicitous questions, spreading doubt and uncertainty?

On New Year's Eve, rather than simply wait for Ludwig to slip away from the family celebrations at the palace, I decided to host a lavish party. Amidst swathes of tartan and wreaths of holly and mistletoe, I toasted in the coming year with a handful of infatuated young students. Following a dinner of glazed duck, we retreated to the drawing room. When they began to tease me about my dancing career, I looked around at their eager young faces and kicked off my shoes.

In a burst of exuberance, I demonstrated a fandango in its authentic form. The power of the dance coursed through me, the frustrations of the past year animating my every step. When I tossed my head, my hair tumbled down my back. I gathered up my skirts. My fingers became hummingbirds, and then exotic flowers unfurling in halos around my head. I closed my eyes. For a few precious moments, I was in a gypsy cave in Spain, the future still a rosy dream. Once more, I grew dizzy with the sound of applause.

Amidst a raucous clamour of stamping and cheering, the students hoisted me on to their shoulders and paraded me around the drawing room and straight into the crystal chandelier in the middle of the ceiling. The next thing I knew, I was sprawled across the floor with a splitting headache and blood trickling from a cut in my forehead. In the story that spread rapidly through the city, I was dishevelled and the students were *sans* trousers.

The following week, I appeared at the theatre in a new gown of midnight-blue velvet that offset to perfection the bright new diamonds I was wearing. The heavy jewellery circled my wrists and throat and nestled in my hair. With the slightest movement, I sent off shards of light. As I sat down in my box, a ripple of disapproval swept through the auditorium.

After two years in Munich, I felt like a bird in a jewelled and gilded cage. Everywhere I went, I was gawped at and taunted. I was aware of every look, every slight. *When passion is at its height, collect jewels.* Ellen's irritating little maxims kept popping into my head. I remembered my first sight of the high-class courtesans at the Italian Opera House in Covent Garden. How worldly they had seemed, how impervious to snubs and slights.

From my plush velvet-upholstered box in the upper circle, I surveyed the upturned murmuring faces of the audience. I knew perfectly well what was being said. I was the whore of Babylon brought into their midst. I was the witch who had enchanted their beloved king. The New Year celebrations at my house *had* grown a little boisterous, it was true, but the subsequent stories had been blown out of all proportion. Nobody was paying any attention to the production of *The Enchanted Prince* that was being enacted on the stage. I shrugged and glanced over at the royal box. Even I had to admit that my chances of being accepted at court were completely ruined. I fingered the diamonds circling my throat. Luis, at least, had not forsaken me. The gold and silver settings were from Paris, the large faceted diamonds from India.

As I turned my neck, I could feel the weight of the diamonds pressing down on my head. Whilst the audience whispered about the small fortune the king must have spent, I tried to repress a smile. In the royal box, next to the queen, Ludwig struggled to retain his composure.

For that one perfect evening, I felt omnipotent, untouchable. As I surveyed the upturned faces of the audience beneath me, laughter bubbled up in my throat. If the Archbishop of Munich wished to honour me with the title of the goddess of love, I would embrace it. "There is no longer a Virgin Mary in Munich; Venus has taken her place." I remember preening myself, his words spinning around my head like a halo. Every eye in the theatre was focused in my direction, every thought, every whispered exchange revolved around me. "If your divinely appointed king worships at my feet, what does that make me?" I whispered. Let the old order come crashing down; let the conspiracy of kings crumble; let the privileges of title be stripped bare and exposed!

In my mind's eye, the evening was already captured for eternity. I was an image rolling off the presses and appearing in every newspaper in Europe. I was a best-selling reproduction sold at newsstands throughout the land. I was a picture on a magic lantern slide, my silhouette projected into the gloom of a hundred grubby music halls. I was a shimmering spectacle in a metropolitan panorama, a luminous, perpetual mirage fluttering endlessly in the darkness. I was a masterpiece in the style of the French romantic painter,

Eugene Delacroix; a life-size, full-length portrait rendered into glowing, vibrant life in oil and tempera and linseed. In a hundred years' time, I would adorn the walls of a private salon, the midnight-blue of my gown smouldering against velvet upholstery the colour of deepest claret. With an immense chandelier of flickering candle-light behind me, my face and neck and throat appear smooth and pale as alabaster, and each diamond sparkle into a thousand tiny lights. An evening stretches into a lifetime, a fleeting second into perpetuity. No matter what happened next, no matter where I went, I would replay that moment over and over again.

End of Act I

Interlude

With the coming of spring, the first intimations of revolution had already begun to reverberate across Europe. In every city, in every town, the whispering grew louder. Across Bavaria, plots thickened and tempers flared. In coffee houses and bierkellers, arguments became volatile. A raised voice provoked a scuffle; a simmering undercurrent of discontent erupted into looting and arson.

ACT II

Scene Eight

INDIGO CASHMERE

(Skirts ripped and torn, blood-splattered
and caked in mud and manure)

Chapter 32

On a stark and wintry morning in 1848, an altercation in the bazaar began to attract a crowd. It was the beginning of February, and the temperature had dipped to minus five. On the other side of the city, at the rear of a palatial mansion in Barerstrasse, a voluminous cloud of condensation issued from a kitchen door, and a temperamental white Pomeranian named Zampa slipped outside.

At the front of the house, in a drawing room hung with green watered silk from Paris, a woman was clipping articles from a diminishing pile of newspapers. In an ashtray beside her, the tip of a black cigarillo smouldered. By her feet lay the gutted and discarded pages of a month's supply of newspapers from London, Paris and Berlin.

From far away, beyond the tall windows with their metal grilles, beyond the wrought iron gates and the two uniformed bodyguards, beyond the sweep of Barerstrasse with its swathe of poplar trees, drifted the barely audible sound of a distant crowd.

As I picked up the cigarillo, I felt suddenly self-conscious. For a moment there, I had been imagining myself as a character in a play. It was becoming a little too easy to drift into make-believe, to confuse fantasy with reality, to believe the stories the newspapers printed.

I contemplated the pile of cuttings in my lap.

"Now who shall I be today?" I mused.

In the vast expanse of Venetian mirror above the fireplace, I caught sight of my reflection. Tangled wisps of black-brown hair and expressive, almost masculine eyebrows framed a face that looked pale, almost peaky. If the crowds outside burst in now, they would be sorely disappointed, I thought. Dark clouds scudded across the surface of the mirror, and as my reflection fell into shadow, I recalled a young woman with swollen eyes and bruises beneath my clothes. My mother's voice resounded inside my head: "Well, what exactly did you expect?" she whispered. In the mirror, Lola, or Eliza or Marie jolted backwards as if she'd been slapped.

"I am Marie, Countess von Landsfeld, and don't you forget it," I snapped, but my words echoed mockingly back at me as I spoke.

I opened a scarlet cuttings album on to a virgin page and reached for a nearby pot of glue. All morning, I had been determined to ignore the noise outside, but it had grown steadily louder, wheedling its way into my consciousness and jangling my nerves. Ludwig may have lavished me with wealth and a title, but he couldn't dissipate the animosity towards me that was sweeping the city. For more than three days, I had been unable to leave the house. I was trying to concentrate on pasting up my latest batch of cuttings when Susanne burst into the room.

"*Es der hund!*" she cried. "Zampa's run off again! *Ach nein,* Madame! You can't go out there. *Bitte,* I beg of you."

Chapter 33

I had always embraced change, electrical storms, a forest fire sweeping all before it, yet when the end came, it caught me off guard. At the very point that I was attempting to reconcile myself to flawed reality, the entire fragile edifice came tumbling down around my ears. Within a week, the balance had swung a hundred and eighty degrees. One day, I was gazing down from my velvet-lined box in the theatre: the next, I lay helpless beneath the thrashing hands and feet of a murderous crowd.

I *knew* that I shouldn't have gone outside. Susanne had pleaded with me not to go. But the moment I heard that Zampa was missing, I felt compelled to find her. Zampa was a white Pomeranian with a diamanté collar and my name stamped into a silver tag around her throat; I couldn't leave her out there on her own. For over a week, there had been outbreaks of rioting all over the city. All that morning, an angry rumble had echoed in the distance. As the commotion grew louder, I feared what might happen to my little dog if the crowd got hold of her. The mood outside was ugly. I could hear it in the low ominous bellowing and the outbursts of chanting.

I opened my eyes with a start, arms in the air, palms curled into fists ready to fend off an assault. My eyes flicked about in nervous confusion. There were ashes smouldering in the grate, an ivory hair-comb lying discarded on the floor. When I registered that I was in the drawing room, I fell back against the chaise in relief and exhaustion. Susanne was splashing my face with lavender water. The back

267

of my head throbbed with the dull insistence of metal against wood. When I tried to move, it felt heavy as weighted lead. My ears were ringing. Hadn't I been outside? In Barerstrasse? Looking for something? A wave of panic broke over me. My skin grew clammy with sweat. I couldn't breathe.

I had been searching for Zampa. Running through the streets, calling her, calling her, my heart beating so fast, I could feel it throbbing in my ears and filling my throat.

"Zampa?" I whispered.

I felt a wet rasping tongue on my cheek. Zampa, apparently unscathed, sat up eagerly on the chaise beside me, her ears cocked, her tail wagging, her silky white coat sleek and clean. As I scooped her up in my arms, I caught a glimpse of a filthy and pathetic creature in the mantelpiece mirror, her clothes in shreds, her bare feet smeared with dirt.

I was about to demand an explanation when I saw her eyes widen with horror and disgust. "What the hell do you think you're looking at?" I wanted to scream, before the truth dawned on me. I swallowed hard and fought back the impulse to weep. I looked like some pitiful wretch who survived on scraps. A scavenger, a beggar, somebody decent people would go out of their way to avoid. My hair was a tangled mess of muck and straw. My dress was ripped and caked in manure, one sleeve torn at the shoulder, the other missing altogether. The tattered remnants of my petticoats were black with grime. A bruise was coming up on my cheek. What had happened to my shoes, my stockings, my beautiful cashmere shawl?

In brief nightmarish flashes, it all started coming back to me. There was a horse rearing up, a sea of grasping hands, blows raining down, fists, teeth, a mounted gendarme beating a path through the crowd. Waves of terror crashed down over me. I could hear shouting, and scuffles breaking out in the *strasse* beyond the house.

My eyes darted around the room seeking out intruders. I could hardly breathe. My chest heaved. I gasped at the air. The windows rattled with the impact of a huge mass of people. The sound of chaos permeated the house, yet the drawing room displayed a still, almost timeless orderliness. Everything was as it should be. Nothing was out of place. There was Susanne hovering uneasily by the door, and Ludwig's face slipping in and out of focus beside me. Susanne kept wringing her hands in her apron: I could feel the agitation emanating from her like static.

Ludwig clasped my hands, his lips moving rapidly. He was trembling and gulping at the air like a fish on a dried-up riverbed. The lines on his face were more deeply etched than I remembered, and he looked drained and pale, as if his skin might be cold to the touch. He repeated the same sound once, twice.

"My God, they could have killed you," he cried.

He kept babbling about republican plots, about ministers undermining his authority, but I hardly registered what he was trying to say. I felt his fingers pressing into the flesh of my arm, noticed his eyes anxiously scanning my face. *Why don't they all just go away*, I thought. *Why can't they leave me alone?* I folded my arms around Zampa, buried my face in her coat, and allowed her to lick my nose. I closed my eyes and listened to the sound of her little heart beating. If I concentrated hard enough, perhaps I might be able to make Ludwig and his incessant prattling fade away.

After a fitful night's sleep, I woke to the caterwauls of the crowd reverberating throughout the house, as if some gargantuan beast was prowling about outside. There was no fire in the grate, and the curtains were still closed. When I rang the bell, nobody answered. I called out into the empty hallway, but there was no response. I had a chill, eerie sense of being alone and drifting in the world. As I pulled on a robe, every muscle in my body screamed out in protest. Walking through the deserted corridors of the house, I felt like a spectre roaming an empty ship. Though all the windows were locked and most of the curtains drawn, a collective howl penetrated the house and resounded along the hallways. Zampa ran from room to room, wagging her tail and barking. Bands of tension tightened around my chest and throat. I peered out of an upstairs window, and then promised myself I wouldn't do so again. The entire *strasse* seemed to be filled with a seething mass of people. Despite the cordon of armed police surrounding the house, the crowd was pressing nearer.

In the drawing room, I found a note from Ludwig regretting that he'd had to return to the palace. When I went into the kitchen, I discovered the few remaining servants huddled around the stove. When I tried to issue orders, they simply gawped at me.

"Oh, don't trouble yourselves," I muttered, "I might as well do it myself."

Every hour or so, a messenger arrived with further news. Ludwig had dismissed both his government and all his ministers. The university had been forcibly evacuated: all students who were not permanent residents of Munich had been given forty-eight hours to leave the city. Soldiers patrolled the streets. Lines of armed police surrounded the palace.

Time stretched, then retracted. Night came, then went. The following afternoon, I was sitting in the darkness of my drawing room in a feeble puddle of amber light emanating from a single oil lamp. I didn't know how many hours I had been sitting there for, nor even how many days I had been confined to the house. My entire body ached, every muscle, every bone, even the surface of my skin felt tender and sore. Beneath my clothes, mysterious bruises adorned my arms and calves and thighs. The swelling on my cheek had subsided, and the bruising had flushed the surface of my skin a pale, translucent mauve. The last time I went to search for the servants, I had discovered that I was completely alone, the house billowing out around me into a seemingly vast and endless honeycomb of uninhabited rooms.

On the octagonal table in front of me sat a small blue glass bottle. From time to time, I picked it up, and then put it down. I could see the thick viscous liquid glinting temptingly at me through the dense ultramarine glass. I had obtained the bottle, which contained a potentially fatal dose of laudanum, in Paris after Alexandre died. It had travelled with me ever since. I had been contemplating the bottle and its contents since the early hours.

As the last slivers of afternoon light retreated into the shadows, I glanced at the glinting blue bottle. *It is only a matter of time now*, I thought. The last messenger to bring any news had burst in with blood oozing from a wound in his head. The royal family were confined to the palace. The police had lost control of the city. Thousands of people were blocking the streets. In the kitchen, the store cupboards and the pantry were bare. The only food in the house, a plate of marzipan, a leg of roast duck and a half-empty bottle of champagne, lay untouched on a tray beside me.

I reached half-heartedly for the marzipan, but when I sank my teeth into a piece of the dense, sticky sweet, a throbbing pain shot through my jaw. Placing the remains of the duck on the floor, I watched Zampa tear off splinters of the dark red meat. If the mob got hold of me, they would rip me apart with the same greedy pleasure. Tipping the bottle of champagne to my lips, I took a cautious sip. The champagne was flat and warm, its wetness sizzling against the ache in my jaw. Outside, the shouting grew wilder and something heavy thudded against the front door. I picked up the bottle of laudanum , and then pulled out the cork.

Let them break in and find me dead, I thought.

The heady aroma of laudanum mingled seductively in the air. I inhaled deeply and imagined drifting into unconsciousness. Who would miss me after all? Ludwig, my mother, Mrs Rae? For each of them, grief would undoubtedly be tempered by relief. The only two people who had truly cared for me, Alexandre and Major Craigie, were already dead. I thought of all the people who would shake their heads and say that I took my life into my own hands years ago— Thomas, George, Ellen. Liszt might raise a wry glass in my honour. Only my old school friend Sophia might shed an honest tear. Zampa barked, then pulled insistently at my skirts. Outside, the stones crashed down. I looked down at my pampered little pooch with her long silky white coat and her trusting black eyes. She had travelled with me from Paris; I couldn't abandon her now. Pressing the cork carefully back into place, I tucked the bottle into a pocket in the side of my gown, then followed Zampa up the stairs.

271

On the first floor at the front of the house overlooking the *strasse,* I opened the glass doors and stepped out on to the balcony. Gazing down at all the upturned faces, something inside me began to slide, and then crack. If I concentrated hard enough, I could transform the uproar into applause. I was a little girl dancing for Sita, my *aya* in India. I was at school with Sophia practising a waltz. I was a dancer on stage before a crowded auditorium. This is what it must feel like to be a queen surveying her people, I thought. The scene before me shimmered, and then began to drift and slip. As a wave of people surged forwards, the police pushed them back, and I felt as if I were watching a tournament or a pageant laid on solely for my benefit. I cradled the bottle of laudanum in my pocket and felt the cool glass against my palm. With my other hand, I raised my empty champagne flute in a rueful salute, and then took an ironic bow.

The crowd went berserk. The outcry was so loud it buffeted the house, knocking me backwards against the doors.

"*Raus mit* Lola! *Raus mit* Lola!" The shouts rang out. "Long live the Republic! Down with the whore!"

My fingers tightened around the bottle in my pocket, and I gazed up into the wide, blue sky. Far, far below, the people were moving about like tiny figures on a board, the rioters storming the gates and the police charging with bayonets. A line of soldiers opened fire, and the air filled with smoke and a single blast of musket fire. As I stumbled backwards into the house, the balcony doors imploded behind me in a blizzard of splintering glass. An hour later, a final message came from Ludwig pleading with me to flee the country.

The following day, I found myself curled up in the corner of a strange, pokey little room in the attic, my knees tucked beneath my chin, my heart thumping loudly against my ribs. Through the semi-darkness, I tried to identify my surroundings. There were bare floorboards, a faded quilt covering a narrow bed, Susanne's black gown and white apron hanging from a hook on the wall. For some strange reason, my lacquered fan from Cordoba lay discarded in the middle of the floor. The noise from outside was so loud, I felt as if I was caught inside the jaws of some monstrous bellowing beast. Daylight came with creeping lines of light beneath the curtains and along the bottom of the door. When I peered out of the window, I saw bullets flying, blood spurting from wounds, a girl felled by a stone. In the midst of it all, a coal merchant clambered on to the gates. When he waved a noose in the air, the crowd bawled their approval. I winced and then slid back down to the floor.

My neck was already mottled with a ring of purple and yellow bruises after the last time I ventured out. My skin felt distended and raw; the slightest touch made me flinch.

I had witnessed a hanging in Newgate once. As the thief swung from the rope, he lost control of his bladder and bowels. His tongue stuck out of his mouth, fat and swollen and black.

With one hand I gently cradled my throat, with the other I reached for my pistol, which was lying on the floor beside me. The volume of noise from outside bounced through the house like a hurricane, shaking the walls. The knot in my stomach twisted tighter. I couldn't move. Fear nibbled at my fingers and toes. My ears began to itch, then my nose. My eyes remained fixed on the door. I listened for sounds in the house: a creak of the stairs, a squeaking door, footfalls. Zampa was cowering and whimpering beneath my skirts, her eyes terrified circles of yellow-white.

One, two, three, four; one, two, three, four. Two pairs of slightly grubby, naked feet were pacing back and forth across the wooden boards: one pair of feet was big, the other small. Bridie was showing me how to toddle across the floor, ready to catch me should I fall. *One, two, three, four; one, two, three, four.* Our four bare feet padded across the floor. I needed to concentrate on every step. Bridie's big hand felt solid and warm around mine. Only the firmness of her grip was keeping me upright. If she let go of me, I would wobble, then fall. *One, two, three, four; one, two, three, four.* I kept tracing the patter of footsteps methodically back and forth.

Stories like mine always end in tragedy; any cheap novel or newspaper commentary could tell you that. I heard the sound of wooden doors splintering, and myself laughing hysterically at the madness of it all. All of a sudden, I understood what I had to do. What did I have to lose? I thought. My life, my house, my jewels? What did it matter, what did any of it really matter?

The moment I stepped outside, I gulped in the fresh crisp air. It was a bright morning, a fine mist shimmering in the first tentative rays of sunlight. In the far distance, I could see the ring of mountaintops that circled Munich. Beyond the gates, members of the nobility jostled for space with draymen and blacksmiths. Dark pools of blood stained the flagstones. In every direction, I saw a swarm of angry, shouting faces and jerking fists.

Cobbles smashed down into the courtyard. Youths began to climb over the walls.

"*Raus mit* Lola!" the chants rang out.

"Death to the Spaniard! Death to the whore!"

With my pistol in my hand, I pushed open the front doors of the house, and then climbed the marble steps around the fountain.

"Here I am. Kill me if you dare!" I shouted.

The crowd stared. I glared back.

"Go on then, do your worst," I jeered.

Before me, I saw a sea of faces twisted in jealousy and resentment and rage.

"Well, what are you waiting for?" I screamed.

One stone hurtled through the air, then another.

"Bad shot," I cried.

A stone struck my arm; another grazed the side of my face. I raised my pistol and aimed directly at the man with the noose. He was so close I could see his breath. I saw the black eyes of muskets pointed at me, fists clutching stones, the dangling noose. *This is how my life will end*, I thought. *A stone smashing into my cheek, unseen hands tugging at my skirts, a hundred trampling feet.*

I steadied my aim, and then took a last deep breath. As I released the trigger, I was suddenly thrown off course, and the bullet ricocheted into the air. I felt myself plummeting backwards into an inky blackness. I tried to break free, but I felt suffocated. I couldn't breathe. As dense shadows loomed down over me, I felt almost relieved. *It will soon be over*, I thought. *Nothing will hurt me any more*. The struggle would finally be over. Darkness enveloped me. Like a heavy and voluminous old cloak, it stifled and engulfed me.

Chapter 34

By the time I fought free of the hairy stinking black horse-blanket I had been snared up in, the decision had already been made. Two military officers had abducted me in Barerstrasse, then bundled me into a waiting carriage. As we sped through the outskirts of Munich, they handed me an envelope containing a ticket and documentation. My passage out of Bavaria had already been booked. Ludwig had almost certainly saved my life, only to succumb to pressure and banish me for ever. Why didn't he just leave me to the lynch mob and save himself the trouble? I thought. On the shores of Lake Constance, the steamship that awaited my arrival was fittingly named after him.

It was a grey and desolate day. Though it was hardly afternoon, daylight was swiftly fading. As I stepped on to the gangplank, I stared down at the icy water lapping the side of the boat. Whenever the two military officers tried to steer me by the elbow, I slapped their hands away. Halfway up, I insisted upon viewing the deportation papers again. Tears welled in my eyes. This was no terrible mistake. There at the foot of the page was Ludwig's distinctive signature. Should I doubt it for a moment, he had also enclosed a letter directing that I wait for him in Switzerland. I stared out across the lake. In the distance, I could see the icy peaks of the Swiss Alps. Rain stung my cheeks, the wind whipped up my skirts.

Despite my pleas, my lapdog, clothes and jewellery were all left behind. My only luggage was one small battered valise that had travelled with me since I was a child. It contained a single change of clothes, three of my journals, a jewelled brooch in the shape of an exotic butterfly and a ring with a red glass stone.

As the ship set off across the lake, a handful of onlookers gathered silently by the dock. The men removed their hats. A woman crossed herself. Alone in my cabin, I spread my few meagre possessions across the bunk, and then stripped off my filthy, dirt-encrusted clothes. I sat down on the edge of the bunk, naked and frightened and alone. I felt raw and forsaken and utterly exposed.

In Switzerland, I camped out between dustcovers and broken-down furniture in the semi-derelict Chateau l'Imperatrice, the former home of the Empress Josephine. A month later, my precious little Zampa was brought to me. The next week, my jewellery finally turned up at the chateau, in two armoured reinforced trunks. Locking myself in my bedroom, I checked the contents, and then donned the diamond tiara, necklace and bracelet that Ludwig had given me. As I inspected myself in the mirror, I reflected upon my situation. Ludwig continued to make all sorts of promises, but he was confined to Bavaria. The slightest rumour that he intended to visit me provoked further outbreaks of rioting.

Noticing a single wiry grey hair in my coiffure, I swiftly plucked it out. I was twenty-eight years old. Divorced. I had not danced in public for more than two years. All my costumes, my shoes, my castanets, my guitar, my sheet music remained in Munich. I had no family and considerably more enemies than friends. My house in Barerstrasse had been ransacked, and much of the furniture smashed. Outside Bavaria, I had no income, no assets, no savings, few possessions. What had happened to my treasures, my cuttings albums, my Spanish shawl, my lacquered fan? I thought of my beautiful crystal staircase, my dressing room full of gowns, my box at the theatre. *Perhaps it really had all been an illusion, a dream*, I thought. I had been offered a glimpse of opulence, only for it to be snatched away.

Peering more closely into my mirror, I no longer saw a dancer, nor the mistress of a king. Deep within my eyes, I glimpsed a small, bewildered child. Staring back at me from the looking glass was Eliza Gilbert, aged seven, sent far away from home, with a name tag pinned to her coat. I ripped the necklace from my throat. What was the point of fame, status or riches, if at heart I was still that dreadfully neglected little girl? Turning abruptly away from the glass, I threw the diamonds into my jewellery box and slammed the lid.

I remembered my last day in England, my sailing tickets for Hamburg clutched tightly in my hand; the last cautionary words of Ellen, my maid, resounding inside my head.

"Meddle with the truth at your own expense, not mine," she had said. "Believe your own lies, and I dread to think what will become of you."

Chapter 35

At the end of a back street in Munich, at the top of some winding rickety stairs above an ironmonger's store, the door to a storage room had been left slightly ajar. The room was piled high with old trunks and boxes full of rusty door handles and hinges, the air gauzy with cobwebs and thick with dust. A large fragment of broken mirror was propped up, at eye level, on a pair of wooden stepladders. Hanging in the middle of the room, from a hook in the ceiling, was an exquisitely beaded silver dance costume.

The costume was shimmering and silvery, its layered skirts falling like luminous petals from a nipped-in waist. A shroud of white muslin had been rolled back over the padded hanger, revealing a tiny bodice and diaphanous skirts. On the floorboards beneath it sat a pair of silver satin slippers, scuffed at the heel and toe. A matching waist-length white mantilla trimmed with silver lace hung from a length of silver ribbon.

In the particles of light struggling in through a tiny casement window, the glistening surface of the costume sparkled and gleamed. The slightest breeze from the doorway ruffled the shimmering silver skirts, and the bodice seemed to swell with energy and vitality. In the middle of the gloomy, dust-laden room, the costume came magically to life, as if some invisible presence had taken possession of it, as if a trace memory impregnated into the fabric had sprung unexpectedly forth. Animated by some inaudible music wafting in the breeze, the costume rippled and danced. In the flickering half-light, it undulated and languidly swayed.

Scattered across the floor were reams of censored and forbidden newspapers. In some, all references to Lola Montez had been completely blacked out; in others, the name still blazed across the headlines.

On the pavement outside the shop, Lola's maidservant Susanne looked quickly from left to right before pulling a key from her pocket and unlocking the door. At her feet was a battered old portmanteau. Before the house in Barerstrasse had been completely ransacked, she had managed to retrieve a few precious tokens.

End of Act II

Interlude

A revolution is a mysterious thing, an almost alchemical process, a quickening, a collective hysteria, a communal impulse to sweep everything before it. Imagine a whirlwind, a tornado. Overnight, a meek little seamstress can become a virago, a bone-weary coalman demand change, an under-appreciated servant girl develop ideas above her station. The wheel invariably turns. The waning moon waxes again. A dancer spins. With every turn, she stirs up the wind. With every circling gesture, she unsettles the air.

ACT III

Scene Nine
A SET OF JOURNALS BOUND IN DRESS REMNANTS

Chapter 36

*T*he *Life of Lola Montez* opened as a play at the Broadway
Theatre in Manhattan. She played herself, of course. It
was her life, after all. She conceived it and directed it.
She chose the costumes; she wrote the lines. With a click of her fingers, the drapes opened and swung back. In an instant, she became
the central actress in her own unfolding drama. Every night she re-
enacted her life all over again. The auditorium fanned out in front
of her in a dazzling sweep of veined marble and gilded baroque
flourishes. The chorus in their finery poured in from the wings. Vast
gas chandeliers cast a bluish light; candles in their sconces flickered
with a warm glow; jewellery glittered. On the opening night, more
than three thousand people stared up at the stage.

Poised centre stage, Lola could feel the anticipation building
steadily into a frenzy. She really didn't need to do anything except
remain motionless and wait. With her swirling skirts and black
mantilla, she conjured up a volatile mixture of emotion and
restraint, of primitive passions barely contained. She exuded the
unmistakable whiff of revolution, the thrill of dissent, an atmosphere charged with gunpowder and flaming torches, a new straining at the seams, a delicious hint of all sorts of previously
unimaginable possibilities.

She raised her castanets above her head and then paused. As the
staccato sound of wood against wood echoed around the theatre,
the audience let out an audible sigh, as if they had all exhaled at
exactly the same time.

On and off the American stage, in the theatre and between the pages of the newspapers, Lola was a major attraction. No longer a novelty turn within an evening of entertainment, she topped the bill. One or two dances in the interval would no longer suffice. As an actress, she could take the leading role in a play *and* open and close with a dance. It really was the best of both worlds; she could present both the countess and the dancer.

Within a fortnight of her arrival, she had dropped any pretence of a Spanish accent and thrown herself wholeheartedly into the melting pot. She even began to enjoy the sound of her own strange hybrid of a voice, though she still had a little trouble projecting it from the stage. In a land full of opportunists, there was no longer any need for authenticity. Depending on her mood, she claimed to be various combinations of Spanish, or Irish or Scots. Like thousands of immigrants before her, she grasped the opportunity to start life all over again. Why remain still, when motion changes everything? Out of chaos comes life; from stasis comes a deadening, a slow, lingering tedium. There was nothing left for her in Europe. She was insatiable for strangeness, new sights, new people, the undiscovered, the unexplored, the unknown. She lived in a dream of how life could be: always bigger, brighter, more radiant. "Reality" was a little like an unwanted inheritance, a neglected brass vase; it needed polish, it needed extra shine, it was better left behind.

In those first few days in Manhattan, she heard Irish voices everywhere: Sligo, Dublin, Wexford, Cork. In the docks, she turned at the sound of a familiar accent and saw an Irish couple selling chestnuts and toffee apples. She stepped towards them and was about to make enquiries, when she realised where she had seen them before. She recalled a wretched dark-haired couple being evicted from the Ballycrystal estate. She remembered a thin and sullen woman, barefooted and wild, who had averted her eyes. This woman stood with her hands on her ample hips and looked Lola straight in the eye. Lola smiled apologetically and moved on. On the way to the hotel, she caught a fleeting glimpse of a woman who looked uncannily like Bridie. She almost called out, but wasn't about to make the same mistake twice. As the woman drew nearer, she saw a plump smiling matron in conker-brown boots on the arm of a prosperous merchant. New York was full of this new breed, it seemed. In checked waistcoats, plaid shawls and shiny new boots, these brand-new Irish-Americans were proud and boisterous and brash.

Everything was new in America; everybody was reborn: it was here that mattered, now that counted. From New York, Lola embarked on a tour of the north-eastern states, honing and refining her act along the way. American audiences wanted something that reflected their own experience. She performed a Tyrolean dance, a Bavarian folk dance, a Hungarian czardas, a Spanish cachucha before she realised that nationality and origin no longer mattered: what was required was a synthesis of all things European. America was crying out for something iconic, something that could easily be reproduced over and over again. Theatre roles came and went: Lady Teazle, the Queen of Spain, Charlotte Corday, even the various incarnations of Lola Montez—but a single dance could become emblematic. Americans were clamouring for something fresh, something that was both startling yet hinted at deep roots.

Lola gave them her very own Spider Dance. She took the dance steps from her *Oleano*—that furious *zapateados* of heels that made men shiver with secret masochistic pleasure and women quiver at the breaking of a taboo, at the idea that a woman might actually feel, never mind express, rage or scorn or contempt. With a new name, the ancient and venerable tarantella became a brand new sensation.

A deadly spider gets caught up in the petticoats of an innocent young girl. In peril for her life, she rigorously shakes her skirts. When, at last, the spider falls to the ground she stamps it beneath her foot. In a passionate outpouring of triumph and relief, she celebrates her narrow escape.

It was a raw and emotional dance, at once simple yet brimming with ambivalence. In Boston, the newspapers strongly advocated a boycott; in Philadelphia, the advance publicity cautioned that it was not suitable for respectable women; in Connecticut, the first charge of indecency was made; in Pennsylvania, a number of gentlemen hurriedly escorted ladies from the auditorium. Often Lola played to a black house—that is to say that there was no feminine presence at all—though in New Orleans, the theatre was packed with women who threw flowers on to the stage. (Of course, those Southern ladies, with the veins of Hispanics and Creoles running through their veins, knew a thing or two about passion and fire, but that's a different matter.) One of Lola's favourite cuttings was from the *Alta California*, where the reviewer sweetly admitted that any indecency might be of his own making, rather than inherent to the display upon the stage.

> *Madame Montez shakes the spider from her skirts with barely a glimpse of ankle never mind thigh! The piquancy is all in the suggestion of what might happen behind closed doors. When she crushes the spider with such gusto all sorts of lewd and lascivious images were conjured up in my mind. Let them arrest girls for indecency for dancing the polka in France! It shall not happen here. We are Americans, not Europeans, lest we forget. Should we ban her for putting ideas in our heads or frankly confess that she merely touches upon thoughts and sensations that are already there? Gentlemen, I suggest the latter.*

As news of the Spider Dance spread, so did the advance publicity. Lola had become the very antithesis of elegance and feminine refinement, the dark shadow of every meek and respectable woman quietly attending to her tapestry. After a night at the theatre, many of the male members of the audience went home and looked askance at their wives. Was that a sparkle in her eye? What did she mean by that slightly raised eyebrow or the secret smile playing at the edge of her lips? It was the darnedest thing, but sometimes a dear devoted wife could seem almost too doting, as if the fragrant exterior disguised a more complex truth. God knows, the way things were going, women would soon be demanding the vote! In drawing rooms across the continent, ladies eagerly reading newspapers would hurriedly stuff them behind cushions or beneath their embroidery at the sound of their menfolk's approach. In the privacy of boudoirs and basements and kitchens, mistresses and maids and seamstresses tentatively lifted up their skirts and stamped their feet, enacting a hundred secret versions of the infinitely variable Spider Dance.

Lola played across America, in just about every city in every state, in grand municipal theatres and in two-bit auditoriums above saw-dust-strewn saloons. In the three-year-old boomtown of San Francisco, where disputes were still settled by an exchange of gunfire, she made frequent use of her whip and her pistol. In Sacramento, she challenged an inattentive audience to a duel.

Sacramento was still in many ways a frontier town, and the audience was not unusually boisterous, but when some so-called gentlemen had the gall to snigger at the Spider Dance and upset Lola's concentration, she stopped the music and strode to the edge of the stage.

"Come up here!" she called out, pointing to the pink-faced ring-leader, the theatre being small enough to make out the culprits occupying the best seats in the house.

"Give me your trousers and take my skirts; you're not fit to be called men!"

The audience fell into stunned silence, then erupted into laughter.

"I will speak!" she shouted.

Unfortunately, the hilarity was not entirely directed at her tormentors. Soon rotten apples and eggs were flying through the air. Lola looked out at a sea of male faces who were clearly making sport at her expense.

"I scorn you for the cowards that you are!" she hollered above the din. "I would gladly fight any man who dares to insult me! What do you suggest—a whip perhaps or a pistol?"

The conductor panicked and raised his baton.

Nobody took up Lola's offer.

The musicians started up again and, unable to make herself heard, Lola reluctantly resumed her dance. When a bouquet of roses landed on the stage, she crushed them beneath her foot. Eyes flashing at the audience, the true object of her scorn was clear. Any last semblance of order vanished, and the theatre exploded in uproar. As chairs hurtled through the air, Lola beat a hasty retreat. From the wings, she could hear an equal measure of hissing and applause. When order was finally restored, she danced an encore to a theatre of broken benches and to the accompaniment of the wind whistling through gaping windowpanes.

Later that night, a crowd of several hundred drunken men gathered beneath her hotel window and serenaded her with pots and pans. Leaning out of her window, she waved her fist; they shouted and jeered.

It was a pantomime.

"Three groans for Lola Montez!" they shouted to a cacophony of clashing pot lids.

"You're no gentlemen," Lola chided.

"And you're no lady," they bellowed back.

Lola responded with a challenge. "Come to the theatre tomorrow night and you can abuse me all you like!"

Once everybody had finally gone home, she collapsed into an armchair with a fortifying glass of brandy.

"Oh dear," said Lola's manager. "This is a disaster."

"Nonsense," she replied. "Tonight was worth more than a thousand dollars, you'll see."

The following evening, with the theatre packed to the rafters and a whole contingent of policemen lining the auditorium, Lola made a pretty apology from the stage.

"I am but a poor defenceless woman, much beleaguered and put upon. Forgive me, my beloved Americans, who believe in the expression of freedom as much as I, if in the heat of the moment, I reacted too quickly. I should have known better than to allow the dishonourable and ungentlemanly behaviour of a small cabal of mischief-makers to so unsettle me. When I stamped upon the bouquet, it was within the long and ancient tradition of crushing the spider. Truly, I meant to cast no aspersions nor call into question the sentiments of the good people of Sacramento, whom I hold close to my heart. Ladies and gentlemen, if you wish me to go on with my dance, you have only to say the word."

The audience replied with a roar of approval, and Lola reciprocated with a double encore.

For the rest of her run in Sacramento, ticket sales doubled, and she had no more trouble. If she challenged the audience on the basis of their gender, it was because that was exactly what they did to her. For one precious night, she released them from the obligations of chivalry. They should have been grateful to her!

Of course, Lola had subdued, thoughtful moments brimming with doubt and regret. Nobody is all ego; nobody is really larger than life. Like everybody else, she had days when she felt like a snail without a shell. Days sitting motionless in darkened rooms. Days when the light hurt her eyes, and even the sound of the maid whispering seemed too loud. Days when she couldn't leave her hotel room, when she couldn't summon the smile, the presence, the essence of Lola Montez.

On such occasions, she retreated between the covers of her journal. It was the one place where she truly let down her guard, where she could be painfully, nakedly, consistently herself. The most recent was bound in a piece of soft sea-green suede that she had purchased in London. Earlier versions were covered in remnants of her favourite dresses: peacock blue silk, shot taffeta in golden yellow, a moody olive green velvet, a section of salmon pink quilted satin. In them, she recorded her secret thoughts and fantasies. Throughout her childhood, the practice had sustained her to such an extent that her main relationship was with herself. Through all the movement, the endless travel, from childhood to adulthood, it had been the single connecting thread.

Before the opening of the first Broadway show, she had hovered in the wings, waiting for her cue. Dust rose from the drapes. The chorus were flapping about. The director bellowed. His assistant cowered. The stagehands made minor adjustments to the set. From the peephole at the side of the stage, Lola's eyes scanned the auditorium. The orchestra were murmuring among themselves in the pit. Occasionally, an instrument sounded: a triangle, a rumble from a tuba. Twice the conductor tapped his stick. In the stall aisle, she noticed a young woman being displayed on the arm of a promenading gentleman who nodded and smiled in attendance. With gently sloping shoulders exposed above a frothy, soft-hued gown, the young woman looked as pale and demure as a swan. Her neat head was bowed and acquiescent; bashful eyes swept the ground; a milky face displayed the slightest of smiles. Lola watched the man treating this frail creature with equal measures of care and disdain. He led her by the elbow. Might she stumble? Might she fall? He steered his charge into her seat as one might a child. Lola watched intently. She remembered being such a woman once in another time, in a life she left behind.

Chapter 37

Inland from San Francisco, the road climbs higher, until, at about two thousand feet above sea level, the foothills level out into a lush green valley. With the peaks of the Sierra Nevadas in the background and the ocean away off in the distance, Grass Valley felt as if it were located near the top of the world. There was a spirit of optimism about the little town that wasn't merely a consequence of the gold permeating the rock. The air felt pure, and the view communicated a sense of expansiveness that Lola could feel take root inside of her. The sound of the mills pulverising quartz gold echoed across the valley, creating an atmosphere of purpose and industry. It was a boomtown, and it suited her perfectly. Everything was new; anything was possible. Men became prosperous by dint of hard work or luck. Deep shaft mining and industrial processing works dotted the landscape, but to Lola they were infinitely beautiful. The old world was being swept away and with it the old constraints. Grass Valley was an active, vibrant place reverberating with the sound of the waterwheels and steam engines. On every side, the crushed ore was yielding up its treasure, with fine filters of gold sparkling in the light.

Main Street consisted of two rows of slatboard houses, a saloon, one restaurant, a bowling alley, a bookstore and a bordello: the only hotel had bunk beds for prospectors. In the little theatre above the saloon, Lola performed for an audience so starved of entertainment they willingly paid double the usual admission. Miners rubbed elbows with rude fellows in new suits and old

291

chaps in fading finery. Mine owners and managers squeezed in with actors and musicians. Even the girls from the bordello stuck their heads around the door.

Playing to the intimate nature of the surroundings, Lola stepped to the front of the tiny stage.

"We are all prospectors here," she said with a little curtsy. "We are all kings and queens. Look at me: a countess bowing humbly before you."

That first night, the downfall of Ludwig was particularly popular, and the Spider Dance provoked offers of assistance to capture the spider. By the end of the evening, Lola had already made her decision. Grass Valley would be a good base from which to cover the western states and she had already begun to invest extensively. She had learned her lesson from Ludwig: a king can bequeath a fortune, but he can also take it away. Further up the valley was the Empire Mine, the richest in California, and it was there that she staked her claim.

The moment Lola laid eyes on the little wooden house in Mill Street, she knew that it was meant for her. It was painted white, and it had a verandah all the way round the outside, just like the bungalow she remembered from her childhood in India. As she gazed out across the mountains, the vista seemed to meld together elements from the past—the foothills of the Himalayas, the Bavarian Alps surrounding Munich, the views of the Spanish Sierra Nevada that had lent the ancient city of Granada such a shimmering magical air. When she created her new home, she found herself making it for the little girl she had once been. In the garden, alongside native cactus plants, she planted amber bignonia and golden trumpet flowers, big, bright blooms that reminded her of India and Spain. There was a hammock on the porch and a swing hanging from a tree. She bought a dog, a horse and a green parrot named Polly. Soon she was living with a menagerie of animals: turkeys, chickens, two goats, a pig, a pair of lovebirds. Every week, somebody brought her something else. One week, she rescued a

292

cinnamon bear cub from a travelling circus; the next, a neighbour brought her a wild cat with a mangled foot.

On Saturday mornings, she gave dancing lessons for three local girls. "Stand up straight, be tall, be proud," she entreated them. She never ran away from Eliza Gilbert again. If people accused her of being childish and impulsive, she didn't care. Visitors arriving from Europe expecting a grand countess found a tanned woman in a calico frock digging in her flower garden instead. When Piotr Steinkeller emigrated from Poland, he made a point of looking her up.

"Why, you're black as an Indian!" he cried. "I hardly recognised you."

Of course, in a small town it was easy to get into altercations, and Grass Valley was no exception. Henry Shipley was the editor of the *Grass Valley Telegraph*, and wielding such power had obviously gone to his head. Though he was still a young man, he was already jaded and cynical. Every week he gleefully abused visiting performers between the pages of his newspaper, but then he had the nerve to insult Lola. A petty feud had been brewing for weeks, but for Lola, this really was the last straw. She was out of the house in an instant. She found him in the Golden Gate Saloon on Main Street with his nose in a whiskey, though it was only ten in the morning.

"You dare to call me a hypocrite!"

"If it isn't the mighty Montez," he sneered.

"I demand an apology!"

When he refused to retract his libel, Lola set about him with the sharp edge of her tongue and reinforced her argument with her whip.

"*That* is for every career you have destroyed. *That* is for abusing your position, and *that* is for having the nerve to insult me in print with adjectives that would more accurately describe your own miserable disposition. Insolence indeed!"

On the third lash, Mr Shipley caught hold of the whip. He was about to throw a punch, but according to Lola, the spirit of her Irish ancestors took possession of her left hand and she got in first.

When her fist caught his eye, Mr Shipley staggered, then bowed. "Lola Montez makes the front pages again!" he gloated. "You really must try to be less predictable, my dear."

With the landlady of the Golden Gate standing solidly between them, the fight was essentially over. They continued to trade insults both there and later in the press, though Lola had to travel to Nevada City to offer her account. Shipley was incorrigible, but it was a small town, and he benefited from the boost in sales. Who triumphed? Let us just say, he retreated before her. At public gatherings, they traded insults and banter, both claiming the ultimate advantage, though Shipley tended to err on moral victory, having lost the floor. The truth was that they were dependent on each other whether they liked it or not. Lola provided an endless source of material for him, and he maintained an audience for her. There is an art to publicity, but one needs to tread carefully. Once the machine starts, it develops its own momentum, especially with syndicated stories. It is like spinning around in a hall of mirrors; it's all too easy to become giddy and reckless, to lose sight of your original purpose.

One of the reasons Lola had bought the house in Grass Valley was in order to settle down and complete her memoirs. Newspapers would print the slightest sliver of a story, but book publishers required something more substantial altogether. Dashing off racy letters to newspapers was effortless, but dredging up her own thoughts and memories required a level of reflection that did not come easily. Everybody wanted to read about her exploits in Europe, but those dizzy, exhilarating days already seemed distant and remote. Lola felt as if she were recovering memories from a dream. In *The Life of Lola Montez*, she had circumvented any difficulties by imagining herself as a character in a slightly farcical play. With its success, a number of publishers were now offering generous sums for a definitive biography.

The first time Lola sat down at her desk, the words stumbled on to the page. From the moment she left London, she realised, she had begun to lose her way. In her second attempt, she went further back and retrieved Eliza Gilbert. There was no escape from the past, she conceded. No matter how fast she kept moving, her childhood was always there waiting for her. Once she understood that, the words slipped easily across the pages. She felt like a mole burrowing tunnels through the ground; once she started, she couldn't stop.

Lola Montez was born of Eliza Gilbert as surely as the dun and brittle carapace splits open to release a beautiful vision of itself. Eliza was the dreaming pupa: Lola Montez, the fluttering butterfly, the first splash of living colour, the manifestation of a schoolgirl's reveries. When Lola looked back upon her life, she saw not one story, but two, one unfolding inside the other. She was like a famous figure with the two aspects in conflict, one with the urge to pull forward and ever onwards, the other with an eye fixed firmly on the past. Her mother had abandoned her at the tender age of seven, and in response she felt compelled to take on the entire world. If she tried to live beyond society's love or approval, it was because she needed it too much. She hadn't entirely forgiven her mother, but she had learned to become a little kinder to herself. As the memoir neared completion, she could almost imagine Lola and Eliza walking hand in hand: Lola, resplendent in a crimson flamenco costume, Eliza in a bright Indian silk dress of orange and peacock blue.

One day she was sitting on the porch watching a fat bumblebee feeding on pollen and fertilising a clump of yellow lilies. Weighed down by the sacs of powdery saffron clinging to its legs, the bee hovered uncertainly before dipping deeply into the flowers. Lola remembered her lessons with Carmen in a dusty cave in the Moorish city of Granada in Spain. "You must find the core," she said. "You must strip everything away. When you find a raw quivering thing, then you can begin." *It's true*, Lola thought. *What else can I do, but begin and begin, then begin all over again.*

Scene Ten

FINAL EFFECTS

(Addendum)

Chapter 38

After almost two years in Grass Valley, unsettling stories from around the globe began to seep into Lola's thoughts like seams of gold quartz building up through rock. In Ireland, India and the West Indies, fortunes and reputations had been made and lost, leaving famine, mutiny and rebellion in their wake. It was only a matter of time before America followed suit: in California, the economy was already faltering. Now, with the discovery of gold in Australia, a whole new world was opening up. Prospectors and speculators of all types were scrambling to its shores: entrepreneurs, miners, troupes of actors, good-time girls. Alluring tales of this vast continent of red earth and rich resources filtered steadily back to Lola's bungalow in Mill Street. Accounts of gold-fever and turbulence, of pit owners and miners starved of entertainment, of high fees and rich pickings proved irresistible. Between the first days of spring and the onset of summer, Lola assembled a troupe and set sail.

In Australia, the European settlers had successfully conquered many aspects of the red continent, swathes of Sydney and Melbourne hardly differed in appearance from fashionable London, but at least one ever present reminder of the wild and untamed underbelly remained. In the most unexpected places, in drawing rooms and parlours, from behind curtains or beneath pianos, the most fearsome spiders might pop up or dash sideways or scurry up the wall. In laundries and pantries, in bedrooms and privies, the hairy huntsman and the whitetail lay in wait or lurked. In Australia, there were spiders for every occasion, it seemed; the grey house spider, the cupboard spider, the brown trapdoor spider. Australian tarantulas could grow as big as the palm of a man's hand, and the wolf spiders had eight eyes that glowed green in the dark. There was even an Australian relative of the black widow: if it didn't actually prove fatal, the sting of a female redback could certainly induce spasms and fits.

With native inhabitants of this calibre, Lola's Spider Dance took on an unexpectedly vivid life of its own. Suddenly in theatres across the continent, there was an enactment of the burgeoning nation's worst fears. For audiences already attuned to the very real dangers posed, Lola's star turn acquired a heightened level of urgency and passion. After arriving in Sydney in the middle of a stormy Australian winter, she was soon playing to packed houses. At the Victoria Theatre, she presented a showpiece that had been choreographed to dramatic perfection.

"Spider, spider, spider!" the men in the audience cried out, clamouring for the arachnid to be found and to be cast out.

Imagine a lithe and beautiful young woman entangled in the filaments of a spider's web. As the fibres wrap themselves around her ankles, she becomes more and more confused. A sinuous and hypnotic music fills the air. As it slows, the young woman discovers an invader within her petticoats. She attempts to shake it loose, and then re-examines her skirts. The spider climbs higher. The woman reels and spins in a flurry of skirts. Like a woman possessed, she wriggles and itches. The battle becomes hectic, and the tension builds. The woman dances with abandon and fire, until she succeeds in shaking the spider on to the floor. In a furious outburst, she stamps it beneath her foot. At last the deed is done. The threatening intruder is completely vanquished. Abruptly, the tempo of the music changes from staccato to mellow. The woman smiles in pleasure and delight, and a brimming love for the miracle of life seems to flow through her body, animating her movements.

Audiences were held spellbound by the force of passion displayed upon the stage. Caught up in the drama unfolding before them, they could almost see the spider. As it fell to the ground, they sighed with relief. When it was crushed so decisively beneath such a dainty and feminine foot, they stared horror-struck. The creature that had threatened all sorts of unspeakable liberties was unequivocally dead, but a new spectre had arisen: the sight of a beautiful woman pulsing with vehemence and vigour. Flowers rained down upon the stage: the applause was rapturous.

Lola really didn't need to reveal any part of her person in order to create a scandal. Simply to show the spider invading her skirts, to expel it and then to extinguish it beneath the ball of her foot: that was enough. It was a perfect drama in three parts.

Once upon a time, in the Middle Ages, as the Crusades swept across Europe, a strange hysteria took root in southern Italy, and then spread rapidly across rural Italy and Spain. Out in the fields at harvest time, scores of women were afflicted by the bite of the tarantula. As the poison swept through their bodies, they were thrown into uncontrollable spasms. The only known cure was to dance, and motley bands of musicians gathered by the field gates waiting for their services to be called upon. All day and all night, the poor afflicted souls spun round and round until they had sweated the deadly poison out of their systems and collapsed exhausted upon the ground.

This was the source of the tarantella, in which couples danced round in circles and women swished their skirts and stamped rigorously upon the ground. As to the origins of the dance, social historians claimed that it dated back to the Dionysian rituals, but that with the onset of the Crusades, the expression of desire had become a disease. Certainly the affliction seemed to strike most forcefully at seeding and harvest times, when the ancient orgiastic dances of fertility would once have taken place.

In America and Australia, men flocked to the theatre in droves, though many pointedly excluded their womenfolk. What exactly did they think they were protecting them from, if not from the very idea that women might possess innate desires of their own? What is

299

a tarantella without a spider, and what might that most ancient of creatures evoke? In the realm of the symbolic, the spider seems to touch upon something from the murky depths. What is black and hairy, and creeps about under the cover of darkness? What else might lurk in our box of unutterables? Our dark box of taboos? Let us consider the spider once again. In tales of ancient Greece, Arachne wove the infidelities of the gods into tapestries. The goddess Athene, outraged that a mere mortal had dared to challenge divine supremacy, punished Arachne by turning her into a spider. Thus from antiquity, the spider and the expression of sexuality became inextricably entwined.

Consider the spider. In her darkest form, she devours her hapless mate. For that most voracious of creatures, the black widow (and the redback, her Australian counterpart), the act of reproduction becomes a tantalising dance of death, yet the male willingly offers himself up and is drawn in. Look again at the men packing out the theatres as they alternatively hurl abuse or compliments, torn between ecstasy and outrage.

As Lola toured the cities and outposts of Australia, the Spider Dance developed a number of dramatic twists and turns. Instead of being shaken free, the spider succeeded in applying its sting first. As the venom coursed through her system, Lola became enfeebled or reeled distracted from the stage. In this startling new version, she was impelled to keep dancing until the poison was flushed out, or she would die. The performance took on a new level of urgency. Audiences watched with alarm as she danced to the point of exhaustion. More than once, she collapsed mid-performance. At times, it seemed that the battle might be lost. Once she fell down and lay motionless whilst the music played on. Minutes dragged by, until the stagehands had to lift her bodily from the stage. There were other misfortunes along the way. Squabbles broke out among Lola's theatre troupe, money was lost, actors disappeared. In Victoria, the Bendigo Theatre was struck by lightning in the very middle of a show.

Lola had just begun her performance when a roll of thunder rattled through the theatre. There was a blazing flash, then an almighty explosion. A ball of lightning smashed through the roof tiles and crashed down on to the stage. There was a second flash, then a stench as of gunpowder. The fireball hit the boards, narrowly missing Lola, who managed to jump out of the way. The stage split in two. The gauze scenery caught fire. The theatre filled with smoke. Ladies screamed. Stagehands ran about. The manager bellowed for buckets of water. Sceneshifters tried to beat back the blaze.

In the midst of it all, Lola stepped to the front of the stage. As the curtain dropped down behind her, she raised her hand.

"Let us not be afraid!" she entreated. "Imagine that the thunder and lightning is part of the performance. The old order is falling down, but a new one will rise up, mark my words! Now let us continue with the show!"

The curtain rose up to reveal a smouldering set, flashes of lightning intermittently illuminating the extent of the damage. From the pit, a single violin struck a note, and Lola began to dance. Swaying from side to side at the front of the broken stage, she stared up at the sky, silently daring the elements to strike her down, half hoping for a final blow to put an end to it all, once and for all. In the midst of devastation, she danced on. It could have been Pompeii or the end of the world and she would have carried on. As she lifted up her skirts, the audience steadily evacuated the building. Unable to tear their eyes away from the unnerving spectacle on the stage, they retreated step-by-backward-step until the auditorium was empty.

Lola concluded the evening more or less intact, with only a few scratches and bruises to mark her fall, but she was hesitant about performing the Spider Dance again. In her hotel room afterwards, she sank gratefully into a hot bath and closed her eyes. Her dancing days were essentially over; she didn't need an act of God to tell her that. Every bone in her body ached. She felt faint, her feet throbbed, piercing pains shot through her head. Every performance left her feeling empty and wrung out. Afterwards, she took longer and longer to recover. Where once the Spider Dance had invigorated her, now it consumed her and wore her out. The truth was that a tarantella required the stamina of a young woman, and she was no longer young. At thirty-five, she struggled to summon up the energy and fire required. With the sound of thunder and lightning still crackling in the distance, she languished in the bath until long after the water had cooled. The time had come to hang up her dancing shoes or to find a successor.

Australia proved conclusive in a number of ways. Not only was it the natural resting place of the Spider Dance, it was also the land of whips. As Lola toured the vast continent, her whip-cracking alter ego made regular appearances in the local newspapers. She won whips in draws; she obligingly posed with them for photographs; she occasionally incorporated them into plays. In Ballarat, a small town outside of Melbourne, Victoria, she got caught up in another showdown with yet another newspaperman. It was the same old story. When Henry Seekamp set himself up as a moral guardian of the community at Lola's expense, the rest was perhaps inevitable. On Main Street in Ballarat, the dancer and the editor battled it out with horsewhips, then fists. In an unequal draw between the petite dancer and the sprawling drunkard—why was it that so many newspapermen seemed so desperately fond of drink?—it was the editor's reputation that came off worse. He was reduced to grabbing at Lola's hair and skirts in the middle of the street for all to see. When the two were finally separated, a group of onlooking miners pilloried Seekamp with rotten tomatoes and spoiled fruit.

"Shame, shame," they cried.

It was also in Ballarat that the tables finally turned. When Lola questioned the box office receipts, the theatre manager's wife laid into her with a whip and then her fists. Mrs Crosby was a solidly built lady who, unlike Mr Seekamp, felt no compunction to hold back. She beat Lola so severely that the whip broke, and then she finished off the job with her fists. Dented and bruised, Lola beat a hasty retreat. She had learned her lesson the hard way, and she never took up a whip for the sake of a publicity stunt again.

On the last leg of her tour, the Spider Dance attained a new level of immortality. Lola had already developed the dance to the point of pastiche; George Coppin merely took it a step further, opening the doors to a whole string of burlesque versions. They say that imitation is the sincerest form of flattery, and George Coppin certainly took some trouble over his transformation. In a figure-hugging black gown with an extravagant skirt of flounces, he took to the stage of his own theatre in Melbourne and struck a Lola-esque pose. Strange to say, it is often the most masculine men who take pleasure in feminine fripperies, and George Coppin was no exception. A tall man in his late forties, he was broad at the shoulder and wide of girth, with considerably more than the one requisite chin. On his balding head, he sported a rather dashing wig of black curls, which he tossed extravagantly about until they bounced. As the music began, George Coppin sashayed to the front of the stage.

Australia might no longer be a prison colony, but as with many once male-only institutions, a long and honourable tradition of cross-dressing remained. Though he was more pantomime dame than diva, George Coppin entered wholeheartedly into the dance. His attitude was haughty, his poses statuesque, though his belly protruded from his tight black dress.

"Spider, spider!" the audience cried out.

George Coppin danced like a man possessed. Stomping about the stage, he threw up his skirts to reveal miner's boots and hairy legs. When he pulled an enormous hairy black tarantula from beneath his skirts, the audience whistled and cheered.

"Death to the spider!" they shouted. "Out, out, out!"

George dashed the spider to the ground. With the audience egging him on, he jumped up and down on it with both feet. At the conclusion, he brushed his hands together in satisfaction, one foot resting triumphantly upon the squashed tarantula. Stepping to the front of the stage, he dropped into a lumbering curtsy.

"I am but a poor, defenceless woman, much abused and put upon," he speechified in a high-pitched, squeaky voice. "Men try all sorts of guises to get beneath my skirts, but I am such a helpless creature, what can I do?"

Tucked away in the wings, Lola stifled a fit of giggles. She had provided George Coppin with her sheet music and taken him through the steps, and, for all his playacting, he had offered a creditable version. Lola was already making preparations to leave Australia, and with it, her career as a dancer. It had fallen to George Coppin to provide her swan song. His Spider Dance was certainly memorable. For a so-called parody, he had fully savoured the role, imbuing his performance with considerable urgency and fire. In one fell swoop, the Spider Dance had become as quintessentially Australian as corked hats and billycans.

Lola left Australia with a menagerie of birds, including another talking parrot named Polly III and a white lyre bird, and plans for a change of career. In this new phase, she intended to launch herself as a lecturer and lady author. On the sea journey back to America, she gathered together the outline of her first two proposed lectures. One would be on the fine art of publicity, the other on the ancient origins of the venerable Spider Dance.

Chapter 39

Lola's new career proved to be highly lucrative, garnering high fees and audience figures, in addition to a previously unimaginable sheen of respectability. She stepped down from the theatrical stage and up to the podium with surprising ease. Upon her return from Australia, she toured America, England and Ireland, speaking on a range of topics from politics to beauty and fashion. Often she used autobiographical material, talking about Lola Montez as if she were talking about another person, in another lifetime. (In private she increasingly used the name Eliza.) Though she had retired from the exertions of dancing, the neuralgia and fainting fits grew steadily more frequent and severe. She had been about to embark on a third lecture tour, when her increasingly fragile health took a turn for the worse.

In an apartment in Greenwich Village, two middle-aged women eyed each other warily across the drawing room. It was October, and there was a fire smouldering in the grate. The hostess sat very still alongside it, blue eyes blazing from a pale, gaunt face. With one hand gripping the arm of the chair and the other the marble top of a walking stick, she seemed suspended in time, caught between the effort of standing up or remaining exactly where she was. The visitor, who appeared a decade or so older, hovered uncertainly by the door. Still wrapped up in her cape and bonnet, and with her nose pink from the cold, she looked slightly windblown, as if she had arrived by the forces of nature rather than her own volition. From behind her, an icy draught from the hallway swept into the room and lowered the temperature still further. Evidently the two women were not on the easiest of terms.

Still rooted in the armchair, Lola's fist tightened around the walking stick until her knuckles turned white. Her face twitched, as if she were struggling to translate her thoughts into words. When she finally spoke, it was with some difficulty.

"To what do I owe the pleasure?" she asked in a strange, hollow voice.

Mrs Craigie responded with a forced little smile. "I had to come," she said.

The two women exchanged a rather formal and awkward embrace, before Lola indicated the chair opposite. "Please do have a seat," she said.

Mrs Craigie peered at her, then coughed. "You look well," she said, though this clearly wasn't the case. Lola's dark and rather modest merino gown hung loosely from her torso, he collarbone jutted from her kneck, and her skin looked as pale and flimsy as tissue paper. Draped protectively around her shoulders, a luxurious mauve cashmere shawl only served to emphasise the frailty of her appearance.

Lola's nostrils flared slightly. "I am afraid news of my death was a little premature," she said.

At the beginning of the summer, on a glorious sunny June morning, Lola had woken up to discover that she was unable to speak or move. Three days later, she slipped into a coma. Ships sailing for Europe carried news of her death. The funeral arrangements had already been made when she miraculously opened her eyes. After a great deal of effort, she managed to get out of bed, but she was a dumb and dribbling wreck—wiping her mouth compulsively on her sleeves and unable to take care of her most basic needs. From this infantile state, she had painstakingly taught herself how to sit up, then move her limbs, then mouth words. Gradually she learnt to string sentences together, to wash and dress herself, to walk with a stick.

Throughout the summer, she had fiercely grasped hold of each blessed day, squeezing every ounce of enjoyment out of the sight of a patch of blue sky or an opening flower or the song of a blackbird. Over the course of three months, she continued to push herself until she could move around her bedroom without the aid of a walking stick. Not once in this seemingly never-ending process of rehabilitation had she drawn a scrap of comfort from the thought of the woman who was now sitting in front of her.

Mrs Craigie settled down in the chair opposite Lola, divesting herself of her bonnet and cape. She was a handsome woman of fifty-five, dressed in yards of rustling black taffeta. Where once she had been girlishly slight and her daughter full of womanly curves, the situation was now, rather starkly, the reverse. Lola was all ribs and elbows, whereas her mother had the plump and complacent appearance of a prosperous and slightly formidable widow.

"My dear Eliza," she said.

"You have come from England, I gather," said Lola.

Mrs Craigie nodded. "Fifteen days by sea," she said.

"You came all that way to see me?"

"The newspapers said you were dying."

"That's why you came?"

Mrs Craigie looked hurt. "That's not what I meant. I thought we might make amends. After all, you are the one who wrote to me."

"That was twelve years ago."

Mrs Craigie looked at the floor. "I am here now," she said.

Lola regarded her mother's face and decided to give her the benefit of the doubt.

"Forgive me," she said. "I was not expecting you, that's all. Let's have some tea, and you can tell me about your journey."

One of the unexpected consequences of Lola's new choice of career was the level of social acceptability that it had bestowed upon her. Lola, who cared little for the niceties, found herself welcomed into the bosom of society: ladies who would once have made a point of snubbing her, now embraced her. Even her mother, it seemed, felt able to partake of her company.

Over the course of tea and lemon seed cake, the two women made polite conversation about the weather, Mrs Craigie's journey and the differences between London and New York society.

"So you never considered marrying again?" enquired Lola.

"Major Craigie left me well cared for. I will never stop mourning his death," Mrs Craigie rather piously replied.

"So I see," said Lola, glancing at her mother's voluminous black skirts.

She bit her lip. "I was dead to you once. What has changed now?"

Mrs Craigie brushed some invisible crumbs from her lap. "You are not what you were."

"Perhaps you prefer me like this," said Lola, her voice shaking.

"Why do you keep twisting my words? I have come all this way to see you. Isn't that enough?"

"So you did receive my letter?"

"The life you were living then. . . You can't really have expected me to reply."

"Well, yes, I did hope that you might. For some women, the bond of motherhood might have been enough."

Mrs Craigie couldn't contain herself any longer. "After all the shame you put me through!" she said, rising slightly from the chair. "All the gossip and the scandal for all those years! People whispering! The absolute disgrace of it! I had to move back to England where nobody knew the connection."

Lola shrank into the chair, pulling the mauve shawl around her bony shoulders. Bands of tension tightened across her chest. Pressing a hand against her sternum, she struggled to regulate her breathing. The air felt close; she felt too hot; the walls of the rooms seemed to be bearing down upon her. How could she ever have thought relations between them might be any different? In the opposite armchair, her mother seemed to almost glow with self-righteousness. Lola remembered the last time she had seen her, more than twenty years previously on a quiet residential street in Calcutta.

She could still vividly recall the look on her mother's face, her jaw set, her eyes giving nothing away. It was as if she, and not Lola, had been betrayed. Lola had watched her mother from the carriage as it pulled away. The coachman headed for the docks and Mrs Craigie had retreated into her townhouse without a backward glance. It was the second time her mother had sent her away, and Lola had vowed that she would never allow that to happen again.

"I was never good enough for you," she said quietly.

Mrs Craigie looked distraught, her eyes moistening with tears. "I'm here now, aren't I?" she said. Pulling a crumpled yellowing envelope from her purse, she turned it over in her hands.

Lola recognised her own handwriting on the front.

"You kept it?" she said.

"We have no kin but each other," said Mrs Craigie, quoting from the letter.

Lola fell back against the chair in hopelessness and exhaustion, her heart beating against her chest like the wings of a trapped bird. She closed her eyes for a moment, and a small bud of hope opened up amidst all the hurt and confusion. *Perhaps it isn't too late to make amends after all*, she thought.

When she opened her eyes again, she noticed that her mother was surveying the drawing room.

"I didn't imagine you would be living like this," she said.

The drawing room was spacious and respectable, with décor that was more inclined to neutral than ostentatious.

Lola shook her head imperceptively. "What did you imagine?" she said quietly.

"Well, you do seem to be living rather modestly, all things considered."

"Indeed," said Lola. "All things considered. I seem to be an endless source of disappointment to you."

"Why do you persist in taking this tone with me when I have come all this way to see you?" asked Mrs Craigie.

"I can't help but wonder *why* you have gone to such trouble."

"Surely you could live more comfortably," persisted Mrs

Craigie, glancing down at the envelope in her hands, her thumb absentmindedly stroking the Munich postmark.

Lola finally understood. "I have lived in a palace with a crystal staircase and another once occupied by the Empress Josephine, but these days I am happy enough to live within my means."

"Within your means?" Mrs Craigie squeaked. "Countesses don't live like this!"

"This is perfectly respectable, isn't it? I should have thought you would be pleased. Ill-gotten gains quickly dissipate, it seems. I was generous to others, as others were to me."

"You can't have frittered everything away?"

Lola laughed. "Is your concern for me or for yourself?"

"I *am* your next of kin," said Mrs Craigie.

"I have already made arrangements," said Lola.

"But I am your mother!" protested Mrs Craigie. "I gave birth to you! I won't ever forget that, though it seems you already have. I don't understand why you have to be so hurtful. You always were an unnatural child."

"You know something," said Lola. "I forgive you."

"You forgive me! I did everything I could for you and you threw it in my face!"

"I asked your forgiveness once, and you chose not to reply. The time is long gone when I need ask anything of you. I am sorry if I have been such a constant cause of embarrassment to you."

Mrs Craigie smiled appeasingly and switched tone. "You need to rest, poor thing! I am staying in New York for a few weeks. When you are feeling a little better, perhaps I can call on you again?"

With the aid of her walking stick, Lola managed to stand up. "It seems I meet your standards now, but I am afraid you don't meet mine. When I needed a mother, you weren't there. I certainly don't need one now."

"You're sending me away?"

"It seems so," said Lola.

Mrs Craigie compulsively smoothed down her skirts. "Be sure your sins will find you out," she muttered.

"Are you suggesting that I have brought my condition upon myself?"

Mrs Craigie pursed her lips. "Only you know the answer to that."

Lola limped over to the door with some difficulty, and held it open. "I am sure you can see yourself out."

Long after the sound of her mother's footsteps faded away, Lola remained standing in the hallway, one hand clutching her stick and the other the handle of the drawing room door. She listened to the sounds in the street: footsteps, a carriage rumbling by, a hawker shouting his wares, a couple of children shrieking with laughter as they ran along the pavement, a tapping stick, the raucous cawing of a swooping crow, the rustle of wings.

Consider the spider, that most ancient symbol of the dark feminine. If not completely fatal, the sting of the female black widow can bring on spasms and fits. Should the necessity arise, she is perfectly capable of devouring both her offspring and her mate. Mrs Craigie returned to England after a couple of weeks, without effecting a reconciliation with her daughter. She continued to write intermittently, but Lola never replied. Following the visit, Lola struggled to continue with her recovery, but within three months, she caught pneumonia and died. Ultimately, it was the sting not of a spider, but of a mosquito, that took her to an early grave. Evidently, the malaria she had first contracted in India had permanently damaged her health, the recurring attacks she suffered from throughout her adult life very probably led to her premature death. No mother should bury her own child, so the saying goes. Certainly Mrs Craigie did not return for the funeral, nor was she acknowledged in Lola's will.

Lola's mother was not the only person to imply that Lola had brought her condition upon herself. Many of the newspaper obituaries posited her death as a morality tale against the emancipation of women. *Those who dance with the devil, pay the price*, declared one. Maybe Lola did tempt fate one too many times, or perhaps some people just don't make old bones. In Paris many years before, a grieving Alexandre Dumas had publicly pronounced that her love was a deadly curse. In the end, though, it proved to be her mother, and not Lola, who possessed the fatal touch.

End of Act III

Epilogue

*L*ola Montez died at the age of forty-one and was buried in Brooklyn's Greenwood cemetery beneath a plain white headstone inscribed with the name Eliza Gilbert. Among her papers was a photograph of a dark-haired woman with even features and a determined set to her mouth. The woman was slender and petite, with a firm jaw and a pleasant, if unremarkable, face. Surely this couldn't be the famous beauty? The voluptuous enchantress? The exotic muse? According to the scribble on the back, the portrait was taken in New York in 1851 when Lola was thirty-two. The fiery Spaniard who had inspired a rhapsody, a duel, a revolution was obviously an Irishwoman. It was as plain as the features of her face. Only the eyes, large and widely spaced, hinted at a capricious and lively intelligence.

Of her fabled jewellery collection, all that remained was an old-fashioned looking ring with a large red stone. The ring, which was mentioned in the journals, had apparently belonged to her mother. According to Mrs Craigie, Lola's father had presented her with a ruby betrothal ring: it was only after his death that she discovered that it was made from plated brass, inset with a piece of faceted red glass. Lola's executors sent the ring for evaluation as a matter of routine. When the jeweller examined it, he became extremely agitated. The setting was a fairly modest pressed gold plate, that was true enough, but the gem was a rare curiosity. At the end of the century, dark amethysts from the coast of Malabar were still being passed off as rubies. Because of their scarcity, oriental rubies, as they were known in the trade, had become extremely valuable. It was possible, the jeweller conceded, that a less experienced *merchant might not have recognised it. When the ring was finally put up for auction, it was purchased anonymously by a hopeful young actress seeking a talisman.*

In the cemetery, beneath the modest white headstone, fresh red camellias began to appear overnight, and a curious phenomenon swept America, then Europe. In theatres and music halls, a steady procession of young women began to emerge, each claiming to be the true daughter of Lola Montez. The most compelling claim was made by an enterprising young Bavarian woman named Susanne, who arrived in America in the months following Lola's death. In her possession were a number of items that had certainly belonged to Lola, including two large suede-bound cuttings albums and a striped pink and white hatbox, which contained a Spanish shawl, two mantillas, a lacquered fan and a carved mother-of-pearl comb.

Susanne's speciality was a recreation of Lola's most famous dances, whilst dressed in the original costumes—a shimmering silvery dance costume from Paris and a black velvet costume from London, with an iridescent skirt of crimson, violet and blue. Susanne was a nondescript, almost mousy young woman, yet when she danced she was utterly transformed. Audiences stumbled from theatres, describing a vivid and starkly feminine sensuality, an electrifying presence, a vibrant and elemental force.

"The final revelation is that lying,
the telling of beautiful untrue things,
is the proper aim of Art."
Oscar Wilde

Acknowledgments

I am indebted to Bruce Seymour for his definitive biography and Max Ophuls for his inspirational film; to Brian Keaney, Bill Hamilton, Kevin Graal, Faith Evans and Vincent Woodcock for their invaluable insights at key stages; to Desmond Graal for his knowledge of Spanish and German; to Bryan Holdsworth for technical input; to the *Escuela de Baile d'España* in London and Ron Hitchens (*La Argentina*) for their knowledge of the history of flamenco both in Spain and England; and to the Tyrone Guthrie Centre in Monaghan for allowing the space and time to begin to write the first draft.

With special thanks to Steve MacDonogh and Brandon, without whom Lola would not be making such a glorious comeback—and to Lola herself for allowing me to write about Spain and Ireland, two countries I hold close to my heart. Finally, I would like to express my deepest gratitude to my friend Kevin and to my sister Bridget, for their unfailing encouragement and support.

MORE OUTSTANDING FICTION FROM BRANDON

BARRY MCCREA
The First Verse

"An intoxicating tale of a young man drawn into a bizarre literary cult... A clever satire of literary criticism, it's also a coming-of-age (and coming-out) tale, a slick portrait of 'Celtic Tiger' Dublin and a compulsive thriller." *Financial Times*

"Entertaining, smart, and very, very readable."
The Irish Times

"An audacious, kaleidoscopic blast." *Sunday Business Post*

ISBN 9780863223808

EMER MARTIN
Baby Zero

"An incendiary, thought-provoking novel, like a haunting and spiritual ballad, it moves us and makes us care." Irvine Welsh

In an unheard of country, each successive Taliban-like regime turns the year back to zero, as if to begin history again. A woman, imprisoned for fighting the fundamentalist government, tells her unborn child the story of three baby zeros – all girls born at times of upheaval.

ISBN 9780863223655

MARY ROSE CALLAGHAN
Billy, Come Home

"The slim, moving novel depicts the life of Billy Reilly, a schizophrenic man whose gentle nature and fragile psyche are no match for life in modern Dublin... Without becoming mawkish or preachy, Callaghan delivers an effective indictment of society's failure to care for a vulnerable minority." *Publishers Weekly*

ISBN 9780863223662

MORE OUTSTANDING FICTION FROM BRANDON

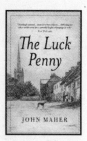

JOHN MAHER
The Luck Penny

"John Maher confirms himself as one of Irish writing's bright stars with this meditation on death… [A] superbly executed story about bereavement told through characters that intrigue from the first… *The Luck Penny* is an outstanding Irish novel for the wider English-reading world." *Sunday Tribune*

"An expertly crafted, tender tale of grief, language and land… A richly rewarding read." *Metro*

ISBN 9780863223617

DAVID FOSTER
The Land Where Stories End

"Australia's most original and important living novelist." *Independent Monthly*

"A post-modern fable set in the dark ages of Ireland. . . [A] beautifully written humorous myth that is entirely original. The simplicity of language is perfectly complementary to the wry, occasionally laugh-out-loud humour and the captivating tale." *Irish World*

ISBN 9780863223112

WILLIAM WALL
No Paradiso

"In addition to the author's alert, muscular style, his painlessly communicated appreciation of obscure learning, his vaguely didactic pleasure in accurately providing a sense of place, many of these stories are distinguished by a welcome engagement with form . . . In their various negotiations with such tensions, the stories of *No Paradiso* engage, challenge and reward the committed reader." *The Irish Times*

ISBN 9780863223556

MORE OUTSTANDING FICTION FROM BRANDON

Drago Jančar
Joyce's Pupil

"Jančar writes powerful, complex stories with unostentatious assurance, and has a gravity which makes the tricks of the more self-consciously modern writers look cheap ... Drago Jančar deserves the wider readership that these translations should gain him." *Times Literary Supplement*

ISBN 9780863223402

Nenad Veličković
Lodgers

"Nenad Veličković offers a beautifully constructed account of the ridiculous nature of the Balkans conflict, and war in general, which even in moments of pure gallows humour retains a heartwarming affection for the individuals trying to survive in such horrific circumstances." *Metro*

ISBN 9780863223488

Chet Raymo
Valentine

"Such nebulous accounts [as we have] have been just waiting for someone to make a work of historical fiction out of them. American novelist and physicist Raymo has duly obliged with his recently published *Valentine: A Love Story*." *The Scotsman*

"[A] vivid and lively account of how Valentine's life may have unfolded. .. Raymo has produced an imaginative and enjoyable read, sprinkled with plenty of food for philosophical thought." *Sunday Tribune*

ISBN 9780863223273

MORE OUTSTANDING FICTION FROM BRANDON

AGATA SCHWARTZ AND LUISE VON FLOTOW (eds)
The Third Shore
Women's Fiction from East Central Europe

The Third Shore brings to light a whole spectrum of women's literary accomplishment and experience virtually unknown in the West. Gracefully translated, and with an introduction that establishes their political, historical, and literary context, these stories written in the decade after the fall of the Iron Curtain are tales of the familiar reconceived and turned into something altogether new by the distinctive experience they reflect.

ISBN 9780863223624

EVELYN CONLON
Skin of Dreams

"A courageous, intensely imagined and tightly focused book that asks powerful questions of authority . . . this is the kind of Irish novel that is all too rare." Joseph O'Connor

"Astoundingly original . . . a beautiful novel, which will move you by its courage in delving into controversy and its imaginatively spun revelations." *Irish World*

ISBN 9780863223068

PJ CURTIS
The Lightning Tree

"In revealing Mariah's story, Curtis creates an elegiac and moving portrait of Irish rural culture. While the narrative looks backwards over Mariah's extraordinary life, this is also a hugely relevant piece of writing for anyone visiting the region today, as Curtis is highly adept at recreating the mystical and complex atmosphere of life on the Burren, a rugged and wild landscape that remains largely untouched by modern life." *Sunday Telegraph*

ISBN 9780863223471